FEED BACK

MIRA GRANT

orbit

www.orbitbooks.net

ORBIT

First published in Great Britain in 2016 by Orbit

1 3 5 7 9 10 8 6 4 2

Copyright © 2016 by Seanan McGuire

A CIP catalogue record for this book
is available from the British Library.

ISBN 978-0-356-50807-8

Typeset in Garamond 3 by M Rules
Printed and bound by CPI Group (UK) Ltd, Croydon, CR0 4YY

Papers used by Orbit are from well-managed forests
and other responsible sources.

MIX
Paper from
responsible sources
FSC® C104740

Orbit
An imprint of
Little, Brown Book Group
Carmelite House
50 Victoria Embankment
London EC4Y 0DZ

An Hachette UK Company
www.hachette.co.uk

www.orbitbooks.net

And we're back.
This book is dedicated with joy and gratitude to
Kathryn Daugherty and Leslie Stewart.
There are so many sides to every story.
The two of you helped so much in writing mine.

Book I

Boom Tomorrow

It's not what's true that matters. It's what people remember when the dust dies down.

—BEN ROSS

You haven't experienced real joy until the first time you've improvised a zombie trap from six yards of chicken wire, a bunch of old lumber, some string, and a guinea pig. I mean damn, people. That's living.

—AISLINN 'ASH' NORTH

My mother was a goddamn national hero.

She lived in Oakland before the Rising, and she was there when everything started going down. Just her, my grandma, and four kids. I was the youngest. Four years old, full of piss and vinegar and random fits of defiance. Too big to keep locked in a playpen, too small to understand what was happening, or why Mama cried all the time, or why the apartment was suddenly full of guns and strangers. I don't remember much about those days. It's just flashes, little glimpses of things my mind has mercifully decided I don't really need to know.

I had two brothers once. I know that. I still have a sister. She was seven in 2014, and she wrapped herself around me like a blanket, and we both rode out the storm.

The world will never know what my mama did to save us. Just trust me: She was a hero.

We buried her this morning. Her name will never appear on the Wall.

—From *That Isn't Johnny Anymore*, the blog of Ben Ross, May 16, 2039

One

The world isn't so good with funerals anymore.

Deaths, sure; we have plenty of those. We can give you death in any shape or size you want. Good death, bad death, slow death, fast death – the modern world is the fucking Amazon.com of dying. Maybe it wasn't like that before the Rising hit and the dead started to walk, but hey, guess what: All that shit happened, and now we're the rats in the wreckage, living and dying in the aftermath of our parents' mistakes.

2014. That was the year when everything changed, when a bunch of bored jerks broke into a lab and let a nifty synthetic virus out into the world to have a party in the stratosphere. Only the virus didn't stay up there, where it wasn't hurting anybody. It dropped back down to Earth and got to work infecting people. Maybe that would have been cool – I've never had a head cold or a stuffy nose, and I understand that those were right annoying – but it met up with another nifty synthetic virus, and the two of them hit it off right away. They got right to the business of having babies, and like all babies, these ones took after both sides of the family. They got their airborne daddy's communicability. They got their slower, stealthier mama's adaptability. And then they got the world as a birthday present. Where Kellis-Amberlee walked, the dead got up and joined in the fun.

So yeah, we're real good at dying. Every human on this planet has been in a full-time immersion course on the subject since the summer of 2014. What we're not good at is burying our dead without putting a bullet between their eyes first.

I'd been waiting across the street from the funeral home for the better part of an hour, fussing with the hem of my floral sundress and wishing for an excuse to go do something else. Anything else. Taxes? I'm there. Trip to the licensing board to explain why my tracker sometimes went offline for no apparent reason? Okay, I'm your girl. Cleaning out my in-boxes on the various social media sites that I was supposedly curating for the team? All right, let's not push it. Although it still might have been easier on my nerves.

Loitering has been illegal essentially forever, even before the Rising, although it used to be more erratically prosecuted. People got more nervous about it once we started coexisting with zombies, since now the weird guy who's been standing on the corner for the last hour watching the traffic lights change is potentially getting ready to eat you and your entire family. The patrol cars had been circling the block with increasing frequency, and I was pretty sure all the local CCTV cameras were focused on me, waiting for the moment when I did something actionable. Again, technically, loitering was actionable: I was breaking the law by staying exactly where I was. But the local cops would have needed to get out of their vehicles to mess with me, and that would have put them out in the open. Nobody likes being out in the open.

Well. Most people don't like being out in the open. The majority of the human population would be perfectly happy living and dying in hermetically sealed little rooms, never seeing the outside world again. Most people are pretty terrible, really.

A patrol car appeared around the corner, slowing until it was creeping along at maybe three miles per hour, the officers inside watching me suspiciously through the closed window. They were getting bolder, which meant they were getting ready to ask why I was mooching around the streets alone, with no visible weaponry. I stayed where I was, crouched gargoyle-style atop a weird modern art piece that had been installed to commemorate local victims of the Rising, and dipped a hand into my purse.

Before the dead walked, that sort of thing could have gotten me killed. Reaching into a bag while under police surveillance was likely to be interpreted as reaching for a gun – and back then, just *having* a firearm in the presence of the cops was considered a totally valid reason for them to start shooting. If the Rising hadn't happened when it did, the police would probably have triggered a civil war. That would have been even nastier than the zombies, if you ask me. At least zombies were acting on hunger and instinct and blind need, not racism and paranoia and carefully nurtured power trips.

The patrol car slowed to a stop as I pulled out my license and held it out for both them and the nearest cameras to see. The thumbnail photo of me had been taken right after a bad haircut and a worse bar fight, which was why I kept it: Given my line of work, if someone was ever trying to identify my body it was a pretty sure thing that I'd be covered in bruises and rocking some seriously hideous hair.

'Aislinn North, journalist, license number IQL-33972.' The 'I' identified me as a journalist of foreign origin, granted permission to work on American soil. 'I'm waiting for my colleague, Benjamin Ross, who is currently engaged in a legal visit to the Oumet Brothers Funeral Home.' I nodded meaningfully toward the building on the other side of the street. 'This is a public street. I don't have to file any paperwork to be here, and as a licensed journalist, I'm exempt from local vagrancy and loitering restrictions. Now shoo. I'm working.'

I grinned, revealing the gap where my left incisor had been prior to a nasty encounter with a man who thought that running a zombie dog-fighting ring would be a great way to spend his twilight years. Ben always says I'd be more photogenic and pull better ratings if I got it fixed, but Ben can stuff it. I don't have the time or patience to mess around with dentures and bridges, and given the odds and how I tend to do my job, I'll probably be a zombie someday. Being a zombie with unbreakable titanium implants in my mouth seems like an asshole thing to do. Besides, I hate dentists. They act like everyone is a walking biohazard zone, like it's somehow our fault that they decided to go into a profession that involves blood.

The policemen stared at me, mouths open and eyes wide, before hitting the gas and roaring down the road, probably breaking several municipal speed laws in the process. I didn't know for sure. Northern California's weird local regulations were a little outside of my comfort zone. Give me a small town in the Irish countryside, surrounded by rolling hills and burial mounds, and I'm your girl. Give me a city that should have been abandoned during the Rising, where the skyscrapers are just one more excuse for people to lock themselves away from the natural world, and I can rock it. But the suburbs of California? Nah. Unsafe, uncool, and not my favorite place to kill an afternoon.

The doors of the funeral home opened as the mourners began emerging. There was no reception line for people to tell the family how sorry they were: That had been handled inside, followed by the line for the blood tests that would clear them to go back out into the world. No one looked around or even hesitated as they beelined for their respective cars, unlocking the doors, sliding inside, and shutting themselves in the latest in the series of boxes that defined their lives. I would have been impressed by how efficient they were, if I hadn't been so busy shaking my head at their cowardice.

'World didn't end when the virus hit, you assholes,' I muttered, shifting positions atop the statue. The bronze was warm where it touched my skin. I could have stayed where I was all day long, bored but comfortable.

Fortunately, I didn't have to. The crowd finished flooding into the parking lot, and there was a moment of chaos while they all tried to leave at the same time, cramming their cars into the exit without stopping to think about the fact that this was going to slow *everybody* down. I tapped the camera attached to my dress strap, zooming in on gridlock. The footage might be useful for something later, if I could go for a tight enough focus to keep people from realizing that it had been shot at a funeral home. No one likes to be reminded of the finality of death, and footage that forces that reminder never plays well. Kinda ironic, given how well the finality of death plays for an audience when it's up and walking around, taking bites out of the neighbors. A good zombie video is still money in the bank, even all these years after the end of the old world and the beginning of the new.

The last car pulled away. The funeral home was still, save for a few crows that had landed on the lawn and were now pecking at the grass. They took wing, cawing frantically, as the door swung open one last time and a tall, angular black man in an even blacker suit stepped out, his hand up to shield his eyes from the sun.

I didn't wave. I didn't move. Ben was always trying to take in as much of his environment as he could. His defense against the so-called glare was just as likely to be his attempt to steal a moment to get the lay of the land. That was my cue to blend in as much as I could, settling into the deep, utterly practiced stillness that had seen me through my childhood.

Ben scanned the street for a few seconds before his eyes focused on me. Raising one hand, he signed 'okay' in my direction, signaling that I had been well and truly spotted. I nodded, coming out of my crouch and sliding down from the statue.

The soft thump when I hit the sidewalk was almost obscured by the sound of wind rustling through the eucalyptus trees. I reached up and patted my former perch fondly. Much as I'd hated being here, the statue had been a good place to kill the afternoon, and I was going to miss it, at least until I found something else to sit on, some new high ground to claim. There was always new high ground. It was all a matter of knowing how to look for it.

'Ash,' said Ben, once he was close enough to speak without shouting. He never did enjoy raising his voice, not even in an emergency. 'Any trouble?'

'Some local cops got a trifle too interested in me when I didn't move for an hour, but I showed them my license and they moved on,' I said. 'I'm guessing I'll have a ping from the licensing board by the weekend, reminding me that the police are not here for my amusement and should be treated with respect. Aside from that, there was nothing. No shamblers, no ramblers, no major local alerts. We missed a few little stories. Someone broke into a mini-mart near Mount Diablo – they named the mountain after the devil, Ben, this is where you've brought me – and someone else started a fire when they tried to cremate their dead parakeet. Nothing worth chasing. Hell, I wouldn't even have turned my camera on if we'd been there.'

Now Ben looked amused, despite the pain lurking in his dark eyes. He was asking about the news because that was who he was: That was how he coped. I was less clear on why I was going along with it. Ben might be all about repression, but I've never seen the point of it.

Maybe that's why we're still married, apart from all the nonsense with immigration and then his mum getting sick and everything. I'm afraid that if I divorced him without someone else standing ready to take my place as terrible influence, he'd crawl into his own head and never come out again.

'You know,' he said, 'I don't think I've ever seen you turn your cameras off.'

'True,' I said, blithely. 'Did you know that border guards have scramblers in their collars to keep their faces from showing up on video? It's like they think people would illegally film the customs process.'

Ben raised an eyebrow.

'This is where you point out that, one, I *do* illegally film the customs process, and two, Mat unscrambles that sort of shit in their sleep, and so what's the big deal? I'll tell you what the big deal is, Ben. The big deal is how it shows an essential lack of faith in the population.' I crossed my arms and pouted as exaggeratedly as I could. 'Am I not an American citizen now? Do I not deserve the benefit of the doubt?'

'You've been an American citizen for less than two years,' said Ben. 'Talk to me again once you've been tapped for jury duty and lost a week to sitting in a little box, staring at a bunch of grandstanding attorneys who see you as their ticket to a top-rated Internet talk show.'

I snorted, but I didn't argue. The fondness of attorneys for shoving journalists in their jury box was well documented, even if being a journalist had been a get-out-of-jury-free card before the Rising. Making us serve was a way to punish us for our tendency to film whatever the hell we wanted – which had led to a whole lot of convictions over the years, including a few murder cases, which had become notoriously hard to prosecute since Johnston's Law made manslaughter impossible in high-hazard zones and Willis's Law made 'he was a zombie when I shot him' a valid defense. Kellis-Amberlee activated in the blood almost instantly upon disruption of the body's electrical systems, no matter what caused the disruption. Shoot somebody in the forehead and they'd die without reanimating, but any blood tests you cared to do would still show that boy howdy, they'd sure been a zombie when you took them out. Naughty, naughty zombies, always trying to eat the living.

Journalists screwed that up. Journalists did weird shit like strapping cameras to crows in order to get overhead shots of the city, and sometimes that meant we turned a misdemeanor 'you shouldn't discharge an unlicensed firearm after nine o'clock in a school zone' into a rare felony 'you shouldn't kill people, it's rude.' So the attorneys made us suffer for our sins whenever they could, knowing we'd chase the story as soon as the verdict was in and we were legally allowed to get into the meat of it. Sometimes that made the attorneys look like heroes, because it was a better story that way. Sometimes it got them out of their crappy public service jobs and into something cushy and media-related, where they never had to be in an open courtroom again. Either way, it wasted a lot of our time, and that was what they lived for.

Ben rubbed his face. 'No word from Mat?'

'Mat's busy,' I said. Mat was always busy. A planet-buster comet could be falling from the sky and the people of Earth could be scrambling for their shelters, and Mat would hold up a hand and say 'Sorry, come back later, this hard drive isn't going to reformat itself.' If I hadn't been so fond of them, I would probably have started keeping water balloons in my purse. 'But I did hear from Audrey. She says, and I quote, "Tell Ben we got this. He can take all the time he needs."' I smiled serenely. 'You see? They got this. This has been gotten. We do not need to rush back. Want to go for a milkshake? I could commit crimes that would get me deported for a milkshake. Twice if the shop had violet on tap.'

'You shouldn't drink violet milkshakes,' said Ben. 'Nothing consumable should be that shade of purple.'

'And yet I drink them anyway. Come on, Ben. Let's go to Berkeley and have something nice before we head home. You can have boring vanilla and pretend it makes you morally superior. Maybe we'll get lucky and a bunch of zombies will attack the soda fountain while we're there, and then we can be Johnny on the spot for a story right in the middle of the Masons' home territory. Can you imagine the looks on their faces?' I was laying it on a little thick, but that didn't matter as much as getting Ben to agree to do something – anything – apart from heading home and wallowing in his sorrow.

Wallowing is dangerous. Wallow too much and you can forget what it means to do anything else. Maybe that's not so bad for some people, the ones who live in gated subdivisions with guards at the gate and snipers standing at the ready, but for people like us? People who go out into the world and bring back the facts of the matter, whatever those facts happen to be? Wallowing gets us killed. There's no room for grief in this post-Rising world, where bodies are cremated as soon as they hit the ground to keep them from getting up and going for the people they used to love. There's only room for moving on, putting the sadness behind us, and letting the world back in. It sucks, sure, but it's the kind of suck that keeps people alive.

'Heh,' said Ben, a smile tugging at the corners of his mouth. I beamed at him. His smile died instantly, replaced by something far more familiar: regret. 'You know, my mama would have been happy to have you at the funeral.'

I stopped beaming. 'Ben, don't.'

'She liked you. I know she always said she didn't, but she didn't mean it. She didn't like what you represented, that was all. She knew you didn't mean me any harm. Sometimes she even said you were a gift from God, since you gave me an excuse for good Christian charity.'

'I don't want to have this conversation.' Not in public: not where some asshole with a camera could come along and turn *us* into the news. Everyone in the business knew what our deal was. I'd talked about it on my blog more than once. That didn't mean that some people wouldn't be happy to come along and start muckraking, trying to prove that we had never even been friends; that everything about our relationship was a business arrangement, and not true, if platonic, love.

Ben's face fell. 'Ash . . .'

'Milkshakes. Come on. Milkshakes, and distance, and time. I'm sorry about your mother, we all are. We want you to take the time you need to get all the way better. We can cover for you for at least a week before anyone notices, if that's what it takes. Mat says they can spoof your email address and handle all of the merch orders, if you want them to. We're just waiting on your word. I'll even talk about your mother with you, if that's what you want me to do, but please, not here. Not on the street, not where we don't know who's listening. Please.' I gave him my best pleading look.

I'm good at pleading. I've had a lot of practice at pleading. Pleading with his image over the Internet, trying to convince him to help me get the hell out of Ireland before I lost my mind. Pleading with the agents at border control on both sides – America to let me in, but not before I'd pled with Ireland to let me *out*. Our population was never the highest. After the Rising, when the Catholic majority really got to work grinding out the hellfire and brimstone, a lot of people chose to leave. Between that and the zombie sheep, it was no wonder the government started limiting migration *out* of the country, while simultaneously opening the doors to anyone with Irish heritage who wanted to come home, live under a religious hegemony, and produce oodles of fat Irish babies. Fun for the whole family!

And all of that had only been the warm-up to pleading with his mother not to contest our marriage, which had offended her all the way down to the marrow of her bones. Her youngest son had been the light of her life, the last piece she had of the good, clean world before the Rising. She'd been waiting for years for him to find a wife and start giving her grandchildren. Instead, he'd come home from an unannounced trip overseas with an Irish expatriate who was only marrying him for the citizenship, and who had no intention of either sleeping with him or bearing his children, even via artificial insemination. I'd been a real shock to her system, and if there was one good thing about this situation, it was that we'd been married for so long that I was pretty sure I hadn't killed her.

Well. Mostly sure. She *had* rather been counting on us getting divorced once I had citizenship, and when that hadn't happened, her disapproval had been a bit difficult to bear.

Ben sighed, shoulders drooping. 'I should be crying,' he said. 'I should be a soggy mess in a corner somewhere, going through tissues and confessing all my sins. Instead, I'm standing here with you, talking about ice cream. Don't you see how not right this is? I should be mourning more than I am. I should be *sadder*.'

'None of this means you didn't love her, if that's what you're worried about.'

'But—'

'How many times did you tell her that there's no right way to love? Well, this is the flip side of that. There's no right way to be sad, Benny-boy. Maybe you're going to stop sleeping, or cry every night for the next year. Or maybe you're going to return to business as usual, until one day you turn around and someone's wearing her favorite color, or carrying a bouquet of her favorite flowers, and it breaks you.' I put a hand on his shoulder, squeezing gently. 'The only right way to mourn someone is to remember them. The rest is just trappings.'

Again he smiled, although the expression came nowhere near his eyes. 'How do you know so much about mourning?'

'My mother was a banshee and my father was the cold North wind,' I said. I took my hand off of his shoulder. 'Now come on, what do you say we go and get that milkshake? It's my treat. You can have whatever you want.'

'I say—' Ben paused. 'I say hold on a moment.' He raised a finger, signaling me to wait, before he reached up and tapped the skin behind his left ear, activating his bone-implant phone. Not as disposable as a burner or as attractive as an ear cuff, but no one could take it away from him, and the only way to permanently disable it would be surgical. Better yet, because it was made of lab-grown bone matrix, it didn't show up on most equipment sweeps. Even if the rest of us were stripped of our gear, he'd have a way of reaching the outside world. That was worth its weight in bullets.

I crossed my arms, rolling my eyes extravagantly as he walked a few feet away, lowering his voice. That meant the call was private enough for him to not want me listening in. Rare, annoying, and a good opportunity to sweep the area. I stepped back into my original position in front of the statue and started my scan.

The funeral home was empty, the shuttered windows dark and the parking lot deserted. There was a red dot above the main window, attached to a small black box; a Devlin security system, most likely, hardwired into the local police department's computers. Funeral homes are no more dangerous than any other business that regularly admits large groups of people, and are probably a lot less dangerous than some. That doesn't stop their insurance rates from climbing every time someone gets a bad feeling about them, which has meant some heavy investments in security. The average funeral home is better protected than most banks.

If the red light was on, there was no one left inside: Even the staff had gone home. I switched my attention to the surrounding buildings.

Not many people will voluntarily live right next to a funeral home, despite the aforementioned excellent security. If I wound up in the neighborhood, I would have been asking about storing my valuables in the old embalming rooms. So it was no surprise that the curtains on the apartments to the left were shabby, repaired several times and then pulled tight across barred windows. There was a high fence around the whole structure, apparently wood, but with giveaway metal strips at the top and bottom. It was a steel-core oak model, and there was probably a switch in the manager's office that would allow the whole thing to be electrified at the drop of a hat. Good choice. The only visible trees were eucalyptus, whose high branches and friable bark made them virtually impossible to climb. Even better choice.

The structure to the right was more of an absence: a green field surrounded by a cast-iron fence, allowed to grow wild and weedy. It was surprisingly lush; someone was still watering it, despite California's perpetual drought conditions. That meant it was the property of either a church, a private school, or both. Churches could afford to water empty lots. They had a good income from their apocalypse-panicked parishioners, and their tax breaks meant that they were always looking for something else that they could write off. Private schools were sometimes more strapped, but almost all of them were playing on the idea of 'normal someday.' As in 'when we reach that normal someday and this all goes back to the way it used to be, we'll have this beautiful, secure space for your children to play in, so give us money, or we might have to sell it.' It kept the donations coming in, and it kept the idea of the virus-free promised land alive in the minds of the rich.

Something was moving in the field. I frowned and took a step toward the street, pulling a mag from my pocket. It was a single lens mounted on a wire frame, like a pair of glasses that had been cut in half. It clamped to the bridge of my nose, amplifying my vision first by a factor of ten, and then, when I tapped the magnification switch on the side, by a factor of thirty.

There was a moment of disorientation as my brain adapted to the virtual split screen of seeing normally with one eye and at a distance with the other. The first several times I'd used the mag it had made me sick to my stomach, unable to cope with such dramatically different visual inputs. Mat had told me sternly that they hadn't designed the system just to have it go to waste; they ordered me to keep trying. Now, I could use it as a sniper scope if I had to, taking the long shot without hesitation and rarely, if ever, missing.

My eyes adjusted. The movement in the field became a man: tall, dark-haired, wearing a brown suit that looked like it had seen better days. He was walking through the knee-high grass with an unsteady lurch that would have confirmed his status as one of the infected even if it hadn't been for the drool on his chin.

I didn't need to activate a camera. The mag was set to auto-record unless I told it otherwise, since anything interesting enough to be looked at in that particular manner was likely to be interesting enough to film. I zoomed in one more time, getting the gruesome details before I pulled the ear cuff out of my other pocket and clipped it to my ear. It pinched the skin a little. I wasn't usually the big communicator of the group, on account of how I couldn't be trusted in polite company.

Ah, well. Desperate times call for desperate measures. I pressed the side of the cuff with my thumb and said, sweetly and clearly, 'This is Ash North, license number IQL-33972, requesting a connection to the Orinda Police Department. This is a high-priority request.'

There was a moment of silence, broken only by a soft buzzing, before a woman's voice filled my ear, asking, 'Ms North, why are you still on the street? My records indicate that the funeral you were observing concluded nearly twenty minutes ago. Please advise your business in the area.'

'Hello to you too, ma'am, and I hope you're having a right splendid day, there in your nice, secure police station.' The infected man was continuing to shamble across the field toward the fence. He had to be following the motion of Ben pacing on the sidewalk to my left. He wasn't moaning yet; his mouth was slack, not tense with the effort of calling for his kin and kind. That meant we had a bit of time before the street became totally unsafe.

'It's been better,' said the woman, biting her words off sharp and crisp, like they had somehow offended her. 'Can I help you, Ms North?'

'You know that big gated field next to the funeral home? I'm assuming something like that would have to be on the local police department's records. Just guessing here, but it doesn't seem like the sort of thing you'd be allowed to overlook.' My zombie was picking up speed, shambling ever faster toward the fence. There was no mistaking the hunger in his eyes. Oh, he was going to be upset when he realized his way was blocked.

'Yes, we know the field.' The first traces of something other than disdain were creeping into her voice. She must have run my license number. I don't have a history of crank calls to the police. I may treat most things like a game, but when the safety of civilians is on the line, I take things very, very seriously.

'Then you may be interested to know that there's an infected man on the other side of the fence. Contained, but of course, we don't know how he got in there. I'd say late forties, medium build, Caucasian, brown hair, eye color irrelevant, due to full retinal retraction, but probably brown, if you're checking the missing persons lists. He's currently alone, not yet in full moan, but he'll get there.' The man's mouth dropped further open, sudden tension tightening the muscles of his cheeks and throat. 'Oops, I spoke too soon. He's moaning. Let's see what he flushes out of the field, shall we?'

Ben had finished his phone call. He moved to stand beside me, giving me a confused look. I tapped the mag with my index finger, and then extended my arms in front of me in the ASL for 'zombie' before pointing to the field. His eyes widened.

"How many?" he signed.

"One, so far," I signed back.

He nodded and dug his hand recorder out of his pocket, moving far enough away that my ongoing conversation with dispatch wouldn't muddle his notes. Mat would have to filter Ben's narration out of mine if we both wanted clean audio, but that was nothing compared to the kind of crap we asked them to do on a regular basis. Once I'd demanded stabilized footage of a bungee jump past a zombie cougar that had managed to get itself stuck on a ledge. Mat had done it, although not without constant complaints. Good times.

'Mat, it's Ben,' said Ben, talking a little too fast and a little too excitedly. 'We've got an infected man in the field next to the funeral home – what? Yes, I'm still at the funeral home. Ash and I were getting ready to head for a milkshake when Rosie called. Yes, my sister. No, she didn't want to talk to Ash. We buried our mother today, that didn't change her mind about anything. Look, can you check local missing persons and infection alerts, see if you can figure out who our walking dead boy might be? It'd be nice if we could get a march on this. Thanks. You're a peach.'

He kept talking after that, but I was in no position to listen: As always, everything was starting to happen at once.

Our infected man was still moaning, now walking at a remarkably brisk pace for a zombie. The moan meant he'd spotted us, and was now sounding the dinner bell for all his zombie friends. That could be a major problem for us if he had friends on *this* side of the fence – or really, even if he didn't. Zombies were stupid in isolation, shambling husks of the people they'd once been, hollowed out by sickness and by instincts the human body wasn't wired to deal with. Trouble was, zombies somehow got smarter in larger groups. Put enough of them together, and they'd start to plan. They'd start to figure out things like ambushes.

Or distractions. That field was totally enclosed. How had our shambling man appeared in the middle of it so quickly? He'd started out just close enough to catch and hold my attention, but far enough away not to seem like a threat. There was a word for something like that.

Bait.

I swore loudly before grabbing Ben's arm and jerking him toward the statue I'd been perching on for most of the afternoon. It was a trio of abstracted bronze people, the metal slippery and not designed for climbing.

Ben nearly dropped his recorder, breaking off in the middle of whatever he'd been saying to demand, 'Ash, what the hell? Let me go!'

'No can do, up you get, I'll explain why later, come on, come on, no time to dilly or dally or do anything but *climb*.' I shoved him toward the statue, looking anxiously around me as I did. When did the street get so damn still? Where were the pigeons, where were the squirrels, where were the little scraps of urban wildlife that hung around the fringes of man's world and signaled safety by not giving a fuck about anything that wasn't unnatural and wrong? Gone, all of them, even the crows, which had vanished from the funeral home lawn somewhere between my spotting the man in the field and right now.

Ben looked like he wanted to argue. Then he started climbing. We'd been colleagues and friends before we got married, and he knew how much attention I paid to my environment. Can't be an Irish Irwin without building a strong degree of situational awareness, after all; the sheep will take you out in a heartbeat if you don't pay attention to the world around you.

'Aren't you coming?' he asked.

'Too narrow; I'd knock you off. Climb faster,' I said, scanning the area again. My mag was still set to magnify. That's why, when I turned to look behind me, it looked like the zombies were inside of grabbing range.

I did not scream. I do not scream. I am not a screamer. I may have . . . yelped a bit. In surprise, not terror. I took a step backward, adrenaline flooding my veins, only for my non-augmented eye to inform me that I was being silly; the mob of infected now running toward me full tilt was in fact at least eighteen feet away.

Not so much better, really. But better enough to make all the difference in the world. 'Dispatch, are you still on the line?' I asked, keeping my voice bright and upbeat and cheerful. We could edit out the yelp. Pitch-shifting the rest of my dialogue would be harder, and would start verging into falsifying the news, rather than just reporting it. I wasn't *against* a little doctoring of the facts if it got me a better story, but there was only so far that could be pushed before people started getting pissed.

'Yes, I'm still here.' The woman sounded much more focused and businesslike now. Shouting in someone's ear will do that. 'Are you in distress?'

'I'm about to be. I have a closing mob of what looks like eleven infected, all about two weeks baked, judging by the state of their clothes and hair; I can transmit visual data directly, if you want to open me a loop into your system.' Mat would be watching for that by now. If the police decided to open a door, our resident techie would be inside in a blink, scooping up everything that could be of use before getting the hell out of Dodge. Mat was good like that.

'What?'

I didn't sigh or roll my eyes. It wasn't nice to taunt people who were just trying to do their jobs, and more importantly, I didn't have the time to waste. 'I said, eleven infected, not in the field, *on the street*, closing fast. You have eyes on the area – they've been watching me this whole damn time. Adjust the feeds to point at my line of sight, or let me into your systems, but either way, get someone out here before we wind up on the evening blog rolls in a posthumous sense.'

I tapped my ear cuff to kill the connection. No sense in letting things drag out and letting her think that the situation wasn't urgent.

She had the IP for my mag, and Mat would be watching like a hawk, waiting for her to open her system for my feed. As for me, I had other things to worry about. I turned. Ben was high enough up now that I could climb after him without knocking him off the structure. I grabbed the first chunk of statue I could get a grip on and started pulling myself up.

A yellow light came on at the bottom of my mag lens: the police dispatcher was plugging into my feed. It was followed a second later by a second yellow light, as Mat seized the open connection and started pilfering the police computer for missing persons reports and local disturbances.

I knew the dispatcher would want facial shots of the zombies. I turned as best I could to look back at the mob without losing my grip on the statue. They were closing fast on my location, and would be in a position to start doing the old grab-and-yank routine in a matter of seconds.

'Sorry, lady, that's all you get,' I muttered, turning my attention back to climbing. Ben had reached the top of the statue and was clinging to its head, terror and fascination in his face. I stuck out a hand. 'Little help?'

'Sorry.' He grabbed me and pulled, hauling me upward just as I felt the wind generated by a reaching zombie's hand as it tried to grasp my ankle. I jerked my foot up, away, before the zombie could get a grip on me.

There was barely sufficient room atop the statue for the two of us. Ben sat loosely, all splayed limbs and absolute lack of situational awareness, while I produced a pistol from my purse and aimed carefully at the lead zombie.

'We're surrounded,' said Ben.

'Yup,' I agreed.

'We're going to have to go through full decontamination.'

'Again, yup.'

'I liked that dress.'

'I liked it too,' I said. 'Pity about all the bleach it's about to soak up.' The fabric would probably survive, but the pattern would be destroyed. My closet was full of lovely dresses that were no longer suitable for wearing on camera, thanks to random bleach-spotting.

'We're surrounded by zombies.'

'Yup.' My initial, adrenaline-fueled count had been correct: There were eleven of them, not counting our friend in the field and anyone who had yet to join the party. I had eight bullets in my primary gun, and another six in my secondary. I normally wouldn't have left the house that poorly armed, but I hadn't expected the funeral of Ben's mother to turn into an outbreak exercise. That would show me.

'Are you about to start shooting?' Ben made the question sound almost academic, like it was perfectly reasonable, and not at all a function of our ridiculous situation.

'Not just now. You don't have ear protection, I only have fourteen bullets, and we're inside the potential splatter range if I'm shooting down with my eyes open. If they find reinforcements somewhere, I'll reassess. Right now, I'm all for sitting tight and waiting for the cavalry.'

'Makes sense.' Ben paused. Then he started laughing helplessly.

I gave him a sidelong look. 'What?'

'My mother would be so offended right now. How dare I get attacked by zombies at her funeral? I should have had the decency to do it tomorrow.'

'Technically, you're not at the funeral anymore. The funeral ended when the last of the mourners went home.'

Ben shook his head. 'Nope. I'm supposed to go home, eat casserole, and be sad.'

'Oh, I'm *so* sorry, I didn't know.' I looked down at the zombies. 'You hear that? You're getting in the way of casserole!'

The zombies moaned. Ben laughed. We waited for the police to arrive.

All in all, just part of a day's work.

There seems to be some confusion among my readership as to the exact nature of this blog, which is kept separate from my front-page articles and published under the 'Ben Ross' byline, rather than the more formal 'Benjamin A. Ross.' Because I do not care for confusion – it's messy, and detracts from the news, which is after all, why we're all here – I thought I'd take a few moments to explain the way things work around here.

This is my op-ed blog. Items posted here will generally be factually accurate, to the best of my knowledge: I say 'generally' because I will sometimes resort to hyperbole, humorous exaggeration, and swearing in an inappropriate manner. This is where I go to remind you that I'm human; that I have opinions of my own; that I will, for lack of a better way to describe things, sometimes fuck up. I'm a person, not just an amiable robot who reports the news.

To those critics who have attempted to use quotes from this blog to prove me intellectually dishonest: Please know that there is nothing wrong with you that being raised by my mama wouldn't have cured before you graduated from the third grade. Now shoo. Adults are talking.

—From *That Isn't Johnny Anymore*, the blog of Ben Ross, September 3, 2039

———

The process of becoming a naturalized American citizen is *fascinating*. I would've done it years ago if I'd understood how many hoops there would be for me to jump through, most of which were incredibly fun, in that 'how did you people ever go from colony to country, much less world power?' sort of a way. I mean, not to teach my grandmother's distant cousins to suck eggs, but I rather think we could have figured out a less inefficient system in twenty minutes with a dry-erase board. While drunk out of our minds on very, very cheap whiskey.

Very cheap. Aged in a toilet bowl.

But yes: As of today I, Aislinn North, am a fully verified citizen of the United States of America, subject to all the rules, regulations, rights, and other things beginning with the letter 'r' that this nation guarantees to its citizens. I am also eligible for a divorce if I want one (and I'll have to want one eventually: While I love my husband dearly, and our marriage was absolutely legitimate and will not invoke the wrath of the INS, he wants children and I do not). Hear that girls? Benny-boy will be back on the market as soon as I meet one of you that he thinks is worth all that paperwork. The line forms at the back door. Don't push.

—From *Erin Go Blog*, the blog of Ash North, September 14, 2037

Two

It took over two hours for the good people of the Contra Costa County Sheriff's Department to organize a police response, get us down from the statue, put us through a thorough decontamination process, take our statements, put us through *another* thorough decontamination process when Ben reminded them that he'd been inside the funeral home before the zombies showed up, refuse to cancel decontamination number two when I pointed out the fact that he'd needed a blood test to get out of the place and I had never gone inside to begin with, refuse to answer our questions, and finally tell us we were free to go.

They did not give us a ride back to our car. That would have been too much like being decent human beings, which was apparently not a part of their mission statement. The sun was long since down by the time we reached the antechamber of the long-term parking garage near the funeral home.

Ben paid the taxi while I paid the ticket machine, verifying the credit card with yet another blood test. There had been some issues recently with people who'd been infected – well, technically, people in whom the Kellis-Amberlee virus was amplifying, which just so happened to make them technically dead in the eyes of the law – maxing out their cash withdrawals at as many ATMs as they could before they fully turned. That way they could pay someone to put them down rather than calling in a police executioner or notifying the CDC. It was an understandable decision. I thought it might be quite nice to be shot by someone who would tell me they were sorry before they pulled the trigger. But once someone's dead, they're not supposed to be making withdrawals, and the banks were starting to get pissy about it. Hence the additional blood tests now impacting the middle class. If you were poor, they figured you didn't have enough for them to give a damn about, and if you were rich, you could buy a few less needle pricks in your lifetime. Only a few. We wouldn't want to start seeming *humane*, now, would we?

I was waiting at the gate when Ben came over to join me. 'All sorted?' he asked.

'All sorted,' I replied, holding our parking ticket up for him to see. I liked that it was still paper, a prehistoric artifact in a world of apps and plastic and everything digital. I had a collection of folded paper animals made from parking tickets gathered in garages from Galway to San Francisco. It was like a souvenir that didn't cost me anything – well, didn't cost me anything *more*, anyway – and that was a miracle all on its own. 'What took you so long?'

'The driver knew we'd been there during the outbreak, wanted to know if we had any thoughts on how it might have started.' The parking garage proper had two doors, one for the driver, one for the passengers. Ben took up his position on the driver's side. As a passenger, my test results would clear me – or not – a few seconds behind him. That way, if I was infected and he wasn't, he'd be able to get to the car. Forget 'women and children first': Like most security systems, the garage just wanted to know that we were going to get our car out of their precious parking space before we were eaten.

'And what did you say?'

'I gave him my URL, told him to swing by later tonight for more details.' Ben turned his head just enough for me to see the bright slash of his smile as he brought his thumb down on the testing pad.

'Nothing like driving those ratings a little bit higher when you have the chance, huh?'

'You're the one who understands the bloody system,' I said. 'I just point and click and go where I'm told.'

'The day you go where you're told is the day I join the priesthood, because clearly there has been a divine intervention.' The door clicked as Ben's blood test came through clean. 'See you on the other side, trashmouth.'

'Not if I see you first,' I said. He stepped through, and he was gone.

The testing panel hummed softly as it cycled, presenting me with a clean surface to press my thumb against. There'd been some sort of problem with the systems that did the cleaning about oh, five or six years ago, which had resulted in a whole bunch of people being infected. The company that made the cleaning systems went out of business, the families of the dead sued the government for a truly staggering amount of money, and all parties involved hushed it up as much as they possibly could. Even the braver reporters I knew had stayed away from *that* story. It was a one-time manufacturing glitch; it happened because sometimes bad things happen in the world; destroying people's ability to trust the protocols that kept them safe was only going to lead to worse down the road. The party line was good because it was true, and all the Newsies had stayed quiet, and all the Irwins had followed their lead.

Sometimes I wonder whether the real difference between us and the pre-Rising news figures we like to sneer at and claim to despise is a matter of scale. They belonged to big corporations, with all the advantages and disadvantages that came with that position. They made their own rules, sure, but they did it while someone else held the reins. We'll never be too big to fail, and so we get to make our own choices, tell our own stories ... until someone big enough to buy and sell us a thousand times over comes along and shuts us down.

The disadvantage of being independent is the way you're never going to have a safety net. All you can do is fly until you fall – and falling is inevitable. Everybody falls, if you give them enough time.

I pressed my thumb against the testing zone. A hole opened, and a needle bit into my flesh, quick as a whisper. Seconds passed before the door clicked, unlocking itself, a small light set into the frame flashing green. It was meant to be discreet, hopefully preventing a panic if someone turned up positive for Kellis-Amberlee while there was a crowd surrounding them. As if that would ever happen. Even in this brave new world twenty years after the creation of the 'zombie virus,' people are afraid of dying. Call it a quirk of mammalian biology, which is the result of millennia of being the ones who survived to pass their genes along, but people tend to become extremely upset when a machine tells them their lives are over. If someone came up positive in a place like this, they wouldn't step calmly aside and let the rest of the commuters get to their cars while they awaited their inevitable execution. They'd freak right the fuck out, and with good reason.

I stepped through. Ben, who was waiting on the other side, frowned.

'You have that pensive look again,' he said. 'Ash, what's wrong?'

'Nothing's wrong,' I said. 'I am a paragon of cheer and pith, like a busty leprechaun imported from the land of sexy accents to boost your site ratings.'

Ben snorted. 'Now I *know* you're upset about something. You only go full Irish when you're trying to distract me from the way you're actually feeling. What's wrong?'

'No, wait, I want to unpack one of those phrases before we get all touchy-feely.' We started walking, passing rows of parked cars. Many of them were in long-term storage, paid for by the month and marked with blue stickers on their rear taillights. A lot of them were pre-Rising 'classics,' the kind of thing that looked great on a movie set or a garage floor, but didn't add much protection against the living dead. 'What do you mean by "full Irish"? Am I only half-Irish when I'm eating cereal and drinking orange juice? Does beer activate additional Irish? What about soda bread?'

'You don't like beer.'

'Yes, and that's one of the many reasons I felt the need to flee my fair homeland. It was a matter of self-preservation. What were you trying to say? I'm trying to sort out whether to be offended or amused.'

Ben flashed me a quick smile as he pulled the car keys from his pocket. 'Which side of the fence are you coming down on so far?'

'Amused, with a small side order of "this is why I play to stereotypes sometimes, because it's fun to watch you squirm,"' I said. 'Could still change, depending on your explanation. Grab a shovel, start digging, see how deep you get before you hit bottom.'

'What I meant was exactly what you just said: Sometimes you play to stereotypes, usually because you're annoyed or deflecting or trying to knock the person you're talking to off their game.' Ben stopped next to his car, a sturdy old Volvo that looked like a relic of an early era, and that had been completely rebuilt internally and externally, even down to the bulletproof glass in all the windows. We were safer in that car than we'd have been in a tank, according to Ben.

Personally, I would have liked the chance to do a little comparison shopping. Tanks get about two miles to the gallon – maybe more if you're running on biodiesel, but converted tanks are even harder to get your hands on than the original kind – and yet you're in a *tank*. You have a gun that can fire depleted uranium bullets like, half a mile. Seems to me that's worth a little fuel inefficiency.

'So "full Irish" means "talking about banshees and the Blarney Stone," then?' I asked, as Ben unlocked the car and we both gripped our handles. This was our last blood test before we got home: needles set into the door locks bit into the heels of our hands, timed to within a fraction of a second. There were no lights. We knew that we were clean when the doors unlatched and we were able to get inside.

'That's right,' said Ben, sliding behind the wheel and clipping his recorder to the dashboard charger. 'You used to do it more, you know. When we first got married.'

'I was a lot more nervous then.' I settled into my own seat, dropping my purse on the floor between my ankles before I fastened my belt. 'I was leaving the world I'd always known behind, and going to live in a foreign country.'

'You make it sound like you were the little mermaid or something.'

'Might as well have been.' I let my head fall back against the headrest, staring up at the ceiling. 'I was just thinking about your mum, that's all. I always wanted her to like me. I figured there'd be time. I'd been wearing her down. She'd almost started to believe that I was genuinely fond of you, not just taking advantage for a green card until I could go through the citizenship process. I figure I was one declaration of intent to divorce from us being friends. Maybe it's selfish of me. I don't know. But I can't help thinking it would have been good for her, too, knowing I really did have your best interests at heart, even if I never had any intention of crawling into your bed.'

Ben hesitated before reaching over and awkwardly patting my knee. It was a charming, pointless gesture, and I lifted my head enough to smile at him.

'She liked you,' he said, as he turned his attention to the windshield and started the engine. The car purred to life around us, silent as a breeze and solid as a boulder. There were advantages to hybrid tech. 'She didn't understand a lot of things about you, like why you had to marry *me* – after I explained the situation, all she wanted to know was why you couldn't have found a nice girl to marry, and left me alone.'

'Because I wanted this to be a business transaction for the both of us,' I said. 'You know that. I get U.S. citizenship, you get an E.U. passport, and we're both in a better position to do our jobs going forward, even after we divorce. Mixing business with pleasure would have just muddled things up, in every possible way.' That, and left whatever sweet girl I'd settled down with always asking herself whether I'd only wanted to marry her in order to get out of Ireland.

No. It was better, by far, to be up-front about what I wanted; to treat every step as the mutually beneficial agreement that it was, and let it end without anyone's heart being broken. Ben and I loved each other. Always had. We just didn't love each other romantically, or as anything more than friends.

'I know,' said Ben, pulling out of the parking space. 'She knew too, after I'd explained it to her a few times. She was trying with you, Ash. It was just that she couldn't figure out how she was supposed to treat you. If she acted like you were my wife, she got angry at you for not doing the things she thought a wife was "supposed" to do – for not loving me the way she wanted you to love me, for not giving her the grandchildren she wanted. If she acted like you were just another of my friends, she felt like she was downplaying our relationship and shaming you for being involved with me, since she wasn't acknowledging you as my wife. So she got confused, and she shut down. It would have happened. Maybe it would have happened the day after we signed our divorce papers, but it would have happened.'

'So she could've liked me as an ex-wife.'

'I think she would have.' Ben slid our paid ticket into the waiting slot. There was no blood test required at this stage, thank God. Past a certain point, it stopped being security and became paranoia.

'That's nice.' I tugged at my ruined skirt, frowning at the bleach stains cutting across my pretty flowers. 'I was also thinking about that outbreak today. The infected used that man in the field as a decoy. I'm sure of it. Do we have our missing persons reports yet?'

'Let's find out.' Ben cleared his throat before saying, slowly and precisely, 'Dial Mat.'

'Dialing Mat,' said the car's built-in phone system. It had a pleasant preprogrammed female voice, factory standard, designed to be as universally non-offensive as possible. According to Mat, it was based on the lead actress from some short-lived science-fiction show that had come to a crashing halt when basically the entire cast got eaten at the 2014 San Diego International Comic-Convention. This is the sort of weird trivia that permeates our lives, and makes our teammate the top-rated pub trivia competitor in the Bay Area.

There was a beep, followed by a click as Mat's voice came over the car speakers. 'What is your wish, o master?' Mat asked, voice light and eager.

'Missing persons reports,' said Ben. 'What do you have?'

'Hi, Mat,' I said.

'The beauteous Ash speaks! My ears and fingers and other bits are blessed beyond measure!'

I rolled my eyes. 'I am fully equipped to break several, if not all, of your bones without breaking a sweat or getting deported. I'm a citizen now. Threats of wanton violence are back on the table.'

'I've met you ever. Threats of wanton violence were never *off* the table.' Mat paused long enough to chuckle at their own joke before continuing, 'I pulled all missing person reports filed in the last three months, basing my start date on the apparent spread of malnutrition and gangrene amongst the mob that swarmed you guys. It's fascinating. Two or three people vanished in that area every two weeks during the sampled time frame. No universal factors – age, race, gender, occupation, it's all over the map, with a few glaring omissions.'

'Let me guess,' I said. 'No police, journalists, children under six, or caregivers.'

There was a pause before Mat said, 'Okay, you are not allowed to be psychic. If you become psychic, I quit, and you can find yourselves a new pet genius. One who isn't creeped out by the thought of the Midwich Cuckoos rummaging through their brain like it was a jewelry store bargain bin.'

I snorted.

'Mat, focus,' said Ben. 'All these people disappeared in the same neighborhood, and no one noticed?'

'I didn't say "neighborhood," I said "area." The difference is both scale and geography. I pulled from a three-mile radius, which crossed two municipal lines and included a stretch of unincorporated but occupied land, butting up on the Clayton exclusion zone. These people are living in the backyard of the zombie apocalypse. No one has lived out there for *years*, and coyote sightings still happen frequently enough that I'm not going to sleep tonight.'

'So we have some muddled geography, we have some bad police communication, we have some bad luck . . . all right, I'll buy this,' said Ben. 'Ash, what are you thinking?'

'I'm thinking those zombies used happy boy in the field as a decoy,' I said, promptly. 'He was supposed to hold our attention while the rest of them got close. That's some pretty sophisticated thinking for a bunch of deadies, but not beyond what we've observed in clinical settings.' Zombie sheep were arguably *smarter* than the regular kind, as all their prey instincts switched over to making them better predators. 'So they find a field, right? Maybe it started with someone who'd been infected and didn't want to get shot before they converted, but didn't want to hurt anyone either. They run to a place that seems enclosed enough to be safe. I figure there have to be gates. Mat?'

'On it,' said our techie. I could hear typing in the background, lightning fast. Mat never did anything slowly if they could help it. 'All right, I've got a full blueprint of the location, and the most recent Google Earth map files. Looks like they photographed everything fresh about a month ago.'

'Perfect. Find the gates, and then start comparing the photographs of the fence around them to the ones taken oh, say, a year ago.'

'What am I looking for?'

I glanced at Ben. He was watching the road, but he was smiling: the small, satisfied smile he always wore when a plan was starting to come together. I loved that smile. It meant we were about to cash in on the world one more time, putting chicken in the pot and butter on the bread.

'You're looking for differences in the shape of the fence,' I said. 'It can't be too obvious, or someone would have noticed by now. A few bars missing, a little rust – there should be distortion in the top bar, since it won't be supporting the same weight as everywhere else.' Metal fences were a good start, but there were so many things that could damage them, ranging from vandalism to erosion. Being so close to the Clayton exclusion zone meant there was a large low-income population. Someone could have looked at that field and thought the metal was just going to waste. I couldn't blame whoever'd done that for trying to protect themselves. I *could* blame them for not finding a way to call in an anonymous tip about vandalism to the local police. The police ignore graffiti but pay attention to things like broken fences, broken walls. Everything is connected. By making themselves safer, our hypothetical thieves had made the field less safe, and they had allowed that situation to endure.

Mat sounded awed as they said, 'There are three breaks, all under the tree line; they aren't visible during any of the spring or summer pictures, but they're pretty plain during autumn and winter, if you're looking for them. How did you *know*?'

'We had troubles back home with people raiding National Heritage sites, looking for materials they could use to shore up their own homes.' Ireland was a developed nation like any other: We had our cities, our small towns, and our villages. But we also had a long history of isolated homes, of burial mounds and carefully preserved henges. Some people had ridden out the Rising far from any other living human, and they'd done it by learning to improvise their defenses from whatever they could find.

'So someone steals a few bars, and someone in the process of converting makes it inside the fence before they fully go over,' said Ben, picking up the thread. 'Where did the rest of the zombies come from?'

'Well, you're starting with two here: the biter and the bitee,' said Mat. 'When you only have one zombie, they want to multiply more than they want to feed.'

'And a fully converted one probably couldn't figure out how to get into the field,' I said, thoughtfully. 'You have one zombie in a field, one zombie outside of a field. The one outside is hunting, it tries to hide.

The one inside has nowhere *to* hide. Someone stops to stare, thinking they're safe and can report the trapped zombie later—'

'And the zombie outside the field grabs them,' said Ben. 'They have a hunting strategy.'

'They would have needed to replace the zombie inside the field at least once if they weren't feeding it,' said Mat. 'The infection doesn't leave you alive long enough to account for some of these missing person reports.'

'We know zombies can herd,' I said. 'Zombie sheep are worse than collies. When their friend behind bars started getting peckish and unwell, they just brought him a cup of recently slaughtered soup. As to why I asked about the groups I did, if any of *them* had been snagged, someone would have taken action. The zombies just got lucky in that they only took folks no one would go searching for.'

'Well, this is horrible,' said Mat. 'I'm going to keep running the data I have here, see how much of this flight of fancy I can verify. How far out are you guys?'

'Just passing Lafayette,' said Ben. 'We'll be home inside the hour.'

'I'll put the kettle on,' said Mat, and killed the connection, leaving us in silence.

Ben broke it first. 'If they can find the facts, it's my story and your quick report.'

'And if they can't, it's my story, since I'm allowed to fudge the details, and your quick report,' I countered.

'Deal,' said Ben, with a nod.

I grinned.

Ben and I met through a baby blogger site, an aggregator that paid aspiring journalists by the page hit for their best work. It also took a ludicrous number of rights, including the right to repost in perpetuity, reverting only when the site chose to purge their archives. Since they'd had a few of their babies go on to become pretty big names in the world of Internet journalism, they were notorious for *never* purging their archives. They would hold on to every crumb for as long as they could, waiting for the day when the byline underwent an alchemical transformation and turned to gold.

The pay was crap, the management was corrupt, and everyone who wrote for them knew it going in, but none of us gave a damn, because we were making *news*. We weren't just farting around on our own private blogs and web hosts: We were part of a real, respected family of sites, with the aggregator name branded on every report and lunatic stunt like some sort of badge of honor. We also knew the one good thing about the aggregator's fame-chasing ways: They'd never try to keep us after we said we were ready to move on to bigger and better things. They *wanted* us to move on to bigger and better things. That way, they could milk our time with them for all that it was worth.

Ben had been part of the Factual News division, writing dry, insightful, biting pieces on the state of poverty in America, and the way many of the systems that were beneficial to the rich and invisible to the middle class were genuinely ruinous to the poor. No matter how much the world changes – cancer is cured, the dead walk, and the news passes into the hands of the people, where it maybe should have been all along – the poor will always be getting screwed by somebody.

I'd been part of the Action News division, the few, the proud, the willing to do suicidally foolish things in the name of driving up ratings. I was the girl who snuck into Newgrange to watch the solstice sunrise light up the burial chamber of an ancient king, and nearly got eaten and arrested – in that order – for my trouble. I volunteered for the spring sheep shearing, normally an activity reserved for people who'd committed crimes against the government. My willingly exposing myself to animals of amplification weight was considered grounds for committal by my parents, who'd tried hard to make it stick. The fact that I was nineteen at the time had worked in my favor; the fact that I'd still been living under their roof had worked against it. In the end, the judge had decided for them, and I'd been transferred from my jail cell to a nice facility where everyone spoke softly and carried firearms all the time. When I'd started refusing my pills, they had responded by switching to patches and injections – things I couldn't say no to.

The whole time I'd been locked up, Ben had been fighting for me. We hadn't been close friends before that, more acquaintances who occasionally waved to each other in the contributor chat rooms before he went back to dissecting some obscure bit of American history and I went off to race a zombie pit bull for the nearest tree. But he was a good guy, and when the news of why I'd dropped off the web reached him, he'd gone to work. He hadn't hesitated. He hadn't said 'Well, a judge is okay with it, so she must deserve it.' He'd just ... gone to work.

Three months after my parents had me committed, the doors opened and I was free to go. When I'd stepped into the waiting room, unsure of my footing in shoes that had laces and actually gave me ankle support, there had been a slim black man waiting for me, smiling nervously. He did that a lot, I would come to learn: It was one of the ways you could tell that he was anxious.

As soon as he'd seen me, his smile had disappeared, replaced by the neutral expression that meant he was actually relaxed. 'Aislinn North?' he'd asked.

'Who wants to know?' It wasn't the most graceful response, especially given what he'd just done for me, but I hadn't known that; not then. To me, he'd been a Yank and a virtual stranger, and I hadn't wanted to waste the brief minutes of my unexpected freedom on him. I knew my parents wouldn't have agreed to this voluntarily, and there was going to be hell to pay as soon as they got the judge back in their pocket. I was an unmarried woman of childbearing age with no fertility problems, and we were a country that desperately needed its babies.

'Oh, I'm sorry. We hadn't actually ... I mean, you probably saw my picture, but it was the size of a postage stamp. Newsies don't show up in our reports as often as you Irwins do.' He'd smiled again, this time with relief. 'I'm Ben. Benjamin Ross? I thought you might need a friend right about now. A friend who's really, really good at badgering public officials.'

I had blinked. I had stared. And then I had matched his smile with my own.

'Oh, I think we're going to get along *really* well,' I'd said.

His stay in Ireland had lasted two weeks: long enough to see me settled in a new place above a friend's house, and to see my parents slapped with every judicial restriction we could come up with, and a few I was fairly sure he'd invented out of pure pique. They weren't allowed to make decisions about my medical care or mental health; they weren't even allowed to contact me unless I contacted them first. I had my life back, and I had someone new in it.

My girlfriend had given up on me during my second month of incarceration, recognizing the genuine danger she'd be in if she pushed things too far: After all, my parents were demonstrating a new, fascinating way of dealing with a lesbian daughter who insisted on putting herself into mortal danger. The last time I ever heard from Kylie was a week after I moved into my new flat, when I got a card saying 'I'm sorry,' and giving no return address. It had been easier, after that, to let her go. They say the course of true love never does run smooth, and I can't blame her for wanting to protect herself, but once I'd been free, she could have come back to me, and she hadn't been willing to take the risk. That wasn't true love. It was better for both of us if it stopped.

Ben and I had remained close, and when we'd left the aggregator to go freelance, we'd done it together, plotting all the while to get me the hell out of Ireland. Three years later, I had moved to America as his blushing bride, and now, six years after that, I was a citizen. I would trust him with my life. I did, on a near-daily basis.

We turned off the freeway and onto the rough, pothole-riddled road that ran up the backside of Albany to our home neighborhood. Well, calling it a 'neighborhood' might have been overly generous, since we were the only ones who lived there. It wasn't condemned or considered a hazard zone or anything like that; we would have been risking our licenses by living in a place that wasn't cleared for human habitation. It was just that anyone with money had moved to places with better security, and most people without money hadn't been able to afford a house there before things got bad. Since the rich still weren't selling – maybe someday we'd beat back the zombies, and they'd be able to return to their precious Victorians, live under their scalloped roofs, and resume feeling better than all the rest of us – that left most of those homes sitting empty, rescued from the elements only by the yearly efforts of well-paid maintenance crews who came in like the thunder, blasting away grime and repairing slumping porches before vanishing again. They never stayed past dark. No one could pay them well enough for that.

In a land of beautiful, empty shells, our house was unique, because it was a home. It had belonged to Ben's grandparents. His grandfather had been a dentist, and had bought the place with cash back when that sort of thing still happened. Now, with them gone and his mother having chosen a safer life in Berkeley, behind walls that had been enough to keep the monsters out, it was our rent-free do-it-yourself paradise. We paid property taxes, sure, but they were nothing compared to what we'd have been paying if we actually needed to find someplace else to live.

Ben brightened as we turned up the driveway, coasting toward the waiting garage. He hadn't grown up here, but he might as well have, and most of his life's happy memories featured this house in one way or another. There was no better place for him to go after a terrible day.

The house had been built long before modern safety standards had been in place, which had necessitated a few modifications and workarounds to keep abreast of new security regulations. It was a good thing Ben and I were married in name only: Trying to bring the place up to code for raising a school-age child would have required us to sell it just to raise the money. The open garage door revealed a space large enough to park two midsize vehicles, assuming we weren't concerned about potential damage to the paint. There was no room to store anything else. Mat kept their bicycle in the front hall, where we all tripped over it constantly. Audrey would have parked her car on the street if we'd let her, but that would have opened us to the risk of tickets and spot inspections, since the authorities didn't like cars being left out in the open.

The garage door lowered as soon as we were inside. Ben looked at me.

'We're about to get the grilling of our lives as to why we were still outside the funeral home when the zombies showed up.'

'This is true.'

'And then Audrey's going to remember that we buried my mama today and get all awkward about the fact that you're still my wife, and have an obligation to me under circumstances like this.'

'This is also true.'

'I just want to say thank you before all of that happens.'

I blinked. 'Thank you for what?'

Ben's shrug was brief, and slight enough that I would have missed it if I hadn't been looking directly at him. 'For coming with me and then standing back. For being there. I knew that if it got to be too much, all I had to do was call, and that *kept* it from becoming too much. I understand why you didn't come into the funeral home, and I appreciate it. A few of her friends knew about our situation and kept quiet out of respect for her. If they'd started in on you . . . I might have punched someone, and you know I have delicate hands.'

'Like a bundle of yarrow twigs,' I said solemnly.

His snort of laughter was almost a relief. 'I'm just saying thank you, Ash. Let me say thank you before we face the angry hordes of our housemates, all right? It's important and I need to do it.'

'Someday I'll understand why such random things are important to you,' I teased gently. He knew I already understood, and that I wasn't comfortable with gratitude; I knew he needed this, because he always needed this. He'd been old enough during the Rising to remember it, in bits and pieces, which was something I'd been mercifully spared. It woke him up some nights, gasping and clawing at the air. If little rituals of gratitude and appreciation anchored him, he could have them. He could have them all. 'You're welcome. I liked your mum. She was a good lady, and the fact that I'm not a proper wife to you was my fault, never hers.'

Ben smiled. 'Good.' He got out of the car. I followed.

There was a blood-testing unit next to the back door – only one. We could approach it together, but we had to test one at a time, with the door locking for three seconds between uses. Rules and regulations don't always get along with the real world. This one was meant to keep us safe. If I turned up infected after Ben had already gone inside, I would be trapped in the garage, nicely contained and ready for the CDC cleanup crew to sweep in and save the day. But we could have been carrying passengers, and they could be infected. If a zombie was starting from the back of the garage, allowing two tests at a time could have seen up to four people safely through. Restricting it to one meant two people, at best, and one at worst.

Ben pressed his thumb to the pad, wincing as our outdated security system drove a needle that was slightly larger than it needed to be into it. He was going to be getting a good chunk of his mother's estate – it was all being split between him and his sister – and while most of that money was already quietly earmarked for weapons and equipment upgrades, hopefully there would be enough left over for a new door security system. Something modern, that used micro-needles and cooling foam to take the pain away, and didn't lock down the whole garage every time it needed to be rebooted, which was about once a week. It was a good thing Audrey almost never went out, or we would have been in serious trouble.

The door clicked open, the light over its frame going from red to green. Ben stepped through, and it slammed shut with enough force to break faces and fingers. We'd wedged a pool cue in it once, just to see what would happen, and the damn thing had broken the wood clean in half. When the system said 'one at a time,' it meant it.

I stepped up to the pad, glared at it for a moment, and put my thumb down. The needle stabbed into my flesh with more force than had been necessary in years, seeking a large enough blood sample to allow for thorough testing. I clenched my jaw, forcing myself not to flinch. There were no cameras on me now. I could have cried if I'd wanted to. Most of my online persona was crafted from the idea that I was cheerfully immune to pain, a manic pixie dream girl with a gun in each hand and a winsome sundress riding up my knee. I hated the archetype, hated how much I'd learned to smile through broken bones and bruised muscles, but oh, how the money rolled in.

Everybody's got to have a gimmick, and sometimes the one you have to go with isn't the one you would have chosen under any other circumstances. If it put food on the table, I was willing to keep trading on my dignity, at least until our big break came and I earned the ratings that would let me make my reports while wearing proper trousers.

The light flashed green. The door unlocked, swinging open for me. I stepped through into the warm, cream-colored hallway, my shoes scuffing on the hardwood floor, and smiled to myself, allowing my shoulders to unlock. I was finally home. Whatever happened here, I could handle it.

A head appeared through the kitchen entrance, hanging at a diagonal angle that meant its owner was clinging to the doorframe. 'What took you so long?' demanded Mat. 'We started the debrief like, *seconds* ago.'

'I was negotiating with the garage security system,' I said primly. 'When you say "the debrief," you mean . . . ?'

'Audrey made soup, and we're going to eat dinner.'

I rolled my eyes. Mat smirked.

No one's sure how old Mat is, aside from 'somewhere in their midtwenties' and 'too young to remember the Rising firsthand.' It's never seemed like vital information, and so we haven't pressed the issue. What would have been the point? It wouldn't have changed anything. It would just have made Mat uncomfortable. Like many of us, they had things in their past they didn't want to talk about.

At the moment, Mat was wearing lipstick the color of watermelon flesh, and had glittery bows clipping back their midlength blue-and-green hair.

'Female pronouns today?' I asked, putting my purse down on the table outside the garage door.

'No, neutral,' said Mat. 'I just felt like dressing up.'

'Fair enough,' I said. 'I'll be down in a few minutes. I need to put this in the bin' – I indicated my ruined dress – 'and put on something a little less apocalypse-chic.'

'See you.' Mat's head retracted back into the kitchen as I turned and walked toward the stairs.

It was good to be home.

One of my colleagues posted an op-ed piece yesterday about the debt Internet journalism owes to Alexander Kellis, creator of the virus he called 'Alpha-RC007' and the rest of the world called 'the Kellis flu,' and Amanda Amberlee, the first person whose cancer was cured by Marburg Amberlee. And it's true: Their lives, and their deaths, created the world that allowed bloggers to step out of the shadow of the professional news media and be respected in our own right. But if I start thinking of it like that – if I start thinking of my career as something built on the back of a martyred scientist and a dead child – I'll have to find something else to do with my life.

Dr Alexander Kellis never did anything wrong. He observed strict lab protocols, filed his research with the appropriate authorities, and was trying to create a better world for everyone. His cure was designed to be infectious in part to guarantee that it couldn't be hoarded: No one would be able to keep it from the poor, or the politically unsavory, or the incarcerated. He trusted his medical colleagues. He didn't trust the politicians who so frequently controlled them. Like other members of his generation, he remembered a time before guaranteed medical insurance for the poorest members of society, and he knew that some would always be trying to take that fragile safety net away. His goal was a new safety net, eternally circulating, incurable and impossible to take away. What he got was a dead husband and professional disgrace. What he got was a rope around his neck, tied there by his own hand. His immortality is his name associated with the most feared disease in the world.

Colds and flus killed thousands of people globally every year. We don't thank him as a savior. We condemn him as a mass murderer.

Amanda Amberlee was innocent in all of this: She was just a girl who got sick, got diagnosed with cancer, and was lucky enough to be admitted into a clinical trial hosted in Denver, Colorado, administrated by Dr Daniel Wells. Dr Wells was the man who figured out how to use gene treatments to hollow out the Marburg virus and use it as a delivery system for the most effective cancer treatment the world has ever known. Dr Wells was the one who designed the virus, intentionally, to remain dormant in its hosts even when there was no cancer to fight; he built a stealth weapon, cloaked in proteins that mimicked the human immune system, tricking our bodies into becoming battlefields.

Dr Wells did not intend his virus to be airborne or transmittable outside of laboratory conditions. Had he been more careful in his clinical trials, less inclined to race toward immortality, he might have seen the signs of mutation, and he might have stopped it. The Kellis cure would have been benign without Marburg Amberlee to weaponize it into the virus we fear today.

Of the two men whose work became Kellis-Amberlee, there is little doubt that the lion's share of the blame should lie with Dr Wells . . . and yet there are few, outside of the medical field, who remember his name. Instead, we remember the name of a doctor who worked to benefit the lives of the poor and the disenfranchised, who was victimized by bad reporting and 'activists' who didn't understand the risks when they released his life's work into the atmosphere. We remember a little girl whose only crime was in not wanting to die.

History has always slept on a bed of bones. Do not idealize the monsters who put them there.

—From *That Isn't Johnny Anymore*, the blog of Ben Ross,
August 7, 2039

Three

My room was on the second floor because that was the highest habitable point in the house: high ground again. If there had been an attic, I would have worked out a way to shove a bed into it, and been proud of myself for the thought. Being that high up helped soothe the last of my ruffled nerves, and I came downstairs twenty minutes later, wearing a fresh sundress – this one patterned with sailboats and saucy mermaids, their painted lips puckered like they were getting ready for their underwater selfies. The old one had gone into the rag basket, to be used in Audrey's perpetual attempts at mastering the ancient and apparently difficult art of oil painting. One day she was going to burn the whole place to the ground by lighting a candle next to the wrong laundry basket, and then we were really going to be up shit creek without a paddle.

The sound of conversation and typing drifted from the kitchen. I followed it. Like all good Irwins, I'll take the path of least resistance whenever possible, if only because the path of least resistance is often where the action is. Also, the kitchen smelled like chicken, rosemary, and cinnamon, which meant the action was probably delicious.

All three of my housemates were already in the kitchen. Mat was sitting at the table, typing rapidly. Ben was leaning over their shoulder, pointing at something on the screen. Mat slapped his hand away. Ben laughed. Audrey was at the stove, stirring the soup as she balanced on her tiptoes, arching her feet like she was wearing imaginary high-heeled shoes. She was the first to notice me, picking up on some small sound or change in the atmosphere, and she was smiling as she turned.

I smiled back. It was reflexive: I couldn't help myself if I tried. Audrey was the sort of person you wanted to smile at. She was beautiful, with soft curves and bleach-streaked black hair cropped off just below her chin – too short to do much with, long enough to get in her eyes. She was a few years older than the rest of us, but you'd never know to look at her. Good genes and better lifestyle choices kept her fitting right in. As usual, she was wearing torn jeans and a paint-splattered plaid shirt that she'd probably stolen from either Mat's or Ben's closet. Her eyes lit up when she saw what I was wearing.

'You finished the mermaid dress!'

'I did!' I spun, showing off the way the skirt flared. 'I have more of this fabric, too, in case this one goes the way of the last. All the Scotchgard in the world can't protect you from as much bleach as I got hit with today.'

'Aw, poor baby,' she said. 'Soup's almost ready.'

'Awesome.' I turned my attention to the table, pitching my voice louder as I asked, 'So what's the story? Did we get it right, or did we miss the mark?'

'You got it *so* right that I'm asking you to pick my lottery numbers this week,' said Mat. 'Look at this.' They turned the laptop, enough for me to see the screen. A schematic of the fence was sketched there, drawn blueprint-style, white on a slate background. That was good. That looked official, and people would respect it.

Red 'X's marked the fence line in four places, one of them only about five feet from an official gate.

'Missing bars,' said Mat, turning the laptop back to face themself. 'They were removed sometime between the beginning of December and the beginning of January. There were a few pretty intense rainstorms in the area during that window, which would have made great cover if someone was desperate enough.'

'Someone is always desperate enough,' I said, hooking out a chair with my foot and sinking down into it. 'Have the police released a statement?' Overlooked vandalism in a residential area, leading to deaths, was a *very* big deal. Some heads were going to roll over this. Not ours, thankfully, which meant we could just sit back and enjoy the show.

'No, because they haven't found the holes yet.' Ben looked briefly triumphant. 'We can get the jump without technically breaking any laws, since they never told us to keep quiet. How long will you need to splice a report together?'

'About two hours, if Mat can help with the noise levels. Hey, Mat, can you help with the noise levels?'

'For you, oh shrieking banshee of my heart, anything. If only because I don't want you to kill me in my sleep.'

I smiled serenely. 'Now that's a person who knows what side their bread is buttered on.'

Mat laughed. Sometimes it seemed like Mat had been laughing ever since Ben had brought me home.

There are genderfluid people in Ireland, because there are gender-fluid people everywhere in the world. Some folks aren't boys *or* girls, or they switch between those states on a regular basis, sliding toward whatever direction currently serves as their soul's magnetic north. I don't understand it like I should; I was born a girl, I've always been a girl, and one day, when I misjudge a situation a little too badly, I'm going to die a girl. As for home, well, part of the post-Rising return to deeply religious values – not that Ireland ever slid that far away from them – was the suppression of our trans and nonbinary populations. If there's not room for lesbians, there's sure not room for people who refuse to settle down and be good little members of whatever sex the doctor called out when they were born. So yeah, it was weird for me when I met this brightly smiling, intentionally androgynous Newsie who said they wanted me to use neutral pronouns except when they said otherwise. Some days Mat wore a dress and wanted to be called 'she'; some days Mat wore overalls and wanted to be called 'he.' Most days, Mat wore skirts and fitted men's shirts, stompy boots and leggings, and wanted to be called 'they.'

The adjustment was hard. I'm not going to lie about that. I'd had ten years to get accustomed to the idea that when I thought about love and sex and growing old with someone I loved sleeping in the bed beside me, I thought about a girl, and not a boy like my parents wanted me to. With Mat, I had about five minutes to decide whether I was going to embrace the singular 'they,' or be one more in the long line of assholes who had looked at someone else's life choices and said 'nah, my comfort matters more.'

I've never much cared for assholes. Mat was Ben's housemate and best friend, and that was what had mattered when we met, and that was what mattered now.

Besides, there was something to be said for having your own tech genius on the premises. If it had wires and a plug, Mat could take it apart, remove half the pieces, and put it back together in working order. Our water heater was a Frankenstein creation of panels and pieces that didn't make any sense, but somehow provided us with endless hot water and some of the best water pressure I'd experienced outside of a government sterilization facility. Our roof was a sea of solar panels and our attic was a battery farm. It would take a six-day thunderstorm with no sun getting through before we'd have to pull a drop from the municipal grid. Add that to the fact that Mat ran the only combination grease-monkey and makeup blog currently in operation, and we had plenty of reasons to appreciate their presence.

'This is a good example of municipal neglect,' said Audrey, giving the soup another stir. 'There's no way that could have gone unnoticed if the checks that are supposed to happen were actually being performed.'

'Someone's been skimming the money that was supposed to go to inspections,' I agreed.

'Naughty,' said Audrey. 'Are we going to expose a corrupt civil service department, or just go for the vandalism and need angle?'

'Vandalism and need; the issue is both that the holes were made and that they weren't noticed, but mostly, it's that they were *needed*,' said Ben firmly. 'The local government's doing the best it can on limited resources. More than half the population is living in poverty, and would move if they could afford it – that exclusion zone again. I can't condone vandalism that leads to death. We need to be careful never to look like we are. But we also need to make it clear that this situation arose because of inequity of resources. If the people who stole those bars had been able to keep themselves safe without breaking the law, don't you think they would have?'

I didn't say anything. Ben always thought the best of people: It was part of his charm, that and his endlessly outstretched helping hand. I knew more of the darker sides of humanity. There would always be thieves and liars and cheats, people who didn't think the rules applied to them. We were acting on the assumption that the fence had been vandalized by someone who needed to increase their home security, and it was a good assumption; it was a *comfortable* assumption, one that left us with a sympathetic villain. But it could just as easily have been a middleman, someone who promised the poor and the desperate whatever they said they needed, only to go out and steal it for them. Those people were the scum of the earth. They overcharged for vital necessities, and when they were called on it, they said they'd been 'forced' by the people they supposedly served. It was a bad scene all the way around. Better to stay with the narrative that left everyone at least a little bit sympathetic, and leave the shadows alone.

Audrey put a bowl of soup down in front of me, the ceramic hitting the table with a thump. I blinked, first at it and then at her. She smiled.

'Eat,' she said. 'I know you missed lunch.'

'Yes, ma'am,' I said, and picked up my spoon while she was passing bowls to the others.

Audrey wasn't our chef: She was our Fictional, the third arm of our unbalanced tripod. She wrote hard-boiled pre-Rising crime sagas, following a group of fictional detectives through a series of seedy underworlds and dockside dives. She had a good following, and stood out from the pack by eschewing romance in favor of brutal murders and quippy one-liners. Her most popular detective, Li 'Lethal' Jiang, had been optioned by a small film studio, and was now appearing in a series of direct-to-download serials. And oh, how the money rolled in. Audrey could have bought her own place, hung her hat with any blog site in the country, and she stayed with us in our weird little collective, where we all took turns doing the chores, and someone else was always in the downstairs bathroom. It was a nonsensical choice on her part.

Love makes us do stupid shit sometimes. Audrey settled next to me at the table, bumping her shoulder against mine. I grinned at her around my spoon.

Audrey joined our blogging team a year after Ben and I got married. I fell in love instantly, which led to some serious 'this is a bad romantic comedy masquerading as my life' complications when she realized that I was flirting with her. She was smart, pretty, accomplished, and knew how to make the best potato leek soup I'd ever tasted: I never stood a chance. She, on the other hand, had some fairly strong objections to dating a married woman. When Ben and I had first sat down with her to explain the nature of our relationship, she had thought it was some sort of cruel joke. Then, slowly, she had come to understand the facts – why we had married, why we had *stayed* married, and why it was important that we *look* married, at least in the eyes of the INS.

And then she had kissed me in the hallway as we were on our way to our respective rooms, and I had been well and truly fucked.

In public, the three of us were poly, Ben married to me and dating Audrey, me married to him and dating her, her dating the both of us and smiling serenely when anyone commented on how she was a home-wrecker. It was a pretty fiction. If I'd been even slightly interested in boys, or if Audrey had felt that way about Ben, it might have worked out. As it was, we were still keeping it up now that I had my citizenship, waiting for . . . I don't even know. For the right time. For Ben's mother to die. For me to stop worrying about being deported. For *something*.

If I was being honest, most of the waiting had been on my part. Audrey had made her intentions toward me clear ages ago, and was just waiting for me to catch up.

Mat scrunched up their nose, looking at their laptop. 'Well, damn,' they said, with deep frustration.

I looked up. 'Can't scrub the sound?'

'What do I look like, an amateur? I've already scrubbed the sound. It's in your in-box, ready to upload. All I needed to do was isolate that dispatcher's voice, and that was half done before you hung up the phone. No. It's the Ryman campaign.'

Everyone went quiet.

Senator Peter Ryman was the golden boy of the Republican Party. He was also young enough to believe in freedom of the press. His campaign was trying to be 'edgy' and 'modern' by bringing their own blog team along for his run at the White House.

'What about it?' asked Ben cautiously. Mat had been a big advocate for us putting our applications in, which had required a *lot* of paperwork: proof of our license status, proof of our firearms training, and in my case, consent to a deep background check by the Ryman team, since I had only recently become a U.S. citizen. If they had found anything they didn't like, they could have contested my naturalization – and since my commitment was a part of my record, I'd been on pins and needles until our applications were filed.

'We didn't get it.' Mat looked so morose that it was all I could do not to burst out laughing. It's not nice to mock the pain of others, but the fact was, none of us had been banking on this opportunity the way

Mat had. Sure, it would have been nice to spend a few months basking in the limelight of someone else's problem, and the ratings would have been incredible – we could have done all the house renovations we had to keep putting off – but we'd never really been in the running. An Irish expatriate, a black man, a lesbian, and a techie who didn't want to be nailed down to a gender? Not the sort of thing that says 'we'll sell you to the masses' to a political campaign.

'Sorry, Mat,' said Ben. 'Any idea who did?'

'Give me a second.' Mat settled in to type, ignoring the soup cooling by their elbow. I calmly leaned across the table and pulled the bowl to me. Audrey looked amused. I shrugged. If Mat wasn't going to eat it, there was no sense letting it go to waste.

'You know, it's probably good that we didn't get it,' said Audrey. 'I mean, we would have been following the *Republicans*. Can you imagine them trying to deal with us? It would have been a disaster of epic proportions.'

'Disasters make the news,' said Ben.

'How many Irwins are at this table?' asked Audrey. 'One. One person at this table intentionally and voluntarily puts herself in danger for the amusement of others. I don't want to *be* the news, ever. I want to live a long, happy, peaceful life, figure out how to oil-paint so that it doesn't look like dog poop on canvas, and maybe see China one day. Becoming the news gets you dead.'

'Or it gets you famous,' said Mat. 'Okay, get this. The winning team hasn't been announced yet, but Georgette Meissonier just cancelled her attendance at all local events and locked down her group's firewall, and Georgia Mason has resigned from Bridge Supporters.'

I straightened. Shaun and Georgia Mason were journalistic royalty. Their parents had survived the Rising and become two of the world's first fully accredited Internet journalists. Stacy Mason had virtually written the book on what it was to be an Irwin, and her son had followed in her footsteps. No one took a risk like Shaun Mason. No one took a hit like him, either. We'd been on a few of the same group expeditions. I'd flirted with him because the cameras loved it, and he'd flirted back with exactly the same level of interest – the sort of thing that turned off like a switch had been flipped as soon as the cameras stopped rolling. He was a consummate professional, and everyone who knew his sister said she was even colder and more wrapped up in her work.

'If they were submitting an application, why did we bother?' I asked. 'They probably got it on the strength of their family name alone. They didn't have to *try*.'

'Come on, Ash. They're people like anybody else. I bet they have the same problems we do.' Audrey leaned over to rest her head against my shoulder. Her shampoo smelled like apples. 'This would have been a great opportunity for anybody. You can't blame them for trying.'

'I can blame them for anything I like, but since I didn't want this opportunity anyway, I am choosing to take the high ground and say I hope they will have a wonderful time,' I said primly.

Audrey laughed. 'Good girl.'

'Please, stop,' said Mat, in a monotone. 'The cuteness is toxic and will destroy me. Stop, stop, stop.' They looked up from the laptop and frowned. 'Wait, where did my soup go?'

This time, Audrey wasn't the only one laughing. Sure, we didn't get the gig of a lifetime, but it didn't matter. There would be other gigs, other opportunities to show what we could do. Our collective was getting stronger all the time. One day soon, the world would know what we could do. We would find a way.

The soup was delicious, and the conversation around the table quickly devolved into the usual post-op chatter: how to cut the reports, how to describe the situation well enough to make it thrilling without making it seem exaggerated or unrealistic. People who'd never been in a field situation were always happy to say it couldn't have happened that way, even when there was video footage available. Saying the footage hadn't been doctored didn't help; unless you got *incredibly* lucky with your raw take, everything was doctored in some way. A good techie would adjust the light levels, filter the sound, even stabilize the camera after the fact to make the action clearer and easier to understand. All good things, except for the part where it meant that digging into the file's metadata would inevitably find evidence of tampering. There was no clean video in the world anymore. Hell, some cameras tampered as a matter of course, which meant their footage was automatically inadmissible in court.

Audrey eventually excused herself to go upstairs and get to work on her latest Lethal Jiang adventure. It was my night to do the washing up, and so I tied an apron around my waist and got to work while Mat and Ben kept arguing about the best way to intercut the pan shots of the area that I'd taken while he was inside the funeral home. It was a pleasant backdrop to the slosh of running water and the clatter of silverware. This was what home was meant to sound like.

Neither of them looked up when I called good night and made for the door. They were sunk in their own little world, the pair of them, and they wouldn't surface until they'd negotiated the best use of our limited video. I wasn't concerned. I knew I'd get all the juicy action shots, the man moaning in the field and the hands reaching to pull us down from the statue's head. I'd even get the jittery, bouncing footage taken during the climb. I could craft a fabulous narrative from that, and let Ben have the dry, boring bits about civic responsibility and crumbling infrastructure – the sort of thing that got the older generation's engines revving, as they continued to think of the world as something we could reclaim one day, and not just something to survive. He looked at zombies and saw a walking metaphor for man's inhumanity to man. I saw zombies. I liked it that way.

Audrey was propped up on pillows in the bed when I slipped into the room. She looked up and smiled, her reading glasses resting on the end of her nose and her tablet balanced on her knee. 'They down there burning the house down?'

'Not tonight,' I said, reaching behind me to unzip my sundress. It fell to the floor in a puddle. I stooped to retrieve it and hung it over the edge of the laundry basket, making my motions slow and deliberate, aware of how closely Audrey was watching me.

By the time I'd finished undressing and pulled my nightgown on, Audrey's glasses and tablet had somehow found their way to the nightstand. She reached for me, smiling. I came to her, and we came together, and for a little while, the world was reduced to the two of us. Nothing more, nothing less.

Eventually, we slept.

Audrey woke before I did, as was her wont; she was sitting up in the bed, glasses back on her nose, tablet back on her knee, when I rolled over and opened my eyes. 'Good morning, sleepy girl,' she said. 'It is currently eight thirty Pacific Standard Time. It's Mat's turn to make breakfast, so I suggest cereal. And Ben is going to drag you out of here by your foot if you don't get up and get your report online within the next hour.'

'Good morning to you too.' I rubbed my face with one hand, yawning. 'How did we get a deadline?'

Wordlessly, Audrey turned her tablet so I could see. The chat function was on, and a line of messages ran all the way down the right-hand side of the screen. All of them were from Ben. They had started at seven o'clock, and grew increasingly urgent as time passed. By the time I caught up to the present, he was yelling in all-caps, demanding she pour ice water over my head and questioning her devotion to something called 'Sparklemotion,' which was always his go-to when he was really pissed off. My friends are weird.

'Okay, okay, I'll get up.' I rolled over again, this time so I could swing my feet around to the floor. As usual, my body protested every action. Some Irwins train themselves to wake in an instant, going from cool slumber to battle-readiness without missing a beat. I hate those people. I am a slow, bleary creature when I wake up, like a bear struggling out of hibernation. If I ever woke to zombies in my bedroom, I would be a dead woman.

It was different in the field. In the field, I was more like an exemplar of my profession, powered by adrenaline and energy drinks, rarely stopping for longer than it took to back up my files and run back into the bush. I just slowed down at home, dropping my guard and allowing myself to catch up on all the sleep I didn't get when I was working.

I stood, removing my robe from the floor and slipping it on. Even that seemed like too much effort for this uncaring hour of the morning. Audrey, who had probably been awake well before Ben started messaging her, watched with tolerant amusement. I blew her a kiss and slipped out of the room. Time to take care of the necessities, before my darling husband decided to beat my head in with his laptop.

The house we shared was technically big enough for eight if we went by the number of bedrooms available, and not by how many people we could stand sharing living space with. Despite that, there were only three bathrooms, which was a large part of what defined our normal cap. It was hard to like *anyone* very much when they were between me and the vital necessity of peeing.

Ben had the master bedroom, naturally, since it was his house. Audrey and I were down the hall, in the space between the office I shared with Ben and the room we used as Audrey's art studio. Mat slept on the ground floor, surrounded by rooms filled with buzzing equipment and endless dry-erase boards. The last bedroom was maintained for guests, and had been decorated by Ben's mother, who'd always insisted the rest of us had no idea what 'welcoming' looked like to a normal person. Maybe she was right. I didn't really know. Her selections had been pleasant and non-offensive and reminded me so much of the institution that I'd never been able to spend more than a few minutes in that room before I had to flee.

Ben was sitting at the kitchen table when I came down the stairs. He looked up at the sound of footsteps. Then he actually slapped the wood. 'Did you take a sleeping pill or something? I was starting to think you were *dead* up there.'

'Don't be silly, Benny-boy,' I said, walking past him to the fridge. 'There would have been screaming if I'd died in the night. You know Audrey doesn't sleep armed.' A point of loud and frequent dissent between us. I loved her very much. That didn't mean I slept next to her without a gun close at hand, in case the worst happened. She said she loved me too much to think that way. Some nights I couldn't sleep for fear that my heart would stop in the night, and I would reanimate and eat her.

'Don't call me Benny,' grumbled Ben, refocusing on his laptop.

That wasn't like him. Well, the objection to the nickname was like him — was exactly like him, in fact — but the grumbling and the glaring were unusual. I paused in the process of fishing the orange juice out of the fridge, turning to give him a thoughtful, narrow-eyed look. 'Something wrong?'

'The news about the Masons is all over the blogosphere,' said Ben. He was glaring at his screen. 'The story we got yesterday was *good*. It was like a last gift from my mama. And now we can't get any damn traction, because all the aggregators care about is sucking up to the golden children before they decide who's going to get their stories.'

'Joke's on them, mate,' I said, closing the fridge. 'Nobody's going to get those stories.'

Ben raised an eyebrow as he turned to face me again. At least he didn't look mad anymore. He was always easier to deal with when he wasn't railing against the injustices of the world. 'Explain.'

'You've met Georgia Mason, yeah?' I carried the orange juice over to the table and sat. When Ben nodded, I said, 'And I've met Shaun. He's a professional, and he tries to play it private, but there's a few things he can't hide. He loves his sister. He loves his work. He *hates* his parents.'

Ben blinked. 'But ... they're the Masons,' he said, sounding confused.

I swallowed the impulse to sigh. Ben had been raised by a doting mother and a loving older sister, both of whom had wanted nothing but the best for him. In a weird way, he'd had a sheltered life. Add the fact that Stacy and Michael Mason were celebrities, thanks to their place in the hierarchy of the news, and it shouldn't have been a surprise that he was confused when I said Shaun hated them. Somehow, it still was. Ben and I had been married for years, and we'd been friends even longer, but I kept expecting his naïveté about certain things to drop away and reveal the realism beneath. It kept not happening. Maybe it never would.

'Shaun wants out of his parents' house, which I assume means Georgia does too, since I can't see those two ever splitting up,' I said. 'They're not going to go to an aggregator. Cuts profits, reduces control. They're going to go independent. Watch. You'll see baby bloggers going dark over the next few weeks as the Masons approach them.'

Ben slanted a glance at his laptop, as if expecting an email to suddenly appear.

This time, I did sigh. 'They're not going to hire us, Ben. We're too much of a package deal, and we have too much of a reputation for getting stubborn when people don't want us to tell the story the way we want to tell it. They may respect us professionally, but we're not getting tapped for this one.' And privately, I liked it that way. If Shaun and Georgia Mason put together their online 'dream team' by gutting the bottom levels of the world's blog sites, all those people would enjoy long, lucrative careers as People Who Work For the Masons. I didn't want that. I wanted my own byline, my own headlines, and I didn't ever want to be in the position of putting my bosses' needs before my own.

Call me selfish if the label seems to fit, but I've had more than enough of people making my decisions for me and pretending that those choices were the right ones.

Ben looked briefly disappointed before he shook his head, and said, 'I guess you're right. It still feels like we're being left out of something amazing.'

'Mmm,' I said, and took a swig of orange juice from the carton.

Wiping my mouth, I suggested, 'Give it a few days. I'll post my footage of the zombies coming at us, say it took longer than expected to confirm the fence angle. Maybe we can go back, shoot in the field if the police don't have it totally locked down, or just get some shots of the burn they've probably done by now. We can give this story new legs if we have to. It's not like "oh no, there was a zombie" is something that's time-sensitive anymore.'

'I guess you're right,' said Ben. 'Again. Stop being right. Twice in one morning is creepy, and I don't like it.'

'Sorry, buddy. I'm planning to be right for the foreseeable future.' I toasted him with my orange juice carton. 'Something's going to come along and change the world for us. You'll see. Something always does.'

Ben didn't say anything, but he was smiling as he bent back over his keyboard. It was a small victory. Sometimes, that has to be enough.

Li Jiang slunk around the corner of the alley, placing her feet with the exquisite care of a housecat walking on the sidewalk after a storm. She made no sound, and the gun in her right hand remained pressed low against her thigh, a firm, constant reminder that however defenseless she might appear to the onlooker, she was more than capable of living up to her lethal nickname.

According to her sources, Blackjack O'Neil's men were camped inside that bar, waiting for their next shipment of terrified pre-teen girls to arrive. Once they had those children in their foul clutches, the auctions would begin. Her only source of relief was the knowledge that Blackjack didn't allow his people to 'sample the merchandise,' as it were: All of those children would remain untouched until they were delivered to their new owners. Which meant they would be untouched forever, because she was here to bust up their party.

Silently, she walked toward the bar, and death followed in her footsteps.

—From *Shadows on the Bay of Blood*, originally published in *Wen the Hurly Burly's Done*, the blog of Audrey Liqiu Wen, August 3, 2039

———

According to the nice people at Border Control, the majority of Americans will never travel outside of their home country, with the most recent numbers showing that only thirty percent have bothered getting and maintaining passports for international travel. Of those thirty percent, most use their passports to travel to

Canada for cheap drugs, or to Mexico for cheap access to beautiful beaches and well-secured vacation resorts. The remainder? Well, Border Control couldn't tell me how many of them were journalists, but I'm betting the number is pretty high.

Look, I get it. Plane travel is scary, cruises are scary, anything that involves leaving the house like, ever, is scary. Life is scary! Life is *supposed* to be scary. Before the whole zombie thing, we used to tell people to face their fears and seize life, to go out and experience new things and come home full of wonders.

I get that I'm an Irwin, and that for many of you that will make me the definition of unreliable when it comes to safety advice. But I'm also an Irish girl who moved to America because I wanted to face my fears. I wanted to see everything this world had to offer me. I haven't been disappointed.

Let me tell you, you have no idea what you're missing. So maybe it's time for you to get out there and find out.

—From *Erin Go Blog*, the blog of Ash North, November 3, 2039

Four

My predictions were naturally correct, because I am a genius: The Masons announced they were forming their own blog site, the aggregators fell all over themselves begging for something they could syndicate, and a little judicious editing allowed us to bring our story of municipal neglect and zombies in supposedly secure fields to the prominence it deserved – middle of the road, nothing that was going to fund a new mortgage, but it spiked into the top twenty a couple of times, which made Ben happy, and it got me a bunch of new subscribers, thanks to my suicidal good cheer in the face of the undead. Mat did a series of patriotic makeup tutorials inspired by the major candidates for President. The Congresswoman Wagman design was surprisingly tasteful, even though it involved a distressing amount of feathering, while the Governor Blackburn design had been immediately added to my bag of tricks.

The less said about the design for Republican candidate Governor Tate, the better.

It had been almost two weeks since we buried Ben's mother, and I was enjoying a lazy afternoon of lounging on a high branch in Briones State Park with a fishing pole in one hand, trawling for zombies. It wasn't that hard: All I'd needed to do was put a chunk of rotting chicken on the hook and cast off into the brush. The Kellis-Amberlee virus couldn't thrive in poultry, but the smell still attracted the infected, whose need for protein to rebuild their bodies was sometimes strong enough to overwhelm the virus's single-minded need to spread.

My ear cuff beeped. Since my cameras were rolling, I forced myself to keep smiling as I tapped it to activate, and said, 'Little busy here. Surrounded by sweet boys who want my hot bod.'

There was a brief pause while Audrey parsed this. Then she asked, 'How many zombies are we talking here?'

'Four so far. I heard movement in the bushes, so I'm hoping to flush one more out before I start shooting.' There had also been some tech employed before I came into the area. I wasn't saying that on the record. My ratings would be better if people thought I'd gone in blind.

There was another pause. 'Ash, are you in a tree again?'

'I am, yes,' I confirmed. 'It's a very nice tree. Very supportive.'

'Don't you remember what I told you about zombie raccoons?' Audrey sounded more worried than annoyed. That was nice. I didn't need her yelling at me while I was in a tree surrounded by zombies. Call me paranoid, but it didn't seem like the sort of thing that would make me *safer*.

'Yes,' I said obligingly. 'You told me they can climb trees and eat my delicious brains from above. I have yet to see one. I am disappointed in your dangerous Californian wildlife. Next time I emigrate, I'm moving to Australia.'

'It's illegal to shoot zombie koalas.'

'It might as well be illegal to shoot zombie raccoons, for as many of them as I've actually seen.' I cast my carcass-on-a-string into another patch of underbrush and reeled it slowly back toward me, bringing one last zombie shambling into view. According to the infrared mapping I'd done before climbing my tree, there were no more large infected creatures in the area – and my tree, while connected to the forest, was separate enough that any zombie raccoons drawn in by the noise would have needed to approach from the ground. Was this going to stop me from teasing my girlfriend about her excessive paranoia?

Nope. Teasing made for good audio, and the trouble with solo missions is the lack of people to torment. But as always, I had every intention of making it home again. Making it home was practically my specialization in the field.

'Look, okay, I don't want to think about this too hard, so when you finish doing whatever it is you're doing right now, can you please come back? Ben's calling an all-hands meeting, and for once it's not because somebody clogged the shower drain and left it for the next person to deal with.'

'Be still my beating heart. Be home in an hour.' I tapped my ear cuff to break the connection and pulled a knife from my dress pocket, leaning forward to cut the line on my fishing pole. It had been contaminated by contact with the dead; disposable things are never worth the effort of cleaning them. Maybe that's not the most environmentally friendly attitude to take, but anyone who had a problem with it could go get my fishing gear back from the zombies if they were that displeased. It was going to be no skin off my nose either way.

Five zombies milled around my tree. Two were busy ripping the rotten chicken apart and shoving it into their cavernous maws. They both looked up at the sound of my rifle barrel snapping into place. One had the hook dangling from his cheek, like the latest in punk accessories for the modern zombie. Both had dead, expressionless eyes. Looking at them was more like looking at sharks than people: cold killing machines, living only to consume. That was what Kellis-Amberlee did to the human brain. The virus wiped the mind clean, replacing human emotion and intellect with hunger and raw need. It was a set of primitive instincts that must have still been lurking in every one of us, waiting for the virus to come along and let them out.

My gun's internal silencer kept my first shot from being *too* loud, but nothing portable can actually silence a gun like they do in the movies. Flocks of crows and pigeons launched themselves into the air from the trees all around me as soon as I pulled the trigger. The cameras mounted in the upper branches would catch the flurry of wings;

I'd use that footage for the 'child-safe' version of my report, which would drive up hits on both videos, as people wanted to pretend they cared more about artistry and adventure than they did about gore. Everyone knew that wasn't true. But the hits went up, and the money rolled in, and the bills got paid. As long as those things happened, we could all be happy.

Shooting five zombies who were in the preliminary stages of a mob was no trouble, especially not with my marksmanship scores. I almost felt bad about it. Here they'd been going about their undead business in a secluded park, sucking down squirrel guts like they were spaghetti, and I had to come along and ruin all their fun. I was a big meanie. I still clicked clear pictures of all five zombies in addition to my moving footage. There were survivors' organizations that would sometimes pay for confirmation that a loved one was finally resting in peace, and the California Forestry Department had a standing bounty for zombies of any species killed within the bounds of a state park. I might be able to get paid twice for every one of those kills, in addition to the money from my reports. That was part of my motivation for shooting where I did, in both senses of the word.

Being an Irwin meant shouldering a greater percentage of the financial burden than Ben. Audrey made more than I did. Mat and I were close to parity, thanks to their makeup tutorials and fondness for setting things on fire to prove how sturdy they were. Mat was more of a Bill Nye Newsie than a Michael Mason: They still told the truth at the exclusion of all else, but they did it by getting down in the dirt and *proving* it. It was a rarer exemplar of the breed, and wow did it hold people's attention.

I was unhooking my rig and preparing to climb down from my tree when something waddled out of the bushes, moaning in an odd, guttural tone. My eyes widened with delight.

'No *way*.'

The zombie raccoon heard me. It looked up, bloody saliva dripping from its jaws, and made a chittering sound that still managed to come across as a moan.

'Hey, audience,' I said brightly, glad I was wearing my mag, and hadn't yet retrieved my cameras from the neighboring trees. 'I give you the finest example I've seen of California wildlife: the undead, uncommon raccoon. Say hello to Mr Stripy. Now say good-bye to Mr Stripy's head.'

A bullet designed to kill an infected human did a number on the skull of an infected raccoon. It was certainly impressive, and would have been enough to turn my stomach only a few years ago. Fieldwork hardens a person fast. It's that, or get killed because you were busy barfing in the bushes when you should have been watching your back. As my friend the raccoon had just demonstrated, no matter how well you thought you knew the terrain around you, it was always going to hide a few surprises.

It took about ten minutes to tear down all my non-disposable equipment and get the plastic booties over my shoes and tied off at the knee. Carefully, so as not to rip them, I dropped to the contaminated ground. Bits of bone and brain matter were everywhere. I'd need to call in the incident to the rangers so they could come out with hoses and sterilize the site as best as they could. They couldn't bleach the soil without killing the forest – something they were loath to do, although that was changing, generation on generation, as people forgot what it was to view large green spaces as anything other than death traps. They could still remove the bodies and keep the crows from carrying off the carrion, which could lead to secondary infections. Poor crows. They lived in a world that was basically a walking buffet, and half the time they were denied the best bits.

My car was parked at the top of a high ridge. It was a zippy little thing without most of the security features built into Ben's, surrounded by blinking hazard lights intended to notify any law enforcement who came by that there was a working Irwin in the area. Supposedly, that would keep me from coming back to find that my vehicle had been towed. In reality, if I'd pissed off the local cops badly enough, recently enough, my lights could 'accidentally' wind up deactivated, and I could be walking home. There was a reason I tried to be reasonably well behaved when dealing with the police. Being arrested was one thing. Walking home without a large enough collection of bullets was another.

The lights – and the car – were intact when I got to the top of the ridge. I opened the trunk, tossed my gear into the waiting plastic bag, and slammed it closed before producing a blood test from my purse and jamming it against my thumb. The need to do this before I could get into the vehicle was never going to strike me as anything but stupid. If there had been zombies on my trail, stopping for a blood test would have gotten me killed. As it was, it meant thirty seconds spent stationary and exposed, unable to get to my guns, which were already in the trunk – and that was part of the regulation. Since my gear had been in the field, it needed to be isolated before I could check out clean. What if one of those bits of brain had ended up on my scope, and got on my hands *after* I'd taken my blood test? Nope. Too big a risk. Much safer if I stood around outside and unprotected, hoping not to die before I could get back into my car, where the clean guns were.

The lights on the test flashed green, the proximity unlocking the car doors. I flung myself into the driver's seat, slamming the door behind myself with sufficient force to rattle the glass. It was over-dramatic, but it made me feel better, and that was what mattered.

I tapped my ear cuff. When Audrey answered, I said the three little words that mattered more than anything else in our world: 'I'm coming home.'

'Good,' she said. 'Hurry.' Then she killed the connection, and I hit the gas.

Traffic jams are a thing for the big highways on the major commute routes, not for the back roads that run too close to the state parks, and certainly not for the surface streets that lead into the low-income areas. I kept the needle at the speed limit the whole way, cruising comfortably past burned-out storefronts and fenced-off hazard zones.

It's interesting. The Bay Area balances havens for the rich next to blasted hellscapes for the poor, and no one ever seems to think it's strange for some people to have everything while others have to depend on a crumbling, unreliable public transit system just to afford the blood testing units required to let them keep going to work. The country has been in a state of high economic inequality since before the Rising. Some people have even gone so far as to say that it *caused* the Rising, since a lack of trust for authority and the media helped motivate the Mayday Army to release Dr Kellis's yet-untested cure into the atmosphere. So it would have been reasonable to think that maybe after the dead walked, things would get better for the living poor.

Being reasonable doesn't make a thing true. Sadly.

The garage was open when I came around the corner. Mat must have activated the tracker in my car and used it to estimate when my route would get me home. It was a cute trick. Risky as hell, but cute, and I appreciated it for what it was. There were two black sedans parked in front of the house, and a black van parked across the street, in front of one of the empty houses. That gave me a little more pause than the open garage door, the first traces of concern spider-walking down my throat.

Audrey wouldn't have sounded so calm if the INS had decided to revoke my citizenship and toss me out of the country. We had several coded ways of saying 'run,' just in case the need ever arose. She hadn't used any of those codes. And Ben hadn't tried to contact me, hadn't sent an email or pinged my phone. Whatever was going on, it wasn't about deportation. It couldn't be about eviction, either: His grandfather's will had been perfectly clear, and Ben owned the house, no strings attached. So what the hell was going on?

I pulled into the garage and killed the engine while the door was sliding closed behind me. There was nothing I could do to make the blood test that would let me into the house cycle any faster, but if there'd been a way to bypass it, I would have. My friends – my *family*, however dysfunctional – were in that house, and whatever was going on, they needed me.

The light flashed green. The door clicked open. I swung it wide, and froze as the two large, black-suited men in the hallway pointed their service pistols at me. One was aiming for my head; the other was aiming for my heart. It was a good cover pattern when dealing with the living, and that didn't make me feel *any* better about it, thanks.

'State your name and business,' said the larger of the two men.

I blinked at him. Then I let go of the door, which slammed closed with its usual bone-snapping force. Both men jumped. I folded my arms, narrowed my eyes, and said, 'My name is Aislinn North, and it seems to me that my business is my business, given I've just entered *my* home. Who would you be, then? Are you the local goon squad, come to explain to us why we should be considering joining your church before the dead walk? Because I hate to be the one to break your bubble, but the dead are already here.'

'Ash!' Ben's voice was welcome. The edge of 'oh God no she's going to start a bar fight' was familiar, and enough to make me relax, just a bit. He wasn't worried about me getting shot; he was worried about me nutting somebody and needing a full decontamination. 'Ash, it's okay.' He shoved his way between the two men. 'These gentlemen are security for our guest. I'm sorry they greeted you like this. We're going to talk about that. For right now, can you go and get yourself cleaned up? We have a lot to go over, and we need your input.'

The urge to break protocol and throttle him thoroughly was strong. But it was Ben's job to see to our interests, and to keep me from committing any federal crimes. I glared at him as I nodded assent.

'If you gentlemen would let me get to the stairs, I'll be heading for my room to change and decontaminate,' I said, as mildly as I could. 'I do that better when no one's aiming a gun at me, as it turns out. Not sure where that quirk came from, but there it is.'

The two men exchanged a look before glancing to Ben. Then, slowly, they lowered their guns and stepped to the side, allowing me access to the stairs.

I did not flee. Fleeing would have implied that I was frightened, and I wasn't frightened. I was . . . unsettled, and annoyed, and highly motivated to get the hell out of there. So I didn't flee, but I did take the stairs two at a time, and I didn't look back until I got to the bathroom and shut myself inside. The door auto-locked, beginning the mandatory post-field decontamination process.

Our home security system was old enough that we'd all learned not to go to the bathroom just as someone was getting back to the house: If Audrey had been seized by the need to pee as my blood test was processing, she could have been caught in the decon cycle intended for me, getting locked in the downstairs bathroom until my checks came back clean. It had happened before, and while we were a lot more careful about it now than we used to be, none of us had any doubt that it was going to happen again. It was just part of the reality of living in our situation.

Carefully, I stripped to the skin, dropping each article of clothing into the white biohazard hamper that fed directly to the washing machine in the basement. Even my bra had to go in, which was *hell* on my lingerie. Every female Irwin I knew participated in a twice-yearly bra drive to replenish our underwear drawers. Asking people to give us money for dainties was a little grubby, but otherwise, we'd have been holding our tits whenever we had to run, thanks to the total lack of elasticity.

Before I closed the lid on the hamper, I twisted the dial to 'delicate.' It didn't make *much* of a difference, but at least the delicate cycle used color-safe bleach, and could extend the life of my average sundress by two or three washings – long enough for me to sew a replacement.

Sometimes I wondered if male Irwins had these problems. Most of them seemed to default to the classic 'tank top or muscle tee and khaki pants' uniform, and nobody was going to notice if those got a little bleach-stained or torn or had to be replaced in the middle of a video. Female Irwins, though — we all had to have our 'gimmick.' If we didn't, we weren't really trying, and viewers might decide we weren't strong enough or fast enough or clever enough, let's go check that other guy, what's his name, *he's* a real journalist. There was no official ruling that said tits and ass were what sold the news, but we knew the score. Humanity had made a lot of changes since the Rising. It hadn't become a completely new beast.

The shower turned on as soon as I stepped inside, and the stall door clicked, locking behind me. I'd stay put through a full sterilization cycle, or . . . actually, there was no 'or.' Unless I wanted to take a sledgehammer into the shower, I'd stay put through a full sterilization cycle. Hot water blasted me, just barely this side of scalding. I closed my eyes and turned my face into the spray, enjoying this brief moment of normalcy. It wasn't going to last. It never did — and indeed, as I finished the thought, the bleach cascaded down, blanketing me, washing away any fomite traces of Kellis-Amberlee that might have somehow been able to find their way onto my skin.

I'm a natural redhead. Maybe that's a cliché, but tell it to my genetics, which decided I would look better with too many freckles and hair the color of a good tikka masala. Add regular bleaching and chemical treatments to try to repair my damaged follicles, and I usually look like I spend a lot more time in the sun than would be a good idea for someone with my complexion. Skin cancer isn't a concern anymore, thankfully. Sunburn still is, and always will be.

Decontamination showers last a minimum of six minutes, assuming you hit all your marks and rinse all your creams and soaps away with the maximum of efficiency. I've been doing this long enough that I have it down to a science, and by the time the shower beeped for the first exit window, I was long past clean and sliding down the hill toward polished. I hit the button to kill the cycle. The door unlatched and swung open, releasing billows of steam into the bathroom and highlighting one of the issues with my having been herded into decon like a zombie being steered into the killing chute: I had no towel, and I certainly had no clean clothes.

As if on cue, there was a knock at the bathroom door. 'You decent?' called Audrey.

'You said I was pretty damn good last night,' I called back. 'If I've been downgraded to "decent," we're going to have words.'

She opened the bathroom door and let herself in, holding an armload of fabric toward me. There was a towel on the top of the pile. I grabbed it and started drying my face and hair as quickly as I could manage. Audrey watched me, something between tolerance and trepidation in her expression. It was an odd combination, especially for her. I slowed in my drying and lowered the towel, eyeing her warily.

'What?'

'Don't freak out, all right? We needed to get you into decontamination as fast as possible because of our guests – they might have decided to leave, or they might have decided to shoot you, and either way would have been bad – but I'm up here to get you ready to come down, and to tell you not to freak out.'

'If I'm getting deported . . .'

'If you were getting deported, I would have met you in the garage, and we'd already be fifty miles from here. Screw decontamination.' Audrey's expression hardened for a moment, turning icy cold. Then she shook her head, and the moment passed. Thankfully. She was *scary* when she got like that. 'I just need you to promise not to freak out, all right?'

'All right. I won't freak out.' I resumed drying. 'This is definitely weird, however. On the scale of one to "alligators in the basement," I feel like we're trending closer to "alligators" than anything else.'

'Not a bad choice of words,' said Audrey. She took a deep breath. 'Does the name "Susan Kilburn" mean anything to you?'

'Sounds like the girl I dated when I was in sixth form, but her name was Karen, and I doubt she'd come to America just to throw our lives into a tizzy,' I said.

'She's the governor of Oregon,' said Audrey.

'All right, that works as well,' I said. I dropped my towel, taking the panties from the pile she was holding. She'd arranged everything in the order in which it was to be used, which was remarkably clever; I usually just carried an armload of jumbled fabric in, dumped it on the sink, and picked out what I needed.

The panties matched the bra that had been sitting beneath them. I felt the first prickle of excitement. If this was something that needed me properly put together all the way down to the skin, then this was something *big*.

'She's one of the three primary presidential candidates being put forth by the Democrats this year,' said Audrey. 'It's her, Governor Frances Blackburn out of Maine, and Senator Eliot York out of Illinois. No one's sure who the front-runner is going to be, but Governor Kilburn is definitely in the running.'

'All right,' I repeated agreeably, and pulled my bra on. I was still damp; the fabric stuck to the skin, forcing me to spend more time arranging myself than usual. Maybe that's why I missed the frustrated look on Audrey's face, and the way her smile had frozen, becoming more of a rictus.

'Ash,' she said.

I kept fighting with my bra.

'Aislinn,' she said.

I looked up. 'Yeah?'

'Governor Susan Kilburn, one of the Democratic candidates for President of the United States of America, is sitting in our kitchen, enjoying Mat's attempts at small talk, while Ben tries not to hyperventilate,' said Audrey patiently. 'Now, I recognize that murdering you widows Ben and leaves me without a girlfriend, but if you don't get your clothes on and get downstairs in the next five minutes, I'm going to consider it. Are we on the same page now?'

I stared at her for a beat. Then I grabbed my sundress, abstractly pleased to see that she'd fished the patriotic one from the back of my closet – white fabric, red and blue stars. I'd worn it to my citizenship ceremony, and then on my first zombie hunt as a genuine American Irwin. The bleach damage was minimal, and as long as no one was staring at my ass, they probably wouldn't notice.

'Oh, good,' said Audrey. 'You're finally moving.'

'Do I need shoes?' I demanded. 'I don't think I have time to blow-dry my hair, can I go downstairs with wet hair *and* no shoes? Is there some sort of deportation offense in appearing in front of a presidential candidate with no shoes?'

'I don't think anyone's going to be looking at your feet,' said Audrey. She picked up my discarded towel and hung it on the wall to dry while I was still struggling into my sundress. Then she folded her arms, giving me a critical up-and-down look. 'You'll do. You look like you've just come out of the field, but under the circumstances, that can only be a good thing. Now come on.'

She turned to open the bathroom door. I leaned past her, using my longer arms to push it shut again before she could get out into the hall.

'Audrey, breathe,' I said. 'How serious is this?'

She looked at me for a moment. Then she leaned up, kissed me, and smiled. 'This could change *everything*,' she said. 'Now come on. Let me out, and let's go meet the woman who's going to make us famous.'

I took my hand off the door. Audrey slipped out into the hall and I followed her, feeling a little awkward padding down the stairs in my bare feet.

The men who'd met me at the garage door were standing in the kitchen doorway when we arrived. Each of them was holding a blood testing unit. I stared.

'Is this a joke?' I asked.

'No, ma'am,' said one of the men. He held his blood testing unit out toward me. The other offered his to Audrey. 'You must have a clean bill of health before we can allow you to enter.'

'I took a blood test to get into the house.'

'Yes, ma'am.'

'I just finished a full decontamination shower. I smell like bleach.'

'Yes, ma'am.'

'There is no *possible way* I've been exposed to live-state Kellis-Amberlee between the bathroom and here.'

'Yes, ma'am.' Through it all, the man continued patiently offering me his blood testing unit.

Audrey already had her thumb on the unit that was intended for her. She looked my way and rolled her eyes. 'Just do it, Ash. This is going to take forever if you try to argue with them. These are not men who have a "negotiation" button.'

'Bloody Americans,' I muttered, and pressed my thumb down on the testing pad.

I'll give them this much: Their technology was much more advanced than ours. I didn't feel the needle go in, just the soft chill of the cleansing foam hitting my skin and preventing even that hairline prick from bleeding. The lights on the top of the test flashed between red and green for several seconds before settling on green, marking me as uninfected. That was a lie – we're all infected – but I wasn't an immediate danger, and that was essentially the same thing.

Audrey had already passed her own blood test by the time I was cleared, and was waiting for me, twisting a lock of her hair anxiously around her finger. She dropped her hand when the men stepped aside, and smiled at me before stepping into the kitchen. I followed. I had followed her this far; I really had no excuse to turn and run away now.

Ben and Mat were sitting at the kitchen table with a stranger. She looked to be in her late thirties, although the truth of that was anyone's guess: With enough money, aging can become practically optional, at least on the outside. Her skin was smooth and unwrinkled, and her hair was a perfect shade of chestnut brown that could only have come out of a bottle; otherwise, the bleach damage would have been visible. She had a strong jaw and a mouth that looked designed for smiling, which was probably all that had saved her from a nose job when her political handlers got hold of her. Her nose was strong and slightly squared off at the end, and it balanced her face completely.

Her clothes were more of a surprise than her carefully considered physicality: When I'd thought about meeting a prominent U.S. politician — which, to be honest, I hadn't done very often — I had never considered them showing up in my kitchen in a Willamette University sweatshirt and comfortable, broken-in jeans.

She stood when I entered the kitchen, and reached for me, offering her hand. 'You must be Aislinn North,' she said. 'We've been waiting for you. I'm sorry not to have called ahead. I'm Susan Kilburn.'

'I'm sorry to have kept you waiting,' I replied, my manners kicking in despite everything. Her handshake was firm without being overbearing. I wondered how many hours she'd spent practicing that before settling on the right amount of pressure to apply.

Susan — Governor Kilburn — it was so hard to know what to call her. Yes, she was trying to become the next President of the United States, but right now she was standing in my kitchen looking like she was going to start pumping Mat for makeup tips. As for the rest of my team, they weren't helping. Audrey was behind me, where I couldn't see her face. Mat looked starstruck, like they couldn't believe they were breathing the same air as a woman who might one day hold the highest office in the country. And Ben had just plain shut down, reverting to the perfectly neutral expression he used when he was trying to process what was going on around him. No help there.

Thankfully, she seemed to understand how strange this situation really was. She smiled, sat, and said, 'It's no concern. If I'd called ahead, I'm sure you wouldn't have been out in the field. But since your fieldwork is what makes you so appealing to me, I wouldn't have wanted to interfere with your report. That goes for all of you. I'm not here to get in the way of what you do. If anything, my visit is intended to be about the opposite.'

'Which is why you said you wanted to wait until everyone was home before you told us what was going on. Not that we don't appreciate your visit — we just know better than to think this is a social call,' said Ben. 'There's pressing the flesh, and then there's trying to individually visit every voter in the country. One of them works, the other gets you killed.'

'Yes, but if the other got me elected, I'd consider it anyway,' said Governor Kilburn, and laughed.

'We're all here now,' said Audrey. There was a thin edge to her voice that might have been inaudible to anyone but me. She was excited, and trying to hide it. 'Do you want to let us know why you dropped by?'

'Of course.' Governor Kilburn looked around the table, her expression smoothing out until it had become regal, political — the face of a President in waiting, a woman who was poised to become a commander in chief. 'I'm assuming you've all heard about the blogger contingent attached to the Ryman campaign over on the Republican side of the fence.'

'We put in an application, ma'am,' said Ben. Governor Kilburn raised an eyebrow. He shrugged, unrepentant. 'Politics are one thing; work is another. My family has always voted Democrat, but if following a Republican around the country for a year would change my status in the blogging world, I'd do it.'

'I'd eat live eels,' said Mat, not to be outdone. Audrey and I turned to blink at them. They grinned briefly.

'There are no live eels in my offer, I'm afraid,' said Governor Kilburn, pulling things back on track. 'I'm here *because* you put in that application, although I wasn't sure you'd admit its existence to me. I have access to certain data from the Ryman office—'

'Did you hack the competition?' asked Mat, sounding enthralled.

'Peter is an old friend of mine,' said Governor Kilburn. 'We announced our intention to run on the same day. *That* was a fun phone call. After he'd chosen his team, he thought I might want to follow suit, and since his people had already done all the background checks and baseline vetting, he didn't see a problem with giving me the data.'

'Peter – you mean Senator Ryman?' I asked. 'You're on a first-name basis with the competition?'

'We're not competition yet,' she said, with a quick, feral grin. 'He has to take his team's nomination, and I have to take mine. Until we reach that point, we'll do whatever we need to do in order to support each other, because it's always better the devil you know in a situation like this one. Right now, we're just two people gunning for the same job. Maybe one of us will get it, and the other will get a cushy cabinet position for the next four years. Maybe neither of us will get it, and we'll wind up drowning our sorrows in his wife's excellent sangria while we plan for our next shot. Either way, we're still friends until we no longer have that luxury.'

'He gave you his data,' said Ben. 'You mean he gave you all the applications he'd received for his campaign bloggers.'

'Yes, and the guidelines he'd used to vet them,' said Governor Kilburn. 'He was explicitly looking for package deals, groups that already knew how to work together *and* represented all the major areas of Internet journalism.'

'A Newsie, an Irwin, and a Fictional, in other words,' said Audrey.

Governor Kilburn nodded. 'Within the loose definitions you set for yourselves, exactly. The team that was his second pick didn't have a true Fictional; they had someone who generates memes at a rate that I would think was exaggerated if I hadn't seen the man's work myself. How anyone can caption that many cat pictures *every day*, I will never know.'

'Hey, Jonny does good stuff,' said Mat.

I snorted.

'Wait – the folks over at Brag Bag came in second?' Ben frowned. 'Their Factual News Division has been fined several times for inaccuracy in guaranteed reporting. If he had people vetting the applicants, they should never have made the top ten.'

'Well, there were fewer "complete" teams applying than Peter would have liked; fewer than twenty percent of the applicants actually covered all three branches of the news *and* had the necessary licenses *and* had the necessary firearms training, *and* had no arrests or convictions that would interfere with their being able to serve the potential future President of the United States,' said Governor Kilburn. She had a light, conversational way of putting information down in front of you, like she was just reminding us of things we already knew. I could see it serving her well on the campaign trail. I could also see it getting damn annoying in extremely short order. 'Several promising candidates were knocked out due to felony convictions in their immediate families. Bloggers aren't required to have security clearance, but we have to know that no one close to them could present a problem.'

'Where did we rank?' I asked. It was a bald, borderline rude question. Someone needed to ask it, and the nice thing about being the team Irwin was that 'someone' was almost always going to be me.

'You would have come in second, but you were disqualified,' said Governor Kilburn.

'Why?' demanded Audrey. 'We have no arrests, no convictions, no outstanding warrants. Half of us don't even have *families*.'

'At the time the application was filled out, Mrs North's naturalization was under a year old. In the eyes of the Secret Service, she was still a foreign national.'

My knees felt suddenly weak. I didn't look at Ben. I *couldn't* look at Ben. Our relationship had cost him as much as it had given me. He'd managed to find a few girlfriends who were fine with the fact that he was married to another woman, but none who were willing to keep going out after he made it clear that they'd be dating in secret, or that she would be publicly dating me as well. He'd had uncounted fights with his mother about being married to me, and what it was going to mean for his chances of having grandchildren. If I had cost him the gig of a lifetime, just by existing, I didn't know how I was going to live with myself.

'I read the application requirements myself,' said Ben stiffly. 'They indicated that they were open to all journalists, regardless of nationality, who were living legally in the United States, or who did the majority of their reporting for U.S. audiences. I know several teams with members in Mexico or Canada who also applied.'

'Their applications were accepted and looked at the same way all the others were,' said Governor Kilburn. 'Being a foreign national wasn't an automatic disqualification. It was just . . . a black mark, of a sort, that had to be outweighed by everything else in order to go away. In Mrs North's case, her prior citizenship combined with her involuntary committal was too much for Peter to risk. He's a conservative man in many ways. He had the opportunity to work with an all-American team – how do you top a brother-sister pair and one of the last evacuees from Alaska? The people he picked were the ones he saw as the best possible assets.'

'This is a very circuitous way of telling us why you're here, ma'am,' said Ben. His voice was even stiffer now. He knew me well enough to guess what I was thinking, and from the way he kept glancing in my direction, he didn't like it one little bit.

He'd always been my greatest cheering section. That was just the sort of friend he was.

'Not really,' said Governor Kilburn. 'Mrs North is an American citizen now. The things for which she was committed are not crimes in this country; if anything, they're marks in her favor. She fled here because she wanted the right to live her life as she saw fit, and she lived within the system until we accepted her. Mr Ross, you live in the home of your grandparents, and you survived the Rising under the care of a single mother who had lived through one of the most racially and economically troubled decades our nation had ever known. Miss Wen graduated at the top of her class from Yale before choosing to write crime fiction for a living. And, ah . . . ' She stumbled.

There was only one member of the team left. I decided to take pity on her. 'Just "Mat" is usually fine, right, Mat?'

'Yup,' agreed Mat. 'Sometimes I think about going to medical school, just to get a gender-neutral salutation.'

'I find that "Governor" also works for that problem,' said Governor Kilburn.

Mat laughed. 'Well, once you're in charge of the country, maybe I'll run for your job.'

'Fashion bloggers are common. Fashion bloggers who come with an intact group that touches all three branches of the news are exceedingly rare. Mat's presence on this team gives you an edge I don't think Peter took into account. Part of being conservative is a rather rigid approach to gender roles in society.' Governor Kilburn shook her head. 'He would never have seen a makeup artist as an advantage against the opposition.'

'Clearly he is a man who has never beheld the raw cosmic power of really good eyeliner,' said Mat primly. They sounded utterly offended. 'I take it back. I didn't want to work for him anyway. No one who can't see the vital importance of what I do deserves to have me fighting for them.'

'Which is why I want you all to be working for me,' said Governor Kilburn.

You could have heard a pin drop in the silence that followed, although I wasn't sure why, even as I held my breath along with everyone else. There was no other good reason for her to be here, in our kitchen, talking to us. She *had* to be here to offer us a job. And yet hearing it, actually *hearing* it leave her mouth, was like the whole world tilting on its side and laughing at us. This couldn't be happening. This was the sort of wish-granted, lottery-won moment that happened to other people, people like the Masons, people who lived enchanted lives. It didn't happen to people like *us*.

Audrey recovered first, thank God. 'What are your terms?' she asked. She wasn't technically in charge – inasmuch as our collective had a 'boss,' it was Ben, who was generally responsible for finding us jobs and figuring out ways to leverage our collective skills into better pay and wider exposure. At the moment, though, Ben was overwhelmed with too many things in too little time, and so she was stepping in, covering for him. That was what she did. That was what we all always did for one another. It was our job, our real job, the one that everything else was built around.

Governor Kilburn swung her attention around to Audrey. The friendly, conversational pose was gone, replaced by pure business. I liked her better this way. It felt more like I was seeing a real person, and less like I was seeing a persona designed by focus groups and market needs. 'You follow my campaign. Starting in two days, when I launch my campaign, and staying with me until my race ends in either the White House or defeat. I sign contracts with your team and with each of you individually. If one of you elects to leave before the contract term is up, it is the responsibility of the team to replace you with someone who covers a similar area of the news inside of forty-eight hours. If they fail, I am allowed to hire your replacement myself. You get access to the inner workings of my cabinet, and to any nonclassified briefing. You—'

'All briefings,' said Ben abruptly.

Governor Kilburn stopped. 'I beg your pardon?'

'We get access to all briefings. We won't post things you tell us are vital to national security, but we need to know the whole picture, even if we're only reporting on parts of it. If you want us to do this, you need to let us do it.' Ben leaned forward. He was still stiff, but he was coming out of his shock, and coming quickly up to speed on the situation.

That was the trick to dealing with Ben. Sometimes he took a while to process things, but it wasn't because he was slow. More the opposite. He was considering all the angles, looking at all the ways a thing could go. By the time he was ready to move, he was going in for the kill. It would have made him a terrible Irwin. He would have been a smear on the pavement before the end of his first urban expedition. But it made him a *fabulous* Newsie, and there was no one I was happier to have at my back. No one.

'We'll sign a single group contract, and handle dispersion of rights and funds within ourselves. No one's going to find themselves caught between two masters,' he continued. 'I'm assuming, since you have access to Ryman's data and you've clearly decided that we're the team for you, that you've already done a deep background check. We're going to get some scrutiny when you announce us as your blog team. I do not want our backgrounds being used to score political points. We aren't here to prove how open-minded or progressive you are. We're here to do a job. We'll do it very well, if you let us. We'll walk if you don't.'

'Well,' said Governor Kilburn. She looked briefly amused. 'What if I say your terms are too strict, and that my offer's off the table?'

'Then I respond by suggesting you get your friend on the phone and ask him what sort of terms he got from the Masons,' said Ben. 'I know Georgia Mason. She's not a friend, but she's a professional colleague, and if the deal she struck with Senator Ryman isn't considerably more rigid and detailed than the one I'm offering you, I'll eat Aislinn's cooking.'

'I can't cook,' I said, recognizing my role in this little drama. 'It's sort of like a traffic accident in a pot. Sometimes you can pick out individual ingredients. Mostly not. It's criminal what I do to a potato. Actually criminal.'

'So I'm not going to get anything better, is that what you're saying to me?' asked Governor Kilburn.

'Actually, I'm assuming you already made that phone call, and just wanted to see what we'd do if you offered us something that looked good but was going to leave us hurting later,' said Ben. 'Am I close?'

'Very,' said Governor Kilburn. 'Full access, but a member of my staff gets to read everything before it goes live, and can flag things as dangerous to either national security or to the viability of my campaign as a whole. You're here to document, not to undermine.'

'We don't delete the things we hold back due to campaign

concerns, and we reserve the right to publish them once the campaign is over,' said Ben.

'If I'm President when the campaign is over, you agree not to publish anything that would undermine my ability to do my job,' countered Governor Kilburn.

'You can't forbid us to criticize the President,' said Ben. 'That's an unfair request for you to make, and I'm reasonably sure that it would be an illegal contract for us to sign.'

'I'm not asking you never to criticize me,' said Governor Kilburn. 'I'm asking you to agree that, should I win, you will not write articles saying I can't govern effectively because I have a tendency to spend Sunday mornings in my pajamas, eating cereal out of the box and watching the Top Forty video countdown. To choose a completely nonspecific example that you cannot possibly prove without signing on for my campaign.'

'CMT or VH1?' asked Mat.

Governor Kilburn turned to blink at them. 'I beg your pardon?'

'Are you getting your rock on with the dulcet all-American tones of Country Music Television, or do you prefer the pre-Rising nostalgia of VH1? It's not a *hard* question.'

Governor Kilburn hesitated, looking around the table like she sensed a trap about to snap shut. Finally, she said, 'CMT. I like the blue jeans and big hair, and the fact that they think writing love songs about shooting zombies in the head is a good idea. There's a sort of postapocalyptic good cheer about it that just makes me feel better. Sunday mornings are my private time. I'm allowed to spend them however I like, providing nothing is on fire.'

'Right answer,' said Mat. They turned to Ben. 'We should take the job.'

'We'll agree not to use personal information we learn to intentionally damage your credibility, providing you will agree that sometimes, that personal information may be relevant to your job.' Ben's lips twitched as he fought a smile. 'For example, were you to miss an important presidential event because there was a convention at Dollywood—'

'Dolly Parton was a hero of the Rising, and I dare you to tell any red-blooded American girl who's ever felt bad about her wardrobe differently,' said Governor Kilburn. She wasn't fighting her smile. 'Agreed. I can have my men draw up the contract within the hour.'

'And that's . . . that's it?' I couldn't keep my disbelief out of my tone. 'You're not going to ride us about my committal, or try to censor us, or anything?'

'I understand that sometimes those who mean well will start making decisions about your mental health without consulting you, Mrs North,' said Governor Kilburn. Her tone was gentle, but her left hand touched her right wrist in a way that was all too familiar to me. I'd seen that gesture before, during support group discussions, when people tried to explain their reasons for attempting suicide. 'There's no reason for that to be held against you now. Your past is a foundation, not a crime.'

'Except when there are actual crimes in your past, which thankfully, there are not,' said Audrey. She hadn't been talking much through all of this. That was . . . unusual. I gave her a sidelong look, noting the laser-like focus she was directing toward Governor Kilburn. I almost never saw Audrey look at someone like that. It was rarely, if ever, a good sign when she did. 'I want your guarantee that anything which comes up in our background checks that is *not* relevant will be left where it was found. No surprises.'

'No surprises,' agreed Governor Kilburn. She raised her chin fractionally, looking at Ben. 'Do we have a deal?'

'One last question: Did you already run through the list of concessions we might ask for with one of your aides, and decide that we were worth the risk?'

Governor Kilburn smiled. 'Why, you sound like you think of me as a politician. It's possible I called Peter and asked what *his* journalists had demanded before deciding how I was going to structure this meeting. We both have something to offer each other, here. You can bring my campaign to the attention of the people who don't care much about anything that happens off-line – and frankly, Peter needs the competition. I can bring you to the attention of the world. Let us make each other's lives better.'

'My mother always said not to trust people who come offering you something for nothing,' I said. 'Leprechauns aren't real, and what looks like a pot of gold is probably nothing but proof that you've been drinking too much. We're not the only journalists in the world, and you'll forgive me for being a bit wary until we have a working relationship.'

'Oh, I'm not offering you something for nothing,' said Governor Kilburn. 'You're going to work hard. You're going to sleep in hotel rooms and trailers. You're going to get so sick of my company that you're going to want to scream. But in exchange, you'll get money, you'll get exposure, and you'll get the chance to be part of making history for a change. Don't you get tired of chasing stories? Come with me, and you'll be able to sit back and watch the stories come to you. You were willing to work for Senator Ryman, even though you all have political leanings that put you much more on my side of the fence. So lean.'

'We're in,' said Ben. None of us objected. He'd seen our decision in our faces, heard it in the questions we were asking; it had been his job to make the final call, because sometimes slow and rational was the only way to approach the race. I went in too hot, Mat went in too careless, and Audrey went in too wary. Ben was our balancing point, the way that we took all those traits and turned them into something useful.

Governor Kilburn smiled and offered her hand across the table. He took it and shook, twice. 'I'll have my people send over the contracts tonight. Review them, sign them, and send them back to me. I'll have transport in front of your house the day after tomorrow at oh-nine-hundred hours precisely.'

'Where are we going?' asked Mat.

'Colorado,' said Governor Kilburn. 'I'm giving a speech in Denver about the importance of rebuilding our past and reclaiming our future. What better place to begin than in Amanda Amberlee's hometown?'

'You are not wasting any time, lady,' said Mat admiringly. They turned to me. 'Can we keep her? I promise to walk her and fill her cereal bowl every morning.'

'That's between you and the governor,' I said, making my voice as prim as I could manage.

'We'll find our own transportation, if you don't mind,' said Audrey. 'I'll be a lot more comfortable knowing that I'm not driving some-one else's car.' The thought that someone else – someone not on our team – might be doing the driving was unacceptable, and so she was ignoring it. I admired that about her.

'Fair enough,' said Governor Kilburn, laughing as she stood and collected her purse. 'I know the footage you shot of this meeting isn't covered by our contract, since you haven't signed anything yet, but I'd appreciate it if you'd remember that we're going to be working together for a while. Please don't cut together anything we're going to butt heads over later.'

'Us, shoot footage in our own kitchen?' Audrey pressed a hand to her chest, eyes widening in exaggerated shock. 'What sort of monsters do you take us for?'

'Journalists,' said Governor Kilburn. She cast us one last smile, and then she was out of the kitchen, her hired security following close behind her. From the looks they gave us as they made for the door, we were neither expected nor invited to follow. So we just stayed where we were.

Audrey and I had been standing through that entire encounter. My knees were shaking, more from unnoticed adrenaline than from exhaustion. Still, it seemed like something should be done about that. I sat down, only realizing when I was halfway to the floor that

I should probably have aimed for a chair. Too late now. I sank into a cross-legged position, pleating my skirt demurely over my knees. It was an automatic gesture, trained into my muscle memory by hours of drills. If I was going to make wearing a skirt into the field my gimmick, I was going to make damn sure no one saw my panties without an engraved invitation.

Audrey pulled out a chair out and dropped bonelessly into it, resting one elbow on the table for stability. She lifted one bare foot and balanced it on my shoulder, staying in contact. I didn't push her away. In that moment, I needed it as much as she did.

'Did that really just happen?' asked Mat.

'Pretty sure,' said Ben. 'How many cameras did we have in here when she showed up?'

'Six,' said Audrey.

'Then we cut together an intro, we make it as human and appealing as we can without actually trending into dishonesty, and we wait for those contracts to show up,' said Ben. 'If we sign, we post the "guess what we're doing" video, and we open that bottle of champagne we've been saving for a big score.'

Almost timidly, Mat asked, 'No, I mean it. Are we really going to do this? Are we going to, you know, go on the campaign trail and be all exposed and visible to the world? Like, is this it?'

'Yeah,' said Ben, with a smile that transformed, bit by bit, into an open grin. He was a beautiful man when he smiled that way. No one could deny that. 'This is it. We're going to be journalists for the maybe future President of the United States of America.'

'I need to pack,' said Mat. They stood and fled for the hall, moving fast enough that I suspected 'packing' was a cover for a mild panic attack. I couldn't blame them. I was considering freaking out a little bit myself.

'I need to go buy a truck,' said Ben. 'Maybe an RV. Something big enough to house us all for however long we're on the road.'

'I can make a couple of calls,' I said. 'Remember Mallory? The

Irwin who died last month? Her family's been looking to offload her field wagon. It runs on biodiesel, and it has a shower.' I was willing to do a lot of things in the name of the news. Traveling in a van that didn't have a shower was not one of them. Give me clean hair or give me death.

'Do that,' said Ben. 'You can have up to two-thirds of the emergency bank account without consulting with me.'

I nodded. 'I think I can get it for half.' Maybe less. Mallory's family had never cared much for her career, but they knew how important it had been to her. Knowing that her rolling fortress was going to be going back into the field instead of being stripped for parts would help them get over losing it.

'This is going to be good for us,' said Audrey. She didn't sound fully convinced.

I reached up and squeezed her ankle. 'We're going to make names for ourselves, and then we're going to make so much money that we'll be able to buy the houses on either side. We can start bringing this neighborhood back to life. In the good way, not in the "shambling zombie wants to eat your brains" way. We can upgrade the security systems.' And we'd have an RV. I was already starting to think of ways I could make that work for me, once the campaign was done and we were looking to get back to normal.

'People say money doesn't fix everything, but I'm looking forward to proving them wrong,' said Ben. His smile faded. 'I just wish this could've happened a month ago. Mama would have loved to know that I'd be taken care of. That my sister will be taken care of. Between her inheritance and me being better off, she's never going to have to worry again.'

'Your mother knows,' I said automatically. Then I grimaced. I've been agnostic at best since leaving Ireland: The Church failed me pretty badly, and I wasn't in the market for a replacement. But old habits die hard, and I'd grown up believing my dead relatives watched everything I did. Somehow this didn't make them all perverts, not even when I'd started experimenting with my sexuality behind the old Tesco warehouse with Siobhan from down the street. There were many aspects of Catholicism that just got stranger when viewed from the outside.

'I hope so,' said Ben, apparently missing the wince. He stood. 'I need to start sending emails. We're going to need to steal a play from the Masons and put together a wider team, or there's no way we'll be able to stay on top of this thing once it gets rolling.'

'And since Governor Kilburn is such good friends with "Peter," she'll be watching to make sure that we perform as well as, if not better than, his pet bloggers,' I said, wrinkling my nose. 'Oh, goody. That's just what I always wanted: a competition against the golden children. Is it too late for me to change my vote?'

'It was too late the second you came downstairs,' said Ben. 'Good night, Ash.'

'Sleep well, if you ever do,' I said, and stayed on the floor with Audrey's foot resting on my shoulder as I watched him walk out of the room.

Once we were alone I looked up at her and asked, 'Is this going to be a good thing, really, or is this the worst thing we've ever agreed to do?'

Audrey leaned down to rest her forehead against mine. It left her twisted like a pretzel, her leg caught between our bodies. She seemed perfectly comfortable that way, and so I didn't say anything. Some of the angles she viewed as normal were impossible for me, and I was in the best shape of my life. Damn the naturally flexible. Damn them all to a lifetime with me.

'Probably both,' she said. 'We're not just going to make the news anymore; we're going to *be* the news, and that isn't always as much fun as people think it's going to be. We're going to get jealous assholes writing articles about Mat's "real" gender, and why you left Ireland, and whether we're all perverts for sleeping together, even though we're actually not.'

I pulled back a little, untangling myself from her until I could get the distance I needed to look into her eyes. 'That's not all we're going to get, Aud, and you know it.'

She looked away.

'We need to talk about this.'

'There's nothing to talk about.'

'Someone's going to find out.'

'So let them find out. I didn't break any laws. I didn't do anything morally wrong.'

'You walked away from your entire life and changed your name so you could join a blogging collective in Alameda. I'm eternally grateful that you did that, honestly I am, but there are going to be people who think it's odd. And Kilburn knows, you know she does. She paused when she said "Yale." She knows.'

'Fuck those people, and fuck Kilburn if she has a problem with this.' Audrey shook her head, looking back to me. 'Fuck them forever. They can eat a bucket of assholes for all I care. I'm not going to do full disclosure, and no one can make me. I'm a Fictional, remember? We have different journalistic ethics.'

'No one can make you, but somebody might do it for you, and I'd rather it be your choice. What is it Ben always says? "Try to stay ahead of the story." I don't want you to get behind this one.'

'Your concern wasn't enough to make you tell the governor no,' said Audrey.

'Because I knew what that look on your face meant. You'd already told her yes. I worry about you. I love you a lot. I'm not going to start protecting you from yourself. That isn't my job.'

'Not yet,' said Audrey. 'When this is over, when we have all the money and all the fame and can write our own tickets, I want you to do something for me.'

'Anything.'

She smiled. It didn't reach her eyes. 'I want you to get a divorce.'

I blinked. 'From Ben?'

'Unless you have another husband sitting around, yes,' said Audrey. 'You have your citizenship now, we've been prepping the "Ben wants kids" excuse, and I want to stop being the other woman. I'm not saying I want to get married right away – we still need to figure some things out, and maybe you need to be attainable for a while before I go proposing – but I want it to be an option. You're a *citizen*. You have nothing to lose by divorcing him, and maybe it would be good for him. He might actually get out and date again. He's lonely, you know. He's not waiting for you to change who you are, but he made you a promise, and he's hurting himself keeping it.'

I was silent for a moment, working my way through her request. It had been coming for a while. I'd seen it in her eyes, and heard it in her laughter. But this had already been an evening full of surprises, and I hadn't been expecting another one.

Audrey stood. 'Thought so,' she said, and walked out of the kitchen.

I almost jumped to my feet and ran after her. In the end, I couldn't make myself move. I just sat there on the kitchen floor, staring at the cupboard, and waiting for the future to begin.

Book II

If You Want It,
Come and Get It

The thing about the past is in the name: It's the past. It may shape us. It may inform us. It may be the foundation on which we are built. But it's dead. Leave it in the grave, and live for the living.

—AUDREY LIQIU WEN

One day we're going to look back on this and laugh. Assuming we, you know, manage to live that long.

—AISLINN 'ASH' NORTH

When my team got passed over for the Ryman gig, I'll admit, I was disappointed. I thought we were some of the best in the business, and would have been a real asset to his campaign. I still think that, although the folks at the newly minted After the End Times are doing a really excellent job of documenting their candidate. I look forward to following their progress.

But my mama always told me that when God closes a door, He opens a window. Our window is Governor Susan Kilburn, originally from Spokane, Washington. She moved to Oregon in her late teens, when she started attending Willamette University with a dual major in economics and environmental science. She fell in love with the area; after graduation, she stayed, went into local politics, and eventually became the governor of her beloved jewel of the Pacific Northwest. She's smart, canny, and good at working all the angles. The perfect environmentalist. She's also in the running to become the Democratic nominee for the next President of the United States of America ... and she chose us. That may prejudice our reporting a bit. When someone who may one day answer to 'POTUS' asks you to serve, it's hard to say no.

Governor Susan Kilburn cares about her state. She cares about her country. She's willing to cross party and ideological lines to do what needs to be done for both state and country, and she under-stands the thin web that connects us all. She's not perfect — everyone has skeletons in their closet, and I'm sure she does as well — but in the end, I think she may be the best option we're going to find.

Let's hope we can document her path all the way to the White House, and beyond.

**—From *That Isn't Johnny Anymore*, the blog of Ben Ross,
February 5, 2040**

Five

Governor Kilburn's people ran in every direction, frantically prepping the site for her arrival. If it had been possible for humans to spontaneously develop the power of flight, they would have done it, just so they could be sure their lighting and security rigs were properly set up. It was sort of impressive, in that 'someone has just kicked a nest of wasps, and now we're all going to pay for their carelessness' kind of way.

Mat was in heaven. They'd been talking with the local techs all morning, babbling rapid-fire about things like the bearing capacity of the temporary wireless and the number of electric charges in the fence. It was sort of adorable. It was also sort of intensely frustrating, since we were surrounded on all sides by forest, and I wasn't being allowed to go running off into it with my hands in the air and a big 'COME AND GET IT' sign taped to my chest. We'd been attached to the campaign for three weeks. We'd been on the road for two. I hadn't seen a single dead person during that time, and I was starting to get twitchy about it.

Audrey patted my arm with one hand, eyes never leaving the preparations around us. 'There, there, Ash, there, there,' she said. 'I'm sure you'll find something horribly dangerous to play with soon.'

'I didn't say anything,' I said, giving her a narrow-eyed look.

'You didn't need to. I know what it means when you start looking at forested areas the way you usually look at my boobs. We have a three-day break after this, while Governor Kilburn does private donor dinners. I bet we can find you a hole in the fence and a good poking stick.'

I abandoned my glowering to give her a warm smile. 'You really get me.'

'I really do,' Audrey agreed. 'Have you noticed the blind spots in their motion detectors? If everything wasn't electrified, I'd be worried.'

'I know, honey,' I said, and leaned my head against her shoulder. Audrey *liked* security systems. Audrey especially liked security systems that had been constructed with triplicate redundancy, making it unlikely that a single failure could endanger anyone who was supposed to be protected. It was one of the few day-to-day reminders of the life she'd walked away from, the one she didn't like to discuss and didn't want me thinking about any harder than I had to.

I didn't have all the details of who she'd been before she came to us – before she came to me. No one did, except for Audrey. But it had left her very aware of the bars on the windows and the locks on the doors, and ever eager to add another layer.

Not that Governor Kilburn's campaign lacked for security. It was just that it was part of the American political machine, and was hence innately divided against itself. Blame the need for any major political candidate's coffers to be continually reinforced with sweet, sweet cash. Public events, like the speech we were about to cover, were open to everyone who wanted to show up. They were also broadcast live on the governor's website, and dissected and remixed for posting on our site. It was campaign as theater, and she was very, very good at it. The private side of things was sometimes open to us and sometimes not. A certain amount of 'behind closed doors' footage was included in our contract; it humanized the candidate without weakening her, and it would have been silly to hire a team of bloggers and refuse to give us access. But some events were still off-limits, usually because they involved people who'd donated such an obscene amount of money to the campaign that they had essentially bought her time for an evening in the process.

Supposedly, there were limits as to how much money an individual or concern could give to a candidate for office. In practice, those limits were as easily circumvented as the data rights management software on a new video game. There were the super PACs to worry about, of course. On top of that, people wrote checks in the names of pets and children, gave gifts that could be traded for monetary value, and generally made it clear that they were willing to pay for the President they wanted. Governor Kilburn never looked *happy* about those dinners, but she went. I couldn't blame her. If someone waved a million dollars in my face and said it could be mine if I'd eat a plate of their private chef's spaghetti, I'd be reaching for the fork.

On those 'private donor nights,' we were free to do whatever struck our fancy. Ben spent them updating his reports with new information and hiring more support staff – coders, baby bloggers, forum moderators – for our site, which was growing by leaps and bounds, thanks to our sudden elevation to 'second biggest concern in the blogging world.' The Masons were ahead of us in ratings and respectability, but we were closing the gap fast. They'd had a head start. They had more name recognition. We had a candidate who was willing to get into water balloon fights with kids. We also had Mat's makeup tutorials, which were starting to take on a distinctly patriotic flair. Mat was making weekly trips to Sephora for red, white, and blue eye shadows, and had been ordering custom lipsticks, stains, and tars from various online vendors at a terrifying rate. By the time we reached the actual election, I fully expected to be surrounded by people who looked like they'd been eating blueberry popsicles for months.

'Candidate on site, repeat, candidate on site,' said a member of the governor's security team, speaking into his wrist as he rushed past us, like he was afraid he might otherwise make eye contact with a filthy journalist and have to stop for a chat. Some of the security staffers were lovely people, like John, who spent a lot of time drinking whiskey and discussing law enforcement with Audrey when he wasn't on duty, or Amber, who had the dirtiest sense of humor I'd ever encountered on someone who wasn't an Irwin. Those people were outnumbered by their stiffer, more professional colleagues, who really didn't like the fact that they had a bunch of wild cards running around. Mat's refusal to go to binary pronouns confused them, Ben's insistence on asking endless questions annoyed them, and Audrey's tendency to dismiss their security protocols as insufficient pissed them off.

For once, I wasn't the most irritating member of our team. It was great. I was thinking of making myself a 'yay, I'm the good child for a change' ribbon. Something big and flashy, like I'd just won the first prize at a church bake sale.

'Guess that means we have to get to work,' said Audrey, with a small, barely muffled sigh. She was a Fictional, but she was also the best-informed when it came to law enforcement and judicial procedures. Ben used her a lot for the candidate's public appearances. Having her to translate the parts that were outside his usual wheelhouse made the process more pleasant for everyone involved.

'Whee,' I said agreeably, and followed her to the small press pen where Ben and Mat were already waiting.

Today's event was being held in a wide, beautifully manicured park that was also, according to Amber, the official Portland rose test garden. People from all over the world brought new rose cultivars here to see whether they'd perform in the real world the way they performed in hothouses and horticultural labs. Roses were the most popular flower on the planet, thanks to their versatility, hardiness, and ability to scratch the ever-loving crap out of anyone who got too close. I would have thought thorns and their tendency to draw blood would make roses *less* popular, since it could turn a thriving garden into a hazard zone, but it turned out people really appreciated having an organic line of home defense. If blood appeared on the roses, they got rooted out, burned, and replaced with an electric fence essentially overnight. Until then, the yard could be regarded as halfway safe. Roses were also one of the few symbols of conspicuous consumption left to the average home owner. After all, if you could afford to replace your landscaping at the first hint of contamination, you must have been doing pretty well for yourself.

Folding chairs were set up between the cordoned-off flower beds, creating tiers of seating. The best seats were right up front, where no flowers would block the view of the governor. Those were reserved for friends, family, and people who'd already donated a lot of money to her campaign, but could potentially be convinced to open their wallets a little further. Oregon was all about the bottom line. The rest of the country was going to be about the politics.

There was a big press pen at the back of the venue, for local bloggers or newspaper people who wanted to show up but hadn't been able to secure a personal interview or permission to take photos from closer up. The small pen at the front was reserved for our team, the governor's official photographer – Herc O'Halloran, who treated every photo shoot like it was going to win him a Pulitzer – and two junior bloggers who'd won a competition at their high school. They huddled together, terrified and elated in equal measure, eyeing the rest of us with the sort of wariness that I normally only saw in the feral cats that stalked our neighborhood. Both of them wanted to go into Factual News, and had been treating Ben like he was the second coming of Anderson Cooper. Ben was pretty confused by this sort of adulation, but he'd been going gamely along with it, probably in part because he didn't have any other choice.

With the candidate imminent, the two teen journalists had returned to their seats. One was taking rapid photos of everything around him, including, I suspected, the air, while the other was whispering into a handheld recorder, face pale and eyes darting from side to side like she expected an attack at any moment. I plopped myself down in the seat next to Ben, checking that my sundress was draping correctly over my knees before I crossed my ankles and flashed him a bright smile.

'Hello, oh handsome savior of the journalistic world,' I said. 'Have you passed the wisdom of your long, long lifetime on to your new acolytes?'

'Stop,' he said, heatlessly.

'She's not going to,' said Audrey, as she took the seat on my other side. 'You know she's not going to. She never stops. She's like the Energizer Bunny of being a pain in the ass. Why do you continue to try to make her?'

'I believe in miracles,' he said.

I looked around and frowned. 'Where's Mat?'

Ben actually cracked a smile at that. 'You're not going to believe it,' he said. 'I was here when it happened, and I almost don't believe it.'

'Mat has decided to retire from journalism and become a full-time makeup artist,' I guessed.

'Mat has returned to their home planet,' said Audrey.

'Ash is sort of right,' said Ben. 'We were getting settled for the event when Chuck came over and asked Mat to come help with makeup.'

I breathed slowly in as I pulled the mag from my pocket and got it seated on the bridge of my nose. It was almost time for the fun to begin, and I didn't want to miss a frame. 'You're kidding.'

'My hand to God,' said Ben, holding up his left hand like he was taking a Boy Scout oath.

'Damn.' I shook my head. 'We may lose Mat over this campaign after all.' Chuck was Governor Kilburn's campaign manager. He made sure she was dressed for whatever event she was heading into, that her hair was always perfect, and that her makeup was never either too aggressive or too understated. He was, in short, the final arbiter of her public image, and if he was trying to sneak Mat away from us, we were going to be in for a fight.

'Don't worry,' said Audrey, bumping my shoulder with hers. 'Mat might think they'd like to live the high life of movie stars and politicians, but the first time someone asks them why they're taking apart the toaster, they'll come running right back to us.'

'We are a safe harbor of blessed madness in this wonderland of excessive sanity,' said Ben gravely.

Three security staffers appeared at the front of the venue as if by magic, lining themselves up with the posts between the podium and the rose beds. They were trying to be unobtrusive. It was a nice trick for a group that averaged almost six feet in height, and came with more guns than the average bodybuilding competition. The music started a moment later, a twangy, country-accented cover of some pre-Rising pop song that I didn't recognize but knew I'd heard before. It was always something I'd heard before. If you asked the politicians of the world, the age of good music ended in the summer of 2014, before Taylor Swift dropped her first heavily political album. They wanted to evoke a more innocent, less zombie-filled age. Maybe it worked. I didn't know; I wasn't the target audience.

The applause followed the music after about thirty seconds, when Governor Kilburn appeared from the side of the rose garden and made her way toward the podium. She was casually dressed in jeans and a dark pink sweater with a draped neckline. I wondered how many of the people watching this live would recognize her red rose earrings as connected to the latest *Sailor Moon* resurgence. I tapped the arm of my mag, zooming in on her ears. Pop culture reporting wasn't so much my thing, but we probably had a baby blogger on staff by now who would be happy to dig into the governor's media tastes for a fluff piece. Or hell, maybe not so fluff. You could tell a lot about a person by what they chose to entertain themselves. If Governor Kilburn was a secret *Sailor Moon* fan, we could be looking at a girl-power campaign of celestial proportions.

The applause died down as Governor Kilburn stepped into position and cast a practiced smile at the crowd. Someone from the back shouted, 'We love you, Susan!' Her smile cracked, becoming less technically perfect and a hell of a lot more sincere.

'I love you too, Portland,' she said, leaning a hairbreadth closer to the mic. 'You have no idea how good it is to be home.' Cheering. 'We would have made this a morning event, but I wanted to go by Powell's before I had to pack and get on the road. There's a lot of country to cover. I needed something to read – and hopefully, I'll have a job soon that takes up a lot of my time.' More cheering, this time accompanied by laughter. It was clear she knew her audience. It wasn't as clear whether she'd be able to work a crowd like this outside of Portland.

It was almost too bad that we hadn't come on to the campaign somewhere other than the West Coast. This was her home territory: This was where she was at her most comfortable, and most likely to succeed. We could learn a lot about her under ideal circumstances while we were here. Finding out how she performed under pressure, on the other hand – that was going to require a change of venue. We'd get it soon. The campaign was slated to leave for Montana in the morning, all of us either packing into the equipment trucks or hopping onto a chartered flight to our next stop. In the meanwhile, it was all about her comfort zone.

The paperwork on Mallory's RV was still going through. Audrey was planning to fly back and pick it up as soon as it was ready for us. It was going to be a few days, and the campaign needed to move.

The cheers died, replaced by an expectant silence. Governor Kilburn had clearly been anticipating that. She smiled, a little ruefully, a little entertained – and I didn't even want to think about how much time she'd spent practicing that combination in her mirror – as she leaned against the podium and said, 'But I suppose you're not here today to hear about my book-buying habits. You want to know what my plan is for this country. You want to hear my reasons for running, and your reasons for maybe casting a vote in my favor come November. So I guess I'd better get started.'

The crowd laughed again, but it was a shorter, sharper sound: They were hungry to hear what she was going to say. These people weren't her friends. Ben would probably be able to explain the social structure and political landscape of Portland to me later, and that was all well and good, because it would give me context. It also wasn't important. You don't survive as an Irwin without learning to recognize predators when they're encroaching on your personal space. Every person here was a predator. Every person here wanted to rip something out of the governor.

Even us. We wouldn't have been in this pretty garden, surrounded by these pretty people, if we hadn't wanted something. Maybe we were less predatory and more parasitic, here to feed off of her without killing her, but we were still looking for a free meal, just like everybody else. I needed to hold on to that. It wouldn't do for me to start thinking that our goals were somehow noble.

Besides, the governor was speaking. I wrenched myself out of my thoughts and back into the moment, trying to look like I had been fully present the whole time, and not susceptible to woolgathering and distraction. Even though I totally was.

The governor was talking about her economic plans for the West Coast in general and the Pacific Northwest in specific. The whole evergreen corridor had been ravaged by the Rising, which had left small towns abandoned and big ones severely damaged, while providing plenty of places for the infected to hide. The economy was still struggling to recover in all but the fanciest of areas. And I'm sure all that would have been absolutely fascinating if I'd cared in the slightest. The American political process was vague and irritating as far as I was concerned, filled with senseless posturing and even more senseless promises that neither side was intending to keep. Maybe it was disingenuous of me to agree to work with a politician when I didn't care about politics. I didn't mind. The whole 'parasite' thing again. Ben and Audrey would get genuine career boosts from this. I would get exposure, and free transport to places I'd never seen, where I could poke at more zombies with sticks.

I reached up and tapped my mag, zooming in on the roses behind the governor. They were lovely. Looking at them would keep me from zoning out completely, and since they were in the same general vicinity as she was, I'd even look like I was paying attention to her speech. Ben wouldn't have to lecture me later about professional comportment, Audrey wouldn't be disappointed, and I wouldn't have to listen to the words 'economic stimulus' more often than absolutely necessary. It was a win for everybody.

Portland was the perfect environment for roses. They thrived here, in the cool and the damp. Even the variants bred to do well in more extreme environments thought Portland was the place to be, putting out more flowers than I'd ever seen before in one place. It was verdant and calculatedly wild, and I loved it.

I was starting to wonder if Mat and I might have time to sneak away and do a quick photo shoot for my blog gallery, which was part slaughterhouse chic and part pin-up fashionista, when one of the roses moved. Not a lot. It didn't crash to the ground or explode into petals. But it *moved*, and not in a way that could be explained by the wind. I sat up straighter, zooming further in on the patch of flowers. Nothing moved. Nothing even looked out of place.

Until something did. A branch twitched aside for a moment, revealing what could have been a patch of dirt, or could have been a patch of dirt-covered skin. I looked around me, trying to be unobtrusive. Ben and Audrey were watching the governor, expressions rapt with concentration. The two junior journalists were even worse. The boy looked like he was witnessing the birth of a new religion, while the girl was actually crying, slow tears running down her cheeks as she was overwhelmed by the historical significance of the moment.

Carefully, trying to look casual and not at all like I was about to go investigate a potential zombie in the roses behind the governor, oh no, not me, I stood. My mag was still magnifying everything on one side of the world, forcing me to focus more than normal on walking without falling down. Ben took his eyes away from Governor Kilburn long enough to give me a quizzical look. He wasn't happy; that much was clear from the way his eyebrows drew down toward his nose, making him seem to be frowning even as his mouth remained in a neutral position.

"Sorry," I mouthed, and mimed powdering my nose. Ben scowled. I was going to get a lecture later about not guzzling the pre–political speech lemonade just because it was there. That was fine. If he was giving me a lecture, I wasn't being eaten by zombies, and everything was right with the world.

I picked my way through the chairs to the back of the press pit. There was a narrow stone pathway there, wending its way deeper into the rose garden. I could slip away unnoticed from here. I still hesitated.

Zombies almost never traveled by themselves when they had any choice in the matter. Numbers made them smarter, and made it easier for them to take down their prey. No one knew why quantity increased quality where the infected were concerned, but everyone knew it happened, and that zombies of different species were happy to work together after they were fully converted. Sure, I'd only seen one shape that *might* have belonged to a human being, but that didn't mean there was only one zombie in the roses. Dogs, raccoons – anything capable of crossing the forty-pound threshold could be lurking in there. And I was wearing a sundress.

My online persona was a carefully crafted blend of femininity and casual danger. The keyword there was 'careful.' Yes, I climbed trees and filmed myself bare legged and fishing for zombies, but I had thick canvas trousers and steel-toed boots on standby. I never went into an active hazard zone without armor, even if I had no intention of using it outside of an emergency. Even the fancy shoes I sometimes wore had been designed for dancers, with thick, square heels that looked higher than they were, thanks to some tricks of paint and perspective.

Most of our equipment was back in the truck, along with the rest of the governor's security team. I considered walking over and asking them to accompany me. I dismissed the idea as quickly as it had come.

If there was nothing out there, I would be seen as flighty and willing to waste everyone's time. Not a good way to start our association with these people. I had my comfort revolver strapped to my thigh, and it had eight bullets, which would be more than enough to either get me out of trouble or notify everyone in earshot that they should be thinking about providing backup. I pulled the revolver from its holster and disengaged the safety.

'Ash, what the hell?'

I jumped, only years of training and discipline keeping my finger from seeking the trigger as I whirled to face Mat. They were standing behind me on the narrow path, a makeup bag over their shoulder and a quizzical expression on their face. Today's eye shadow was all about green: pine green, emerald green, even the slightly too-bright shade that I had identified as matching the hills outside my hometown of Drogheda. Mat had blended them until they looked like a plume of bright feathers, creating a look that would have seemed wide-eyed and startled even if Mat hadn't actually been surprised.

'Mat,' I said, forcing my shoulders to unlock. 'You startled me. You armed?'

'Uh.' Mat looked nonplussed by my question. 'I am outside and I have a blogging license, so yes, I am armed. But it's a small three-shot ceramic gun, so maybe I'm not where you should be looking for firepower? Also the question is freaking me out, so maybe you should explain it a little bit?'

Of all my backup options, Mat was the one I was least happy about. They were a Newsie and a shut-in, and while I trusted them to watch my back – mostly – I didn't have much faith in their aim. Which looped me right back to 'I can't go looking for backup without getting accused of being a hysterical female,' and that sort of thing always pissed me off. Mat was going to have to do.

'I saw something in the roses,' I said. 'I'm going to check it out before I get anyone else involved. And you're going to come with me. Congratulations!'

Mat blinked. 'I do not like this plan.'

'I don't like the plan where I say I saw something and it turns out to have been just a leaf, and they never trust me to do my job again.' I shook my head. 'It'll be fine. Worst-case scenario, there's a zombie in the rose garden, and we put it down as quietly as we can. The governor's speech doesn't even get interrupted. Best-case scenario, it was a squirrel.'

'A squirrel,' said Mat flatly.

'Terror of the garden. Now come on.' I turned to start down the path, trusting Mat to follow me. They might not be the bravest of my teammates, but we worked together because we had each other's backs. If I said I needed them, Mat would come.

Sure enough, footsteps behind me on the path told me I had gambled correctly. I glanced back to see that Mat had drawn their gun and was holding it low against their hip, a grimace on their lips. I was going to have to apologize to them when this was over. Oh, well. Cookies and beer usually made up for whatever I'd done wrong *this* time.

The path wound gently between the patches of roses, with their suddenly ominous-looking thorns. If there *was* something dangerous out here, one scratch could be all she wrote for my existence as a thinking member of the human race. The roses were planted far enough back that we should have been safe, but I still stayed as close to the center of the path as I could, compressing my body to take up as little space as possible. Mat was staying in my wake, letting me forge the trail deeper into the garden. I didn't blame them. I was the Irwin here, and they were just my backup as we walked into a potentially hazardous, definitely sketchy situation.

Because of the curvature of the trail, I didn't realize where we were in relation to the governor's event until the sound of laughter and applause drifted back across the roses. We were almost directly behind the podium, some thirty feet back amongst the foliage. That meant that the movement I'd seen was about five feet ahead of us.

I motioned toward that part of the garden before reaching up and
tapping my mag, returning the world to normal magnification. If we
found anything, I wanted to get clear footage. If we didn't, well . . .
we were about to start pushing into the bushes. I didn't need a spider
the size of a baseball suddenly projected in front of my eye.

Mat nodded at my gesture, setting their mouth into a thin, hard
line. They didn't like this. They were still going to go along with it.
I had definitely chosen the right team when I chose to go with Ben.

Narrow dirt paths were beaten through the rose beds, making
it possible for the gardeners to come and go without cutting
themselves. I stepped gingerly onto the nearest of them, walking
sideways as I made my way into the flowers. My skirt caught a few
times, snagging the fabric, but pulled loose when I tugged. I kept
on going. There had been no further movement, and nothing was
making any noise. Whatever I'd seen had been nothing. We were
going to be just fi—

The hand reaching out of the bushes to my left struck like a snake,
grabbing a hank of my hair before I had a chance to react. I twisted
away as hard as I dared, trying to make a split-second decision about
the best way to go. I could fall backward into the roses, but I didn't
know whether there was another zombie behind me, or whether my
grabby friend had scratched himself on the thorns. I could infect
myself in my efforts to get away.

He was *definitely* going to infect me if I gave him the time to reel
me in and get me within reach of his teeth. I only had a few seconds
to react, and I took the option that might mean one or both of us
made it out of this little patch of hell alive.

'Close your eyes!' I shouted. I didn't wait to see whether Mat had
listened to me. I just jammed the barrel of my gun against the zombie's forehead and pulled the trigger, turning my face away at the last
moment in case of splatter.

The gunshot rang across the garden like an alarm bell. The zombie's fingers released my hair. I turned back just in time to see him

collapse backward, hitting the ground in a heap – and to see his four friends come shambling through the bushes.

'Aw, balls,' I said. 'Mat?'

'Yes?' The Newsie's voice was a pained squeak. I felt bad about that. I'd feel a lot worse if we both got eaten.

'Run,' I said. We turned and fled, moving through the roses as fast as we dared now that we knew they were a transmission vector. One good thing about being among the living: We could still move faster than the dead.

I see I've picked up a bunch of new readers since my makeup tutorials were featured on CNN (that is a sentence I am allowed to write now, what is this strange new world), so I thought I should give you the rundown before we go any further. Hi, I'm Mat Newson, and this is my op-ed slash diary column. I babble here. This is the babbling place. The opinions and thoughts and things I can't always support with hard data or wipe away with a makeup sponge place. It is not required reading for the rest of the site, or even for the rest of my material. It *is* the place for finding out what's new with me, for keeping track of my public appearances, and yes, for getting first crack at any giveaways I host. This is also where you suggest topics for future makeup tutorials. I love you all, but those comment threads are like kudzu! I can't keep them trimmed enough to be useful.

As for me, I'm twenty-seven years old, genderfluid, and prefer 'they/them' pronouns. Some of you will probably scowl right about now and mutter 'but "they" is always plural' to yourselves. And to you I say that Shakespeare disagrees. 'They' has always been used as a generic singular when the gender of the person being spoken of was unknown. Since my gender is unknown from moment to moment, unless I have personally, specifically, and recently told you differently, the singular 'they' is my preference.

One of my blog- and housemates, Ash, is from a pretty conservative part of Ireland. She had never encountered anyone who publicly identified as genderfluid before she met me (although, since she had the Internet, she had heard of the concept). She slipped up a lot when we first met. She always apologized, and she always tried. That's all I'm asking any of you to do, all right? Just try, and keep trying. You'll get there someday.

I believe in you.

—From *Non-Binary Thinking*, the blog of Mat Newson,
February 5, 2040

Six

We ran and the zombies pursued, because that's what zombies were designed by an accident of science to do. A world where zombies didn't chase wouldn't be all that compelling, I guess. Mat demonstrated a previously unknown talent for running like their ass was on fire, pulling quickly out in front of me and racing for the presumptive safety of the governor's security staff. I focused less on speed and more on avoiding the various obstacles in my path, the reaching rose briars and the bumps in the pavement. The last thing I wanted to do was run into a kill box with an open wound. They'd shoot before they saw that it was a scratch, and they'd be entirely right to do it.

I glanced back. The zombies weren't pursuing anymore. We'd run too fast, and there were closer, nonmoving targets available. The group – still not moaning – had turned, moving in silent unison through the roses and toward the governor.

My gunshot hadn't been as loud as I had originally thought. The muzzle was designed to dampen noise, and the governor was in a carefully designed sound bubble, defined by her speakers and by the natural acoustics of the area. Which was all a fancy way of saying that they hadn't heard us, and that they were about to be in serious danger.

'Aw, *fuck*,' I said, with all the sincerity I could muster. I came skidding to a stop, cupped my hands around my mouth, and shouted,

'Mat! Run faster! Tell security we've got a situation – and ask them not to shoot me, all right?'

Mat cast a terrified look over their shoulder, eyes widening as they realized what I was about to do. But they didn't argue. They didn't try to tell me I was being stupid. They just nodded, and kept on running.

The roses were planted far enough back from the paths that I was able to run full tilt for most of the way, dodging between briars when necessary. The last thing I wanted to do was create a secondary biohazard while I was trying to deal with the first one – although that did beg the question of where the first had *come* from. I'd been recording since I stepped into the garden. I tapped my mag as I ran, setting it to wide panorama. Maybe the camera would catch something I'd missed, some point of access for the infected. Because I couldn't believe the governor's advance team had managed to miss something as huge as a zombie mob in the middle of the rose test garden. It didn't make *sense*.

And then it didn't matter if it made sense or not, because I was on top of the remaining zombies, and I had more important things to worry about. 'Hey undead fuckos!' I shouted, sliding to a stop about six feet behind them. Close enough to be able to call my shots, far enough away to be out of grabbing range. It was still closer than I liked, especially without body armor and a face shield, but there were too many people on the other side of those bushes for me to get picky.

Those high school kids were going to be going back to their teacher with a much bigger story than anyone could have anticipated – assuming I was quick enough on the draw to give security time to react. If we all got eaten, nobody was going to be writing the official reports.

The zombies turned at the sound of my voice. Even a smart mob isn't *intelligent*; the quirk of the viral structure that gives them more brains in a bigger group can't work miracles, thank God. Hearing a human within plausible reach was pretty much always going to supersede the chance of a human on the other side of a bunch of prickly bushes. Zombies don't feel pain the way unconverted people do, but they understand concepts like 'the path of least resistance.' Zombies, like shit, will always flow downhill.

The lead zombie made a questioning sound that was halfway to being a moan. I smiled encouragingly.

'That's it. You're getting the idea. Come on, big boy, moan for Ash. Make a big wide sound so that nobody back at base thinks this is some sort of a hoax.' I shifted my aim slightly, pointing the muzzle of my gun at the zombie *behind* the lead zombie. I wanted to lure them away. That meant not slowing them down any more than I had to.

I'm not the best marksman in the world. I don't compete on an international or even regional level. But I *am* a trained Irwin, and at any sort of close range, I'm lethal. Like military snipers and big game hunters before us, we learn to set our adrenaline and our emotions aside before we pull the trigger, because to do otherwise would be to waste a bullet and maybe get ourselves killed. In the words of a pre-Rising author, I do not aim with my hand. I aim with fifteen years of hard training and solid experience, and I very rarely miss.

I pulled the trigger. A hole appeared in the center of the zombie's forehead. She had time to look puzzled, like this hadn't been on her calendar for the day, and then she was falling backward, nearly knocking over the zombie behind her. I followed that shot with another, this time aiming straight up into the sky. All the built-in muffling couldn't stop that one from ringing like a bell over the rose garden. Feedback squealed from the speakers. The governor must have jerked forward when she heard the sound, getting too close to the mic and setting up a following alarm.

Good. I was going to need the backup.

The lead zombie didn't like being shot at. He finally opened his mouth and set up a moan, low and cold and chilling. There was something about the way zombies moaned that hurt the mammalian ear, some deep, ancient note that spoke of bloody seas and dangerous jungles. What was worse, the moan of a zombie could – and would – attract *more* zombies, turning a small mob into a big one faster than you could say 'George Romero was right.'

On the plus side, nothing living can moan like a zombie, even if someone was fool enough to try. It's not possible. So anyone who heard this would know I was in serious trouble. I was hearing it. I knew very, very well just how much trouble I was in.

I took a step backward, adjusting my aim again. This time, I was focusing on the lead zombie. The others had taken up his moan, and were reorienting themselves on me. At any moment, the rush would begin, and zombies can be dismayingly fast at short distances. That whole 'not feeling pain' thing again. They didn't *care* if they were running on blown kneecaps and shattered ankles. They kept coming until their bodies gave out and dropped them on their faces, and even then, they'd do their best to crawl.

I pulled the trigger. The zombie lurched forward at the last instant, and my bullet went whizzing off past his head, vanishing uselessly into the bushes. He was still moaning, and I could hear other moans coming from elsewhere in the garden. We weren't alone. I did the only sensible thing.

I turned and ran again, and this time I didn't look back.

More zombies appeared from the rosebushes as I flew past, their hands reaching for me, their faces clotted with dirt and bits of ground cover. Adrenaline had turned me into a lean, mean, running-like-hell machine, and I was intending to keep going for as long as I possibly could.

Maybe I should have spent a little more attention on where I was going. My toe caught a bump in the path and I went sprawling, hitting the ground with enough force to knock the air out of my lungs and slap the mag off my face. It flew another three feet or so before wedging in one of the neighboring rosebushes. My knees were on fire. I was more than relatively sure that I'd skinned them, and depending on where the zombies had been walking – depending on where the hazard zones in this bucolic little setting were hidden – those scrapes might be the end of me.

There wasn't time to dwell on that. There wasn't time to get my breath back, either. I rolled over, lifting my shoulders off the path, and opened fire on the advancing zombies, grouping my bullets around their heads and throats. I was missing as often as I was hitting, but there weren't that many of them. I might still have a chance.

Assuming, that was, that the cavalry arrived before the zombies crawling out of the flower beds around me managed to grab hold. I fired again and again, until the hammer clicked on empty. It had taken less than ten seconds. My lungs were still aching from my impact with the pavement, and I didn't have to be a genius to know that my body wasn't ready to run. Not yet. Not soon enough.

The remaining zombies moaned as they advanced. I struggled to sit up, hoping that my mag had landed so that I was still on camera. I wanted my entry on the Wall to document something awesome, and not just an incoherent scream fading into silence.

'Well come on, me boyos,' I said, in my most exaggerated accent. My American audience would be delighted. My family back home would be mortified. It seemed like the right note to go out on, all things considered. 'I haven't got all day.'

Then the skies opened up behind me, and thunder rained down on the zombies.

The hail of bullets was thick and fast, and so plentiful that the smell of gunpowder overwhelmed the smell of roses in under a second. I curled into a tight ball, lacing my hands behind my neck as I protected my mucous membranes by pressing my face hard against my thighs. I remembered my skinned knees too late to get into any sort of defensive position; I would just have to hope that my sundress would keep them safe from any back splatter. It was a small, vain hope, but it would keep me from freaking out until someone could produce a blood testing unit and clear me.

The gunfire stopped. I raised my head.

Zombies littered the path ahead of me. The rosebushes looked distinctly moth-eaten, with branches blown off and leaves shredded into virtual confetti. The bodies sprawled on them didn't help. There must have been at least fifteen zombies scattered around the place, some out in the open, others still half-buried in the soil they'd been dredging themselves out of. Which didn't make any *sense*. Zombies never waited long enough to reanimate for burial to occur, and why would anyone have buried their loved ones in the rose test garden, anyway?

The only way these zombies could have been where they were was for someone to have put them there, on purpose. And that opened a whole new horrible line of thought that I didn't want to dwell on just yet.

'Aislinn North, please remain where you are,' said a voice from behind me. I recognized it as belonging to John, Audrey's drinking buddy. That was good. If someone had to shoot me, I wanted it to be someone who wasn't actually a part of my team. Ben would never have recovered, and Audrey . . .

That wasn't how I wanted Audrey to remember me.

'Remaining,' I said amiably. My gun was already on the path. I pushed it away with my toe, showing that I was unarmed.

'Please use your fingers to show me the following numbers. Six. Three. Four. Seven. Two.'

I followed instructions. I didn't use my thumbs. It was important, when proving that you weren't a zombie, to do exactly as you'd been told. He hadn't said 'use your hands,' he'd asked for fingers. Maybe ignoring that fine line wouldn't have been sufficient to buy me a bullet, but I had taken enough risks already today. I didn't feel like taking another one.

'Stand and turn. Keep your hands low. Do not make any sudden moves.'

I stood and turned, keeping my motions as slow and fluid as my skinned knees and bruised ribs would allow, resisting the urge to do a little pirouette. Yes, it would look good on camera, and yes, that was usually a major concern, but under the circumstances, I was fairly sure my audience would forgive me a moment of caution. Anything to keep myself from ending up on the Wall for a few minutes longer.

John and Amber were in front of me, their guns drawn and pointed in my direction. The barrels seemed to have expanded when I wasn't looking, becoming sightless eyes large enough to swallow the world. I stood straighter, letting them look me over.

'Your knees,' said Amber. There was regret in her voice, but it was outweighed by professionalism. We were friends, of a sort. She still wouldn't hesitate to pull the trigger. 'What happened?'

'I ate path,' I said. 'Running too fast, hooked my foot, down I went. The infected were a considerable distance behind me at the time, and approaching via a different route. The odds of my having landed in a biohazard are slim.'

'Slim odds are still odds,' said John. He took a hand from his gun and dipped it into his pocket, producing a plastic-wrapped blood testing unit. 'Catch.'

He lobbed the unit at me underhand, and for one heart-stopping moment, I couldn't decide what I was supposed to do. If I didn't catch it, I was showing reduced manual dexterity, and they might shoot me. If I caught it, I was moving quickly, and they might shoot me. No matter what I did, it seemed like 'and they might shoot me' was remaining on the table.

At the last moment, instinct took over for intellect. My hand lashed out, grabbing the test unit before it could fly past me. The plastic crinkled under my fingers, cool and reassuring. This was what normalcy felt like. This was my ticket back to the land of the living.

The reassuring feeling lasted only for as long as it took for my eyes to find Audrey and Ben at the back of the crowd that was growing on the garden's edge. He looked terrified. She looked resigned, like this was something she had long since come to terms with. I wasn't sure which was worse: the thought that I was about to break his heart, or the fact that I had apparently broken hers so long ago that she no longer felt the need to weep for me.

'Open the bag,' instructed John. 'Remove the testing unit. If you check out clean, we will remove you to a secondary site for decontamination and further testing.'

This was all standard procedure, as was his not saying what would happen if I failed the test. No one who'd passed the exam to become a working journalist needed to be told what would happen if they couldn't get a green light on one of these little boxes. 'Just do me a favor, all right?' I said, as I removed the plastic and dropped it, still cool and crinkling, to the ground by my feet. 'If you have to shoot me – and you shouldn't have to shoot me, but we all know how much power "shouldn't" has in a place like this – can you clear the area first? I don't want certain people to see it.'

'We'll make sure they're out of here, Ash,' said Amber. She nodded toward the unit in my hands. 'Now do it.'

I sighed, popped the lid off the test, and jammed my thumb down on the sensor.

Kellis-Amberlee is a tricky asshole of a disease. The terms 'infected' and 'uninfected' are technically inaccurate, because we're *all* infected, every mammal on the planet, from the moment that we take our first breath. It's in the air. It would be better to say 'active' and 'inactive,' because that's the real difference: Is the virus in your blood sleeping the sleep of the terrible and the just, or is it awake and breaking everything it finds? Except that sometimes active virus is a good thing. Marburg Amberlee was created to cure cancer, and it still does that, activating and taking out any cancerous cells as soon as they register with the virus. Do a blood test while your native viral load is busy taking apart a tumor, and you may get a false positive. You may also get a bullet to the head, because the people who have the guns don't have time to worry about nuance. Nuance is for other people.

The lights on the top of the testing unit began to cycle, flashing green to amber, amber to red, and red back to green again. After five repetitions of that pattern, the red dropped out, until only the amber and green were left, flashing with increasing speed. Finally, the amber dropped out. The green flashed three more times and settled on a steady brightness. I pulled my thumb away and held the unit up, showing everyone in range the light.

'I am not presently infected,' I said, in a clear, calm voice. Americans sometimes interpreted my accent as a slurring of my words, and so I enunciated each word with all the precision I could muster. Anything to keep them from deciding it was safer just to shoot me anyway. 'I am standing with skinned knees in the middle of a biohazard zone, and I would *really* appreciate a change of scene right about now, if you don't mind.'

'Place the test unit in the bag. Press this to your neck.' John threw me another object. I caught it, looked down at my hand, and grimaced.

'A dermal patch? Is this a sedative?'

'In a sense,' said Amber. 'It's a sedative when it knocks you out cold, right?'

I glared at her. She shrugged.

'The governor is on the property, Ash. She's not going to move until we have the situation in the garden cleaned up and under control. We can't walk you past her when you might be contaminated. If we knock you out, we can roll you in sterile sheeting and carry you without risking exposure. It's better this way for everyone.'

Right. 'Who's going to be on cleanup?'

'Not your concern. Take the patch, or we have to treat you as belligerent, and you know how that ends.' Amber looked genuinely concerned. 'I promise you'll be safe.'

'And everyone knows *that's* a promise that always gets kept.' I looked at the plastic box in my hand. The dermal patch inside was barely a scrap of flesh-toned tape, but I knew it would deliver a punch strong enough to put me under for hours. Otherwise, why bother?

Ah, well. Anything was better than a bullet to the brain.

'Tell Mat I dropped my mag somewhere around here. Maybe it can be sterilized.' I sat down on the path, cross-legged, smoothing my skirt over my bleeding knees. Then I popped the box open and removed the patch, peeling off the backing material before slapping it flat against my neck. 'If not, I'm going to need a new one before we roll out. Oh, and make sure Ben knows that . . . that the zombies . . . they were crawling . . . out . . . of . . . the ground . . .' I was aware that my speech was slowing down, but I couldn't seem to do anything about it. The world was getting fuzzy around the edges, filled with shadows that didn't line up or make any real sense.

I blinked, trying to make the dark spots at the edges of my eyes go away. It didn't work. If anything, it did the opposite: When I opened my eyes again, the spots had tripled, chewing away at my vision like termites gnawing on a house.

'This stinks,' I said, as clearly as I could, and closed my eyes again. I didn't feel myself fall backward. I didn't feel myself hit the ground. I didn't feel much of anything that followed, which was probably a mercy.

When I opened my eyes for the second time, John and Amber were gone, replaced by a clean white ceiling with domed lights, glowing beatifically, like the eyes of Heaven. I blinked. The ceiling remained. I sat up. Nothing restrained me or restricted my movement. That was good. The blanket that had been covering me fell away, and I looked down to see that my sundress was gone, replaced by a simple blue hospital shift.

'You're awake.' The voice was Audrey's. I turned toward it. The face was Audrey's as well. She was sitting in one of those hard plastic chairs that are standard issue for first aid stations all over the world, her hands clenched tight in her lap, white-knuckled and unmoving. She lifted her chin slightly, looking at me. 'Say something to prove lack of compromised faculties.'

'The burial tombs at Newgrange date back to the Neolithic era, and are maintained to this day by the National Heritage Foundation, even though tourism has been way, way down since zombies started using the tunnels as a place to hide from the elements,' I said. 'Good place to spend a Sunday. Are we okay?'

'Well, let's see,' she said. 'You snuck off to investigate an outbreak without notifying me or Ben. You took *Mat*, of all people. You know Mat only has their field certification because we insisted. You nearly got yourself eaten. You *did* get yourself grabbed.'

I reached up instinctively to touch my hair, expecting to find that it had all been burnt off in the sterilization process. My relief when I found it intact must have shown in my eyes, because Audrey snorted, hard.

'You're lucky,' she said. 'If I hadn't insisted on being present while they decontaminated you, you would've woken up with a buzz cut, and it would have served you right. What were you *thinking*?'

'That this was an important political event, and you didn't need to be dragged away from it because I was bored and feeling jumpy.' My knees had been covered with a thin layer of spray skin, sealing them and keeping contaminants out of the scrapes. I bent them experimentally. The faux skin pulled but didn't tear loose, feeling more like a very tight bandage than anything else. 'I sure as hell didn't expect a full-scale outbreak back there. I was thinking there'd be one, maybe two zombies at the most, wandered in from some trail we didn't secure properly.' I froze. 'The decon – did I manage to tell them to check the flower beds before I went under?'

Audrey nodded sharply. 'You said, and I quote, "they were crawling out of the ground." Everyone assumed you were high as a kite from the sedatives they'd slapped on you, but Amber passed your message on to Ben and me, and we insisted there be a ground check before they razed the place. I told them you're foolhardy, not foolish, and that you know a security breach when you see one.'

'And?'

'And they found evidence that fifteen zombies had been buried in the rose beds that morning, with straws to let them breathe.' Audrey shook her head. 'They were comfortable enough, and well-fed enough, that they didn't start moving until they smelled food. From there, it was a short distance to setting up the moan. The rest of the zombies came out when they heard the dinner bell.'

'Which means someone put them there.'

Audrey raised an eyebrow. 'Yes, because the rest of us were going on the assumption that a bunch of zombies could have buried themselves completely, *under* the roses.'

'You don't understand.' I shook my head, trying to clear away the last of the fuzziness from the dermal patch. I still felt too shaky to stand up, much less get as vehement as I needed to. 'I know what a garden clean and cleanse looks like. I've *done* them. If those zombies had pulled themselves out and gone for the press conference without me stumbling into the middle of things, no one would have been able to tell what was preexisting damage and what had happened during the outbreak.'

'What?'

'Cleaning and decontaminating a garden, if you want to keep using it *as* a garden afterward, involves removing the first twenty-four inches of topsoil.' Which could be all the topsoil, and some of the hardpack underneath. It wasn't uncommon for a garden that was going to be replanted after an outbreak to be made up entirely of imported dirt, new earth that had never known that land before. Bit by bit, we were re-creating the world. 'If the zombies were buried shallowly enough that they could pull themselves out, they can't have been down much below that. All the signs would have been eliminated in the decontamination process.'

Audrey was quiet for a moment. Finally, she said, 'You're saying this wasn't just planned, it was planned because no one would be able to know for sure that the zombies had been buried after the fact.'

'Yup. It was a trap.' I finally ventured to stand up. My knees wobbled, but deigned to support my weight. That was nice of them. 'I'm assuming they burned my clothes?'

'Even your bra.'

'Damn. I was still breaking it in.'

'Fortunately, you have a girlfriend who loves you very much.' Audrey reached under her chair and produced a green cloth bag, which she tossed past me onto the bed. 'Bra, underpants, sundress. Shoes are under the bed.'

'Have I told you recently that you're an angel sent from Heaven to remind me of God's love?' I opened the bag. She had packed a bleach-streaked sundress that had originally been printed with bright-winged macaws. They looked like ghosts now. That was a good thing. I kept a few damaged sundresses around as a way to project 'I have been through hell' without actually wearing things that had been torn or shot. There was pleasantly shabby, and then there was a bullet hole revealing the color of my underpants.

'No, but maybe you should consider it.' Audrey held herself perfectly straight for a moment more before she sagged, letting all her tension out. She stopped blinking back her tears at the same time. They ran unchecked down her cheeks, stopping me cold.

'Oh, hey, aw, no, Audrey, no.' I dropped my clothes and stood again, crossing to her as quickly as my wobbly legs allowed. 'Don't cry. I'm fine. See? All my bits are still where they were when we got up this morning. I am a completely intact Aislinn. So don't cry. Please?'

'You weren't supposed to run off and nearly get yourself killed at a *garden party*,' she said. When I was close enough she latched on, pressing her face into my shoulder. I didn't resist or try to pull away. It took a lot to upset Audrey like this. When it happened, it was best just to let her ride it out. 'You were supposed to be safe when we were working the political circuses. How the fuck do you do these things?'

'It's a natural talent that I've spent years honing,' I said. 'Don't cry, love, don't cry. You knew I was a scorpion when you picked me up, and I'll always do my best to sting my way back to you.'

'Garden party,' she repeated, like those two words somehow summarized everything that was wrong with my approach to the world – and maybe they did, for her. In what should have been a perfectly safe setting, I had still managed to go charging off and find something dangerous to get involved with.

Speaking of settings ... I pulled back enough to look around us. The walls and ceiling were white, which was normal for medical facilities – supposedly the appearance of absolute cleanliness was good for people, made them feel safer, but it was really about making it easier to bleach the place down to its bones. The shape of the room beneath the paint, though, that was subtly wrong. The corners were curved.

'Since I don't think we've fallen into one of those old Lovecraft stories, I'm guessing we're not actually inside a real building,' I said, looking back to Audrey. 'Where are we, love?'

'That took you longer than I expected it to, and you can stop calling me "love,"' she said, reaching up to wipe her eyes with the heel of her hand. 'You only do that when you're trying to make up for upsetting me.'

'Or when you're naked, don't forget about the naked.' I stood, walking back to where I had abandoned my clothes. I'd feel better when I was dressed. Naked with Audrey was fun when we were alone. It wasn't the ideal when I was in a place I didn't know, at the mercy of people I couldn't see. 'Forgive me my quirks, and tell me where we are. Have a heart, love.'

'If I didn't have a heart, I would die when my blood stopped circulating through my body,' said Audrey. 'We're in the site's private medical trailer. They have a lot of older folks who insist on coming here for their "constitutionals." Portland natives who came here before the Rising and say they'll be damned before they let a bunch of zombies chase them away from something that they love.'

'Which probably doesn't stop them from having nervous fits every time they hear a noise they can't explain coming from the big, scary green world,' I said. I dressed quickly. There are people who like to say that female Irwins are just about eye candy, because we can't *possibly* know what it's like to prepare for the field: not with our breasts and our long hair and our girlish, girlish ways. Those people have never worked with a female Irwin. Half of us eschew the trappings of femininity, because not everyone is that kind of girl, and running around the wilderness harassing the legally dead tends to attract the girls who aren't. The rest of us exaggerate those trappings for the camera, going with victory rolls in our hair and lace-up corsets around our waists. What the people at home never see is how those corsets have Kevlar in their seams, protecting us from the world. They don't understand how we've learned to put ourselves together in under a minute, because sometimes the story won't wait.

Every Irwin is a badass in our own way. The job demands it. But if you want to know who the scariest person in the group is, look for the one who's been fighting zombies without smearing her eyeliner.

'I'd kill for a compact right about now,' I said, reaching behind myself to zip my dress.

'Like this one?' asked Audrey, producing a clamshell from her pocket. 'You're going to need to apply foundation and walk at the same time. If you're awake and well enough to be dressed, we should be joining the debriefing already in progress. Mat is probably starting to twitch by now. They don't like answering questions they haven't already scripted.'

'And they probably don't *know* all the answers; I was the one who saw the first zombie and took off running.' I took the clamshell from her hand and clicked it open, checking my makeup. My lipstick was a lost cause, but my eyes were good; I had a bit of a smoky lid thing going, probably from where I'd slammed into the garden floor. Decontamination always gave my skin a lovely glow. I snapped the clamshell shut and tucked it into my pocket. 'Good enough for now. Let's go ruin some days.'

'You've already done an *excellent* job of that,' said Audrey. She held out her hand. I took it, and she used me to pull herself out of the chair, bouncing to her feet with the sort of enthusiasm that should be reserved for small children and cartoon tigers. 'I don't think I've ever heard so many people shouting at each other about nothing. It would have been impressive as all hell, if you hadn't been sedated at the time.'

Which meant Audrey had missed out on some primo people watching because she was busy worrying about me. 'Sorry about that,' I said dolefully.

'You are a walking natural disaster,' she said, and opened the trailer door.

Outside was a parking lot. Not literally: There were no dividing lines to show the cars where to go. There was just a *lot* of pavement, stretching out in all directions until it encountered the square, boxy shapes of the park management buildings. There was also a crowd of security people, John among them, waiting for us.

Audrey was the first one out, her usual mask of professional indifference firmly in place. It was always amazing to me how quickly she could shut herself off from people she didn't feel had earned the right to see her at anything but her best. Not that her cold, working face was really 'her best' – it was her most practiced, maybe, but there were a dozen versions of her that I liked better, and most of them were smiling.

I was smiling. I was smiling like my face was going to split in two, like I didn't have a care in the world, because I knew my team. Even with me unconscious and Audrey attending, someone would have set up a camera, and I was going to want this footage to reflect the version of me that was acceptable to my public. I was just like Audrey, in my way. It was just that I was on the inside of my plastic smile, and I never had to look at it and feel it break my heart.

'Miss Wen; Mrs North,' greeted John, with a nod for first Audrey, and then me. He sounded like he'd been running hard since the garden, and didn't expect to stop any time soon. 'Can I get you both to take a blood test for me before I accompany you to the governor?'

'One second,' I said. 'How far away is the governor? Is she in one of those buildings over there?' I pointed to the structures on the other side of the parking lot.

John nodded.

'And are we going to have to take another blood test when we get there, to prove that we haven't become mysteriously infected between this door and that one?'

John nodded again. It was hard to read his expression behind his glasses – I hate people who hide their eyes all the time, unless there's a medical reason for them to do so – but I thought he was amused. That was a good thing, because I was about to balk.

'Grand. Then we're going to pass on the blood test now, if it's all the same to you.'

Several of the security personnel tensed. A few of them reached for their weapons. John raised a hand and they all stopped. Good: He was in charge here. That was going to help. 'Why are you refusing basic precautions, Mrs North?' he asked.

'Because we just came out of a sterile medical facility. I passed a blood test before decon, and I know that means I passed another blood test *after* decon, because that's how this sort of thing works. That means we know I'm not infected. Audrey was required to take a blood test before you let her go in there with me.' I didn't know that part for sure, but it was an extremely safe bet. Putting someone unconscious in a room with someone whose infection status was unknown wasn't just irresponsible, it was criminal in multiple states – including this one. 'Since we didn't get infected by stepping through the door, and we're unlikely to become infected by talking to you, I'd rather keep a bit more of the blood inside my body, and only get tested once. If it's cool with you.'

John was silent for a moment – long enough for me to start to think that no, it *wasn't* cool with him. Then the corners of his mouth twitched, betraying his amusement. 'If either of you so much as blinks in a way I don't like, you're going to wish you'd taken the blood test,' he cautioned.

'Probably not, since I'm pretty sure that was a threat, and people who've been shot don't usually wish for much of anything,' I said amiably. 'But sure, we'll go with it. Our regrets will be many. Now can we get moving?'

We got moving.

The walk across the blacktop felt like being marched to the gallows. John led the pack, and the rest of the security staffers fanned out around him, forming a bubble around me and Audrey. They stayed at least six feet away at all times, sometimes as far as eight or nine. If I moved toward them, they stepped away, maintaining their distance. I considered toying with their formation, but dismissed the idea as a bad one. I didn't need to antagonize a bunch of heavily armed, highly strung people who had just had a firsthand demonstration of how dangerous their job was actually going to be.

Besides, if I was being honest with myself, they weren't the only ones who were nervous. I had just come terrifyingly close to winding up on the Wall. The adrenaline had had more than enough time to leave my system while I was sleeping off the sedatives, but that hadn't done anything for my lingering, absolute denial. Now, with time moving around me again, the denial was wearing off. I could have died. I had gone into a bad situation without sufficient preparation, and I could very easily have died.

The Wall is the great virtual monument where the last moments of everyone who has died due to Kellis-Amberlee are preserved. Facebook status updates, random tweets, blog posts, even snippets of home video, they all go up there, building this constantly shifting landscape of heartache and longing and loss. Anyone who chooses to become an Irwin accepts that one day, their face will appear in the rolls of the dead, a hyperlink beneath it summarizing their life and everything that it contained. But that doesn't mean it's something that most of us aspire to. The suicidal and the foolish don't last long in our community. They get their fifteen seconds of fame, they get their lasting place on the Wall, and the rest of us move on.

I started to shiver. Audrey put a reassuring hand on my arm, stabilizing me and lending me what strength she could. I cast her a thankful look. She smiled. That was all I needed in the world.

John stepped aside when we reached the building where the governor and her people – and presumably, the rest of *our* people – were waiting. 'Ladies first,' he said. He somehow managed to make the clichéd old phrase sound ironic, like it was the last thing he wanted to be saying. I decided to forgive him.

'Aren't you a gentleman,' I said, and stepped forward to press my palm against the testing panel.

Bad luck: This one included voice recognition. A snippet of nursery rhyme appeared on the screen. I cast John an alarmed look before I read, 'Wee Willie Winkie ran through the town, upstairs and downstairs, in his nightgown.'

As I'd expected, a red light began flashing above the row that was verifying my blood.

'My accent's throwing it off,' I said desperately, resisting the urge to rip my hand away. That could result in a false positive, which would, in turn, make it legal for any of the surrounding men to shoot me in the head. 'It thinks I'm slurring. Do you have an override for this thing?'

'Security clearance John Englund, personal staff of Governor Kilburn, identification number four two seven zero two, alpha gamma zeta,' said John, stepping up next to me and speaking in a slow, clear voice. 'The subject currently undergoing analysis is an immigrant from the Republic of Ireland. She is not able to pass the voice verification due to accent, not due to infection.'

The red light continued to burn above my blood testing strip. Audrey was already done. She stepped back, holding her pin-stuck hand to her chest and watching with wide, solemn eyes. She knew as well as I did how dangerous voice recognition systems were for me. This could be a very big problem.

Then the light blinked out. The flashing lights of the blood analysis settled on green. I jerked my hand away like I'd been burnt.

'Sorry about that, Mrs North,' said John, stepping into position at the testing panel I had so recently vacated. He slapped his own hand down. 'We've already adjusted all the governor's personal testing systems to account for your accent. In the case of systems at facilities where she's speaking or making public appearances, we'll either suspend voice analysis or make sure you're traveling with someone who has the clearance to deactivate it for you specifically.'

'Much appreciated,' I said. We both knew I'd be having a minder for any event that required us to use a voice analysis system: They simply couldn't afford to make places *less* secure during a major political campaign. But at least they were acknowledging that this was a problem, and taking some basic steps to fix it. That was more than some would have done.

The lights flashed green. John nodded to his team, indicating that they should begin their own tests once we were gone. Then he opened the now-unlocked door and motioned us inside, to where the next phase of our already complicated day was waiting.

Li Jiang was a statue in her stillness, carved from the bones of the earth. It would have taken better than human vision to see the way that she was trembling, so slight and subtle was it, so tied to the marrow of her bones. The slim redheaded woman who sat on Li Jiang's bed, watching her, had no such supernatural gifts. Grace had paid for her passage to America by sitting in a pirate ship's smoke-filled hold, repairing damaged uniforms worn by mercenary men. Her eyesight would never recover from that ordeal.

But she didn't need to see Li Jiang to know that her lover was hurting. The pain was written in every move the other woman made, every turn of her head and every flick of her fingers. That was why Li had gone so still. She was trying to conceal how much she was hurting and, as was inevitable, she was failing in her quest.

'I just don't understand why it always has to be you,' said Grace, her sweet brogue sliding through the room and across Li Jiang's skin like a caress. 'Aren't there other detectives in this God-forsaken city? Can't someone else take the bullet for a change, and leave you here with me, not broken and bleeding for the sake of someone else's war?'

'But that's the trouble, Grace,' said Li Jiang. She still didn't move. She felt as if she might never move again, as if stillness had become her fate. If so, she welcomed it. Still things must eventually move past pain. 'It's never someone else's war. As soon as the place where you stand becomes part of the battlefield, the war belongs to you. I am only doing what I promised you the day that we met. I'm protecting what matters most to me. I'm protecting my home, and all the love that it contains.'

Grace began, silently, to weep.

—From *Blood on the Hanging Tree*, originally published in *Wen the Hurly Burly's Done*, the blog of Audrey Liqiu Wen, February 5, 2040

Seven

The room contained a large oval table, the sort used for committee meetings and public interest groups the world over. This one was probably used most often to discuss the types of rose that would be planted in the now-ravaged test gardens: serious horticultural discussions of thorn and leaf and blossom quality. Those people were going to be pissed when they heard what had happened.

In the present, the table was occupied by the governor, her campaign manager, her head of security, and six other people from the campaign, only a few of whom I recognized, and those only vaguely. Ben and Mat were already there, sitting to flank two empty chairs, which were no doubt intended for me and Audrey. Everyone turned to look at us when we entered the room.

I considered smiling brightly and saying something pithy. Further consideration showed that I didn't have the energy. 'Sorry for the delay, all,' I said, walking over and dropping myself unceremoniously into the seat next to Ben. Audrey followed, sitting down between me and Mat. We were a united front once more. That made me feel a little better – enough to flash a cocky grin as I said, 'Turns out your med staff picked some pretty high-grade sedatives for your security team. Go team.'

'We're glad you and Miss Wen were able to join us, Mrs North,' said Governor Kilburn. She sounded stiffer than I was accustomed to. I wondered if that was what fear sounded like in the good governor. 'I'm also glad you weren't hurt.'

'I'm not,' said Chuck. The stocky little man glared at me, folding his arms across his barrel of a chest. Chuck looked like the sort of man who wrestled bears for fun. In reality, he was a social engineer and image manager who did cross-stitch to relax and owned five bearded dragons, which had the run of any room he stayed in. Walking in to talk to the campaign manager and finding him completely covered in lizards was definitely an experience. 'What the hell possessed you to go haring off after danger without alerting *someone*? Is this the kind of behavior we can expect from you for this entire campaign? Because it's not too late for you to be replaced, you know. There were thousands of bloggers *panting* for your job. I'm sure most of them would be thrilled to operate under a more restrictive contract.'

'Chuck, that's enough,' said Governor Kilburn.

I raised my eyebrows and turned to Ben. 'Think he's been sitting on that one for a while?'

'We've been hearing variations on the theme since we sat down,' said Ben, chasing his words with a quick flash of teeth. 'Good to see you. We didn't get your mag back, but Mat pulled all the footage before the cleaning crew destroyed the data storage unit. You've got some good material.' We had to manually switch to cloud storage for our raw recordings when we were on the road, weighing the risk of losing something material against the risk of getting hacked. Apparently, I had made the wrong call this morning.

'Bully for us,' I said. 'It's always nice when the stupid shit I do pays to replace the good stuff I inevitably break.' I settled in my seat, assuming as casual a pose as I could manage, and turned my attention back to Chuck. 'Governor Kilburn was speaking. All the security staffers I could see were busy making sure no one tried to pick her off while she was explaining her grand vision for the nation. You were totally out of the picture. Who would you have wanted me to tell? More importantly — and dig way down for the answer to this one, really *think* before you give your answer — what would you have done if I'd said something? Would you have given me permission to investigate? Would you have summoned some goons to watch my back? Or would you have told me I was borrowing trouble out of boredom, and ordered me back to my chair, where I would have had a front-row seat for the zombies boiling out of the roses and chowing down on a presidential candidate? Because I don't think I need to tell you which outcome *I* would be betting on here.'

'She's right,' said Governor Kilburn wearily. 'Chuck, it's time to stand down, because you're not going to win this one.'

Chuck looked incensed. 'I don't think you understand what this little muckraker did today! She—'

'Discovered an active outbreak and alerted us to its presence before anyone could be hurt,' said Governor Kilburn. 'She's being hailed as the hero of the hour, and not just by her own people. Do you have any idea what would have happened if those zombies had reached the podium before we heard the gunshots?'

'You could have died,' said Chuck, sounding wounded.

Governor Kilburn stared at him like he'd just grown another head. '*I* could have died?' she said. 'I point out the bullet we just dodged, and that's all you can seize on, that *I* could have died? There were over fifty people there! There were *children* there, for God's sake! My death would have been the smallest part of the tragedy — and honestly, it would have mattered in the most part because I would have gotten the largest headline.'

'And because this was an assassination attempt,' said Ben. Everyone turned their attention on him. He quailed slightly, adding a belated 'Ma'am.'

'How do you figure that?' asked Amber. She was leaning against the wall, seemingly filing her nails. I say 'seemingly' because although the file had been moving the whole time I'd been in the room, I hadn't seen it make contact with her nails once. It was a covering motion, something to keep people from looking at her too closely. I had a few similar screen-saver routines of my own. I respected the nail thing, though. The file could be used as a weapon if things got rough, and that was always useful.

On the surface, her behavior looked unprofessional, and maybe it was: Maybe that was the point. Of all Governor Kilburn's people, Amber seemed to have the best situational awareness, and was the first to read any given room. If people underestimated her because she looked like she wasn't interested in her job, well, that just put her in a better position to react when the need arose.

'As Ash pointed out, there were zombies buried in the garden beds,' said Ben. 'What she didn't know — what she couldn't have known, because she was a little busy fighting for her life when she was out there — was that the roses had been replanted after the dead were buried. Someone sedated a bunch of zombies, dug up the rose garden, planted the zombies, and then put the roses on top of them as cover.'

'Which makes it an assassination attempt exactly how?' demanded Chuck.

Audrey looked at him. 'How is it you're a campaign manager again?' she asked. 'You're not smart, you're not clever, and you're clearly not following the conversation. The governor posted her schedule weeks ago. We've been planning for this launch event since we were hired to follow the campaign. We have *weeks* of interviews, posts, and profiles prepared to go up, all using the rose garden as a source of imagery and metaphor. This was supposed to prove that she was prepared to grow her constituency and grow her influence, all while using a pleasing pre-Rising symbol wrapped up with modern security ideals. Instead, it's become another icon for insecurity. This undermines all our symbolism, which means it *absolutely* undermines yours.'

'That doesn't make it an assassination attempt,' said Chuck. 'It could just be someone trying to destroy our campaign plans.' He sounded unsettled. Audrey often took people that way when she started talking about symbolism and iconography – usually because she was right.

As a Fictional, it was Audrey's job to make the real world less interesting than the fake one, which was no small task, since the real world had zombies, and those were pretty damn compelling, especially when they were trying to chew your face off. She used a thousand literary tricks to manipulate her readers. Some of those tricks worked in the field, too. She was the one who'd suggested that if I was going to wear sundresses all the time, I use fabric that spoke, however subliminally, to my subject matter and the mood I was trying to convey. Even a California winter could become believable if I was running around draped in silver snowflakes.

Roses were hardy, beautiful, and prized in the post-Rising America. The governor had been planning to tie her image to them, using them as a symbol of fiercely dangerous femininity. It had been a good idea, and it might even have worked, if not for the dead bodies shambling all over her garden.

'See, that's the thing about zombies,' I said. 'They don't care if you're campaigning for something, and they don't care if you'll be a better tool alive but humiliated. They care about sinking their teeth into your throat and tearing until all that delicious blood comes out. One zombie might have been an attempt to undermine the campaign's symbolism. This many is an assassination.'

'An assassination with asshole roots,' said Mat suddenly. We all turned to look at them. They had been fiddling with their tablet this whole time, remaining quiet while the rest of us chased the conversation down rabbit holes. Now they looked up, blinking at the sudden quiet.

'I like your makeup,' I said. Mat had clearly had time to freshen up since the garden, and was now wearing eye shadow in a lovely spectrum of pinks and reds. All rose colors. I wondered whether this was their way of working through the trauma.

Mat smiled quickly. 'Thanks,' they said. 'Anyway, I've been checking the victims – the fresher ones – against local missing persons files, and I have five hits. They're all from the assisted living facility down the road. People with mental or medical problems that required them to live under extra security.'

I blinked. 'Wait. *Five* people disappeared from one facility and no one said anything?'

'Most of those homes are so overloaded that you could make off with twenty and no one would say anything after the proper reports were filed,' said Mat. 'The duty nurses were upset, and they're the ones who called it in. Everyone else just kept up with business as usual.'

'Are there any other homes like that near here?' asked Ben.

'No, not that I can find,' said Mat.

A sudden terrible thought struck me. I looked toward Audrey, and saw from her face that she had thought of something similar. Dry-mouthed, I said, 'Is there a home around here for queer youth?'

'The Rainbow Brigade has a halfway house downtown,' said Mat automatically. Their eyes went wide as they shot me a horrified look. 'You don't think . . . ?'

'There were more than five zombies in that garden,' I said. 'If you're going for a population you can winnow without a lot of people raising the alarm, that's one of the big ones. Sadly.'

'Still,' said Audrey.

Mat began to type. I waited, lips pressed into a hard line, to hear what would come next.

Before the Rising, one in four queer teens wound up homeless when they came out to their parents. Just when they needed family love and support the most, they lost it completely. They used to live on the street, gathering in loose tribes, doing whatever it took to stay alive. Then Kellis-Amberlee came along, and homelessness – which had never been safe, for anyone – became the focus of a lot more public attention. Hostels and halfway houses opened all over the world. Mental health care became more accessible, and less stigmatized. I guess when zombies ate most of the homeless population, people finally realized they should start looking after what's left, even if it was just to cut down on the number of potential future victims who might get infected and come after them next.

But that didn't stop teenagers from coming out to their parents, and it didn't stop parents from kicking their kids out. It just meant that a new set of safety nets had to be created, before those kids fell off the ends of the world.

'They've had six kids disappear in the last two weeks,' said Mat finally. 'Three of them, people assumed had gone back to their families. They'd been talking about it, anyway. The other three, there was more concern, but not that much that could be done about it. Resources were limited.'

'Resources are always limited,' I said. 'Check their faces against the pictures from the garden.'

'Someone mined the disabled and queer communities for their victims,' said Ben, looking at the governor. His voice was calm and steady. I envied him for that. 'This is a Democratic campaign. Those are two of the groups that have almost always consistently voted Democrat, even following the changes to the party since the Rising. Someone used your potential voter base as a weapon against you, which means that someone really *thought* about who they were going to use. There are other targets they could have gone after, some that would have been a lot easier to get. They chose those ones because they were both available and personal.'

'Symbolism again,' said Audrey. 'Those kids probably wouldn't have voted. It's all about the *idea* of turning Democrats against you, and taking them away from you at the same time.'

'So you think someone doesn't want me to be President,' said Governor Kilburn.

'Quite a few people probably don't want you to be President, ma'am,' said Ben. 'That's why we're having an election, instead of giving you the job by fiat. But someone was very dedicated to the idea that you could be killed before you got any further than Oregon. The only real question is why.'

Governor Kilburn was silent, just looking at him. Everyone else followed suit. Even me. Sometimes I may talk to hear the sound of my own voice – silence makes me nervous – but I understand the importance of the dramatic pause, and the role it plays in keeping the wheels of the world turning as they should. If she needed a few seconds to come to terms with whatever she was about to say, we were going to let her have them.

Finally, she said, 'There are always threats. It's been part of doing business as a politician, and a female politician at that, for as long as anyone can remember. I turn them over to the authorities, and to my security, and I try to put them out of my mind. It makes it easier to keep smiling for the cameras if I don't remember how many people want to kill me.'

'We have copies, if you want to see them,' said Amber.

Chuck didn't like that. 'They're *reporters*, not the FBI,' he said. 'What good is sharing your darkest secrets with them going to do? Unless you wanted everything splashed across the front page of tomorrow's paper.'

'There you go again, forgetting that we're as deep in this shit as you are,' said Mat. They shook their head. 'I *like* you, Chuck, but you're being way more narrow-minded than I expected you to be. We're not going to report on anything that might get us hurt too. I mean, that's just common sense.'

'And if, as Governor Kilburn says, everyone who runs for office gets threats like the ones she's received, how would our reporting the facts be some sort of shock to the public?' asked Ben. 'We're here to accurately document the campaign, not serve as political advisors, but if you ask me, admitting that there are credible threats only strengthens her position, especially after this attack.'

'Come again?' said Amber. Everyone turned to look at her. She shrugged. 'Okay, look, security's supposed to stay quiet and hug the walls, I get that, but come on. How does this strengthen her position? There's been an attack in a public place. People could have been hurt. People *were* hurt, since the dead guys had to come from somewhere.'

'We know where they came from,' said Mat, in a small voice.

'Which is why coming forward about the threats doesn't hurt anything in this situation,' said Ben. 'The governor passed the threats along to the authorities, according to the protocol, and people got hurt anyway. So now she's speaking out about the danger, and about the cowards who would violate Raskin-Watts by using zombies as a weapon.'

'Ooo, nasty, make it a terrorism charge,' I said approvingly. 'Hit whoever decided to go for the political symbolism where it really hurts.'

The governor sat up straighter. 'You really think this won't backfire? I don't want anyone else getting hurt, but—'

'You still want to be President one day, and that means not sounding like you've accepted too much culpability in the matter,' said Ben. 'We understand. We're not going to lie for you. We're not even going to spin things too hard in your favor. We will find the names and identities of everyone who died because your campaign was starting here, and we'll run obituaries on each one of them. We'll talk about the need to respond quickly and conclusively to threats during the political process, to prevent situations like this one from occurring again. This should never have happened in the first place. I'm not blaming you, Governor, and I'm not going to blame you in my articles. I'm blaming the whole political process. We should have better safeties in place.'

'Aren't you the one who's always saying the world isn't as dangerous as we make it out to be?' demanded Chuck. 'You can't have it both ways. Either it's too dangerous for us to have a simple election, or it's so safe that we should take away the blood testing units in schools. Try to do both at once and you're going to give yourself a headache.'

'There's a big difference between specific danger and environmental danger, which you would know if you weren't all tied up in knots and worried about losing your job,' said Ben. 'This was a tragedy. It's our job to report on it, and it's your job to help the governor move past it. We need her to keep going as much as you do, remember? Without her, we don't have a job.'

'Now that everyone has snapped at everyone else, I'm hoping we've all managed to get that out of our systems, and can move on to doing something productive,' said Governor Kilburn, leaning forward as she put herself back into the conversation. It was smoothly handled. She had clearly been hanging back, giving everyone else a chance to talk. I had to admire that, even if I was one of the people she was handling. 'Nothing we do is going to bring those poor souls back to life, but the journalists are right, Chuck. Whoever did this went for the most vulnerable members of my voting bloc. They wanted to hurt me, and they wanted to send a message in the process. They're trying to intimidate me.'

'Well, they've definitely intimidated *me*,' said Chuck.

'So quit.' The suggestion was made calmly, clearly, and with no indication that the governor was kidding. He flinched. She smiled, trying to reassure. I wasn't sure it was going to work. Most people don't take kindly to being told that they're not needed. 'I enjoy working with you, Chuck. You're damn good at your job, and I feel like I have a better shot at the big white house up on the hill if I have you here to guide me. But if you're going to balk every time you don't like the way things work around here, this isn't going to go well for either one of us. I'm going to get mulish and dig my heels in. You're going to pull all your hair out – and let's face it, honey, you don't have that much to spare.'

Nervous silence from the people at the table who'd been part of the governor's camp since the beginning. My team remained stone-faced. This wasn't our place. We were onlookers, nothing more, in a scene that didn't really need us. And it chafed. I know everyone thinks of themselves as the heroes of their own stories – Irwins maybe more than most, since we're usually the ones risking our necks for the scoop, which makes it hard not to consider yourself the center of the world — but there were better things we could have been doing with our time.

Much better. Almost before I realized I was intending to move, I'd placed my hands on the table and pushed myself into a standing position. Ben and Audrey followed my lead, leaving Mat to scramble to their feet so that we would present a united front.

'Well, this has been fun, but while we've been sitting in here chatting with you lot, everyone else who was at today's ruckus has been getting their footage online, giving exclusive interviews, and basically making a mockery of our so-called "access." So we're going to go now, and get started on doing our actual jobs, while you all figure out what you want to do next. Drop us an email when you know where we're needed.'

'You could be replaced,' said Chuck.

'So could you, and wouldn't that be a funny how-d'ye-do for all of us,' I shot back. 'We need to *work*. We saved your bacon today. *I* saved your bacon today. Rewarding us by keeping us from doing our jobs doesn't do you any favors, but it does piss us off rather royally. And as for firing us, do you really want a bunch of journalists with a vendetta against your candidate out there?'

'You reviewed our credentials alongside the governor when she was trying to decide whether or not to hire us,' said Ben, and his tone was as calm as mine was not, balancing me out. This was his territory as much as it was mine. I would get angry, and then he'd step in, not to defuse the situation, but to cover it with napalm. 'You know what we're capable of. Maybe we're not as fancy as Senator Ryman's pet blog team, but what we lack in prestige, we more than make up for with viciousness.'

Audrey didn't say anything. Audrey just smiled. She had a way of making a simple, nonaggressive expression look like a threat, and she was using it now. As usual, it made me want to kiss the violence off of her face. That would have to wait.

'Go,' said Governor Kilburn. 'Document events. Report the news.

Make the world understand that what happened here today was my responsibility, but not my fault, and that we are absolutely going to do better.'

It was a good line, delivered with enough conviction that I almost believed her. All four of us nodded, with varying degrees of sincerity. Then we turned, still presenting a united front, and walked out of the room.

No blood test was required to exit.

'Well,' I said, as we walked across the wide stretch of blacktop toward the fence. Our cars were on the other side, waiting for us to reclaim them. 'That was bracing.'

'That's a word,' said Mat. 'It has letters and everything.'

'I don't like any of this,' said Audrey. 'We should bail now, while we still have half a prayer of getting out.'

'That's easy for you to say,' said Mat. 'You're a Fictional. Nobody cares if you're associated with real news. I need to get some actual stories under my belt, or I'm going to get kicked out of Factual News.'

Audrey and I exchanged a look. There was a lot Mat didn't know. She shook her head minutely. There was a lot Mat was going to continue not to know.

'No one's bailing,' said Ben. He paused before amending, 'Or rather, I'm not bailing. If you want to bail by yourself, that's your call. But I made a commitment to this campaign, and I'm going to see it through.'

'My bank account made a commitment to all those lovely payments that should be coming my way.' The gate to the parking area *did* have a blood testing unit attached. That was normal, and I was about to slap my hand down on it when the part of my mind responsible for noticing things kicked in and stopped me cold. I froze.

'If you're not going to get pricked, let me,' said Mat, and started to step in front of me.

I didn't think. I just reacted, grabbing them by the shoulders and yanking them away from the testing panel so fast that they lost their footing and went sprawling. Mat's small, deeply offended 'Hey!' was of no real consequence. I was too busy spreading my arms as far as I could, blocking Audrey and Ben from coming any closer to the fence.

'Audrey, I need you to go get John,' I said. My voice came out stiff and almost lifeless: Every word was a zombie, shambling toward its target. I hoped that she could read my tone as the terrified thing that it was, and not as anything else. 'Hurry.'

'Ash, what are you . . . ' She trailed off. I couldn't see her, but I knew her well enough to picture what was happening behind me. Her eyes flicking over the testing unit and seeing the same thing I had. Her mind revving into action, and coming up, inevitably, with the same conclusion. It was so simple that it was almost a miracle I'd seen it in time. Finally, she said, 'I'll be right back,' and turned, and ran.

I stayed where I was, staring at the false front that had been installed atop the standard blood testing unit, and wondered how much worse this was going to get before it started getting better.

The political machine of the United States of America has grown, over the centuries, to an almost perfect model of the dilemma between Dr Jekyll and Mr Hyde. They both have desires, after all, even if only Dr Jekyll is in a place to express his desires publicly and expect them to be catered to. They both have dreams. And they both have engines that must be fed if they want to continue with their work.

We say we want to be the land of the free, yet we quail at the idea of extending that freedom to the poor, who are expected to spend proportionately more of their budget every year on safety accommodations that have not been proven to increase personal or public safety. We say we want to be the land of equality and opportunity, yet we do not tax the rich to make up for those citizens who cannot pay to improve roads, schools, the infrastructure on which we operate. We say we want to make America the greatest nation in the world, and perhaps that's a good thing: We owe the world a debt, after all. Both the Kellis cure and Marburg Amberlee were products of good old American ingenuity, cooked up by American minds on American soil. How many of the dead are ours to claim? There is so much blood on American hands that we may never wash them clean.

We make promises. We make pledges. And we keep our eyes fixed firmly on the bottom line, which is God and king in America, as it always has been, as it always will be. The American political process is not broken. It works exactly as it was intended to, and it will continue to grind good people up and spit them out until such time as someone figures out how to dismantle the great machine.

It is my sincere hope that Governor Susan Kilburn will find a way to prevent herself from being consumed.

—From *That Isn't Johnny Anymore*, the blog of Ben Ross,
February 7, 2040

Eight

False fronts for blood testing units are structurally similar to the credit-card skimmers that caused so much commercial havoc in the years immediately prior to the Rising.' Ben made a suitably dramatic figure, standing in front of the team that was meticulously dismantling the false front, backlit by the floodlights they'd brought in to make their impossible job a tiny bit easier. Really, no one would know he was wearing his emergency suit, or that Mat had used a hair straightener to steam the wrinkles out of it in the women's bathroom.

Audrey was off to one side, as close to the security team as she was allowed, filming every second of the dismantlement and removal. If there was any information to be gleaned from the false front's design, she would capture it and bring it back for the rest of us to go over.

'By slipping a tailored piece of plastic or metal over the top of an existing blood testing unit, the culprit or culprits can modify the unit's original purpose. There was an incident in San Antonio several years ago, where "activists" used half a dozen of the city's blood testing stations as delivery points for psychotropic drugs to make a point about how the media continues to lie to us. Their message was somewhat diluted when one of the women, Heather Lyons, age thirty-seven, suffered an allergic reaction to the drugs she had unwittingly received. She died before paramedics could arrive. She rose, as was to be expected. She then went on a rampage through the neighborhood where she had been shopping, the drugs in her system making her even more aggressive than the average infected.' Ben was only providing background – most of the people who clicked on this report would know the basics, would remember the San Antonio incident as a modern tragedy – but he showed no signs of finding the task either boring or unnecessary. Every word was loaded with the appropriate gravity. If Heather Lyons's family saw this, they wouldn't find anything in it to call disrespectful.

That was always important to him, and it was one of the things that set Ben apart from most of his peers: As far as he was concerned, the worst thing about Kellis-Amberlee was the way it robbed the dead of their dignity. He wanted to give it back, inasmuch as he could, even if it was only one sentence at a time.

That was also one of the things that set Ben apart from me. I understood where he was coming from, but I didn't have time to waste thinking about the dignity of the dead. Not when they were generally doing their best to chew my face off, and I was doing *my* best not to let them. He had luxuries I didn't. That was always and forever the way of the world.

'The pranksters who installed their hallucinogenic false front didn't mean to hurt anyone: They had even disengaged the original testing needles, preventing the impacted door from opening when the test unit was used,' said Ben. 'They were as benign as it is possible for something like this – something that tampers with the essential systems we all depend upon for our safety – to be. Most false fronts have a more sinister purpose.'

I snorted. I couldn't help myself. Then I moved away. There was too much chance that the sound would be picked up by his microphones, and I didn't want to ruin his report. There was no denying the powerful imagery of the men behind him, dismantling the death machine that had been installed to trap us.

It was a simple trick. Take a blood testing unit, preferably a wall panel like the one on the parking lot. Build an identical plastic shell to slip over it, sitting as flush as possible with the original mechanism. Insert a needle array, again, identical to the array in the original mechanism. A well-done false front wouldn't raise any red flags, not even when you started bleeding. But needles can do a lot of things. They're not just a way of taking blood. They're a way of delivering drugs, as Heather Lyons learned to her swift and permanent regret.

And they're a way of delivering diseases. Infected blood was the most common: Gather a bunch of samples the old-fashioned way, with syringes and razorblades. Mix it together, and then set up a bunch of needles preloaded with death. Anyone who used the unit would find themselves going into full amplification, and it only took one. A single zombie was a better delivery mechanism for Kellis-Amberlee than any needle array could ever have hoped to be.

The governor was still on-site, since she couldn't get to the parking lot any more than the rest of us. She could have sent for a helicopter, being the one in charge and all, but she'd elected not to; with her security staff around her, she was as safe here as it was possible for anyone to be, and this way anyone who asked would be told that she hadn't run out on her people. It was a sensible political choice, and I respected her for making it, since she wasn't putting anyone in danger by staying. If her presence had been increasing the risk for anybody else – especially anybody from my team – I would have been shoving her ass onto the nearest air transport, and screw anyone who wanted to argue with me.

Governor Kilburn beckoned me over when she saw me prowling toward her. 'Do we know what the mechanism was intended to do yet?' she asked.

'Not in detail, but it was a good match to the metal; we weren't supposed to see it. And it definitely came with its own needle array. We have to assume whoever put it there was planning to do some damage. We just don't know what kind.' I scanned the fence line. 'What's the camera coverage like in here? Is there *any* chance we got this asshole on film? Because it may be my fabled redhead's temper speaking, but I've the great and burning desire to smash some fingers with a hammer.'

'Please don't smash any fingers with a hammer,' said Amber, coming out of a deep huddle with some of her fellow security staffers long enough to shoot a meaningful glance in my direction. 'If you smash their fingers, we don't get to have any fun with them. You want us to have fun, don't you, Ash? You want us to have lots and lots of fun.'

'Amber, we've talked about this,' said Governor Kilburn. 'You sound like a serial killer when you say things like that. If someone who's *not* a part of our dedicated media team hears you sounding like a serial killer, you won't be able to stay with the campaign.'

Amber flashed her a quick, not entirely professional smile. 'I never say anything where the public can hear me,' she said, and returned to her huddle.

Governor Kilburn signed. 'Sometimes I wonder why I decided to go for this gig. What do you think, Ash? Should we be considering this more terrorist action, or should we be looking at it as a prank?'

'The unit's a standard Apple model, so creating a new shell wouldn't be as hard as we'd all like to pretend it is, but nobody does that sort of false front in a weekend, or because they think it's funny,' I said. 'The thing was properly installed, and connected to the baseplate with the right model of screws. If this was a prank, it was overkill.'

'All right, I need to ask this, and please don't take it as an attack of any sort – I'm too tired and strung out right now to deal with this,' said Governor Kilburn. 'Everyone I've spoken to has stressed how well designed the false front was, and how lucky we are that it was spotted. Now, I know your team had nothing to do with the zombies in the garden.'

'Thanks for not assuming we'd risk our lives, and my life in specific, to liven up a political event,' I said dryly, feeling my eyebrows climb toward my hairline. 'What's your point?'

'Did you, or someone from your team, install the false front on the testing unit to make me appreciate your presence?' Governor Kilburn looked at me solemnly. 'After the day we've had, I'm sure you understand why I have to ask.'

I stared at her for a moment before saying, 'After the day we've had, I'm sure you understand why I have to tell you to go fuck yourself.'

'I do,' said the governor. She sounded serious.

Good. 'Go fuck yourself,' I said, with a sharp shake of my head. 'Do it twice if you need to, just to drive home how incredibly offensive and unnecessary and . . . and *stupid* that question was. We're professionals. We don't falsify the news, because we don't need to. We can make *string* interesting if we have to, because it's our job. We do our jobs. That's why you hired us in the first place. If you'd wanted people who would need to pull bullshit like planting a false face to make a story, you would have found them. You would have gone to them. But you came to us.'

'So how did you know not to follow normal protocol?' The question was calm, even relaxed, but I knew as soon as it was asked that my answer mattered. My answer mattered a *lot*. The small huddle of security guards hadn't moved, but they had stopped talking, going very still as they waited to hear what I had to say.

'The edges were almost perfect. They lined up exactly.' I crossed my arms, looking at her coolly. 'This site is used daily by tour groups, therapeutic excursions, gardening associations, and the staffers who work here. A conservative estimate puts a hundred people through that gate every single day. Seems a bit unbelievable, if you ask me. Most of you Americans are about as willing to go outside where the fresh air lives as you are to gargle with live spiders, but hell, what do I know? I'm just the bloody foreigner who saved all your arses today. Twice. Clearly, I don't count.'

'Last numbers put the test gardens at an average of a hundred and fifteen visitors per day,' said the governor. She sounded grudgingly impressed, like she hadn't expected me to perform this well. The urge to punch her in the stomach a few times was rather strong.

Violence is not always the best solution to problems, but it's usually a good start. Especially when the problems involve human beings. 'Right, so a hundred and fifteen visitors a day. Most blood testing units have an internal cleaning system that keeps their panels and needles in tip-top shape, so you don't have to worry about tetanus or any of those other fun things. Interesting fact about machines with internal cleaning systems: Most people will tend to assume they're taken care of. No need to do anything to shine them up, they're already shipshape.'

The governor looked at me with an expression of dawning horror on her face. I smiled coldly and pressed on.

'The fence around the testing panel showed no signs of bleach-blasting or any other form of aggressive cleaning. The pavement under our feet had no discoloration; I'd say it was last cleaned about a month ago, using nothing more penetrating than a hose. The whole area was in decent repair, sure, and there was nothing about it that should have triggered a deep decontamination – not before today, anyway, and that happened in the garden, not at the gate – but the testing panel? Not a speck of dust. That thing was as pristine as if it had been installed yesterday, which, as it turns out, it had been.' I continued to smile. Sometimes, that was the only thing I *could* do. And sometimes, smiling when I clearly didn't want to was the best way to get my point across. 'I stopped because I noticed how damn clean that thing was, and that made me look closer. When I looked closer, I saw that the screws didn't match the metal fittings around them. Faux bronze instead of faux copper.'

'You could tell the screws were wrong because they were the wrong color?' Amber moved away from the huddle, moving to stand next to the governor. I couldn't tell from her expression whether she was impressed or dubious. To be honest, in that moment, I didn't care.

'It's a very distinctive color,' I said. 'Anyone who's made a study of these testing units would have been able to catch it, if they'd taken the time to look.'

'I assume this means you've made a study of these testing units,' said the governor.

'They use an earlier version of this same model on all the National Heritage Sites in Ireland,' I said. 'I saw a lot of them when I was in the early stages of my career and why are we still talking about this bullshit? You know I didn't plant the false front. Amber's checked her wrist display five times while I've been standing here, so I know that by now *you* know exactly what was loaded into that damn machine. We're still not writing our reports or posting our stories, which means we're losing hits, we're losing revenue, and we're losing our primary reason to stay with you. Your campaign was supposed to be *good* for us, remember?'

'My campaign wasn't supposed to get anyone murdered, and look how well we're doing with that,' said Governor Kilburn. For a moment — just a moment — her veil of professional control flickered, and I saw the woman underneath the politician, even more clearly than I'd seen her when she was sitting in my kitchen. She looked tired. She looked done with all of this. But most of all, she looked like a real person, as confused and frightened and out of her depth as the rest of us.

Maybe that should have made me more forgiving. Since my life — and the lives of my loved ones — were probably still in danger, it just made me want to punch her even more.

'She's right about one thing: I know what was in the false front.' Amber's face was grim. That wasn't encouraging. 'The needles were loaded with small doses of live-state Kellis-Amberlee virus. Enough to cause almost instant amplification in even the largest adult human.'

Governor Kilburn's hand flew to cover her mouth, a look of sick horror filling her eyes.

I cocked my head to the side. 'Does the rest of my team know that?'

'Your hubby's still filming his piece on finding the thing; I figure they'll tell him when he turns the camera off,' said Amber. 'The makeup kid's working the uploads, and your girlfriend . . . okay, she

probably knows, since she's with John, and he's with the team that
was taking the thing apart.'

Which meant Audrey was somewhere nearby, without a protective
suit, in the presence of live-state Kellis-Amberlee. A cold needle of
fear pricked the back of my neck, making the hair stand on end.
'Please ping me if anything happens that I, or any member of my
team, ought to know about,' I said, and turned on my heel and fled,
racing back across the pavement toward where I'd last seen Audrey.

The security team that had been so dedicatedly disassembling the
testing unit was gone. So was Audrey. Ben was still there, lit by his
camera's lamp, speaking quickly into his microphone. When he saw
me he stopped, reached out with one long arm, and caught hold of
my elbow.

I did not punch him in the throat, which showed both excellent
reflexes and admirable restraint on my part. Instead, I came skidding
to a halt, feeling the gravel turn under my feet, and looked at him
without saying a word.

Ben let go. 'Ash. I was hoping you'd come back. The team that
was tearing down that false front you found up and left a few minutes
ago, and they took Audrey with them. Mat's monitoring the security
feeds, but there hasn't been anything to tell us what's going on. Do
you know what's happening?'

Amber hadn't asked me to keep mum about the virus, and frankly,
even if she had, I wouldn't have listened. We were journalists. We
were here to report the news.

I turned toward the point Ben had been speaking to, flipping my
hair expertly back over my shoulder. I didn't smile. A large part of
my video persona was built on knowing when to smile and when to
look as serious as the grave, and this moment was most definitely the
latter. 'Are we live?' I asked.

'Three-second delay,' said Ben. 'Mat's patching the feed as quickly
as it spools, so that we can lose anything that really doesn't work.'

'Good. Mat, patch me in here.' I took a breath, focused on the camera, and said, 'The false front was used to hide a secondary needle array that some clever, horrible folks set up and tipped with Kellis-Amberlee. If we'd put our hands on the thing, we'd have gone into conversion before the lights stopped flashing.'

My throat tightened at the thought. The adrenaline rush – my second of the day – was wearing off, and as always, the crash was threatening to be a bad one. There was a *reason* I didn't linger in the field after the immediate danger had passed. No sensible Irwins did. I forced myself to keep speaking, secure in the knowledge that I was too well trained for anyone to have seen my misery in my face.

'I just got back from a consultation with the governor's staff, during which we discussed their findings, and how I was able to spot the thing in the first place. No one was hurt, and it looks like we're going to be all right.'

'How *did* you spot it?' asked Ben. There hadn't been time to explain before, not with the false front sitting there like a snake about to strike, and the governor's people closing in – at my request – to take over the scene.

I flashed him a tight-lipped smile. 'Trade secret. Now if you'll excuse me, I'm going to go check in with Audrey.' I ducked away before he had a chance to ask me any follow-up questions. He was already talking again as I stepped out of the light.

If I'd been someone who wanted to disrupt a political campaign, and I'd been aware that the campaign was traveling with a troop of professional journalists, I would still have wanted eyes directly on the ground, but I would absolutely have been monitoring all their public reports, announcements, and other updates. *We* were the enemy's eyes in Governor Kilburn's camp, just as surely as we were the eyes of the public, and that meant that certain things couldn't be said on the air.

If the leak was in the governor's security staff, keeping quiet wasn't going to do us any good. But if it wasn't, not saying things like 'hey, we'd all be dead if you'd bothered to sling a little mud around' seemed ill-advised.

A tent had been set up in a corner of the parking lot, springing into existence while I was off talking to the governor. The flap opened as I was approaching, and there was Audrey, plastic scrubs over her clothing and booties over her feet. She moved purposefully toward me, pulling the gloves off her hands as she moved. I didn't stop or slow down. A collision was just what we needed right now.

'We're in trouble,' she said, once I was close enough for her to speak without shouting. There was a cold, hard note in her voice. It was the sound of her past rising up, threatening to overwhelm the soft sub-urban artist she'd been struggling to become. Not even I knew the details of where Audrey came from, but she knew more about police procedure than made sense for a Fictional, and she always wound up drinking with the people who had the biggest guns. Whatever that background was, it was going to come in handy soon. I could feel it down to my bones, and I hated it.

'I know,' I said, and took that girl in my arms, and held her, and hoped that the future would pass us by.

American hotels are deeply weird. I say this from a place of love, and a place of enjoying the way hotel management seems to assume that my truest, deepest desire involves drowning in an endless sea of hypoallergenic foam pillows.

Irish hotels come in two flavors, much like the rest of the country. Either they're very old, built on stone foundations that will endure long past the fuss and bother over this silly 'zombie apocalypse,' or they're very new, rebuilt after the Rising by international hotel concerns that wanted to lure their guests back out of their homes and into the sweet, luxurious embrace of room service and Jacuzzi tubs. Most of our 'modern' hotels that weren't anymore after the dead learned how to walk around have long since been torn down and replaced.

But ah, America. Land of halls without auto-closing fire doors and stairwells that don't actually go anywhere, creating exciting kill chutes for the unwary. Land of large plate-glass windows above the third floor, because there's no possible way the dead will ever make it that far up, not even when the building is covered in climbable filigree or surrounded by trees.

Really, I think the American hotel summarizes everything you need to know about the state of post-Rising security in this country. Blood tests to get into the lobby, blood tests to use the elevator, even blood tests to get out of your room, but Heaven forfend we should rebuild the place to a reasonable standard. That would cost money, and the spending of money by those who have the most of it is a thing to be avoided at all costs.

You will never find a stronger illusion of security, or a less supported reality, than in an American hotel. You will never find a better assortment of room service waffles, either.

Yum, waffles.

—From *Erin Go Blog*, the blog of Ash North, February 10, 2040

Nine

We were still on lockdown at the Embassy Suites three days later.

It was better than it could have been. The governor's staff had booked three rooms for the four of us, letting Ben and Mat sleep alone while Audrey and I enjoyed the seemingly endless supply of hot water in our shower. Our equipment was spread through all three rooms, and we all had key cards to each door. 'Do Not Disturb' signs were respected like hazmat warnings. More than once, when I'd forgotten to take ours down, Ben had stayed stationary in the hall and called my phone rather than risk accidental nudity. So it wasn't like we were being *tortured* or anything. Just being penned up and refused access to the rest of the world, where things were actually happening.

Ben was okay – he had plenty of news to filter through, exclusive interviews with the governor to unveil, and footage to comb – and Mat had done a series of elaborate makeup tutorials based on the victims of the rose garden attack. Even Audrey had gotten into the act, running profiles on each of the people who'd died there, stressing the fact that they were *victims*, they had been *taken*, and most of all, that they had names: names we shouldn't allow ourselves to forget, not after everything that had happened. She was a demon at her keyboard, and every post she uploaded made me love her a little bit more. We were nearing the point of critical mass, and I didn't know what was going to happen after that. My heart would probably explode or something.

But none of that gave *me* anything to do. I wasn't the smart one – that was Ben. And I wasn't the savvy one, or the creative one, or any of the other things my teammates brought to the table just by breathing. I was the pretty one, according to some of my viewers. I was the one who took brainless risks, dangling myself over crevices and hanging out in trees, and there was nothing for me to accomplish here.

I slid off the bed, smoothed my skirt with the heels of my hands, and started for the hotel-room door.

'Where are you going?' Audrey didn't look up from her screen. Her fingers continued to fly across the keyboard, moving so fast that it was virtually a miracle she was typing actual words, not just chicken-scratch shorthand.

'Out,' I said, with a vague wave of my hand that she wouldn't see, but might somehow intuit all the same. 'I figure I'll go see whether John has any news on this lockdown. Governor Kilburn's schedule says she's supposed to be in Montana in two days. Maybe that means we're going to pack up and roll out sometime soon. Or ever. Ever would be nice.'

'Poor Ash hasn't gone zombie-bothering in days.' Now Audrey *did* look up, twisting in her seat to look at me. 'Are you armed?'

'Am I dressed?' I crossed my arms and mock-pouted at her. All my sundresses were made according to a series of patterns I'd worked up, leaving room for the gun at my thigh and the pockets hidden at the waist. It was a rare day when I didn't have enough ammo on me to significantly change my weight class.

'Good,' said Audrey. She turned back to her computer. 'Tell John I said hey, and ask him if he wants to drop by for a hand of poker tonight after his shift ends.'

'Oh, yes, another private poker game is precisely what I need to help me sleep,' I said airily, and let myself out of the room. The door didn't close quickly enough to keep me from hearing Audrey's laughter, and that was fine by me. Sometimes laughter was the sweetest sound there was.

The hotel hallway was deserted. I considered crossing to Ben's door and seeing whether he wanted to come, but dismissed the notion. He was too serious for what I was about to try. Much of my image depended on my seeming too sweet to do or say or think the things I did, weaponized femininity on the prowl. Ben wouldn't help me get the information I needed out of the governor's security team. I needed them off balance, willing to answer my questions, and most of all, willing to help me *move*.

Our hallway was bracketed by elevators, one at either end. There were four halls on this floor, all told. To get to either of the east-west oriented halls, I would need to ride the lobby elevator down to the next floor, which was a transitional level, and switch to their midfloor elevator. Our midfloor elevator only had access to the north-south halls. It was an incredibly inefficient system, especially when you stopped to consider that all the floors connected to the same lobby. Someone trying to get away from an outbreak didn't have time to change elevators over and over again, looking for the magic combination that would get them to safety; they needed to have a straight shot to freedom. And that was exactly what this hotel was designed to avoid.

Security theater is practically the new American pastime. I rode down to the floor below us, switched to their midfloor elevator, and rode back up. Having successfully walked a few hundred feet to travel less than fifty feet from where I'd started, I shot a glare at the closed elevator doors and made my way over to the conference room that had been claimed for use by the governor's people.

The door was propped open. So much for security. As I approached, I could hear voices coming from within, raised in vehement argument.

'—you, we have to get back on schedule!' That was Chuck. He sounded pissed. Poor mite wasn't dealing well with the fact that his campaign had been derailed by something as small as terrorism and attempted murder. 'The governor's approval ratings got a spike when she survived the rose garden attack, but the public is fickle! Blackburn is making real hay out of the fact that she has an open playing field right now!'

'Yes, and we're making real hay out of the fact that we have a candidate who isn't *dead*,' said Amber. I put a hand over my mouth to block the laughter threatening to escape. She just sounded so offended, like she couldn't believe she had to say these things out loud. 'The security sweep is ongoing. We have a lot of data to review before we'll know who did this, or why.'

'The Ryman campaign experienced something similar in Eakly,' said a third voice. Governor Kilburn was apparently coming to her own party. That was both a good thing – she was more likely to be able to approve changes to the status of our team – and a bad one, since she might have firm ideas about how the next few days were going to go, and it was always difficult to talk my way around the policy makers. 'Peter hasn't locked down his campaign.'

'Not just Ryman,' I said, finally stepping into the conference room doorway. All conversation stopped as the people inside turned to look at me, some pleasantly, others with an air of narrow-eyed suspicion that did my heart good. If I was that much of a threat, they couldn't be *that* committed to keeping me penned up in here. It was always best to put the biting dogs in the yard, if you had any choice in the matter. 'They're trying to play it coy and quiet, but we've heard from the team following Congresswoman Wagman, and apparently there was an outbreak at her most recent fund-raiser.'

'Banquet?' guessed John.

'Catered burlesque show,' I said. 'Really nice place, good dancers, *excellent* security. A friend of mine was on the team, which is the only reason I know anything.' And the reason I hadn't actually said anything, despite how nicely this fit into the greater pattern of shit going terribly wrong. Tina was good at her job. More importantly, she enjoyed *having* her job. If I'd gone repeating things she'd told me in confidence, she wouldn't have that job for much longer.

Governor Kilburn sat up a little straighter. 'I'll call Kirsten and see what she knows,' she said.

I blinked. 'Kirsten Wagman? You just . . . have her in your phone? Is there anyone you don't know?'

'Ironically, I'm not very well acquainted with Governor Blackburn,' said the governor dryly. 'We've always been competing for the same votes and the same spots at the table, so she's never felt much like making friends. Whereas my colleagues on the other side of the political divide have always been more than happy to extend the hand of friendship. It's easier if we can argue without hating each other.'

'I am so glad not to be a politician,' I said, although I understood, in theory, why things would work as she was describing them. I got along reasonably well with most of my fellow Irwins, but some of them would always look at me and see nothing but the competition. Every story I broke first was one they hadn't gotten; every risk I got acclaim for taking was a risk that was no longer available to them. Newsies were much more likely to be blatantly friendly toward me. Ben was the one they had to worry about. I was just another potential asset.

'That may be, but I'm sure that if I call Kirsten, she'll tell me what's been going on. She's a smart lady.'

'She wouldn't be running for President if she wasn't,' I said.

'The jury's still out on that one,' said Amber.

Governor Kilburn shot her a sharp look. Amber simply shrugged.

'Permission to speak?' she asked.

'Granted,' said Governor Kilburn.

'In that case, I'm just saying,' said Amber. 'If you were smart, maybe we wouldn't be here. Let someone else take all the risks, while you sit home and enjoy not being attacked by terrorists.'

'Can we sling that word around a little less in front of the journalist?' asked Chuck. 'If we can even call her that. She's more of a shock jock, and you know how the shock jocks love their buzzwords.'

I looked at him flatly. 'If you want to go with me, we can go,' I said. 'Step outside and I'll show you how an Irish girl defends her honor. But since I don't think you'd enjoy that much, maybe you should stop saying things you don't want to pay for.'

'I would enjoy it,' said Amber solemnly. 'I would enjoy it so much that I'd need to get my phone out and record the whole thing. Then I could watch you knocking his teeth out during every staff meeting from here to the election.'

'Amber, I know I gave you permission to speak freely, but please stop for now. Chuck, stop picking fights with the reporters. Mrs North, stop letting Chuck goad you. He's been under a lot of pressure recently.' Governor Kilburn rubbed her face with one hand. 'We all have.'

'Oh, believe you me, his goading hasn't succeeded yet,' I said. 'If it had, you'd know. I'm a bit difficult to miss when I fly into a towering rage. Like Vesuvius, I am. The fact remains that you weren't the only one attacked. At least three of the current campaigns have been.'

'I have no way of knowing whether Tate or Blackburn got hit, but I can start sending out feelers into their camps,' said Governor Kilburn. 'Even if they won't talk, maybe someone internal will.'

'And that's all well and good, really. It still brings us back to what brought me here. Neither of them have locked down their campaigns. Neither of them have put the rest of their schedule on hold while they sit around and argue about whether people are trying to kill them. The show must go on, and all of that.' I crossed my arms. 'We need to be moving.'

'I actually agree with the shock jock,' said Chuck.

'Aw, did it hurt to say those words out loud?' asked Amber.

He shot her a venomous look before refocusing on the governor and saying, 'A political campaign is like a shark. It has to keep moving, or it will die. Right now, your core constituency feels bad about what happened, but let's be serious: None of us died. Your camp suffered no losses, and the people who were used against us were taken from the ranks of those who wouldn't be missed.'

'Careful,' I said quietly. 'Some of us have been those people, a time or two.'

Chuck ignored me. That was probably for the best, if he wanted to get through the rest of his speech without a fist to the face. 'We need to be out there. We need to be in motion, showing people that you're still a contender in this race, and that you will not be cowed by – by—'

He stopped, a sick look crossing his face. Amber realized what was happening before I did. She pounced. 'By terrorists?' she asked sweetly.

'Please do not break my campaign manager,' said Governor Kilburn. She rubbed her face again. 'I'm starting to think he might be hard to replace.'

'But he's right,' I said. 'A political campaign is a lot like a news team. It needs to be generating content constantly – good, interesting content that makes people want to keep coming back. Ben's interview series will hold eyes for a while, but we're getting crushed by Ryman's Eakly incident. They had deaths during the event. That makes them inherently more dramatic in the public eye.' Even though, privately, I felt like the governor's camp had experienced the more *interesting* attack. The senator had been beset by a bunch of zombies outside the fence, some of whom had been killed or infected in violent, frankly clumsy ways. Our attack . . .

Burying the infected under a bunch of prize roses might not be original, and it might result in something out of an old horror comic, but it was *striking*. It was the sort of thing that, had it worked – had we all died, and not started picking the scenario apart with a fine-tooth comb – would have sparked a public panic, and probably closed all the green spaces in the city. There had been urban legends about zombies going to ground in soft earth, under leaf piles, and otherwise burrowing, for decades. This would have been taken as proving all those secondhand accounts true, and if there was anything the American public did well, it was overreact to a change in the undead status quo.

'I wonder if ours was intended to knock us out of the running, while his was intended to make him look good,' I mused quietly.

'What's that?' asked the governor.

'Nothing, yet,' I said. 'I need to talk to Mat, and then maybe it'll be something. Please tell me you're going to let us out of here. We need to move.'

'I'm going to call Kirsten and see what she can tell me about the attack on her camp,' said the governor. 'And yes, I will approve travel plans tonight. We've missed two public appearances, but we should be able to catch up in time for the third. Is that satisfactory to all of you?'

'Yes,' said Chuck.

'Sure,' said Amber.

'Barring a time machine, it'll do,' I said. I smiled quickly. 'Pleasure doing business with you.' Then I turned on my heel and marched out of the room, heading back down the hall toward the elevator. I needed to talk to Mat.

Being an Irwin doesn't mean clinging to facts and figures the way being a Newsie does, in part because we don't *need* facts and figures. We have the infected. We have the fences surrounding the brightest, greenest, most interesting parts of the world, and we have the burning desire to be *in* those places, to dig our fingers into the earth and feel the grass beneath our protective footwear. A lot of the time, we can just count on our cardio and let anything more complicated go. Sure, it means we get written off as the brainless jocks of the blog world – there are even betting pools, run by supposedly reputable sites, taking odds on which of us will die next, and how gruesome that death will be. But it doesn't mean we can actually be *stupid*.

An Irwin who doesn't know how to pay attention to their surroundings is an Irwin who is about to be spread in a thin layer across their surroundings. We may not be the deepest thinkers, but in some essential ways, we're the ones who put the most weight on detail. A scuff in the dirt can be a sign that a zombie has passed through recently. A clean spot on the wall can mean that something is missing.

Navigating the poorly considered elevator system meant it took too long for me to get back to our rooms. By the time I reached Mat's door I was vibrating, bouncing onto my toes every few seconds just to burn off some of the extra energy that I didn't need. I knocked. When that didn't get me an instant response, I knocked again. I managed to wait for almost a five count before I knocked the third time, with both hands, hammering out an urgent beat against the wood.

'I'm coming!' Mat sounded less angry than frazzled. That was probably a good thing. Pissing them off when I needed them to help me wasn't the best approach.

Why did I never think of those things when it would actually do me some good?

Mat wrenched the door open and blinked at me. I smiled as sunnily as I could.

'Hallo,' I said. 'Mind if I come in? I need your big brain to do some simulations for me.'

Mat blinked again. They were wearing a loose green sweater over black yoga pants, and didn't look like they'd been planning to get out of their unmade hotel bed before our evening team assembly. Really, I was doing them a favor by asking them to help me out. Socialization is important.

'Sure,' they said finally. 'Is something up?'

'Only in the abstract sense,' I said, stepping past them and into the hotel room. It was a mess. Eye shadow was smeared on all the pillows, and the bathroom looked like it had been the site of several small, pigmented explosions. I wrinkled my nose. 'Have you let the cleaning staff in here at *all*?'

'My mess is nobody's business but my own,' said Mat, almost

primly. 'As long as I don't live with my mother, nobody gets to tell me I need to make my bed.'

'Ah,' I said, understanding at last. No one gets out of their child-hood unscarred. Some just wear their scars on the inside, where no one can see. 'Look, I was talking to the governor, and I had a thought. Have you been working on a sim of the attack?'

Mat glanced to the side, suddenly shifty. 'What do you mean?'

'Come off it, Mat, we all know you make sims of my best footage and sell them to your buddies.' The mag made my job easier. It also made it a *lot* easier for someone like Mat to create an immersive re-creation of the original experience, complete with stumbles, heavy breathing, and the occasional headlong flight into a tree.

'I don't sell, I trade,' protested Mat. 'Where did you think I got you all that choice *Frozen*-print fabric for Christmas?'

Frozen was the last big Disney movie released before the Rising hit and people started caring more about survival than they did about cartoon princesses. As a result, the merchandise had been somewhat truncated. I had three sundresses made from movie tie-in fabric, thanks to Mat's unexpected holiday generosity. Guilt fueled the *best* presents.

'Doesn't matter,' I said. 'I never gave you permission to use my kin-esthetic likeness for your shut-in friends. I didn't say anything about it because it wasn't hurting anyone, and because I knew that one day, I was going to need you to do me a favor, and I wanted to have as much leverage as I could when that glorious day arrived.'

Mat gulped. 'Leverage?' they asked, nervously.

'Leverage means you do what I want you to do, and nobody gets dangled out a window,' I said. 'Is the simulation finished or not?'

'Sure, um, come over here, and don't dangle me out the window.' Mat motioned for me to follow as they walked to the desk, which had been buried under computer equipment. Most of our servers and relays were bunking with Ben. That had confused me before. Now, looking around at the mess, it made perfect sense. Better a slightly cramped living space than a world where our servers were inaccessible due to wadded-up burrito wrappers.

I sat down on the edge of the bed, where I would have a clear view of the screen, but wouldn't really need to *touch* anything. 'How sensitive is it?'

'Pretty sensitive,' said Mat, waking up their laptop with a click of the keys and beginning to activate programs. 'The default is basically a replay of what actually happened. I'll need a few more days before I can put in the alt mods. You know, "what if the player becomes a zombie," and all that fun stuff.'

'And don't think I don't appreciate the number of times I've become infected on your watch,' I said dryly. 'Can you do a run that removes me completely?'

Mat twisted in their seat to blink at me. 'Come again?'

'You've rendered the environment, and modeled the behavior of the zombies according to standard infected behavior, yeah?' I shrugged. 'So take me out. What happens to the overall sim if there's no player character to find the infected before they reach the governor?'

'I'm not a video-game designer, Ash,' protested Mat. 'I work from the data you give me, not by inventing things from whole cloth.'

'Try,' I said.

Mat sighed and turned back to the laptop, tapping for a few moments. Finally, they said, 'It's going to be rough, but this is what I have.' They pressed 'play.' The sim began.

The first few seconds of footage were pristine and photo-realistic, thanks to Mat having simply rotoscoped the recording from my mag. Video-game design has come a long way in the last twenty years. There's still a great deal of artistry to it, but thanks to increasingly sensitive and intuitive tools, actual artistic ability has come to matter less and less. Blame it on an ever-hungry, ever-expanding market that no longer has any other way to get out of the house.

'All right, now normally, this is where the player – ah, you – would encounter the first infected,' said Mat. 'Since the zombie grabbed your hair, the view would jerk, and then we'd go into the fight sequence.'

'Obviously, that's not going to happen,' I said.

'No, because the zombie doesn't know you're there,' agreed Mat. 'Let me see if I can move the camera.' They tapped something out. The screen shifted, swinging around to face the zombie that initially attacked me. His real face was gone, replaced by the slack, faintly greenish iconography that had defined the video-game undead since long before we'd met the real thing. That was actually soothing. The man who'd tried to eat me had already been robbed of his humanity. He didn't deserve to lose his dignity at the same time.

'We're going to cut to wireframes in a moment, as the AI tries to extrapolate what the zombies would do in the absence of a target,' cautioned Mat.

'That's fine,' I said, and sure enough, a few seconds later, the zombie's face vanished, replaced by a green grid. There was no footage to overwrite. 'Just stay on them, yeah?'

'Yeah,' said Mat. They were starting to sound interested, like this was becoming a worthwhile experiment. In a way, I suppose it was: It was demonstrating the limits of the software. 'The program knows where all the zombies and all the living people are, so that shouldn't be a problem.'

Our wireframe zombie shambled through the disturbingly well-rendered rose garden. As it passed, more zombies appeared, unearthing themselves one and two at a time. 'Some of them took longer to dig their way out because they were buried deeper, right?' I asked.

'Right,' said Mat. 'It was like a timed release system. The deeper a zombie was buried, the longer it took for the smell of people and the sound of moaning to work its way down to them. So they didn't exhume themselves as fast.'

'Meaning no one could accurately predict how many zombies were going to come out of the bushes.' The zombies were almost to the last tier of rosebushes between them and the governor. I sat up straighter. 'Can you run the sim with the zombies *not* moaning?'

'What?'

'They didn't start the moan until I goaded them into it. I've heard about this. Some strains of the virus don't trigger the moan response as early. I can't tell if that means the zombies are more self-confident or if they're just better hunters, but either way, they're better at sneaking up when they're not broadcasting their position all the time.' Which would make this a more successful viral strain, and probably cause it to spread more rapidly through certain populations. Swell. That was going to make my job a *lot* harder, and a lot more dangerous.

If I was right, which I might not be. I was a professional zombie-botherer, not a virologist or research epidemiologist. Those were career paths I'd considered, back before it had become obvious just how isolated my little quirks were going to leave me in our supposedly 'modern' Ireland, but they weren't things I'd pursued. As a scientist, I would have been trapped. The government would *never* have allowed me to leave, no matter how perverse I turned out to be. And I had very much wanted to go, even before my parents had had me committed.

'God, I hope I'm wrong,' I murmured.

Mat looked up from adjusting the sim. 'What?' they asked.

I shook my head. 'Nothing. Woolgathering again. I'll have enough for a sweater soon. Can you run the sim without me, and without the moan?'

'You know, I'm not a custom lab,' Mat said, and resumed typing. 'All right: Try this.'

They hit a key. The sim rewound a few seconds – not going back to the beginning by a long shot, but pulling the figures away from that last rank of bushes – before starting again. This time, the zombies pressed through the roses and spilled into the open area where the onlookers, and the governor, were gathered. The small, computer-generated figures opened their mouths in a moan once they had their hands on their first victims, and not a second before. The people screamed and scattered, following rigid mathematical lines that were nothing like a real crowd in a state of panic, but were close enough to make my point.

'Five,' I said. The zombies were grabbing and grappling with almost everyone. There were enough humans that some of them were getting away. There were enough newly infected zombies that some of them were giving chase. It was not a good situation for the living.

'Four,' I said. The zombies that had stayed behind to deal with their initial targets were beginning to feed. In the presence of so many options, this meant more than a few people were bitten and then flung aside as the dead went after the remaining living. In a state of plenty, a mob will seek to expand.

'Three,' I said. The models of the governor's security staff were shooting at the zombies, but they were distracted by their attempts to get the governor to safety. Professional security workers are required to keep excellent life insurance, since it's generally accepted that they'll die early, and the government doesn't want to take care of their families. That doesn't make them suicidal. It does mean that they're usually willing to put the well-being of their charges ahead of their own, since death is an outcome everyone in their line of work has long since accepted as inevitable.

'Two,' I said. The zombies were everywhere. The security staff couldn't reach any of the exits. They stopped retreating and started calling their shots a little better, thinning out the mob. Maybe that would have been enough to save them, had they already been dealing with the full extent of the outbreak. But there were zombies who had been buried deeper than the others. That hadn't made sense to me at first. Why put a potential asset in the field, only to keep it out of the action? Because it wasn't really being kept out of the action, of course. It was just on a delayed trigger.

'One,' I said, and the last of the infected came lurching out of the rose garden, overwhelming the survivors in a matter of seconds. The security team went down. The governor went down. Mat looked away.

The graphics might not be great, but they were good enough to get their point across, and no one wanted to watch that. Not even me.

And yet I didn't turn. 'We were the wild card,' I said. 'We fucked everything up for whoever did this. Everyone was supposed to die. You can stop the playback now. I know what I needed to know.'

Mat hit the space bar. The image froze. Mat hit the space bar twice more, and the picture was replaced with a collage of adorable kittens. Finally, Mat turned back to me. 'What did you need to know?'

'How bad this was meant to be,' I said. 'Do you have the details on the attack at the Ryman facility?'

Mat nodded slowly. 'Yes. Your reports, Ben's reports ... I was thinking of doing some commemorative makeup designs, but I couldn't figure out whether that would be seen as advertising for the opposition.'

Somehow, I had the feeling that where the makeup bloggers of the world put their eyeliner was the least of the Ryman camp's concerns, but I didn't say anything about it. We all have our own ways of coping. 'Do you think you could draw a sim from that?'

'No,' said Mat flatly. 'I don't have any first-person footage, like I had with you, and the camp had issues with their security cameras. I don't have any way of knowing where the zombies came from.'

Damn. 'Can you pull up blueprints of the venue, anything like that? I have a theory. I'd like to confirm it before I share it with anyone else.'

'Give me a second – I can do the footage that's been released, and I think there are blueprints of the venue online.' A wiggle of the mouse chased the kittens away, and Mat began typing rapidly. 'Since when am *I* your partner in crime, anyway? I'm not the one you're sleeping with. Or the one you're married to. I'm supposed to get a pass from helping you do stupid shit.'

'See, the reason you've been tapped for this mission is simple: You're not the one I'm married to, and you're not the one I'm sleeping with, which means you'll jump straight to "Ash is being weird," instead of going for the more locally popular "Ash is about to risk her neck because she thinks it's funny."' I drummed my heels against the foot of the bed. Thump thump. 'Also, you're the one with the skill set I need right now. I need to know how the outbreak at the Ryman encampment went, and you're the best spatial thinker we have.'

'I'm flattered,' said Mat dryly.

'You should be. If I want a beautiful lie with a noir moral at its center, I go to Audrey. She's my girl. If I want a coherent, logical narrative that fits the facts as we understand them, I go to Ben. He's the best. But if I want to know what the space looked like, if I want to *understand* how that narrative played out, I come to you. Because you're the best, too.' I stopped, waiting to see what Mat would say.

They smirked. That was when I knew I'd won. 'Laying it on a little thick, don't you think?'

'Depends,' I said. 'Are you buying it?'

'No, but I'm willing to consider a lease.'

'Then I'm laying it on just thick enough.' I leaned back on my hands. 'Even if you can't do me a full simulation, I need to know two things. How bad was the outbreak, *really*? Obviously, people died, and that's both sad and tragic, but would it have gone on to be truly terrible if no one had done anything from within the camp? Or would the authorities have shown up and taken care of things?'

'All right. What's your second question?'

'Was Ryman ever in any real danger?' Because Kilburn had been. The governor had been outside, with no one directly behind her: She had been fully exposed. Whoever set this trap had been intending to kill her.

'You don't believe in asking for simple things, do you?' Mat kept typing.

'Simple things are for simple minds,' I said. 'I much prefer simple pleasures, which are for everyone, and only sometimes stain the carpet.'

'Weirdo,' muttered Mat. Then: 'There's not enough footage for a simulation, but I have probabilities. Do you want them?'

'I asked for them, didn't I? Yes. Give me sweet, sweet probabilities, and allow me to make some sense out of all this rubbish.'

'All right. Assuming the Ryman camp didn't underreport the zombies to keep their insurance rates low, or overreport them to make their story seem more dramatic, the outbreak was bad, but not catastrophic.' Mat tapped the keys, more slowly now, adjusting functions of the program without completely resetting it. 'The surrounding area would have suffered extensive losses without the immediate response of Ryman's security crew, but nothing I have here indicates that a firestrike would have been necessary – and it was in a *nice* enough area that anyone who suggested it would probably have been shouted down.'

'Only fry the poor people if you want to stay in office, tra-la,' I said, in a half-bitter, half-mocking tone.

'Money makes the world go round,' agreed Mat. 'As to whether Ryman was in any real danger, he's not Irwin trained, and he wants to live to be President, which means he wouldn't have tried to play hero unless the situation was *very* cut-and-dried. I'm putting a ninety-five percent probability on him staying indoors, away from the action, until the cleanup crews had come and gone.'

'Meaning?'

'Meaning he was never in any real danger. He would have survived even if his people hadn't engaged with the dead. The outbreak started on the other side of a fence, and while there *was* a break in the fence – the footage the Masons got is chilling – it wasn't big enough to allow the zombies to overwhelm the camp. Everyone could have just stayed inside with their doors locked and been fine until the professionals arrived.'

'I see.' I stood. 'Thanks, Mat. You've been a lifesaver.'

Mat turned to look at me, seeming guardedly pleased with the praise. 'What did you want to know all this for, anyway?'

'Ah, see, that's to be a mystery for this age, or at least for this afternoon; I need to talk to Ben.' I blew them a kiss and started for the door.

'Hold up,' said Mat. They grabbed their laptop, yanking out cords without concern for the mess they were making, and hurried after me. I raised an eyebrow. Mat shrugged. 'I'm as bored as you are. Maybe you don't like being cooped up, but I don't like being cut off, and I know you. If you're sniffing around like this, you have an idea. I want to know what it is.'

There was no point in arguing, and there was some virtue to bringing Mat along. The simulation they'd whipped up was nice. Having the whole team on the same page would be even nicer. Which meant . . .

I tapped my ear cuff as I walked. It beeped three times before Audrey picked up, with a mild, 'Are you abseiling down the side of the building right now? Do I need to start gathering bail money for your inevitable arrest?'

'You have so little faith in me,' I said. 'You really think I'd get caught? And no, I'm in the hotel, about to pass the room. Mat and I are heading for Ben's room. Have some things to go over where the attack on the governor's appearance is concerned, and thought you might like to come to the party.'

'Really?' Now there was actual interest in her tone. Whatever she'd been expecting, it wasn't this. 'I'll be right over. Don't start without me.'

'Wouldn't dream of it.' I tapped my ear cuff again before stopping in front of Ben's door and knocking briskly.

'Coming,' he called. The door swung open. Ben looked nonplussed at the sight of me and Mat standing there, Mat still clutching the laptop, me smiling like I was getting ready to win a beauty-and-brutality pageant.

'Hi,' I said. 'Based on the timing of the attacks and the skill shown in placement of the initial infected, I'm pretty sure the people who attacked the Ryman camp are also the people who attacked the Kilburn camp, only they wanted Ryman to survive his attack, and they wanted our candidate to go down in glorious flames. Can we come in?'

Ben stepped wordlessly aside. Mat and I walked into the hotel room. Audrey would be there in a few seconds, and then we could begin our work. Now that we were to be released, she could finally go collect Mallory's RV as well, which would give us a rolling command center of our own. Privacy, and the ability to be alone together: exactly what we needed.

We had so beautifully much to do.

The attack on Governor Susan Kilburn's first (and apparently, last) Portland appearance is being investigated as an act of terrorism. Not all zombie outbreaks are terrorist plots, no matter what some fringe groups may try to tell us: The virus is in the wild, and as such, it will inevitably infect inconvenient people, at inconvenient times. Weddings and birthdays and yes, political rallies will all be the target of an indiscriminating enemy that only wants us for our bodies. So why is this outbreak any different?

This outbreak is different because the zombies which attacked the governor's assembly were all taken from groups that have traditionally voted Democrat, and have faced discrimination from their own families or social groups due to factors outside their immediate control. This outbreak is different because the zombies were, quite literally, planted in the rose garden: They were buried at varying depths, a fact that would have been missed had a standard cleanup crew moved through before our reporter found herself surrounded by infected bodies that were actually rising from the ground.

This outbreak is different because Governor Kilburn was not the only politician to be hit within a narrow time frame, although she was, perhaps, the politician in the greatest danger. It's hard to say for sure, since we don't have accurate sources of information within every political campaign office in the country. But it certainly looks as if some of the attacks were intended to wound, while others, including the attack on Governor Kilburn, were intended to kill.

Why her? Why now? And why is someone choosing to disrupt the American political process in this manner? It makes little sense, and we have less comprehension of the motives that may well be behind it all.

Most of all, I wonder . . . why isn't anyone else up in arms about this? Why aren't people angry?

What's going on?

—From *That Isn't Johnny Anymore*, the blog of Ben Ross,
February 16, 2040

Ten

Super Tuesday and the choosing of the candidates was a week away, and it was anybody's guess which way things were going to go. The governor was still working to regain the ground she'd lost during her impromptu layover in Portland. Her approval numbers were high, if that meant anything: Her opponent's approval numbers were also high, and she and Governor Blackburn had roughly equivalent experience in politics, putting them on a playing field that was temporary, illusory even. Sadly, 'our candidate is better because she performs Journey songs during Friday night karaoke, and she's *awful*; elect her so we can share this with the whole country' wasn't a slogan the rest of the campaign could get behind. More's the pity. Congressional karaoke would have transformed American politics into something I could actually enjoy.

Ben had taken the simulation Mat had designed and my extrapolations from its result and run with them, picking apart the ways in which Portland had clearly been an assassination attempt. It had been enough to buy us some play during a few news cycles, although we weren't entrenched enough to knock the Masons and their crew out of the top slot. They had a better organizational structure, with baby bloggers pumping out content even when their primary team was off-line for whatever reason. It made me want a team of minions to run and do *my* bidding. Too bad that wasn't going to happen for a while. Oh, we had our baby bloggers, but they were still fulfilling contracts to other blogging sites and working for us in their spare time. You needed either money or reputation to start your own site and get that sort of overnight success, and we didn't have either. We just had the Kilburn campaign. This was what would make or break us, and bearing that in mind, it was difficult not to become overly invested in our candidate.

I was sitting in the main section of our new RV, cleaning my sniper rifle, when the vast behemoth of a vehicle came rolling to a halt. I looked up. Ben was napping in the sleeping compartment, the curtains drawn to block the light. Mat was riding with Chuck and a few of the governor's other advisors, presumably to plan the governor's makeup for the week. Mat had been spending more and more time sunk in the belly of the campaign, and while they hadn't missed a report yet, I was pretty sure we'd lost them. This would end with either the White House or a cabinet position for our candidate, and Mat would follow her to Washington D.C., ready to set fashion standards for the political elite.

I couldn't feel bad about that. Mat had always wanted this. I couldn't be happy about it either. The idea had been to strengthen our team, not split it up; we were supposed to come through this more united than ever. And that wasn't going to happen.

Carefully, I put the components I was holding down on the chamois cloth I was using as a backdrop and stood, making my way toward the driver's compartment. There was supposed to be a blood test between the driver and the passengers, but Mallory had disabled it years ago – she'd mostly traveled alone, and hadn't felt the need to prick her finger every time she wanted access to her own things. We had decided not to put it back in place. It would have slowed us down, and we were all living in one another's back pockets anyway. Adding a layer of sham security wouldn't have *meant* anything, but it might have kept us from reaching each other in time if there was an emergency.

Audrey was behind the wheel when I opened the door and poked my head into the cabin. Her seat belt was off, and she was loading bullets into her pistol. She turned toward the sound of the door opening, offering me a quick, almost professional smile.

'Where are we?' I asked.

'Pit stop,' she said, and gestured toward the windshield.

We were parked in front of a neon-encrusted dive bar in the middle of nowhere. The sign out front said this was the 'Painted Rose,' and was capped by an animated hologram of white roses slowly turning red as something – paint or blood, it was hard to say – was drizzled on them from above. As an image, it managed to be erotic and disturbing at the same time. The parking lot was almost empty, which could have meant potential clients felt the same way.

'I see that we've stopped, and I see this is a place that can be accurately described as a "pit," but I think I'm going to ask that question again,' I said. 'Where are we?'

'About sixty miles outside of Vegas,' said Audrey. 'I thought we were going straight through, but the head of the convoy signaled for everyone else to pull over, so I got off the road.'

'Cool,' I said. 'This place looks sleazy, dangerous, and like they probably have great happy hour specials. Let's check it out.' I closed the door connecting the cabin to the rest of the RV. There was a click as the rest of the doors unsealed themselves. They were still locked, but we could exit the vehicle now. We hadn't disabled *all* the safety systems: Some of them were legally required if we wanted to keep driving this thing.

'Maybe we should wait for someone to – and you're already gone,' said Audrey, scowling through the open passenger-side door as I slid down to the pavement. 'If you get bitten to death by zombie rattlesnakes, I'm going to pee on your grave. You know that, don't you?'

'Looking forward to it,' I chirped, and shut the door behind me. She would be along in a moment. I had absolute faith in that. Audrey might get fussy about danger sometimes, but she loved it as much as I did. She just had different ways of showing it.

Even in February, the Nevada sun blazed down, bouncing its heat off the blacktop and making the parking lot feel more like the world's largest open-air pizza oven. I stretched languidly, letting the warmth bake into my bones. People sometimes asked why I'd gone for sundresses, instead of more practical expressions of femininity, like the classic Lara Croft look – cutoff shirts and khaki shorts also said 'pretty, girly, pretty girly' to the viewing audience, but they did it without loose skirts and snappable straps. What I could never quite explain was how much I loved dressing for the sun. It was always gray and chilly in Ireland. Any sun was a pleasure. Here, in America, I could have all the sun I wanted. Sometimes I felt like a solar battery, soaking it all in, waiting for the day when I was finally thawed.

The door slammed on the other side of the RV as Audrey got out. I beamed, turning to face her as she walked around the nose of the vehicle. 'Well, this is charming,' she said. 'Were you thinking of a place like this for our honeymoon?'

'Not enough zombies,' I said.

Audrey wrinkled her nose.

Motion to the right caught my attention. I turned. John and Amber were walking toward us, both wearing sunglasses in addition to their customary black suits. Amber's jacket was unbuttoned, revealing the butt of the gun at her belt. She had her hand resting on it, ready to draw at the first sign of danger. I approved of that. Having multiple people on watch meant that I could relax a little bit.

'Where's Mr North?' asked John, once they were close enough to speak without shouting.

'Ben's asleep,' said Audrey. 'I'd rather not wake him if it's not important, since it's his turn to drive next, and we have sixty miles to go before we get to Vegas.' She raised an eyebrow in silent question: *Was* it important? Did someone need to go wake Ben?

'We're here because a good friend of the governor's, who's going to be catching a plane first thing in the morning, asked if we'd stop for a cup of coffee and to allow the two of them to catch up,' said John.

'The governor asked me to come and let you know, and to tell you you were all invited to join, if you so wished.'

My eyes widened. It wasn't frequent that I was the first to put two and two together and come up with the impossible four. Sometimes, however, the odds were weighted in my favor. We were parked in front of a dive bar in the middle of nowhere, Nevada. There was only one person I knew of from Nevada who had enough of a stake in this election to both be in her home state this week *and* be catching a plane to somewhere else – somewhere like, say, the middle of the country, where she needed to do a lot more stumping if she wanted to stay in the race. Super Tuesday was almost upon us. Congresswoman Wagman was smart enough to be concerned about it.

'We wish,' I said fervently. 'We wish, and Ben will *murder* me if I don't get him out of bed. Murder me to *death*. Wait here, I'll be right back.' I didn't wait to see if they agreed. I just spun and ran down the length of the RV. Slapping my hand against the testing panel next to the main door, I waited impatiently for the lights to cycle green before tearing the door open and jumping inside. I could hear John and Amber laughing as it slammed behind me. I didn't care. We were going to meet Congresswoman Wagman. How could I not be excited?

Congresswoman Kirsten Wagman was a Republican candidate. She and I had a lot of political differences. But she thought like an Irwin, all style in the quest to justify substance, and I couldn't help but respect that. She had seen an opportunity to do some good, to push the agendas of her constituents, and all she'd needed to do was trade her dignity for airtime. That was an exchange that every Irwin I knew was intimately acquainted with.

When Kirsten Wagman had been looking at going into politics – after putting herself through law school by working the pole at a gentleman's club – she realized she could either hide her background or celebrate it, and had chosen the latter. Her breasts had already been excellent, at least if the old file photos were anything to go by.

She'd still gone under the knife several times to improve them, along with all the other niggling little details of her physique that weren't perfectly camera ready. And then she'd burst onto the Nevada political scene, as in-your-face as any man in her position had ever been. Most people dismissed her as uninformed and uninterested in the real issues. Most people weren't looking deep enough.

Under Kirsten Wagman, sex work in Nevada had been fully decriminalized and stripped of much of its stigma. She'd created scholarships for strippers and camgirls, encouraging them to find backup careers for when they needed to get out of the business. She'd improved sex education and safety nets for the poor, and she had done it all while wearing lacy slips and sky-high heels. It was a beautiful act of diversion and distraction, and while I didn't think it would be enough to carry her all the way to the White House – not with most of the journalists I knew gunning for her as making a 'mockery' of the political process – no failures now were going to take away from the successes she was building upon. She was smart as a snake and canny as anything, and she might well be the closest thing to an Irwin that we were ever going to see on the political stage.

The sleeping chamber was dark when I opened the curtain and stepped inside. Ben had sealed all the windows before going to bed. It made sense, from an 'actually getting some sleep' perspective, but it made my job harder than it needed to be. Did I wake him gently, or did I rip the scab off of sleep before he realized I was there?

Subtlety has never been my strong suit. I felt along the wall to the nearest window and jerked the curtain open, letting sunlight flood the room. There were two beds, both bunk, and Ben was sleeping on the bottom bed directly across from the window. He yelped, fumbling for his glasses with one hand as he covered his eyes with the opposite forearm. He tried to roll away, but there was no point to it; the light was everywhere. The light would not be denied.

'Good morning!' I chirped blithely. 'We're parked outside a brilliantly tatty-looking bar, and Kirsten Wagman is inside, waiting to have a drink with us. I rather thought you'd not want to be left out of this one. Get up, sleepyhead, and come meet a political genius.'

Ben lowered his arm enough to squint at me in bewildered disbelief. 'Kirsten Wagman?' he parroted, words thick with sleep. 'The *congresswoman?*'

'The one with the . . .' I made a hefting gesture in front of my breasts, whistling to illustrate it. 'Yeah, that's the one. Come on, she's brilliant, I can't wait to meet her, and getting you up and moving is *making* me wait, so get up.'

'You're serious.' Ben sat up, positioning his glasses securely on the bridge of his nose as he stared at me. 'We've stopped to have tea with a congresswoman.'

'It's Wagman, so I suspect we're having either beer or schnapps, but yes.' I beamed. 'This is the best job ever. Are you awake? Are you coming out? Or do you just want me to take a lot of notes? Spoiler alert: I won't take any notes. Your brand of boring journalism is not appealing to me, and I'm going to do my best to ignore it completely during this amazing opportunity.'

'I'm up, I'm up,' said Ben, finally sliding out of the bunk. He was wearing flannel pajama bottoms patterned with little robots. It was adorable. I knew better than to tell him that: He had a tendency to get annoyed when I commented on his wardrobe, maybe because I kept telling him not enough of it was tear-away. 'Give me five minutes to make myself presentable, all right? And thanks for waking me. I would have hated to miss this.'

'You can have three, because you took so long to get up,' I said, and sauntered toward the door. When I got there I paused, grinned at him, and added, 'You're welcome.'

Then I was out, leaving Ben to the mysteries of his suitcase and a wet washcloth across his face. All of us were prepared to be up and running at a moment's notice – it was part of the job – but we had our own ways of getting there. Ben depended on cold compresses and shocks to the system. Mat slept like a normal person, which was always disconcerting for the rest of us. Audrey believed in a healthy diet, exercise, and naps whenever possible. And I, naturally, believed in stimulants to get myself up and sleep aids to put myself down, on those rare occasions I felt like it was necessary for me to stop. Everyone copes in the manner that works best for them. That's true of the human race, and it's especially true of the news.

Audrey and John were sunk in a deep discussion of the virtues of the various types of whiskey when I hopped back out of the RV. Amber turned to me, a questioning expression on her face.

'Well?' she asked.

'He's getting some clothes on and he'll be right out, he swears,' I said. 'Can we wait just a few more minutes?'

'How about you wait just a few more minutes, and I'll take Ms Wen with me to escort the governor inside?' suggested John. 'That way, she can do that weird "filming everything" you people are so obsessed with, but the governor doesn't have to keep sitting around waiting for her pet reporters to get out of bed.'

I thought about protesting that this stop hadn't been on the schedule, making Ben's nap entirely reasonable and not something he should be teased about. I dismissed the idea just as fast. John was on our side, as much as any member of the governor's camp could be said to be 'on our side.' This wasn't important enough to risk messing that up. 'Sounds good to me. Audrey, does that work for you?'

'Who do you think suggested it?' She leaned up and over to plant a kiss on my cheek. 'See you in the strip club.'

'I've got singles,' I chirped, causing her to roll her eyes in exasperation before she followed John away from the RV, back across the blacktop toward the governor's tour bus. I watched them go. They were laughing again within ten feet of leaving us.

Amber stepped up next to me. 'You know, if I were you, I might find a way to have a date night in all this crazy. You, her, a bottle of wine, a reminder that you really do love her more than you love your beard . . .'

'Huh?' I turned to look at her. 'What are you talking about?'

'Just that you may have the whole "hot femme" thing sewn up, which clearly does it for your girl, but *no* girl likes to be ignored, and John doesn't ignore her.' Amber shrugged. 'I'm not saying she's cheating on you—'

'You'd better not be. Audrey would never do that, and I'm morally obligated to defend her honor.'

'—but I *am* saying maybe she's going to remember she deserves better if you don't step up your game. You're traveling America with a political campaign. You're seeing things most people are happy to leave on paper.' Amber gestured to the desert surrounding us, and for the first time, I really registered the fact that we were standing in the open without a fence. Nothing protected us from roving undead, because nothing *needed* to. Any zombies who found themselves in this unforgiving landscape would most likely die a second, final time before they did any damage.

It was amazing. It was exhilarating. And it was something I'd completely missed in my eagerness to make sure everyone was where they needed to be.

'After this meeting is over, I'm taking a stick and finding a rattle-snake to irritate,' I said. 'And when we reach our next stop, I'm taking my girl out for dinner.'

'Sounds like a plan,' said Amber.

The RV door banged open, cutting off any further conversation about my relationship with Audrey. I wasn't sure whether I should be grateful or annoyed as Ben descended to the pavement. He was wearing fresh-pressed tan slacks and a white button-down shirt. Beads of water gleamed on his hair. They were the only sign that he'd been asleep up until recently; he looked as alert and awake as a man who'd been up for hours.

'I'm here,' he said. There was a beat, and then he asked, 'Where are Mat and Audrey?'

'Mat's with Chuck, presumably, so no one knows, and Audrey went in with the governor's team, so she could film the arrival for you,' I said. 'Amber's going to walk us over.'

'Hi, Sleeping Beauty,' said Amber, looking amused by her own joke. 'Does either of you need anything else before we move? A frosty beverage, a shower, a bucket of tarantulas . . . ?'

'Tarantulas are too fragile,' I said. 'You can't really have any fun with them without killing them, and that's not fair. They never did anything to me.'

Amber blinked, apparently trying to decide how seriously she needed to take my response. Then she shook her head and said, 'Follow me,' before beginning to stride across the blacktop toward the building.

I produced my mag – replaced and newly updated by Mat – and settled it on my face before following her, setting it to record with a tap of my finger. However much useless footage I got, it would all be worth it if I found one image worth using. Ben trailed along behind, his recorder already out in his hand, murmuring impressions and shorthand comments into the microphone. We were ready to work.

Two of the governor's security people were standing by the door, along with two security agents I didn't know. The new agents were wearing sensible button-down shirts in impressively bright neon colors, one in pink, and the other in electric green. I grinned. 'Congresswoman Wagman's detail, I assume?'

Electric green produced a blood testing unit from her pocket and held it out to me. 'Please place your thumb on the panel,' she said.

Pink was doing the same with Ben. He was a big man, and dwarfed my companion without trying. I looked him over, getting a good shot for my records, and did the same with electric green as I pressed my thumb down.

'It's a good color for you,' I said. 'Do you get to pick, or did she assign one to each of you? Because if you get to pick, you might want to try a bright blue next time. It would really make your eyes pop.' Flirting was an automatic thing for me, a nervous tic that kicked in when I was going into a new situation. Amber's comments about Audrey and John were echoing at the back of my mind, putting my nerves on edge. Being a good reporter is hard. Sometimes I feel like being a good girlfriend is even harder.

The light on the testing unit flashed green. The security agent pulled the little plastic box away. 'You're clear to enter,' she said.

'Oh happy day,' I said, stepping to the side to join Ben. Amber was still being tested: The downside of traveling in groups of more than two. I nudged him with my elbow. 'You ready for this?'

'I'm just glad you woke me.' His eyes were constantly in motion, documenting every inch of the building, just in case there was some seemingly unimportant detail that he could pull out and turn into a believable narrative hook. For someone so quiet and seemingly harmless, Ben could be a devastating weapon when he wanted to be. A lot of that was his refusal to ever stop *looking* at things. Even on death's door, he would still be looking, and more importantly – more dangerously – he would still be *seeing*.

'Anytime,' I said.

Ben flashed me a smile as Amber walked over to join us. 'Now that we're all confirmed as among the living, I want to give you two a couple of ground rules,' she said. 'The governor and the congresswoman have been friends for some time – that whole "female solidarity" thing. They will be calling each other by their first names. The congresswoman can be extremely informal when she's at home, and may encourage you to do the same. You will not do the same. While you are grown adults and free to consume whatever you like, we recommend against drinking anything the congresswoman or her staff mixes for you, as they have the alcohol tolerance of professional boozehounds. No uncensored nudity is to be posted in any of your reports. No nudity at all without clearance forms. Am I clear?'

'We're not amateurs, ma'am,' said Ben. 'I appreciate the reminder, but there was nothing there I didn't already know.'

'Ah, but now I've reminded you, and no one can conveniently "forget,"' said Amber, and winked at me.

'Spoil all my fun,' I grumbled.

'Don't worry,' she said. 'There's more fun to be had.' Then, with all the solemnity of a magical candy maker in a children's movie, she pushed the door open and revealed the club on the other side.

At first glance, the place was exactly as seedy and without redeeming qualities as the outside had promised. The floor was plain, polished wood, with drifts of sawdust piled here and there in the corners. There were at least five stages I could see, and thanks to some clever construction work that prevented any door from having a clear line of sight on the entire club, there were probably another five stages I *couldn't* see, obscured by this retaining wall or that spiral staircase. There were four bars, each with their own tap system and back-bar covered in bottles of booze.

Second glance started picking out details. Like how everything was spotless, and the air smelled of pine and rosemary, not anything less savory. Our footsteps echoed in the dull way that meant we were walking on treated plastic, not actual dead trees, which would make the whole place easier to sterilize and less likely to lead to infection. The poles – of course there were poles, a place like this *screamed* for poles – were polished to a mirror-sheen, and the stages were raised enough that no one was going to succeed in grabbing a dancer who didn't want to be grabbed. It was a mousetrap, decorated to look like the bottom of the barrel when in reality, everything was top-of-the-line.

'Cameras on every inch of the building,' I said, eyes tracing the complicated network of wires, cables, and recording devices mostly hidden beneath the decorative molding around the edges of the room. 'That's a panic button cable. See, the gray one? That's going to connect to a private internal lockdown system. I want one for my bedroom.'

Amber turned to look at me quizzically. 'You can tell that from the wiring?'

'Security systems are a hobby of Audrey's which makes them a hobby of mine. Find the panic button, isolate this whole room in military-spec Plexiglas paneling. I wish I could trigger the system just to see it work.'

'Please don't,' said a female voice, from behind me. 'It's a devil to reset, and my insurance gets cranky every time it goes off.'

I turned. The speaker was tall, curvy, and perfect in the way that only lots of money, excellent plastic surgeons, and an image consultant with a degree in graphic design could ever hope to achieve. Her hair was a deep burgundy, like lava, offsetting the deep blue of her eyes, which were expertly lined and shadowed until they seemed twice as big as they could possibly have been. She was wearing blue jeans and a jersey shirt with three-quarter sleeves. On her, that seemed like the most fashionable thing that had ever existed, the style that every woman should have been aspiring to.

Moments like this were why I'd never wanted to become a Newsie. I could never have mustered the self-control. 'Holy shit, you're gorgeous,' I said.

Congresswoman Wagman burst out laughing. 'Oh my God, Amber, baby, what did you bring me? The last honest journalist in the West?'

'Actually, ma'am, I'm the honest one; Ash is the one who doesn't have any filters,' said Ben. He extended his hand. 'It's an honor to meet you, Congresswoman.'

'All right, you can stay,' said Congresswoman Wagman. She took his hand and shook it, studying his face before she returned her attention to me. 'What are your names, little honest journalists?'

'Aislinn North,' I said.

'Ben Ross,' said Ben.

'I resent the implication that there are no honest journalists left,' said a man, stepping up to our group. He looked to be in his mid to late thirties, with sandy brown hair, blue eyes, and the sort of casual posture some people would see as disinterested and others would see as harmless. I saw it a third way: dangerous. Men who'd reached his age without developing a razor's edge behind their eyes weren't innocent: They were just very, very good at concealing their natural defenses. And they were frequently capable of doing damn near anything to get their way.

'Oh, Ricky, you know I didn't mean you,' purred the congress-woman. She waved a casual hand at the man, and said, 'Richard Cousins, head of my little press pool. He makes sure I look good in the news, or at least not terrible.'

'It would be easier if you'd answer criticisms of your public image with something other than videos of your ass,' said Richard. Now he just sounded tired. Maybe he wasn't as dangerous as I'd first suspected; maybe he'd reached the point where he needed to turn to bourbon as a means of handling his life choices. That was a valid developmental stage for many Newsies.

Not so many Irwins. Bourbon was swell and all, but it was also a quick route to getting eaten. I did not endorse any coping mechanism that was likely to end with dismemberment and wearing your inside bits on your outsides.

Congresswoman Wagman made a scoffing sound. I could actually *hear* the scorn. My love for her grew stronger. 'Sweetie, my ass is why the people who don't normally vote for anyone will come out and vote for me. I say "this is what you'll get," and they know I'm telling the truth, so they go ahead and throw in their endorsement. So yeah, you're going to keep getting it. Now.' She waved a hand at us. 'These nice folks are visiting with Suzy. You should show them around, let them get some footage of things they think are interesting, and keep them out from underfoot.'

'Are you trying to get rid of them, or get rid of me?' asked Richard. I couldn't think of him as a 'Ricky.' Maybe 'Rick,' if he lightened up a bit, but that was as far as I was willing to go.

'Aw, Ricky.' Congresswoman Wagman dimpled. I considered sending a thank-you note to her plastic surgeon, who must have spent

months figuring out that precise muscle movement. 'I'm getting rid
of all three of you. Now shoo. Amber, you're with me.'

'Yes, ma'am,' said Amber.

'Um, we have two more team members,' said Ben. 'Audrey Wen
and Mat Newson. Have you already sent them both packing?'

Congresswoman Wagman looked blankly at him before turning
to Amber.

'Cute Chinese girl and skinny genderfluid makeup artist,' said
Amber.

'Ah! Yes, I saw them, and they're here.' Congresswoman Wagman
waved a hand vaguely, indicating what felt like the entire club. 'You're
all going to join back up for lunch, I promise, but first I need a little
one-on-one time with Suzy. It's nice to meet you both. Ricky?'

'I'm on it,' said Richard. He motioned for us to follow him. 'Come
on. I think I know where we can find your friends.'

'Yay,' I said blithely, falling into step behind him. I couldn't resist
stealing one more glance over my shoulder at the congresswoman.
She and Amber were already deep in conversation as they walked in
the opposite direction, heading for a table surrounded by security
agents from both campaigns. Governor Kilburn was in there somewhere, shielded from view by the ranks of the people who were paid
to protect her. She didn't need us right now. I still felt funny walking
away like this.

'You're a Newsie, right?' asked Ben, looking at Richard. 'I've heard
of you. You have a reputation for doing good work. Boring, but good.'

'Mmm-hmm,' he said. 'It's "Rick," by the way.'

'I didn't think you were a Ricky,' I said.

Rick made a face. 'No. Never have been, never going to be. The
congresswoman likes to keep things as informal as she can get away
with, even when we're alone, so she won't accidentally slip up and
reveal her secret plan in the presence of a camera.'

'She has a secret plan?' I asked.

'In the sense that no one ever seems to believe it, yes,' said Rick.

'She's talked about it in every interview I've ever read, and a few that her campaign manager had to dig up and transcribe for me. She wants to improve funding for schools, women's health, vocational planning for children – a few dozen good, solid, philanthropic goals that would benefit the people of this country. She's managed a surprising number of her goals on the state level. I say "surprising" because if you asked most of the people in local politics, they wouldn't be able to name a single one of her successes.'

'But I bet they could tell you what she was wearing every time something came up to a vote,' I said.

Rick nodded. 'Exactly.' We had reached a door labeled EMPLOY-EES ONLY. He pushed it open, not missing a beat as he led us through. 'Wagman is the ultimate Vegas showgirl, only she's not after drunk men's wallets. She's after the whole country. And hell, maybe she's got a chance. Ryman's performing solidly in the polls, but she's been ahead of Tate for most of the campaign, and I think the American people might choose novelty over what they perceive as dignity.'

'Tate's a bit of a tosser, I've always thought,' I said.

'If "tosser" means "flaming asshole," then yeah, you're right about that.' The door fed into a break room almost as large as the bar outside. The only thing that really marked it as a private space was absence: the absence of stages, the absence of dancer's poles, the absence of plastic upholstery on the furniture. Instead, there were overstuffed couches and easy chairs scattered around the floor, creating a comfortable, almost homey atmosphere. There was a bar, flanked by two large refrigerators. A young woman in a U.C. Irvine sweatshirt was asleep on one of the couches, seemingly dead to the world. Good for her.

'You learn to roll with Ash's slang,' said Ben. 'I think she makes half of it up.'

'I'd believe it,' said Rick. 'What's your accent? Australian? Scottish?'

'Irish,' I said. 'If that was a serious question, and not you pulling my leg, you need to get out more. It's not an accent you can mistake for much of anything else.'

'Sorry,' said Rick. He didn't sound sorry. He sounded amused. 'This is my first major Internet news gig. I was a newspaperman for years, and when I went virtual, I had a hard time finding a place that suited me. So actually *hearing* people isn't such a normal thing where I come from.'

'If you're that new to online journalism, how did you land a position with one of the campaigns?' asked Ben. 'We had to apply as a team to have a chance, and the Ryman campaign still passed us up.'

'Not that we can blame them,' I said, drifting toward the bar. I wasn't planning to drink – not this early in the day, and not while we were working – but you could tell a lot about a person by what sort of booze they set aside for their employees. A few labels might unlock the mystery of Kirsten Wagman, or at least give me a place to start. 'They had access to the Masons. Who'd take us over them? Someone who'd hit their head recently, maybe, if the concussion was bad enough.'

'That's Shaun and Georgia Mason, out of Berkeley, right?' asked Rick. His tone was too casual, like he already knew the answer, but wanted it verified by an outside source for some reason.

I shot him a sharp look over my shoulder before meeting Ben's eyes and giving a small, tight shake of my head. Ben nodded his understanding. We might not be married in the biblical sense, but we'd been a unit for long enough to have developed some useful shorthand, especially where prying rival journalists were concerned.

'Depends,' I said, slowing my voice until it was virtually a drawl. 'Why do you want to know? There's plenty of places you can go for information without extracting it out of someone else's press corps.'

'I just thought that since you were from California – the Bay Area, even – that you might know something about them,' said Rick.

'You think the congresswoman is going to get knocked out before the convention, don't you?' Ben's question was mild, but it had teeth lurking behind the seemingly innocuous façade.

Rick paused before he answered. Then he sighed, and said, 'I think she's yoked herself to a gimmick that makes sense on the local level, but is too polarizing at the national level. Some of the things people have said about her – even people who brag about how unbiased and reasonable they are – there's no coming back from that. Wagman knows it, too. She's not willing to concede yet, but I think that's more pride and the hope for a VP nomination than anything else. If Ryman picks her as his running mate, she could wind up in the White House anyway. It's all in which fringe he wants to court. The hard left or the hard right.'

'The Republicans don't really have a hard left,' said Ben.

'Wagman is as close as they get to a hard left, and she'd bring those votes to the table with her,' said Rick. 'So there's still a chance. No point in throwing in the towel before she has to. What about your candidate? You think Kilburn has a shot at the big chair?'

'I think it's going to be either her or Blackburn,' said Ben. I climbed behind the bar, letting him talk while I checked the labels. 'York has been essentially a nonentity throughout this campaign. I can't remember the last time I heard him mentioned in anything other than a full candidate roll call.'

'Even I know that running a virtual campaign doesn't work unless everyone else is doing the same thing,' said Rick. He paused, and while I could no longer see his face, I could hear the confusion in his silence. 'What's your friend doing?'

'Ash is Irish. She has a strong personal relationship with alcohol. Ash? What's your verdict?'

I popped up from behind the bar. 'Not top-shelf, but not rotgut, either. Good selection, good investment bottles, obviously a strong sense of "you shouldn't be drinking anything I wouldn't be willing to put in my mouth." I give it a seven out of ten as hospitality bars go. I'd host a party here.'

Rick blinked at me. 'Seriously? You were assessing the booze?'

I raised an eyebrow. 'Does Congresswoman Wagman own this club?'

'Yes.'

'Is this the employee break room and hence the employee alcohol supply?'

'Yes.'

'Then yes, I was assessing the booze, because the booze is relevant. The booze tells me things.' I hoisted a bottle of bourbon. 'This is a thirty-dollar bottle. Not the best thing you can buy for a place like this, but a long way from the worst. This is Christmas-party bourbon. You pour it for your friends and family, for people you give a crap about. This tells me more about what sort of woman Wagman is than any amount of "oh she gives money to animal shelters." This tells me she's *kind*.'

Rick looked dubious. 'What if it had been the really fancy stuff? The three-hundred-dollar stuff?'

'That would tell me she didn't stock her own bar, and was either too disconnected from the common man to know that you don't need to pay that much for basic social drinking, or was trying to impress people with how generous she was. Neither of those buys you many points in my book.' I put the bourbon back under the bar before leaning forward, resting my weight on my elbows and smiling at him. 'Sometimes the middle of the road is the only decent place to be.'

'You people are very strange,' said Rick.

'You don't know the half of it,' said Ben. 'As for the Masons, yes we know them, but we're not friends. We're not even associates. They're ...'

'Snobs,' I supplied.

Ben shot me a look, sighed, and said, 'They're insular. Neither of them has ever been interested in forming strong outside friendships with other locals. I know they *have* friends, but with a few exceptions, it's always been people who are far enough away that the Masons don't have to worry about being asked to get together and socialize. They've been hiring for their own site since they hooked up with Ryman. I know a lot of Bay Area folks who applied, and only one who was hired. Dave Novakowski, whose big passion is wandering away and nearly getting himself killed in remote locations.'

'Which means he's not so much living in the Bay Area as he is storing his stuff there until the inevitable estate sale,' I said.

Ben snorted, but he didn't contradict me.

Rick nodded, looking thoughtful. 'I heard they were working with Georgette Meissonier.'

I gave Ben an exaggeratedly blank look. He smirked and supplied, 'Buffy,' before he turned to Rick. 'She's their team Fictional. Our friend Audrey fills the same role for us. Do you have a Fictional working with the congresswoman?'

'No. Wagman doesn't need someone to make up stories for her. She can provide the old razzle-dazzle without anyone telling professional lies.'

The role of a good Fictional was a lot more than 'telling professional lies,' but I decided not to get into it. Yes, defending Audrey's profession always made me feel like a good girlfriend – and I was bad enough at being a good girlfriend to want any opportunity I could get to be a better one. At the same time, she didn't *need* me to. She made more money than I did, she had better ratings than anyone else with our group except occasionally Mat, and most importantly of all, she had nothing to prove to people like Rick. Him thinking she wasn't an important part of the news media didn't change her job, or impact how good she was at doing it.

'How many people does Wagman have working for her?' asked Ben.

'Six,' said Rick. 'We're all from Factual News, which makes things unbalanced sometimes – it gets weird when you have six people trying to come up with new angles on the same story. Between you and me, I think a few of my colleagues have already started hunting for new gigs.'

'But you're going to stick it out until she doesn't get the nomination,' I said.

Rick shrugged. 'Someone needs to. Hell, maybe I can get a book out of it. It's definitely one of the more interesting campaigns I've seen since the Rising.'

'And someone tried to kill her, yeah?' I tried to keep my tone light.

Not light enough. Rick stiffened, eyeing me warily before he said, 'I don't know what you mean.'

'That's why we're here, isn't it? Our candidate wants to talk to your candidate about the outbreak at her fund-raiser, find out if maybe that accident wasn't as accidental as everyone wants to make it out to be.' I straightened, pressing my hands against the bar. 'I mean, it's that, or we coincidentally had attacks on three of the five mobile campaigns within the same week.'

'Now, Ash,' said Ben. 'We don't *know* that there wasn't an attack on the York campaign. It's not fair to leave him out of things just because he's a recluse.'

'If there was an attack, no one noticed, including him, so I don't think it counts,' I said. 'For it to matter, someone would need to set his house on fire, drive him outside, and put zombies on the lawn. Not exactly subtle.'

'But York isn't doing well in the polls,' said Rick. Ben and I both turned to look at him. He shrugged. 'The three highest-performing candidates right now are Ryman, on the Republican side, Wagman, also on the Republican side, and Kilburn, on the Democratic side. If you write Wagman's numbers off as people trolling the government — which sadly, I think is the case, hence my not expecting her to get the nomination — your girl and the Masons' boy are our top candidates. And they were both attacked.'

'I appreciate that you're infantilizing everyone equally,' I muttered.

'What?' asked Rick.

'Nothing,' I said. There was a time and a place for telling people off about their word choices: This was neither. As long as he was willing to talk, I needed to be willing to listen. From the sidelong look Ben shot in my direction, he was feeling the same way. We needed to tread carefully.

'So are you saying Tate and Blackburn are nonentities?' asked Ben. 'Tate is polling well. He has strong support among white males age thirty-five to sixty. The pre-Rising generation thinks of him as a visionary.'

'Everyone else thinks of him as a throwback,' said Rick. 'He's too reactionary, he's too insular, he wants to build a wall across the Canadian and Mexican borders. A *wall*. As if the damn fences in Texas and Arizona didn't get people killed during the Rising. He's not going to take the nomination, no matter how well he polls. The Republicans want the White House, and they know better than to put him in front of the nation. I'm betting he'll get the VP nod from Ryman. That gets him to a place where he can push some of his legislative choices, without giving him the power to do any real damage.'

'And Blackburn?' I asked. It was fascinating watching this relative stranger tear down the candidates. It made me want to point him at random people and ask him to talk about them.

'People see her as soft on the dead, thanks to her support of the scientific research community.' Rick made a face. 'It would be funny, if it wasn't so damn sad. She's culturally Jewish – twenty years ago she wouldn't have been able to make it this far in the race because of her background. She doesn't practice, but that doesn't matter. She knows how important it is to her family and the people in her community that their bodies remain intact after death, so she supports the zombie corrals, and the research stations. Places where the infected can be kept and fed and studied and *learned* from. That's the thing. She's not proposing the zombie Club Med, she's talking about keeping more of our loved ones in one piece so we can learn about the disease that took them away from us, and in the process, can prevent little kids needing to gun down Grandma.'

'Isn't she worried about hesitation?' I asked. 'When a zombie's coming at you, you don't say "hmm, what were his religious beliefs," you pull the damn trigger and you keep yourself alive.'

'Oh, she doesn't want to ban our current responses to the dead. She just wants to modify them a little. Enough to allow people who know that they're at risk of amplification to sign certain waivers.'

'We already allow for donating your body to science,' said Ben.

'Currently, science is doing what science has always done: focusing on otherwise healthy males between the ages of eighteen and forty,' said Rick. 'No one wants to think about zombie kids or zombie grandparents. The research stations have the right to turn down any donation and cremate the infected individuals immediately. Anyone who's judged too young or too old or too disabled prior to infection is never going to be a part of their testing pool. There are some blood anomalies that have been shown to lengthen the delay between exposure and amplification, but as they're almost always comorbid with other conditions, the people who have those anomalies don't wind up in the long-term studies.'

I blinked. 'That was . . . really science-y. Can you say it again, without being quite so clinical, so that there's a prayer I'll understand it?'

'Sorry, Irish, but I've been working for Kirsten Wagman for months,' said Rick mildly. 'If there's one thing I've learned to spot, it's someone who's playing dumb to buy themselves more time to think about what they've just heard. The long and the short of it is that Frances Blackburn came into this race with the religion thing against her, since a lot of people are still clinging to the pre-Rising "we're a Christian nation" ideology, and her positions on several modern science topics haven't done her any favors. She's going to get knocked out of the race before the convention, and then your girl's going to have to decide between an all-female ticket and adding a recluse to her platform. Honestly, I don't know which would hurt her more right now.'

'I'd punch you in the mouth for implying that two women can't run this country, except for the part where that's not what you said,' I said. 'You're saying no one would *let* them.'

'Exactly,' said Rick. 'I think we've reached the point where a female President would work just fine for most of the voters. They want to know what she'll do to keep them safe and among the living, and if she has a good answer, they'll follow her. But a female President *and* a female VP? That may be pushing things.'

'York wouldn't be much better,' said Ben. 'He's already indicated that, were he to win, he would make his presidency "modern" by telecommuting to the White House.'

'Which offends some voters, and makes others feel like he's the first sensible candidate we've had in twenty years,' said Rick. 'He'll pull some focus, and he'll probably go independent after he loses the nomination, which will take his voting bloc with him.'

'Sure, but since his voting bloc isn't that big, we're not particularly worried,' said a voice from behind him. We turned. Governor Kilburn and Congresswoman Wagman were standing in the doorway, with Amber and Mat behind them. Audrey and John weren't there. I felt a small pang of concern. I didn't like Audrey being out of sight *and* out of communication for this long. It wasn't clinginess – or at least, it wasn't entirely clinginess. It was the need to know that my team was safe.

And if I kept telling myself that, it might become true.

'Also there's the part where he's not going to get the nomination, because no one's met him,' continued Governor Kilburn. 'People think it's about safety and status, but there's nothing that can replace meeting a person, or even seeing them against a backdrop you recognize. It's why so many celebrities still go to Disneyland, even with all the security and restrictions on showing up at someplace so potentially open.'

'Disney's snipers are amazing,' I said. 'There's never been an outbreak on any of their properties, because the happiest gunslingers on Earth are right there, waiting for an excuse to pull the trigger.'

'And even though it's a robot in the giant mouse costume these days, that photo is still worth a million votes,' said the governor.

'People want their politicians to be sensible, smart, and just a little bit brave. They want us to seem better than they are.'

'Sweetie, they want us to seem better than *we* are,' said Congresswoman Wagman. She grinned lopsidedly. It was a smile I'd never seen from her before. In most of the public footage, she looked like a pageant contestant getting ready to make a run for Miss America. This smile was smaller, subtler, more human in ways I couldn't quite explain, but was pleased to see. 'They want us to be perfect. Superheroes who can cure the zombie apocalypse with a single bill banning reanimation and a perfect photo shoot with the cutest doctor at the CDC. How do you think I made it this far? People want to be sold a fantasy, and even if they balk when they get the final bill, they know what they're paying for.'

'How long have you been standing there?' asked Ben.

'Long enough to hear my Ricky explain everybody's strengths and weaknesses, which I utterly agree with.' Wagman blew him a kiss. Rick flushed red. 'He's a smart boy, our Ricky. When he goes looking for a new job, you should take him on.'

'I think we're pretty full up, ma'am,' said Mat politely, stepping around the two candidates and walking over to stand next to Ben. 'It's not like we're trying to build a news empire here, just a reputation for knowing how to do our jobs better than the next guys.'

'Oh, there's going to be an opening on your team soon, sweetie,' said Wagman. 'Between me and Suzy, we're going to woo you away from the wild frontier of the news and into the sweet embrace of public image manipulation. I've seen your tutorials. I've even tried a few of your looks.'

'Really?' Mat tried not to look too excited. They didn't succeed. 'I could show you some designs I worked up for you but haven't put on my channel yet. I could even show you how to do them.'

'See, and this is why we're going to hire you away from your current masters, who don't understand your genius.' Wagman turned to Ben. 'You're all right with a little head-hunting, aren't you, sugar?'

Ben looked amused. 'We're not Mat's masters. We're a news collective, and everyone gets a voice. If Mat decides to leave us to do your eyeliner, that's their decision, and we'll respect it.'

'I can't leave my team,' said Mat. 'I love them too much. Also, I really, really like taking things apart, and I haven't had many opportunities to do it since the campaign started. I'd dismantle your blender like, six times a week. But I'm happy to discuss some freelance makeup design before we get back on the road.'

'See, this is what I get for introducing Kiki to new people,' said the governor. She didn't sound annoyed: If anything, she was swallowing laughter. 'I saw Mat first.'

'But I saw Mat last, and it's the one who makes the grab who catches the ball,' said Wagman. They were both smiling. They were on separate sides of the political divide, and their campaigns couldn't have been more different, but they were both smiling. There was something beautiful about that, and something sad at the same time. I had watched the news – not us, for the most part, but our peers – trying to set them against each other, calling Wagman horrible names while implying that Kilburn was frigid and loveless because she was an unmarried woman running for the highest office in the nation. And they were smiling, because they were friends.

It's weird, as a maker of the news, to consider how often the news is used to shape reality. Maybe that's why I'm happier as an Irwin. It's not just a lack of interest in the big words and complex concepts that Ben wallows in. It's a desire not to twist the world every time I speak a word. The situations I get myself into might be staged on occasion, but they're still real. Those things really happen, even when the cameras aren't running. That matters, maybe more than I can say.

'Ladies, ladies, there's enough of me to go around,' said Mat grandiosely.

Both candidates laughed, and were still laughing when the door opened and John walked into the room, followed by Audrey. I stood up straighter. She flashed me a grin and made a beeline for the bar, where she boosted herself up and sat down beside me before leaning over to kiss my cheek.

'Hello, Ash,' she said.

Public displays of affection usually weren't her thing; mostly, they were mine, and I'd learned to tone it way, way down. I wondered briefly whether Amber's speech this morning had come out of the knowledge that John was getting ready to express interest in my girl. Only briefly, though. I couldn't blame him for being interested: She was amazing, after all, and I was married to a man, which might cast the seriousness of our relationship into doubt. Audrey was fairly public about her bisexuality, and she was officially dating both me and Ben, at least for the moment. It was only natural that John would have been interested. As long as he'd back down when she said no, I didn't see any reason to get worked up about it.

Besides, she'd chosen me. She always did.

'That is *adorable*,' said Wagman. 'Are they always that adorable? Can I have them, too? I want to dress them in sequins and make them snuggle behind me during my next political speech.'

'No, Kiki, you cannot steal my entire news team,' said the governor. 'We're all here now. We can get back on track.'

'Spoilsport,' said Wagman, and straightened. Somehow, in the middle of the motion, she became a different person. She was still casually dressed and made up like she was heading to a nightclub, but her demeanor was serious and her shoulders were set. She looked like she was about to give a speech before a critical audience, and she was planning to make it a good one. 'Suzy and I have been talking about what happened at her speech in Portland, and at my benefit in Reno. I have to ask that none of what I'm about to tell you be broadcast. Even my own people haven't been allowed to report on this situation.'

'It would be bad for the security of the campaign as a whole, and we don't need to be reducing people's faith in the congresswoman right now,' said Amber.

I paused, looking between the two of them. Then I raised my hand.

Governor Kilburn quirked an eyebrow upward. 'Yes, Ash?'

'Um, sorry to get off topic and all, but I know Congresswoman Wagman is a friend of yours, and I know you have info I don't, and my friend who told me about the attack on the burlesque show said there'd been some restructuring in their security lineup recently, and I was just wondering, Amber, are you related to the congresswoman?'

Amber turned to John. 'You owe me five dollars.' She looked back to me while he was grumbling and digging into his pocket, and said, 'Niece.'

'She's mine, I'm not hers,' said Wagman. 'You could not *pay* me to be twenty-five again. Now, the body of a twenty-five-year-old, that I'd take. Imagine the campaign reform I could do if I didn't need this much foundation to look this good.'

'Huh,' I said. 'All right.'

'I want to state just this once and for the record that I've known Amber since she was a child, and that I knew about her relation to Congresswoman Wagman when she applied for the troubleshooting position on my security detail,' said the governor. 'She is not spying for the enemy. She is not doing an inferior job because she wants me to be eaten by zombies, thus making it easier for her aunt to get the presidency.'

'I would've gone to work for Tate if I was planning to kill a candidate,' said Amber amiably. 'Nobody would believe it was an accident, but at least I'd die a national hero.'

'Now, Amber,' said Kirsten. 'What's our rule about threatening my opponents?'

'Don't do it in front of the press,' said Amber.

'We're getting a little far from the original topic,' said Ben. 'What happened at your event?'

'I was getting there,' said Wagman. She snagged a chair from one of the break tables and sank elegantly into it, crossing her ankles and looking at each of us in turn. 'All right: It was a circus-themed burlesque night fund-raiser. Everyone was supposed to come in costume, even the staff. It allowed for anonymous donations, and for having a little fun with the people around you. No touching, but lots of teasing.'

'Your political events are very, very different from mine,' said the governor.

Wagman shrugged. 'To each their own. In a perfect world, we'd be on the same side of the fence, and we could buddy cop our way to the White House.'

'If you both lose this time, can you run again in four years, and do that?' I asked. 'I volunteer *right now* to be on your news crew.'

'Let's finish this campaign before we bury it, all right, sugar?' said Wagman. 'Anyway, people started rolling in for setup around noon, and we opened the doors at eight. Everyone checked out clean before we let them into the building. That part was important, given how close together we were all going to be. We even had cater-waiters circulating with handheld blood testing units, doing random checks. It made people feel safer, you know? Like we were really looking out for their well-being.'

'Psychology matters,' said Ben.

Mat was frowning. 'How did the outbreak start?'

'What?'

'Um, sorry.' Mat shook their head. 'Continue. I'll catch up in a second.'

Congresswoman Wagman looked at them thoughtfully before she said, 'We had a group of clowns coming to perform at the end of the evening. They cleared the first blood test, at the back door. They cleared the second blood test, at the kitchen, ninety seconds later.'

'Nice gauntlet,' I said approvingly. 'Normally I'd call that overkill, but when you have that many people packed into a small space, I appreciate the diligence. All you're missing is a good eye in the sky camera array and a casino-trained operator.'

'We had three,' said Wagman.

I made a soft squeaking noise.

'No, you may not propose to the United States congresswoman, no matter how sexy you find her taste in security measures,' said Audrey, putting her hand on my knee and squeezing. She sounded amused. That was good. 'You're taken on so many levels that it's getting ridiculous.'

'Can you blame me for finding good visual security sexy as all hell?' I asked.

'If I blamed you, I wouldn't be dating you,' she replied. Across the room, John looked away.

Right: He *had* expressed an interest, and she *had* turned him down. I couldn't blame him – Audrey was awesome – but hopefully this wasn't going to interfere with their professional relationship. I turned my attention back to Wagman. 'You said they passed the first two blood tests. Was there a third?'

'Yes, thanks to the eyes in the sky. Two checks were mandatory, but if both came back clean, the third was optional; it had a release button, controlled by the guard at the door. We wanted people to feel a little naughty, and a little special, when we let them inside. Like they were getting away with something.' Wagman shook her head, an expression of genuine regret on her face. 'The clowns passed the second check, but as they were walking down the employee hall toward the door to the main room, one of them stumbled. Maybe that didn't seem like such a big thing – it was a dark hall, the floor wasn't perfectly level, people trip all the time – but for some reason, it caught the eye in the sky operator's attention. She called the door guards and asked for a third blood test on the clowns. Said they were displaying early kinesthetic signs of amplification. Which, as it turns out, they were.'

'All of them?' asked Ben.

'Three of the five tested positive on the scene. The guards removed them, since none were fully amplified yet; it was better to take them to a sterile location than to risk contaminating a main thoroughfare. I was sitting on a swing inside a giant birdcage when all this was going down, explaining to potential donors how my pretty blue tail feathers represented environmental conservation.' Wagman grimaced. 'I had my team in my ear, talking about removing the clowns, scrambling to fill that spot in the evening's calendar, and we all still thought the show was going to go on. The entertainment had been exposed. That was tragic, but no one else had been hurt.'

Her pragmatism wasn't as cold as it seemed. Kellis-Amberlee could strike anyone, at any time. Because of that, we'd all long since learned how to keep going. It was that, or become like York, locked in his house and stubbornly insisting that he could do anything he wanted without ever breaking the seal on his sterile fastness. Removing the infected clowns had kept everyone else in the building safe. Once that was done, the job should have been over.

The job hadn't been over. I could see that in her eyes. Slowly, haltingly, she continued, 'The other two clowns were being held by my security until they received confirmation that the infected individuals had been removed from the premises. It's standard operating procedure with something like that. While they were waiting, one of the two remaining clowns looked up at the ceiling. He seemed dazed. Disoriented. According to the eye in the sky operator, his pupils were expanding past normal limits, eating into the iris. She hit the alarm. The guards responded, but not fast enough. Both clowns amplified in that hall. Three of my security staffers died.'

'But the infected individuals didn't get through the door,' I said thoughtfully. 'Did anyone know that you had an eye in the sky array?'

'Just my staff,' said Wagman.

'Was it standard? I mean, was this something you'd been doing for a while, or was it something new you were trying? Eye in the sky should be standard for any event in a building that can support it, but I know it's not.' People still had funny ideas about privacy – like the funny idea that they *had* any. Given the satellites, GPS locators in our equipment, and constant data uploads from every blood test taken by anyone in the world, it was a miracle everyone hadn't just embraced the culture of the unending overshare.

'I've always used eye in the sky arrays when I was in a casino that had trained operators on hand, but I've only had my own system since the start of the campaign,' said Wagman. 'We have two technicians who come in with the setup team, and install the system alongside the sound crew and lighting directors. If we can, we get a separate room for the operators. If we can't, they get to share my dressing room.'

Of course she had a dressing room. You couldn't put on costumes like hers in a public bathroom stall. 'The attack on the governor was planned. Somebody *planted* zombies in the rose garden, figuring they'd dig their way out and eat us all once the sound of the humans got to be too much for them to resist,' I said. 'Was this one planned, or did the clowns just run into a streak of bad luck?'

'It was in their makeup,' said Mat.

We all turned to look at them. Congresswoman Wagman blinked. 'Yes,' she said. 'How did you know?'

'Because they were clowns,' said Mat.

'Going to need a little more than that,' I said. 'I hear the words as they leave your mouth, and they don't make any sense, no matter what order I put them into.'

'Clowns wear a lot of makeup, in distinct layers,' said Mat. 'If you're a *professional* clown, you only use the good stuff, because anything else would clog your pores and mean risking a serious skin condition. The only person more concerned with what goes on their face than a clown is a professional camgirl, and honestly, clowns are probably more careful. The thing is, all that makeup starts super crisp and distinct, and then it bleeds together with wear and sweat and time. So if you wanted to poison a clown you could, say, put something in their pancake, and trust the concealer to keep it from fully touching the skin for at least an hour.'

'This is like listening to a foreign language,' said John.

'Yes, but so far the makeup artist is right,' said Wagman. 'Go on, sugar.'

'Kellis-Amberlee can't be absorbed through the skin, thank God, so if someone was going to spike a clown's makeup with the disease, it would need to be near a mucous membrane. Most clowns go base level, pancake white, mouth, if they're the sort of clowns that have big red mouths. Put the virus in the mouth paint. It won't be swallowed right away – not until the layers start to blend and bleed, and the paint on the lips has softened. Is that what happened?'

Wagman had gone motionless. Her voice was still pleasant as she said, 'If I hadn't known you were with Suzy this whole time, I'd be having you arrested on suspicion of terrorism right now. That's exactly what happened. When we swept their van after the incident, we found that their mouth paints had been tampered with – packed full of the damn virus. Those poor bastards were dead before they stepped into the building. It just took a while for their bodies to realize it.'

'So they passed the first two blood tests because they hadn't swallowed any paint yet,' Audrey said. 'Most people will sweat when they have to take two blood tests in quick succession. Test anxiety combines with the belief that if they'd *really* passed, they'd be clear for at least an hour. Everyone claims they feel safer when exposed to repeated testing, but that's not true. So the tests they passed would have resulted in their makeup being warmed, and in some lip-biting behaviors.'

'Infecting three of the five, and starting amplification,' I said, picking up the thread.

Ben had been quiet and thoughtful through this recitation. Now he sat up straighter, and asked, 'Who knew you were hiring these clowns?'

'Everyone,' said Wagman. 'They were well-known here in town, and they were going to be a public part of the evening's entertainment. It was on my team's blogs, and they put it all over their social media. Having them was supposed to show that I supported local artists and local industry.' She grimaced. 'It backfired. Even if we'd wanted to cover up their deaths, we couldn't have, and now there are some local pundits saying I can't keep them safe.'

'But no one seems to be aware that there was an outbreak at your event,' I said, frowning. 'We're talking about eight deaths, all told, and you've just said that there wasn't a cover-up. How the hell did you manage that?'

'You mean my leak didn't tell you?' asked Wagman. She gave me a challenging look. I didn't flinch away. Tina wasn't here, so I didn't need to worry about revealing my source by being too friendly: I just had to keep myself from doing anything that might get her in trouble. Not ideal, but better than it could have been.

Wagman sighed, yielding. 'We had to cancel the rest of the event, of course; pled a kitchen fire and closed down the building. The time stamps of the amplifications were already on file with the CDC. We sent a confirmation notice, and contacted the families of the deceased. But since the CDC doesn't release times of amplification unless there's an inquest, and since no one was asking . . .'

'You just let it ride,' said Ben. He looked at the governor as he asked his next question. 'Congresswoman Wagman, were you not concerned that any of your opponents who learned about this incident might attempt to use it against you? It's not technically lying to the American public, but there are people who would see it that way.'

'Including you, huh, sweetie? Tell me, did you publish every little detail of the attack on *your* candidate?' Congresswoman Wagman shook her head once, fiercely. 'I didn't hide their deaths. I didn't lie about where they happened. I attended their funerals. I've done everything I'm required by law to do, and a few things no one ever legislated, because they would have looked too much like caring. Telling people "this was a concerted attempt to assassinate a candidate for the presidency" earns me nothing.'

'Surely that's not true,' protested Ben. 'Great leaders have always faced assassination attempts. You could improve your public image by stepping up and making yourself look like a great leader. Why else would they be afraid of you?'

'Bless your heart. You're still not answering my question, and you're insulting me at the same time, even if you can't see it.' Wagman leaned forward, her attention fixed on my husband. There was nothing soft or silly about her now: The time for persona and presentation was over. We were looking at the real Kirsten Wagman now, a brilliant political mind who had chosen to trade her dignity for more airtime and hence more attention for the causes she gave a damn about. Dignity was temporary. Improved health care and public housing was ... well, also temporary, but it mattered more. 'I don't want to improve my public image. I'm perfectly happy being the candidate they all laugh at, because it means they're talking about me. If I said "someone tried to shoot me," people would be sorry. They'd talk about what a terrible world this is, and how brave I am. If I said "someone tried to cut my head off," people would be shocked. They'd talk about how hard it is to be a woman in politics, and how noble I am. But if I say "someone tried to use Kellis-Amberlee to kill me and make it look like an accident," people will say I'm lying. The phrase "drama queen" will come out. So will the phrase "attention whore." It's amazing how it's always about gender when people are trying to cut you down without calling you a liar, isn't it?'

'Preaching to the choir,' said Mat.

Congresswoman Wagman wasn't done. 'And if they would stop there, maybe I would think it was worth it – I'd be warning the world, right? Only Suzy already knows. I'd be willing to bet Pete already knows, even if no one in his camp wants to talk to me. Tate and York, fuck them. They can do whatever they want, and it won't be any concern of mine. The only people I'd be "warning" would be the American public, and not only would they turn on me, they would disappear.'

'Kirsten is right,' said Kilburn. 'Most people are already afraid to come to political rallies and events. Things like the rose-garden incident don't help with that. They reinforce the idea that the world is dangerous and there's no way to stay safe without staying locked up. Say that someone's using zombies to intentionally attack political events, and we're done. York gets the world he wants.'

'Any chance he could be behind this?' asked Amber. 'He's a wacky old coot who'd fit in pretty well in a *Scooby-Doo* cartoon. Maybe he's trying to remake the world in his own image by scaring the shit out of the rest of us.'

'I am never going to sleep again,' announced Mat.

'Whoever did this needs more resources than York has, and needs to be free to move around,' said Wagman. 'Much as I'd like to point the finger at that guy – I *hate* that guy – I don't think he's the one.'

'Neither do I,' said Kilburn. 'Whatever's fueling this conspiracy, it's bigger than one candidate.'

'So what do we do about it?' asked Rick. No one said a word, and silence reigned as we all looked uncomfortably at each other. There were no easy answers. Somehow, that was the worst part of all.

Being on the road is interesting. On the one hand, you're surrounded by constant novelty, which I appreciate; as most people know by now, I bore easily, and a bored Irwin is an Irwin who's about to stir up a whole lot of shit for nothing more than the experience of standing in a shit-storm. I am a natural disaster when I don't have something to keep me busy. Travel is definitely good for occupying the mind.

At the same time, travel leaves a lot of big blank spaces on the map, hours upon hours where the doors are closed and the road is rolling by outside, and the green hills of America are all you have to see. America always looks oddly de-saturated to me, like someone has turned the gain down on the entire world. The hills in Ireland are greener. It's not an exaggeration: There's something about the soil that just grows the greenest grass in the world. If there's anything I really miss about my homeland, it's that. How could anyone have access to that much green and not miss it once it's gone?

We're rolling into the Democratic National Convention this week. Either Governor Kilburn will take the nomination and be the official Democratic candidate, or she'll lose, and maybe she'll be someone's choice for VP and maybe she won't, but either way we're likely to be out of a job. So fingers crossed for a Kilburn 2040 ticket taking us all the way home, because I don't want to go back to the real world yet!

—From *Erin Go Blog*, the blog of Ash North, March 11, 2040

Eleven

Cars and tour buses packed the streets of Huntsville, Alabama, turning the place into a virtual parking lot. The Space Center was open twenty-four hours a day during the convention, hoping to lure politicians and policy makers into their brightly lit embrace and convince them to open their checkbooks a little wider. I didn't have a checkbook to open, exactly. That wasn't stopping me. I'd already been on two of the tours and was planning to go back for the paid docent experience, which included a ride in the giant centrifuge. It was all tax deductible, since I could call it a business expense – reporting on space was slightly outside my normal purview, not forbidden – but to be honest, I would have done it without the deductions. Space was *fun*. I hoped they'd be able to operate NASA for a year off these people.

Ben and Mat had been inside the convention center all morning, sending out occasional blip updates and loading their reports directly onto the server. Mat was doing makeup demos near the governor's booth, showing attendees how to get the look that would tell their chosen candidates how much support they had – and because Governor Kilburn was awesome, there were no restrictions on *which* candidate. Mat had done mostly Susan Kilburns, but there had been a few Frances Blackburns, and even a smattering of Eliot Yorks. All of them were free advertising for Mat's services, and hence for Governor

Kilburn's booth. It was a good exchange. I was glad I wasn't the one making it. I would've shoved a mascara wand into someone's eye by now.

Ben's activities were less colorful and more cerebral. He'd been moving from interview to interview, think tank to think tank, all morning long. I could track his movement by calling up his feed and watching the updates, blog entries, and GPS data stream by. My busy bee. I didn't give two shits about most of what he was doing, save in the abstract 'it makes him happy and makes us more valuable to the campaign, so carry on, mighty hero of the news, carry on' sense. Later, he'd try to explain it all to me, and I would smile and nod and remember only what I wanted to, because I had him and Audrey to remember it completely.

Irwins aren't stupid. That's a common misconception about the breed. People think we went into Action News, rather than Factual or Fictional, because we're not smart enough to be on the other side of the desk. I guess maybe that's true for a couple of people, although I can't imagine anyone saying 'I don't like to use big words, guess I'll go risk my life for fun' and being any *good* at it. Being an Irwin is hard as hell, and it requires different kinds of intelligence. Kinesthetic intelligence. The ability to look at a situation, spin it in your mind, and have the solution before the dead guys who are shambling rapidly toward their next meal wind up on top of you. Quick intelligence, instead of slow, because out in the field, slow is the thing that gets you dead.

I'd be bored out of my skull if I was stuck behind a desk all the time, and I'd lose a lot of the qualities that actually make me as smart as I claim to be. I'm not the greenest hill in the field when I'm locked in a room and told to write down the world. Put me outside with a weapon in my hand and a problem to solve, and I'm Ada Lovelace.

The convention center backed up on a large swath of undeveloped land. That wasn't a safety hazard: This was Alabama, and it seemed like even the squirrels carried assault rifles in their cunning little paws. Any zombies that wandered this close to town would find themselves reduced to a fine mist and bleached out of existence before they could do any real damage. On some level, I suspected that was *why* this site had been chosen for the convention center, which was a post-Rising, tornado-proof structure designed to withstand anything short of a direct nuclear blast. It could be used as a shelter for the entirety of Huntsville, if necessary. By putting it where they had, the city planners had made the point that no one here was living in fear. Anticipation of getting to shoot some infected deer, maybe, but not *fear*.

It was a pretty piece of fiction, and as I slid down the soft embankment behind the building, braking with the sides of my feet like a skier to keep from going too fast, I wished them the best with it. If they *really* hadn't been afraid of what might come wandering out of the trees, they wouldn't have surrounded their convention center with six layers of fencing and a state-of-the-art auto-sniper system. The black boxes atop the fencing contained miniaturized rifles, each capable of delivering six shots with terrifying pinpoint accuracy. Very impressive, if you didn't mind all the local birds being shot out of the sky for crossing the fence lines without submitting to the proper blood tests first.

Several of the black boxes swiveled to look at me with their cold, blank eyes as I reached the maintenance gate in the first fence. I checked the blood testing unit for signs of tampering and, finding none, pressed my thumb against the open panel. A small, unobtrusive light half-covered by a half dome came on, flashing red, then yellow, and finally green. I wrinkled my nose, signaling my mag to take some burst photos of the process. It would make good filler for whatever I wrote about the day. More importantly, it would let me study this particular security setup at my leisure, when I wasn't in the field and paying attention to my surroundings. I'd never seen a hooded light before. It would keep my test results private from the people around me, which was good, but could potentially allow me to lie about them, which wasn't.

The unit beeped – an audio cue was even odder than a half-concealed light. Half the time it feels like people are making tweaks to their security setups just so they can say they did it. The gate unlocked. I pulled my hand away from the unit and stepped through. My questions could wait. I had five more gates to clear.

The openings were staggered, forcing the person who wanted to get in or out to walk anywhere from five to fifteen feet along the fence line before they reached the next testing unit. It was a cognitive test, intended to see whether someone was beginning to amplify and hence losing the ability to figure out where to go next. It was utterly, patently pointless, and had probably gotten a couple of people killed. If you checked out clean on one station, you needed to be able to dive through, slam the door, and hit the next checkpoint, not screw around looking for where you were supposed to go. The staggering would give the infected time to spit or bleed on the people trapped inside the fences, turning the living into virtual rats in a cage.

There were no zombies to harry me as I made my way through. Just six pinpricks in quick succession, leaving my thumb feeling bruised despite the cooling foam that accompanied every needle. The last door unlocked, and the black boxes swiveled away from me, no longer interested now that I was moving away from the convention center. It was a small compromise between the 'safety first' people and the 'seriously, we're running out of wildlife, can you not' activists: Anything that tried to move *toward* the center without going through the proper testing protocols would be gunned down, but anything that was moving *away* would be cheerfully ignored.

Getting back in was going to be fun. I looked forward to documenting it.

The scrubby grass and small weeds crunching underfoot were largely unfamiliar, growing as they were in Southern soil the color of dried blood. I wondered idly how many people had moved out of state because they couldn't stand the color of the ground anymore, now that we lived in a world where blood was the enemy and biological waste was a death sentence. Maybe no one had left, and all the people who lived and loved and died in Alabama thought the rest of us were too easily shocked by the world. It was hard to say. But the day was beautiful and the air was sweet, so it didn't really matter.

A cluster of people had formed around a portable Foreman grill in a clearing past the tree line. This wasn't proper forest – more like an orchard that had been allowed to grow out of control when people lost interest in handpicking their own apples. As such, there were wide spaces and clearings everywhere, making it seem like a video-game level, instead of an actual wilderness. Most of the people sat in folding chairs. A few stood, and one was sitting cross-legged on the ground, her eyes closed and her hands resting on her knees.

One of the standers waved as he saw me approaching. 'Well, as I live and breathe,' he said, in an exaggerated Irish brogue that bore about as much resemblance to my accent as it did to a banana. 'If it's not the lovely and talented Aislinn Ross. Top of the morning to you, Ms Ross.'

'Last name's North, as well you know, Karl,' I said. I was trying to sound like I was above his taunts, and I mostly managed it. Mostly. Karl Conway had been a pain in my ass since I'd applied for my U.S. blogger's license. He'd been part of the group that attempted to keep me from certification, claiming my being a foreign national meant both that I shouldn't be taking work from American Irwins and that I wouldn't know how to deal with the unique dangers of the American landscape. It had been the Canadian government, oddly enough, that had come to my rescue; they'd replied to his petition by saying he made excellent points about journalists working on foreign soil, and that they'd be reexamining all those tourist licenses they issued to Americans. Karl had withdrawn his complaint without missing a beat. I'd been licensed, and I'd been ready to let it drop.

He hadn't been. Nothing I did, from hard news to naturalization, could make him stop beating his jingoistic drum and demanding I get the hell out of his country. If ever a man could force my hand to murder, it was going to be him.

'See, where I'm from, a woman takes her husband's name when she marries him,' said Karl. 'It's a sign of respect.'

'Ah, yes, the infamous "respect,"' I said. 'Given your name to any lovely ladies lately?'

Karl scowled. The other Irwins laughed, some ruefully, others with a distinct note of triumph. Karl was about as popular with our community as a bad case of fleas. He was annoying, he was a bully, and he didn't understand when it was time to back off. He was also tenacious and virtually impossible to kill without using a hammer. Everyone knew he was going to be around for a long, long time. Nobody liked it, but most of us were pretty good at learning to live with what we couldn't change.

'Afternoon, Ash,' said the man at the grill. He lifted his head and grinned, his somewhat questionable dentistry doing nothing to detract from the brightness of his smile. A lot of people are scared of the dentist, and with good reason. Even basic cleanings require mild sedation, and a hundred people spontaneously amplify in the dentist's chair every year. It's a very well-paid profession, since it's both essential and incredibly dangerous. For some people, painkillers and a little discoloration are a small price to pay to avoid the needle and the silence. 'We're having chicken and tofu skewers. You in?'

I hoisted my bag. 'I brought supplies.'

His grin broadened. 'Excellent.' Chase Hoffman was one of the best Irwins in Alabama, and this was really his party, since we were guests on his patch. His family had been in Huntsville for the past fifteen generations, and it was going to take more than a zombie apocalypse to move them. The South reminded me a lot of Ireland in that regard. What mattered was how long you'd been there, setting roots into the land. What mattered was where your people were from, where they'd been born and died and where the bodies were buried. Everything else was just the present, and everyone knew the present was only a blink of an eye when set against the great and constant walls of history.

The rest of the Irwins greeted me as I walked over and began unpacking my offering of turkey hot dogs, chicken breasts, and asparagus spears onto the waiting trays. Some of them I knew, by reputation if not by actual acquaintance; others were unfamiliar, and required more attention while I fixed their faces in my memory. It's never good to be introduced to someone I've already met. It made me seem flighty, when really, it was just a matter of my having better things to pay attention to than what face went with which name. The world is made of dangerous things. Hurt feelings are among them, but hurt feelings are unlikely to rip my throat out with their teeth. I prefer to focus on the things that could kill me, not just say nasty things behind my back.

'How's your candidate?' asked Karl, apparently unwilling to let me off the hook with light mockery. Swell. 'She ready to concede?'

'I could ask you the same, you know, with a side order of "how did you convince Blackburn to hire you in the first place,"' I said. 'You seem more like a York man to me. Reactionary, reclusive, slightly misogynistic . . .'

'She's got you dead to rights,' said the cross-legged woman, opening her eyes and smiling benevolently up at him. She turned to me, and extended one hand. 'Hi. I'm Jody. I'm also with the Blackburn campaign.'

'She has two Irwins?' I asked, leaning down to shake.

'I came as a package deal with her Newsie, Eric,' she said. 'He does stunning exposés, I meditate in dangerous places. He's also over there, helping with the barbeque, because sometimes *he* comes as a package deal with *me*.'

Suddenly, I understood where I recognized her from. 'You're Peaceful Demolitions! I've seen some of your videos.'

Jody grinned. 'I am, and I've seen some of yours. You do good work.'

'So do you! So original.' My gushing over Jody was making Karl scowl more. I decided not to stop. 'How'd you come up with the notion? I love a good risk as much as the next girl, but I'm not sure

I could voluntarily close my eyes and think about the world while zombies were clawing at the windows.'

'Liar,' said Chase. 'I've seen those nap videos you did. You sleep in trees, on purpose, in hazard zones.'

'Yes, off the ground and with one hand on my gun,' I said. 'There's a thin line between intentionally stupid and accidentally suicidal, and I try not to cross it when I don't have to.'

'Whereas I play hopscotch with it,' said Jody. She didn't sound ashamed of herself. If anything, she sounded exactly the opposite. I couldn't blame her for that. Her videos were works of art. Occasionally terrifying works of art, sure – even I didn't like watching someone utterly defenseless and exposed for as long as she would sometimes sit, thinking – but beautiful all the same. 'I realized we're all about the running and the screaming, and thought it might be nice to slow things down. Based on my ratings and merchandise sales, I wasn't the only one. I was just the first person to realize there might be money there.'

'Teach me your ways, o wise one,' I said, and Jody laughed, and Chase handed me a turkey dog in a whole wheat bun, and Karl aside, everything was perfect.

More Irwins drifted in. Some of them were with news sites that had come to cover the convention. Others were independents, traveling with their own Newsies. The majority were local or semilocal, and had come for the reason Irwins always came: because they knew that once this many of us were in one area, the party would inevitably begin. There must have been more than a dozen of us there, chatting, eating, and drinking alcohol-free beer, when my ear cuff began beeping rapidly. I put my bottle down on the nearest folding table and drifted toward the edge of the clearing, noting as I did that Karl and Jody, both with Blackburn, and Mo, with York, had done the same.

'You're go for Ash,' I said, activating the connection. 'What can I help you with?'

'Where are you?' It was Audrey. She sounded . . . not tense, exactly, but tightly wound, like she might snap and start spilling kinetic energy everywhere at any moment.

'Out behind the convention center with essentially all the local Irwins, and a few who aren't so local. Karl is here. He doesn't say hello. He does say that I'm a stuck-up Irish bitch, so he hasn't changed a bit. Why? Are you all right? You sound odd.'

'I sound like the candidate announcement just happened,' said Audrey. She paused, long enough for my heart to sink. It was over, then. We were going home.

I'd never admit it, not in a million years, but part of me was relieved. No one tried to kill us when we were at home. We had our space and our things and our world around us, and we knew what we were up against. Let the politicians have their life-and-death struggles over the budget cap and whether people were allowed to keep ponies; I'd go back to my familiar little life, and while it might not be perfect, it was enough. Maybe it was even time to talk to Ben about that divorce. I could make an honest woman out of Audrey, and let her make a better woman out of me.

Audrey was saying something. I jerked back into the present. 'I'm sorry, come again?' I said.

'I said, Governor Susan Kilburn of Oregon is the next Democratic candidate for the presidency of the United States of America.' Audrey still sounded tense, but at least she also sounded amused. She was used to my woolgathering. 'Blackburn came in a close second. Betting pools have shifted over to whether Kilburn is going to be offering her the VP slot, and if so, how long it's going to take her to say yes.'

'Tell Ben she has at least three people on her news team, and while I'm happy to take Jody and Eric – they're an Irwin and Newsie team, and I know Jody doesn't conflict with my area, not sure whether Eric would overlap with either Ben or Mat – we're only working with Karl if he reanimates, because I'd kill him.'

I was speaking too quietly for Karl to hear me from the other side of the clearing, but judging by his posture and the quick, angry looks he was darting in my direction, he didn't need to hear me to know what I was saying. He knew he'd burnt all his bridges with me years ago, and neither of us had any interest in rebuilding. I wondered whether he'd try anyway. This was a big job, and while there are always things for the Irwins of the world to do – people never get tired of watching us risk our necks – big jobs don't come along very often. When you get one, you hang on to it, whatever it takes.

'Karl? The one who said he'd stop making fun of your accent if you gave him a video of the two of us making out?'

'That's the one.'

'Flip him off for me.'

I solemnly swiveled toward Karl and raised my middle finger in silent salute. Then I froze, feeling my blood run cold in my veins. It was a terrible sensation. It wasn't as bad as what was yet to come. 'Audrey, I need you to go find John or Amber. Tell them to lock down the governor and sound the alarms.'

The infected were moving through the trees, and if they were close enough for me to see them, they were also close enough for *them* to see *me*. But they weren't moaning, not yet. Just my luck. Another close encounter with the quiet ones.

Audrey was laughing. 'Is he glaring at you? I bet he's glaring at you. Take a picture.' The true face of her tension was showing itself now. It wasn't concern or dismay: It was giddiness, delight at a job well done, and the belief that things were going to be better now. Even if Kilburn lost, we would have followed her all the way to the final bell. Our careers were made.

If we lived that long. '*Audrey*. Please, listen to me. I love you.' It was a random declaration, and one she'd heard before, if never with quite so much urgency and raw need. She stopped laughing. I stopped flipping Karl off and pointed to the trees behind him. He flipped me off. This was bad. 'Contact security. Tell them a mob is emerging from the trees behind the convention center. Tell them . . . tell them . . .'

If she told them we were out here, would they try to save us, or would they treat us as a firebreak, something to burn when the zombies got too close? The dead were dead. We were the living, and the living, no matter how well trained they are, don't always respond well under pressure. If we were exposed, if we were *infected*, we could run the fences anyway, seeking another few seconds of life before we inevitably died. Irwins caught between a rock and a hard place got smashed. Just like everything else.

'Tell them we're here, Audrey. Tell them we're alive.' I pointed at the trees behind Karl again, more fiercely this time. He must have seen something in my expression, because he turned, and paled when he saw the zombies coming through the wood, and shoved his phone into his pocket before running back toward the others.

Good. I hiked the side of my skirt up and drew the pistol from my thigh holster. It was surprisingly heavy in my hand. I'd held that weapon a hundred times, and it had never seemed so *heavy*. 'Tell them we want to come home. I love you.'

'Ash—' she began. Her voice cut off as I killed the connection.

Some people liked to stay on the phone with their friends and loved ones as they fought, thinking it was better to have the company. I had never wanted that. One day, I was going to die in the field. Maybe I was going to die in this one. If that happened, I wanted to be remembered smiling, not screaming. That was why I always ended my videos with a grin and a wink, no matter how tired I was. Every entry could be the one that went up on the Wall. I didn't want the last thing I did to be sad. Dying was sad enough without helping it along.

Gun in hand, I ran for the others. They were moving fast now, breaking down chairs and producing weapons. No one went for the fence. We all knew there was no point. The same security features that kept everyone inside feeling like they could enjoy being this close to the wilderness would condemn us all, because only the first person would have the time to clear the first gate. Even Karl wasn't enough of a bastard to say 'I want you all to die for me,' and so he held his ground. We all did.

Putting the gate to our backs would have been putting ourselves into a kill zone. As soon as the zombies got close enough, the sniper turrets would start firing, and we'd be splattered. At that point, we'd become targets. I could have climbed a tree, gotten above the action, but that would have meant leaving the others behind. I wasn't ready to do that. Not yet.

Chase stepped up next to me, a shotgun in his hands. I didn't ask where he'd gotten it. It really didn't matter. 'Assessment?' he asked. I shot him a sidelong look. He shook his head. 'Karl came in screaming about how he'd seen them, but I know it wasn't him. Boy would've walked for the fence and said he was getting more beer if he was the only one who knew what was about to happen. So what did you see?'

The zombies were about twenty yards out. Close enough that we couldn't run – not without triggering them to do the same – but far enough away that we had a few seconds of breathing room. We were all professionals. We were going to take every breath the world allowed us, because we knew damn well that these could be our last.

'Five in the lead, unknown number in the back. No moan yet, but they're moving decisively in this direction, which implies that something caught their attention without fully registering as "food." I'm sure that's coming.' Nothing in the world is as single-minded as a zombie that's started moaning. 'Look at their clothes. They're clean. These people amplified within the last twenty-four hours.'

'So they're all fresh.' Chase grimaced. 'Fuck me.'

'Yeah,' I agreed grimly.

Kellis-Amberlee preserved the human body before amplification, keeping us safe from colds and cancer. After amplification, it destroyed everything in its path. Infected individuals generally divided into two camps: newly infected, or 'fresh,' and those who'd amplified long enough ago to start really showing the signs of their illness. Zombies still had the physical limitations they'd had before amplification. They just didn't pay attention to them anymore. They would run on broken ankles and pursue their prey for hours despite bad cases of asthma.

The longer they lived with their disease, the more damage they did to themselves, until they virtually neutralized their potential to do harm. Only virtually. There was no such thing as a 'safe' zombie, and even one that was missing all four limbs and most of its teeth could spit or bleed on an uninfected person, starting the cycle over again. It never ended. It never needed to.

Fresh zombies could run, sometimes faster than the living, because they didn't notice when they broke their toes, blistered their feet, or twisted their ankles. They'd just keep coming, and if the damage they did in the process resigned them to the back of the mob in short order, that was a cold comfort to the people they'd chased down. Fresh zombies could grasp. They no longer understood even simple tools, but their fingers hadn't stiffened and lost manual dexterity, and they knew how to lock them around wrists or tangle them in hair. No zombies were good, but fresh zombies were the worst of a bad lot.

'Think this is a setup?' asked Chase.

'Nope,' I said. 'I know it is.'

Then the zombies were close enough to smell us. The moan went up, and all hell broke loose.

There are a few things all successful Irwins have in common. We know how to defend ourselves. We know the state-mandated firearms well enough to pass our licensing exams, and we know our chosen weapons just as well, if not sometimes better. We know the risks we take every time we go out into the field, and even if most of us secretly believe we're going to live forever, we still accept the fact that this time, this adventure could be our last. We make our peace with that every time we press the 'record' button, because a scared Irwin is a stupid Irwin, and a stupid Irwin isn't going to be around for very long.

That's where the commonalities end. There's no set of standards or guidelines that we all agree to live by, and most Irwins are fierce individualists, convinced that *our* way of doing things, *our* ideas about the world and the dead and the living are more important than anyone else's. A few Irwins choose to work in pairs, or even triplets, but they're rare, and most of us don't understand how they're able to function. We're too busy grandstanding for the camera and enjoying our independence. Which is great for ratings, but not so good when you're trying to fight off a mob of zombies that has a better grasp of teamwork than you do.

There were fourteen of us and an unknown number of them: at least twenty, and probably more, since they were still flowing out of the trees like a terrible river. They were all so *fresh*. How the hell had the people who were targeting us been able to grab so many without being caught? Had we started taking disappearances for granted, viewing them as the dreadful background noise of a life lived in a world full of the dead? And it didn't matter, *couldn't* matter now, however much I wanted it to, because they were closing in on us, and they weren't going to stop long enough for me to get a better look.

Chase's shotgun spoke in thunder, and the zombies answered in moans. Every time he pulled the trigger a head disappeared, vaporized past identification by the bullet. I was grateful for my mag, even as my own smaller weapon opened holes in foreheads and in throats. We'd be able to find out who those people had been, assuming any of us made it out of here.

Jody, the woman who'd made her name with pacifism, produced a lethal-looking assault rifle from her things and began picking off zombies with military precision, making me wish I knew more about her background. The front rank of the dead was denuded within seconds, reduced to so many corpses that wouldn't be getting up a second time. The trouble was, the zombies behind them just kept coming. That was what zombies *did*. They kept coming.

We kept shooting. That was what *Irwins* did, and as the second rank of zombies fell, it began to look like we might be able to win this one. The zombies were too fresh to have tapped fully into the odd, inexplicable hive-mind that powered large groups of the infected, and they moved with jerky, dogged persistence, not splitting up or trying to confuse us. If they'd been a little more advanced in their infections, they could have done all sorts of things to make our lives a living hell. As it was, they didn't have the intelligence for tactics, and we had plenty of bullets.

Bullets, and other things. One of the younger Irwins had been hanging back, staying behind the first rank of shooters. I'd assumed it was because he was scared. Even field-licensed Irwins don't always see real action within their first year, especially if they're under twenty-one when they start. The nastier hazard zones are off-limits until twenty-five, and even the moderate ones don't unlock until a person is past the legal drinking age. I've never been sure why. Drunk people and zombies are a recipe for disaster.

This was a leggy kid, all arms and elbows. He was about nineteen, and he wasn't holding back to let the shooters do their job. He was holding back while he assembled his polearm.

It was a fancy piece of work, too. It looked like a 3D-printed glaive – basically a long stick, in this case made up of separate pieces of screwed-together piping, with a hooked blade at the end. It had probably seemed like a great idea on paper. The action was always five feet away, held at bay by that wickedly designed hook. It had probably seemed even better when he was practicing in his backyard or garage, disemboweling dummies filled with ballistics gel and making war-whoop sounds.

I realized what he was going to do a bare second after he launched himself toward the oncoming mob. '*No!*' I shouted, and the sound of gunfire drowned out my voice, rendering it small and inconsequential. Not that I could have stopped him. He was already moving, racing toward the dead with his glaive held rigidly in front of him, whooping with delight. His head, I knew, would be full of visions of glory, dreams of the headlines he was going to dominate. Humanity has always been happy to reward the daring and the foolish, holding us up like role models when really, we're just illustrations of the best things not to do with your life.

Everyone had noticed him now, including the zombies. A few

people stopped firing, some from visible shock, others from the desire not to hurt the kid, who was one of our own, after all. But not one of us went after him. It felt like my feet were rooted to the blood-colored ground, anchored in place by a weight too enormous for me to ever shift. It was all happening too fast. It was all happening in slow motion at the same time.

He reached the front rank of the zombies, his glaive slicing into the first of them with ease. He whooped as he pulled it loose and whirled it a few feet to the side, cutting the second zombie across the stomach. Its guts fell out with a wet plopping sound, and the zombie went down. Kellis-Amberlee might raise the dead and grant them enhanced blood-clotting properties, but not even it could keep somebody standing after their insides made their first public appearance.

Pulling the glaive loose, the kid whooped again and swung for a third zombie. His foot hit a piece of intestine, and he stumbled, missing by inches.

The zombie that had come up on his side didn't miss. It grabbed his shoulder, yanked him backward, and bit down, ripping a huge chunk out of the side of his neck. He screamed, a high, agonized sound that bore no resemblance to his gleeful war cries. The glaive fell from his hands, making a splashing sound when it landed in the blood that was pooling all around.

The noise broke the spell that this bizarre incident had cast over the shooters. We opened fire again, all of us working together to gun down the remaining zombies. I don't know whose bullet caught the kid, but he fell, a black hole in the middle of his forehead and no life left in his eyes. He wasn't going to be getting up again. That was a small, strained mercy. It was all we had.

Jody screamed.

The sound came from behind me. I whipped around, trusting Chase and the others to cover the hole I had made in our wall of bullets. My eyes widened. All those suppositions I'd made – *we'd* made, since no one had contradicted me – about a fresh mob being too new to plan beyond the moment, they'd all been correct.

We hadn't calculated on there being a second mob, one that had been approaching silently through the trees on the other side, their moans muffled by the sound of the gunfire. *'Incoming!'* I shouted, and opened fire, taking down the first two. Jody had recovered from her surprise. She was firing as well, but there were more of them in this second group, and we were moving toward the point where we would need to reload.

'Fall back!' shouted Chase. 'We don't know how many more are in those trees!'

Retreat went against every bit of my training, which said that I should never run if there was any chance of carrying the day. But there were zombies everywhere, and that kid, whatever his name was, that kid was dead; that kid wasn't coming back. I fired one more time before turning, falling into step with Chase as we ran.

There were zombies ahead and zombies behind, but they hadn't closed the gaps on the sides yet: The way to the open plain between the wood and the convention-center fences was clear. We hauled ass out into the middle of it before forming a circle, some of us slamming new clips into our weapons, the rest just waiting for the dead to catch up.

All except for Karl. He saw his opening, and he took it, weaving around the edge of the second mob and hoofing it as fast as he could toward the fence outside the convention center.

Maybe it was a glitch in the security system. Maybe he was moving too fast, and there was no margin in the biometric scanners; they could have taken him for a zombie, with the way he was racing across the uneven ground. Whatever the reason, he was two feet from the fence and extending his hand toward the testing box when the nearest of the automated snipers opened its blank eye, and a muffled sound like a blast of air being forced through a hose cut through the stillness. Karl didn't have time to react. He fell backward, revealing the hole where his left eye had been, and landed, unmoving, on the ground.

On the ground in front of the gate. Which would now be saturated with his blood. His dead, and hence bioactive, blood. Even if we got past the mob, we couldn't use the gate; we'd be biohazards the second we stepped in what Karl had spilled. No matter how many blood tests we cleared, the convention center security drones would flag us and gun us down.

'Chase, how the hell do we get to the front of the convention center without going through the fences?' I asked the question quietly, not because I was trying to keep it secret – all these people were smart, all these people were reaching the same conclusions I was – but because I didn't dare allow myself to raise my voice. If I started yelling, I wasn't going to stop.

I had no eye protection. I had no leg protection. I wore sundresses into the field on a regular basis, sure, but always when *I* had chosen the field, when *I* had calculated the risks. The rose garden had happened fast and hot and I'd been the one who chose to run toward the danger – me and no one else. Mat had been an unwitting draftee. This time, the danger had come to me, and while I wasn't unnerved enough to forget my training, I was definitely off balance. I just wanted to get out of here alive. I didn't want the perfunctory kiss I'd given Audrey before she trundled off to the convention center and I made for the Irwins' barbeque to be our last. Maybe it was selfish, especially with two people already dead – two people aside from the seemingly endless waves of zombies that were closing in on us – but sometimes selfishness is the truest human impulse of all. Sometimes selfishness is the thing that keeps you alive when everything else fails.

'We have to go back into the woods,' he said. There was a flat, resigned note to his voice, like he'd been circling this conclusion for some time, trying to find any other way to accomplish what he wanted to do. 'There's a maintenance road half a mile in. It connects to the tunnel system used for the landscaping and cleanup crews. There's formalin, flamethrowers, everything you could need to stop an out-break. We just have to get there.'

Get there, with zombies on every side except our rear, where a homicidal fence was waiting to take us down for getting too close, and with most of our ammo already expended. It was an impossible thing for the world to ask of us. It was never going to happen. It was our only chance.

I didn't know most of these Irwins well enough to know their strengths or weaknesses, but I knew what I could see. Like that one Irwin who was built like a small mountain going for a walk. Like Jody, who was tiny and lithe and accustomed to holding perfectly still for long periods of time. Like Chase, who knew the terrain.

And I knew, more than anything else in the world, that I didn't want to die out here. Not today; not like this. 'Everyone!' I shouted, even as the gunshots rang in my ears and my own gun jerked in my hand. The shot was clean; the zombie fell. Three more were waiting to take his place. 'There's a maintenance road half a mile in! We won't all make it there, but we won't all make it here, either! Who's for a rabbit-run to safety?'

The cameras were on, their lenses greedily gobbling up every pico-second of footage. None of this would be lost. Enough of our Newsies knew what was going on that I'd be stunned if half of them weren't already sending up drone-mounted recorders to get aerial shots. All of us wanted to survive this. Fieldwork and death wishes don't go together well, or at least, they don't go together well for *long*, and everyone here had been working the circuit long enough that I had faith in their desire to stay alive. But even more than we wanted to survive, most of us wanted to be remembered as something amazing. There was a reason the Action News reporters of the world took their name from Steve Irwin, a man who never met a camera he wouldn't mug for or a venomous snake he wouldn't pick up and admire. His legacy might have been his family, but his immortality was in his recordings.

Anyone who told me no would look like a coward. Some of them knew that, and had been glaring at me since the words 'maintenance road' had left my mouth. The rest were nodding, some even taking their eyes off the mob to look at me.

'How?' shouted Jody.

'Climb the big guy!' I called back, pointing to Eric. He was easily six and a half feet tall; he'd do. 'Make a mobile sniper's platform! Chase, you know where we're going – I'll take point, keep you covered while you follow and give me directions. I want covering fire. Now move!' I pulled the trigger one more time, and saw the nearest zombie go down in a heap of limbs before I turned and bolted for the tree line. Footsteps behind me told me that Chase was in close pursuit. That, or the zombies were closer than we'd ever thought. Either way, I needed to keep running.

The two mobs hadn't quite managed to merge together, and there was still a narrow avenue between them. I hurled myself down it, shooting when necessary, running for the tree line. A dead man loomed out of nowhere. I put a bullet in his forehead, turning my face aside to avoid blood splatter, and kept on moving. It was the only thing I could do, now that I was committed.

'Keep moving forward!' commanded Chase. I kept moving forward. That was easier than turning, or slowing down: Now that my body was in motion, it wanted to *stay* in motion. I wanted to run forever. If I ran forever, I wouldn't be forced to deal with the things that happened when I was still. I would never be caught. I would never die.

My foot hit a patch of spilled blood and went out from under me, sending me backward. A massive hand closed around my hair and jerked me upright again, sending a bolt of stinging pain through my scalp. The hand let go and I kept running, glancing to the side to see Jody and her human sniper tower pulling up level with me. His was the hand that had stopped me from falling. Eric wasn't looking at me: His eyes were fixed on the path ahead, presumably so he could aim the massive sawed-off shotgun that he had braced against his chest. Jody had her legs around his neck, her ankles crossed at his sternum; she was twisted to face behind her, and her rifle spoke constantly, spitting bullets like curses into the chilly Southern air.

Someone screamed. Someone else swore. All of us kept running, kept shooting, kept doing whatever it took to get where we needed to be.

I didn't see the next of us to die. She was at the rear of the pack, a slight little thing with brown hair in tight braids and camo pants that bulged with too many pockets. I'd seen her before, gracing the mastheads of various small feeder sites – the kind of places that followed other reporters to the news, rather than seeking it out for themselves. Buzzards instead of lions. But she had been smart, and she had been kind, and it wasn't her fault that I didn't know her name. I had learned it and forgotten it on the same day.

I would never forget the way she screamed. It was high and piercing and pained, and almost drowned out a moment later when the zombies increased the volume of their moans and fell upon her, greedy hands ripping into her body, greedy mouths going for her flesh. I hated that we couldn't stop and save her that last agony, even as a small, brutal part of me delighted in the time she had just purchased for us. *She'll be a hero,* I promised myself. *When I tell this story, she'll be a hero.* I could spin her that way, make her a sacrifice rather than a statistic. It was the only thing I had left to offer her.

And it would only happen if I made it as far as the maintenance tunnels. Chase shouted commands from behind me, and I cleared the path ahead while Jody picked off anything that got too close, and the other out-of-town Irwins formed a bubble of moving safe space around him, keeping Chase as safe as we possibly could.

My ear cuff beeped. I ignored it and kept running. This wasn't a good time for distractions. It beeped again, and again, until I realized that it wasn't going to stop; it was either take the call or do the rest of this run with that noise in my ear, gradually wearing down my concentration. Neither option was good, but one was slightly less bearable than the other. I ticked my head hard to the side, opening the connection.

'I'm a bit busy at the moment, darlin',' I said, making my brogue almost as broad as Karl – may he rest in peace, and not merely in pieces – had done earlier.

'You didn't know that it would be me on the phone,' said Audrey.

'Only three people have this channel, and all of you can be a darlin' to me under the right circumstances, my love,' I said. Another zombie shambled out of the trees up ahead. How many of the damn things *were* there? I pulled the trigger and it went down. I was starting to feel like I was in a pre-Rising video game, only there were no extra lives here, no save points or miracle recoveries. There was only the mud under my feet and the taste of cordite in my mouth, the ache in my wrists and the terror in my veins.

I was going to die out here. Somewhere between the shot that killed Karl and the girl whose name I didn't know ceasing to scream, I'd accepted the fact that I was going to die out here. There wasn't any other outcome that made sense. It was terrible. It was unforgivable. But it was the way things were going to be.

'I'm glad you called,' I said, trying not to pant, even as twigs crackled underfoot and the muscles in my thighs began to burn. Years of narrating my own flight through the wilderness was seeing me proud. I sounded almost normal. That was good. I didn't want her to know how scared I was. 'Have I told you recently how much I love you? Apart from those two times on the phone before?'

'Ash, don't be stupid,' said Audrey. 'Just ... just climb a tree, all right? We're watching you now. We're all watching you. Convention-center security is on the way. They just need to clear the fences, and they'll be able to give you the support you need.'

'Aw, should I wave for my mother, then? She'd be proud to see me like this, her little girl all covered in red Alabama mud. Every slaughter should happen here. No one can tell where the bleeding begins. Keep it nice and pleasant for the kiddies.' Another Irwin screamed, the sound cut off by three gunshots in quick succession. I tried not to grind my teeth. That was a waste of both bullets and mercy; yes, it showed kindness to the person who'd been bitten, but it showed nothing of the sort to the rest of us. We needed every bullet and every second we could buy, no matter how dearly they came.

'Ash, come on. Don't be a hero. Come back to me.'

'I'm not trying to be a hero, love. I'm running as hard as I can. I just don't know that it's to be hard enough. I can't climb a tree and leave the rest of these fine folk to die. You wouldn't love me if I did.' My words were getting shaky. Behind me, Chase barked a command to veer left, and so I veered, narrowly avoiding a group of zombies that had shambled out from behind another stand of trees. We'd been running forever. We hadn't been running nearly as long as we needed to. We still weren't safe, and we might never be safe again. 'I do love you. I'd have married you one day, you can be sure of that. I'm not such a fool as to let a girl like you slip through my fingers. I'd have shown you Ireland. It's so green there, you'd think the rest of the world was just imitating the color.'

'Ash. Stop. Don't talk like that.'

'I have to go now, love. Need to focus on the run. You might not want to watch this next bit.'

'Ash—'

'I love you,' I said, and cut the connection, and kept running. I couldn't stop Audrey from watching the feeds that were coming in from our personal cameras and from the hovering drones. She was a big girl. She could make that choice for herself. But I could keep her from hearing me die. My screams would be picked up by the cameras. It wouldn't be the same as being on the phone when it happened.

'Left!' shouted Chase. 'Left, left!'

We all veered left, and there, ahead of us, was a small shedlike structure built into the side of a hill, surrounded by a tiny courtyard shape of fencing and chicken wire. There was room inside for all of us, if only just barely. Hope flooded through me. We might still be all right. If we could get that far, we might not take any more fatalities than we already had.

There were no zombies between us and the courtyard. We ran. There was a blood test on the door to the tunnels, but none on the courtyard itself, which had a solid fence; no zombies would be able to bleed or spit on us once we were inside, and we could go through the test and entry process at whatever pace we needed. I ran inside.

Chase didn't.

'Chase?' I stopped and turned, moving far enough to the left to let the others start squeezing past me. Two more people had stopped – a tall, dark-skinned man in a white tank top, and a thick-waisted, golden-haired woman with names tattooed all around her arms, twisting like snakes. I didn't know either of them by name. I was never going to forget their faces.

'You run like a rabbit, Ash,' said Chase. 'You're going to be amazing. Marry that girl of yours, okay? You deserve a little happiness.' Then he held up his left arm, showing me the long trench that had been gouged out of it. The blood was almost indistinguishable from the mud that covered us all. Only almost. 'I'm signing off.'

'Me, too,' said the woman, and pulled the neck of her shirt aside, showing the hole in her shoulder. It looked like a through-and-through, clean and easy. My confusion must have shown on my face, because she grimaced and said, 'It went through a dead man before it went through me. I'm already getting fuzzy around the edges.'

The man didn't say anything. He just pulled up the left leg of his pants, showing me the tooth marks on his calf.

Three more down. Added to the two we'd lost before we started running, and the two we'd lost *during* the run, and that was seven out of fourteen who hadn't even reached the gate. The seven of us who were left weren't guaranteed to check out clean. Infection was like that. Sometimes it was obvious – teeth against the skin, bullets against the bone – and sometimes it wasn't.

'I'm so sorry,' I said. Then, because it was necessary, and because the zombies were still far enough back to give me the time to be courteous, I asked, 'Do you need bullets?'

'We have them,' said the woman.

'We'll handle it,' said Chase. 'You did good. We got caught flat-footed, and that's on me, but you did good, and half isn't such a big loss, not under the circumstances. Now go do better. I know you can.'

'Chase . . .'

'Shut the gate, Aislinn.' His expression hardened. His pupils were beginning to dilate, but there was still intelligence behind them, and fierce anger. 'Shut the gate, get your people the fuck out of here, and find out what happened. I know you can.'

'I will,' I said, and closed the gate on the three of them. Then I turned, and walked back to the others, and joined the line for the blood testing unit. Someone had done this to us.

Someone was going to pay.

Grace was beautiful in the candlelight, a perfect ivory sculpture of a girl, with hair the color of banked embers and skin like cream. She lay unmoving on her bed, hands folded over her breasts, eyes closed. Her red lashes only made the pallor of her cheeks more obvious; her freckles stood out like they had been drawn on by some careless child, bent only on destroying a priceless work of art. For that was what she was, at least to Li Jiang: a work of art, something unique and irreplaceable.

Li Jiang sat beside her lover's bed, resisting the urge to snatch up Grace's hand and warm it with her own. Their relationship was not a secret among the underworld where they dwelt, but it could still cause them problems when they moved among more respectable circles, and if there was any man who embodied respectability, it was Dr Daniel Keene.

'What's wrong with her?' she asked. 'Why won't she wake up?'

'Your associate has been poisoned,' said Dr Keene. 'The specific toxin is derived from the sap of a rare orchid that grows only in certain climates, and blooms once every twenty years. A single drop is said to be enough to kill the strongest of men. Miss Riley is a stalwart soul, but she is not that strong. I fear it will have already reached her heart, and there is nothing I can do.'

Li Jiang felt as if it were her heart that was in the process of being poisoned, and not her love's. She forced her voice to remain steady. 'For every toxin, there is a counter,' she said. 'Nature does nothing without reason. How can I save her?'

Dr Keene was silent for a moment. 'It will be dangerous,' he said finally.

Li Jiang stood. 'Danger is my only balm,' she said. 'Tell me what to do, and I will do it. Anything. I will do anything, except allow my Grace to die.'

'There is another flower,' he began . . .

—From *Forsake Me, Forgive Me, Don't Forget Me*,
originally published in *Wen the Hurly Burly's Done*,
the blog of Audrey Liqiu Wen, April 15, 2040

Twelve

The convention center's private security staff reached the maintenance tunnels about fifteen minutes after the seven of us made it inside. We could hear the officers coming from where we stood, just past the door. We had already stripped naked, every one of us, checking each other for bites or scratches before pouring bleach over our heads. There was plenty of bleach, at least: Chase had been right about that. Plenty of bleach, plenty of formalin, plenty of bullets. If we'd set up our party closer to the door, we might not have lost anyone at all.

The sound of gunfire announced the arrival of reinforcements. I closed my eyes, the taste of bleach and ashes lingering on my tongue. If they'd been shooting the whole time, there wouldn't have been much left for our backup to dispose of. Nothing but the three doomed Irwins we'd left outside to guard our backs. They'd already been dead when I had closed the gate, even if they'd still been up and alert and talking.

I hoped the zombies hadn't been able to make it this far. I hoped Chase and the others had had a moment – just a moment, because sometimes a moment was everything in the world – to call their loved ones and say they were sorry, that they'd always known it would end like this, but that they'd been hoping it wouldn't end quite so soon. There were always things left unsaid, undone, and I wanted, desperately, for them to have had the time to say at least a few of them.

But they probably hadn't. They'd been Irwins, and every Irwin knew the score. More importantly, every Irwin feared letting their loved ones see them turn. It was why so many of us chose to work solo, or for blog teams that didn't include anyone we really cared about. And then there was me, on a team that included my girlfriend and my husband, both of whom were going to be climbing the walls by now. Sometimes I suspected I wasn't a very nice person.

The door banged open and four people in full riot gear stepped inside. They were holding assault rifles, and those rifles were aimed at us, switching targets with swift efficiency so that even though we technically outnumbered them, there was no chance we'd be able to rush the door before they got multiple shots off. Four more people followed them through, and then we didn't outnumber anyone anymore.

Amber and John came in after the second wave, recognizable by the shapes of their helmets, which were standard-issue among the governor's staff. They were a newer model with a built-in microphone – something Amber promptly put to good use. 'If you have been directly exposed, please move to this side of the tunnel,' she said, her voice echoing effortlessly through the open space as she motioned to the right. 'If you have not been directly exposed, please move to the opposite side. If you are not sure what I mean by "directly exposed," please treat that as exposure, as I have seen your credentials, and there's no way any of you don't know that.'

Nervous laughter followed from most of the Irwins. Five of us moved to the left. Two of us – Jody and her human sniper tower – moved to the right. I shot them a stricken look. Jody shrugged apologetically, spreading her hands in a 'what can you do' gesture.

There were plenty of things she could have done, starting with telling lies. We'd all passed blood tests to get this far, and she wasn't infected – or she hadn't been. She clearly knew something I didn't. She could have touched her clothing since then. She'd definitely touched her face and hair, even if she didn't realize it. There was no amount of training in the world that could kill that hardwired primate instinct. If there had been any blood splatter on her hands or clothing, anything the bleach had missed, she could have tested clean and doomed herself as soon as we got inside.

'Ash? You in here?'

Amber's question caught me by surprise. 'Here, Amber,' I said, raising a hand and waving it for her attention. 'A mite naked at the moment, but it's naught you haven't seen before, I'd assume.'

'I worked for my aunt,' she said, a hint of amusement coming through her amplified voice. 'The human body holds no mysteries for me, even though I sometimes wish it did. Audrey told me to tell you that if you're dead, she's going to murder you.'

'Understood,' I said. One of the officers walked over to me with a blood testing unit. The reason for their number was now clear: There was at least one officer for each remaining Irwin, with a few extra to keep us in their sights. That would allow us all to check out at the same time, and make an exit easier. 'Don't suppose you brought bathrobes or something? My clothes are drenched in mud and bleach, and a bit of vomit, too.'

'Sorry about that,' said the Irwin who'd tossed her cookies – and her share of the barbeque – on the pile of our clothing when the shock hit her.

'Nothing to be sorry for,' I said, and jammed my hand into the blood testing unit. It was a top-of-the-line piece of equipment, designed to get the most intimate and accurate reading possible. Unlike the standard doorway and elevator tests, which only sampled from the base of the thumb, this machine took rolling samples from across the surface of the entire palm, grabbing them from different depths, in case the infection was present and not yet endemic to the system. It only raised the projected accuracy of the test from 99.2% to 99.9%, but that 0.7% increase was worth hundreds of dollars per unit, and millions of dollars in annual revenue. There would never be a test with 100% accuracy. The human body was too complex of a machine, and its changes happened too quickly for any handheld unit to measure.

The needles bit into my palm. I grimaced. For every prick I felt there were another five I didn't, hairline samplers slipping between the cracks in my skin and taking what they wanted from my cells. The whole unit could have been painless, and I'd heard rumors that some units for the ultrarich actually *were*. Supposedly some of them were like acupuncture, making the body feel better, soothing away aches and pains and oh, hey, confirming that the person being tested wasn't a zombie at the same time.

There were no lights on the testing unit. I blinked at it for a moment, bewildered, before lifting my eyes to the mirror-fronted helmet of the officer in front of me. I couldn't tell whether they were male or female, and it didn't matter: They were an impassive representative of the law. If I failed this test, I was never going to take another one.

'Sir, would you like to step outside?' The gender was wrong, but for a single terrible second, I thought the question had come from my guard. It hadn't: It had come from the guard next to me, who was looking at a sad-eyed Irwin who'd confessed, during the barbeque, that he had traveled all the way from Calgary to be at the convention. He'd seemed so happy then, so vital and alive. Now he just looked tired, like something was sapping his life away one drop at a time, leaving an empty shell behind. That wasn't far from the truth.

He looked at the guard and said, 'There were no lights. How do I know what the test said if there were no lights?'

'How do you know what the test said when there were lights?' asked the guard. 'They're a psychological crutch. Their presence changes nothing.'

'There were no lights,' insisted the man doggedly.

I was close enough that I'd be hit by the splatter if they shot him where he stood. To make it this far and then die like that wouldn't just be silly: It would be *stupid*, and wasteful. 'Doesn't anyone have a testing unit with lights on it?' I asked. 'Give the man a little peace of mind before you do whatever's to be done.'

'False positives happen,' chimed another Irwin. 'If he wants a second test, give him a second test.'

I didn't think they were going to go for it. They had all the power, and all the weapons; we didn't even have clothes. But we had press passes, and we had cameras that were still running, even if they were piled in a heap, awaiting decontamination. The officer turned, motioning toward one of the people who were providing cover. The second officer reached into their pocket, produced a more common testing unit, and lobbed it over.

Silently, the officer broke the seal on the unit and offered it to the Irwin who'd asked for it. He pressed his thumb down on the pad. Lights sprang into life atop the unit, flashing red green, red yellow, red red red, and finally settling on a steady, bloody glow.

The Irwin closed his eyes. 'Damn,' he said, in a small voice. When he opened them again he was smiling wryly. 'That's the trouble with Alabama, I guess. I thought it was mud when it hit my cheek. I guess it wasn't. I'll go outside now, if you'll let me.'

'I'll escort you,' said the officer. Her voice was female, and her tone was almost sympathetic.

The other officers stood aside as she walked him to the open door and then out, into the courtyard. The door swung shut behind them. There was a momentary silence. Then three gunshots rang out, only slightly muffled by the closed door.

'And then there were six,' said Jody's living sniper tower.

I looked toward him. 'You're Eric, aren't you?'

'I'm surprised you remembered,' he said. 'Nice to meet you.'

'Think we've met before.'

'I'd remember,' he said.

'You're all clean,' said Amber. To illustrate her point, she reached up and removed her helmet. John did the same. The other security officers did not. I wasn't sure whether that made our people brave or stupid. Amber continued, 'Your clothing will need to be destroyed, but replacements will be provided.'

'What about our equipment?' asked a woman.

'If it can be sterilized, it will be. If it can't be sterilized, hopefully your insurance will cover replacement costs. I hate to be the one to say this, but the convention center wants me to remind you all that you signed waivers before going outside, and they are not liable for any damage to yourself or your possessions.' Amber grimaced. 'They were shouting the legalese after me as I was running for the door to save your bacon, so I'm pretty sure they mean it.'

'Who's handling the exterior cleanup?' I asked abruptly. Everyone turned to look at me, some of them disbelieving, others amused. I shook my head. 'I'm not volunteering, and I'm not looking to cover myself with glory, or with anything else. I want a hot shower and a big glass of whiskey right about now. But those zombies were fresh, and there were *buckets* of them. You don't get mobs like that without an attack, and we'd have heard if there'd been something this close to the convention center. Especially right now, with half the eyes of the country locked on the place.'

'You think this was another setup,' said Amber, slow realization dawning ugly on her face.

I nodded. 'I do. Some of those folks looked like they were wearing name tags. Might make it easy on us, when it comes to finding out where they all came from. Maybe one of the delegations lost a bus and didn't bother to tell us.'

John and Amber exchanged a look. 'I'll see what we can do,' said John. He didn't sound very confident, and that was fine by me, because I didn't actually expect him to accomplish anything.

The Kellis-Amberlee virus switches from its passive helper state to its destructive active state as soon as the blood it lives in leaves the body. Most people are resistant to the virus in their own blood, hence children not amplifying over bloody noses and women not amplifying over menstruation; if it were easy for us to trigger amplification in ourselves, the human race would've ended the first time a woman who'd been exposed to the virus gave birth. We're all infected, sure, but the virus was man-made, and a small handful of the safeguards designed in the original labs are still in place. Thank God for that.

The trouble was, no one is that resistant to anyone *else*. Even identical twins react to the antibodies formed by each other's blood. Every one of those bodies out in the woods represented a huge risk to anyone who tried to study them. A single drop of their blood could spell the end of everything. That's why forensic science, which was huge before the Rising – big enough to be the basis of several long-running television franchises – is all but defunct today. No one wants to handle the dead. Fire and bleach are the solutions, not mass spectrometers and careful slides.

Someone had set those zombies on us. I was sure of it, all the way down to my bones. Things like that didn't just happen, especially not to large groups of trained and heavily armed Irwins. Someone had been trying to throw the convention into disarray, maybe give it a nice framing tragedy to keep attention on the body count and away from whatever it was that was really going on behind the scenes. Whoever it was wasn't going to want anyone getting a better look at the bodies. If I played it up like we *needed* a closer look to learn anything at all, maybe they wouldn't think to ask themselves about all that footage we'd been taking while we were running through the woods.

Our team's drone-mounted cameras were good at picking up and magnifying small details. I knew my personal cameras had been running and uploading the whole time. There was plenty of data, as long as no one thought to seek out and destroy it all before I had finished decontamination and rejoined my team.

'Now that the six of you have been checked out, if you'd please proceed along the tunnel to the first door,' said Amber, clapping her hands together. 'A decontamination suite is on the other side, and there are enough shower stalls for all of you.'

'Our equipment?' I asked.

'As I said, it will be decontaminated and delivered to you, if possible. If something is unmarked, it will be given to the convention center office. You should be able to pick it up in about six hours.'

'All my footage had better be present and unaltered, or you'll be talking to my lawyer,' said Jody, suddenly sweet as pie and smiling brightly. 'I did read the full contract with the convention center, and it said nothing about erasing or deleting footage. That's a solid-state Samsung wrist-mounted recorder. It can stand decontamination procedures up to and including those required to exit an L5 lab. There's nothing that should be done to it here that would compromise the footage, so if something does, I'll know it was intentional. All clear?'

'Are all Irwins this prickly, or is it just your friends, Ash?' asked Amber.

'It's all of us,' I said. 'Answer her question.'

'Whee,' said Amber, deadpan. 'Yes, ma'am, we're all clear, and believe me, I have no intention of altering anyone's footage. Also, I'm not the one in charge of the equipment decontamination, so while it's swell that you're making yourself clear, you're not doing yourself any good by being clear to *me*. Thankfully, I'm also not the person you'd be suing, so I don't feel too terribly worried. If you'd all move, *please*, we can get this show on the road, and we can get you back in decent clothes before your teammates beat down the doors demanding to know what's going on.'

The names of the dead would already have been released, of course; there was no reason to keep those quiet, since once someone amplified, they no longer had any right to either privacy or fair treatment under the law. Zombies weren't human anymore: They were less than corpses, afforded none of the protections once reserved against desecration of the dead. We all knew that. We also knew that our friends, teammates, and loved ones would be clawing at the walls for information, since we weren't transmitting anymore, and our names were not yet listed on the roll call of the dead. We moved.

I kept my steps slow and measured, avoiding the front of the pack, and gradually worked my way toward the back. When I reached the rear I matched pace with the man just in front of me, and said, in a conversational tone, 'How much trouble do you reckon I'm in right about now?'

'I don't know,' said Amber. 'What's your scale?'

'Oh, mild shouting all the way up to divorce and deportation.'

'Can you be deported now that you're a citizen?'

'I'm sure Ben could find a way to have me booted from the country, if he was mad enough. Might involve claiming we were never married in the first place, I suppose.' Which technically, we hadn't been. Despite efforts by the asexual and aromantic communities to have the 'consummation' requirements removed from the definition of marriage in most states, there were still a lot of places where never having had sex could be taken as grounds for an annulment. I loved Ben like a brother. I'd never gone to his bed, and I was never intending to. Our relationship wasn't like that.

'Then you're somewhere in the middle,' said Amber. 'Everyone's intending to yell at you, no one's planning to have you kicked out of the country, at least so far as I know. I've been wrong before.'

'Very reassuring, thanks,' I said.

'Oh, I'm part of the "everyone,"' said Amber cheerfully. 'I should be slamming back mimosas and cheering for my continued employment right about now, not watching your freckled ass march toward the showers.'

'Which we are also required to take,' said John. 'Since we had to go through the same biohazardous wasteland as the rest of you in order to rescue you from the zombie menace. I was looking forward to a day *without* bleach.'

'A day without bleach is like a summer without sunshine,' I said.

One of the other Irwins looked back over his shoulder, laughing. 'Amen to that.'

We were still laughing when we reached the end of the maintenance tunnel. Plastic sheeting had been spread across the space, sliced into dangling ribbons to allow us all to pass. Three more guards in hazmat suits waited there, each holding a clipboard. They were calling names and forming us into lines, positioning us in front of the openings that would presumably lead to decontamination. There didn't seem to be any effort to separate us by gender or genitalia, which was nice: It was always good to have decontamination parties that didn't induce dysphoria in the guests.

I wound up in a line with both Jody and Amber, while John and the human sniper platform were in the next line over. I looked at Amber and grimaced, saying, 'Joking aside, I'm sorry about the decontamination. And the mimosas. I could do with a good strong drink right about now.'

'Alcohol later, decontamination now,' said Amber, and passed through the dangling plastic ribbons. I followed her.

I'd been expecting a standard field decon setup – a chemical shower, a bunch of bleach, maybe some scowling men with guns to make sure we stayed behind the lines until we'd sloughed off the top three layers of our skin. There was a fine line between 'clean enough for the people who set the safety standards' and 'so clean that your skin began weeping blood,' which would take you back over the line into biohazardous. Most of us had been experts at walking that line long before we got our licenses.

Instead, we were walking into what looked like the most luxurious gym bathroom I'd ever seen. Individual Isolette stalls studded the wall; two of them were already engaged, the lights above them burning a pleasant blue to indicate that they were unavailable. A pile of fluffy towels wrapped in plastic waited at the center of the room, along with an assortment of scent tabs. There was even a smiling attendant, dressed entirely in white, her hair bleached to a brittle platinum that looked like it would snap off at the lightest of touches. She held up a towel, offering it to me as Amber moved off to one side and began to strip, dropping each piece of her armor into the waiting bins.

'Hello, and welcome to the Huntsville Convention Center,' said the attendant. 'We're so very sorry that you've been exposed to a bio-hazard. Please, pick your preferred scent profile and drop the tab into your shower as you enter. Your shampoo and body wash selections will be set to match.'

'That's right kind of you,' I said bemusedly, taking a towel. The plastic crinkled under my fingers. I wondered whether there was a way to come back through here with a camera running. This was one of the more surreal things I'd encountered in the process of decon-tamination. 'D'you have something in the fresh grass or clean cotton families?'

'Oh, yes, absolutely,' said the attendant, and positively beamed. Apparently, asking her for additional help was a good thing. 'Select the all-white tablet for clean cotton. Select the green tablet with white spots for fresh grass and sunlight. Either will provide you with a pleasant, immersive cleaning experience that should wash away any unpleasant memories.'

I hesitated in the act of reaching for a green tablet, giving her a wary, narrow-eyed look. 'There aren't drugs in these, are there? I've got work to do, and I've no interest in being given temporary amnesia by a shampoo bowl.'

The attendant's smile didn't waver. 'Psychotropic drugs in shower products are extremely complicated, and can be delivered via spray only. They must be approved ahead of time by the event which you are attending. Currently, we have been cleared for THC and mild anx-iolytics only. Neither is present in the tablets you have requested.' She might be smiling, but the skin around her eyes was tight, betraying her discomfort. She didn't like being this close to me when I'd just come from a hazard zone. She'd been watching me and just me since I approached her. I could still see the tiny movements in the muscles of her eyes as she struggled *not* to look at Amber, who was also in the room, and hence potentially also a danger.

Tormenting the minimum-wage employees is never fair, no matter how cranky I might be feeling. 'Fresh grass is fine, then,' I said, grabbing one of the green tabs. 'Thanks for all your help.'

'Service is a delight,' she said. 'Thank you for your patronage.' Her smile was starting to look frayed around the edges. I headed for the nearest shower stall, dropping my green tab into the slot outside. The door opened, and I stepped inside.

The shower stall was small and pristine. A chute was open on one wall, waiting for my towel, which had apparently been intended only to cover my nakedness until I got inside. That made sense: The point of this shower was to boil the possible infection off of me. Letting me rub a towel I had touched before I was properly clean all over my body wasn't going to help with that process. I dropped the towel inside. A metal door slammed down with so much force that it would probably have taken off a finger if I had tried to put my hand inside. I jumped.

The shower lights came on. 'Welcome, attendee,' said the pleasant voice of the bathroom. It sounded just like the attendant outside. I was suddenly very, *very* glad that I had been watching her eyes closely enough to see her twitching. I didn't need to be spinning myself horror stories about robot civil servants, thanks terribly.

'Hello, shower,' I said.

'I have accessed your medical records, and have determined your ideal temperature range. Do you have any injuries I should be aware of?'

Not on the outside. I was one of the lucky ones: I'd run through hell and come out without so much as a scratch. I'd be hearing the screams for weeks, echoing in my ears every time I let my focus drift, but my body was in fine condition. 'No,' I said.

'Excellent,' said the shower. 'Commencing cleansing cycle.'

The water came on, pouring not just from the showerhead in front of me, which would have been too mundane, and offered too much chance that part of me could go undrenched. Instead, it came from the entire ceiling, crashing down like the wrath of an angry god and soaking me through in an instant. I squeaked, too surprised to do anything else. That was when the water rose up from the floor, hitting my undercarriage with just as much force, and I full-out shrieked. My ego was salved a bit when an answering shriek came from the next stall over. Amber had also met the incredible wall of water.

The floor stopped shooting high-powered jets at me after only a few seconds, and the voice said pleasantly, 'Bleach cycle beginning in five seconds. Please close your eyes and mouth. Please stand with your legs together. Please understand that the management is not responsible for any damage to your person caused by failure to heed these instructions. Please try not to breathe.'

The announcement ended just as the water from above was replaced by a dilute bleach solution – not dilute enough for my tastes, since studies had shown that most commercial bleach balances included substantially more bleach than was needed, and the stuff was murder on my hair. We'd all be blond if the people who set the safety standards had anything to say about it, and then bald shortly after. The folks who'd bleached every last hair off of our heads would just shrug and open a wig factory if we complained. It was about profit margins as much as it was about safety, and *oh*, how the money rolled in.

I kept my mouth shut tight and my eyes shut tighter, counting down the seconds until the bleach was replaced with a citrus-scented rain that stung when it hit my skin, but would help to counteract the damage. There would be lotion on the other side of the shower to offer more intensive repair. Every Irwin I'd ever met had been soft and supple, and smelled faintly of lemons.

'Beginning bathing cycle,' said the shower. The ceiling switched off. The showerhead switched on. I opened my eyes to see three pumps extrude from the wall, helpfully labeled 'shampoo,' 'conditioner,' and 'body wash.' A washcloth was hanging from the body wash handle. It was small, and white, and very, very new. It would probably be burnt after I used it. That was the way of the world: as disposable as possible, because only the very newest things were guaranteed to be as clean as people wanted them to be. You could boil a stone forever, and never get it all the way back to the condition it was in when it began.

Maybe that was a sign we needed to stop trying. Sadly, for a lot of folks, it was just a sign that we needed to find a way to make new stones.

The water ran long enough for me to shampoo and condition my hair and give myself a good once-over with the body wash, which smelled, true to the attendant's word, of fresh grass and sunshine. It was a bit odd, really. When I was done, I dropped the washcloth on the shower floor, and the water stopped.

'We hope you have enjoyed your bathing experience, and we hope you will enjoy your time here at the Huntsville Convention Center,' said the shower pleasantly. There was a click. The back wall swung open, revealing the locker room on the other side. Several of my fellow Irwins were already there, toweling off before slipping into the bath-robes that had been provided.

'Sometimes the world is damn weird,' I said philosophically, and stepped out of the shower. The door swung shut behind me, all but disappearing into the wall.

'Amen to that,' said Jody. She was already wearing her bathrobe. It was too big for her, and she vanished into it like a child. 'Heard your candidate got the nod. Good for you.'

There was something almost indecent about standing here having this conversation when we'd just lost eight people. I nodded slowly. 'Yeah.'

'I'm glad mine didn't.' She looked at me calmly. 'I know you're going to be looking to expand, and that's great, that's good; you're going to need the extra bodies. But don't ask me, and don't ask Eric. We're going home. This has been more than enough adventure for me.'

'Why do you—'

'You know damn well that what happened today wasn't a coincidence, and it wasn't the first time, either. We had two "accidents" while Senator Blackburn was on the campaign trail, and both of them had totally credible explanations, and both of those explanations were total bullshit.'

That was the first I'd heard of this. I tried not to stare.

'Someone tried to kill us then, and someone tried to kill us *all* today,' continued Jody. Her expression was grim. The other Irwins in the locker room were nodding without saying anything. There really wasn't anything that needed to be said. 'This is too dangerous, even for me. It should be too dangerous for you, too. Get out while you can, Ash. You're a good Irwin. You deserve better than the kind of death that turns you into a footnote in someone else's story.'

I wanted to argue with her. I wanted to tell her she was wrong; that no matter how bad things were, they would never be as bad as *that*. I couldn't stop thinking about the eight Irwins who'd died outside the convention center. Six of them . . . I hadn't even known their names. The only one who'd been my friend was Chase; the only one to be elevated above the rank of spear carrier was Karl, and that was just because I'd hated him. The rest really *were* footnotes, at least for now, and even learning their names wasn't going to change that. She was right. She was so very right, and I should have been following her advice – I should have been turning and running for the hills, just as fast as my legs would carry me.

And I couldn't. Ben was committed, Mat was having the time of their life, and Audrey was loyal, and I couldn't leave them, or ask them to leave with me. No matter how much I might want to get the hell out of here, none of them would ever agree to go if even a single one of us was staying behind. That was good. That was as it should be. But that meant my hands were tied.

'Aw, it's not so bad as all that,' I said, trying for a smile that held the right balance of cockiness and regret. I didn't want to look too happy, not with the bodies still warm outside, but I didn't want to show how afraid I really was. 'Maybe the trail had a few bumps and batters, but we're moving up now. Lots of controlled situations and televised debates, less wandering the countryside hoping for a miracle. I'm sure I'll be bored half to death before the election.'

Jody looked at me. Then she smiled a little. There was no balance in her expression: It was pure sorrow, from top to bottom, with no room for anything else. 'I understand,' she said. 'I'd stay too, if I had people I cared that much about who didn't want to go. Just be careful if you can, and save yourself if you have to.'

'Didn't you know?' I opened the nearest locker, pulling out the towel that hung inside, and started drying myself off. 'I'm the last thing I'd ever want to save. I'll get them all out, and then I'll watch it all burn.'

'Then maybe you should start figuring out how to save them before you burn,' she said, and turned and walked away. There was a man at the door, holding a blood testing unit. As I watched, she slapped her hand down on it and, when he nodded, walked past him, out of this sterile, bleach-scented underworld, and back into the lands of the living.

'I smell like a cotton candy factory,' complained Amber, stepping up next to me and opening another locker. 'I thought the pink ones were strawberry, not an ocean of sugar.'

'You'll know better for next time.' I wrapped my hair in the towel, wringing out as much of the excess water as I could. 'Thanks for coming to get us. I know you didn't have to.'

'Are you kidding? I've met your girlfriend. She's a throat-puncher. Looks sweet as anything, talks about painting and urban cycling and the importance of composting, and then she's putting a fist right into your trachea and watching you writhe. It's John you should be thanking. He wanted to stay with the governor.' Amber's hair was shorter than mine, and only took a quick blitz with the towel to be effectively dry. 'I basically dragged him out the door to pull your ass out of the field, and you owe that man a drink.'

'Noted.' The bathrobe provided for my use was soft and plush, and came with matching slippers. I stepped into them gratefully before slipping the robe on and tying it securely around my waist. 'What do I owe you?'

Amber lowered her towel and looked at me, a moment of rare gravity settling over her face. 'Something's really wrong,' she said. 'You know it. I know it. I'm pretty sure your colleagues know it. Find out what it is, okay? I'd like to know that my aunt is safe, and that we're not all going to die out here.'

'I'll try,' I said, and started toward the exit.

The man at the door offered me a blood testing unit. I pressed my palm against the sensor, and was almost relieved to feel the needles biting in. They represented a return to normalcy; they told me I was still a person who could feel and understand pain.

The light flashed green. The door behind him opened, revealing the convention center hallway. Audrey, Ben, and Mat were all there. Ben and Mat were sitting in hard plastic chairs that matched the ones from the Oregon first aid station. Some things are found everywhere. Audrey was leaning up against the wall, head bowed, hair hanging to cover her eyes. None of them had reacted to the door opening. They hadn't seen me yet.

I squared my shoulders, lifted my chin, and stepped out to meet the reckoning.

Book III

Blank Spaces, Blank Faces

Everything is transitory. Even continents die. The question is how much you can accomplish with the time that you have. The question is whether it can ever be enough.

—MAT NEWSON

It's never going to be enough.

—AISLINN 'ASH' NORTH

All right, we're going to start today's look with a neutral white base. No sparkles, no glitter: We're aiming for the color of bleached bone here. Hit your whole eyelid. Extend beneath. If you follow my fingers, you'll see that I'm blending as I apply; that will keep the white from seeming unnatural against your foundation. If you didn't use any foundation, that's all right, this will still thin and smooth the edges.

Now, take your medium brush and use it to evenly apply the pale ash gray shadow to your entire lid. Make sure you don't build up too heavily in any one area, because we're going to be accenting the whole shape of the eye. Take your accent brush, and apply the darker gray to the crease of your eyelid, following the shape of your orbital socket. See how that makes the whole eye pop? This is a great way to draw attention to your look, without getting so overly dramatic that people write you off as a kook.

Once you have the edges of your eye cleanly delineated, go ahead and take your eyeliner. Now, I'm using Urban Decay Blood and Roses, from their liquid liner range, but any good liquid eyeliner is going to work for what we're trying to accomplish. For your top lid, you want a very clean, bold line. Take your time. If you need to use your spoon to guide the brush, there's no shame in that. We do what we need to in order to make ourselves look our best.

Once you have the top lid done, go ahead and draw in your bottom line with one swipe. You want it to be a little jagged, a little drippy. Make it look like you're bleeding. Make it look like you might amplify at any moment and cut those bastards for what they've done. What they've allowed people to do under their watch. What they have willfully ignored. Draw your rebellion on in glitter blood and war paint, and you dare the world to say that you have done anything wrong. You *dare* it.

This look is called the Democratic National Convention. Suitable for day, night, or burning the bastards down.

—From *Non-Binary Thinking*, the blog of Mat Newson,
April 17, 2040

Thirteen

I learned the names of all the Irwins who'd died in the woods behind the Huntsville convention center. There were only eight of them, after all; it wasn't like I was being asked to memorize the phone book. And at the same time, eight was the largest number I had ever confronted. Eight felt like the population of the entire world.

Chase Hoffman, one of the best-known Irwins in Alabama, whose favorite stunt had involved setting up a barbeque in the middle of a hazard zone and preparing turkey burgers while gunning down the walking dead. Marguerite Gates, who'd made it all the way to the gates before stepping back, and whose daughters were both Irwins in their own right, working on the East Coast and mourning their mother with every passing second. David Tilman, who had also made it to the gates, and whose series on animal rescue and the importance of conservation was replaying on half the animal-rights blogs now that he was gone. He could have used the spike in viewership more when he was alive. We never got what we needed when we were still around to put it to proper use.

The kid with the polearm was named George – George Lyman. He'd had his license for just under six months. The girl who'd been pulled down while we were running was Alyson, with a 'y,' no last name attached to any of her reports. She'd mostly done local color pieces. Hannah Woodyard was a political bloodhound who had been considering switching sides to the Newsies. Hal Peters — who almost made it to safety — was a botanical reporter who liked to go out into hazard zones looking for rare flowers and making sure people knew that nature was still out there, still going and still growing, even if we no longer liked to think about it the way that we used to.

Karl Conway, who'd been a bastard and a bully, yet had still deserved better. They'd all deserved better. It was hard to even settle on a tense when I was thinking about them. They were dead, past tense, gone forever, and yet I was watching many of their reports for the first time, introducing myself to the parts of them that had mattered most and had put the strongest stamp upon the world. They were being created anew for me with every link I clicked and essay I devoured, and I couldn't think of them as gone. Not when I was reading their reports.

Reading was about the only thing that took my mind off things. Audrey wasn't speaking to me except when she had to. I'd scared the crap out of her when I went and got myself pursued through the Alabama woods by an army of the dead. Worse, I'd hung up on her when my life was in danger, and worst of all — most damning of all — I'd refused to put myself before the people I was with. I hadn't been willing to climb a damn tree, even if it could have meant saving myself, because it would have meant leaving them in more danger. My reasons had been good. That didn't matter, not really. In all the time we'd been together, I'd never come that close to dying, not even in the rose garden. Before Alabama, on some level, it had been possible to pretend that I was invincible. That couldn't happen anymore.

While I couldn't fully blame her for pulling away, I felt her absence in everything I did. Every morning I woke up hoping that this would be the day when she forgave me. It hadn't happened yet.

Being crammed into a single RV while we followed the governor across the country wasn't helping. Audrey had been finding any excuse she could to ride in the security convoy, leaving me, Mat, and Ben alone with our thoughts – and our security observer, since the governor no longer liked to leave us alone, given the way I kept blundering into trouble. It was understandable, even if having John riding with us meant that we needed to sleep in shifts. I didn't mind sharing a small sleeping area with Ben. It was purely platonic, and if we occasionally dropped into an already-occupied bunk, well. That had happened before when we were on the road. John was another matter. He was a nice enough fellow, but the last thing I wanted was to wake up and learn that I'd become the little spoon for a man twice my size, who I barely knew outside of work.

Mat had been taking solace in driving. Out of the four of us, they were the only one who really understood or cared about cars. I drove because I had to; Ben drove because he had been taking care of his mother for the last several years of her life, and it was easier to get her to her doctor's appointments when he had a car. Audrey avoided driving whenever she could. But Mat . . .

Mat understood what the little clicking noises a cooling engine made could mean, and how to track them to their source. Mat knew how to rebuild a transmission and improve an engine. Without Mat, we would all have been driving electric cars, because none of us had the patience for hybrid engines, no matter how much more economically sound they were. Mat didn't mind being our live-in mechanic; in fact, they were thrilled by the excuse to work on so many different vehicles.

'Look,' they'd explained to me once, wiping grease off their hands, 'everyone looks at the fact that I do makeup tutorials and goes "ah, she's secretly a girl." And then they look at the fact that I love to tinker with cars, and they go "oh, he's secretly a boy." Really, I'm just a person with diverse interests, like everybody else on the planet.'

Mat was happy, the rest of us were happy, and best of all, no one else had to do any of the driving unless they really, really wanted to.

Ben had unfolded the breakfast table from the wall while I slept. We were seated at opposite sides, him tapping away at his latest report, me playing back muted footage of the attacks. I'd been reviewing it for the last week, playing it alongside video reports by the Irwins who'd died there. It looked like I was wallowing. I knew that perfectly well, even as I knew that I didn't have a choice in the matter. I had to know. I had to see.

I had seen. Finally, after days upon days of searching, I had seen. 'Ben, on a scale of sterile environment to that motel in Dublin with the bedbugs, how buggy would you say this vehicle is?' I asked pleasantly.

'Mat swept it last night, and I swept it this morning,' he said, glancing up from his computer. 'There shouldn't be any bugs that don't have six legs and wings. Why?'

'Because I found it. Slave me a window?'

'Hang on.' Ben tapped his keyboard. A blank window popped up on my screen, and I dragged the video I'd been watching into it. Ben frowned at his screen. 'What am I looking at?'

'The zombies that attacked us in the woods? Some of them were wearing name tags. None of us managed to capture any full names, just fragments.' It turned out that running headlong through the woods to avoid being eaten didn't exactly line up perfect shots every time. Maybe there were hackers out there who could have digitally enhanced our footage until it was clearer than reality, but we didn't have one of those. We had Mat, who'd been able to run a few simulations and confirm that there'd been two separate mobs, introduced into the woods at two distinct points – neither of which was remote enough to have been an accident. We had a bunch of different camera angles, which made facial reconstruction possible, even when reading their name tags wasn't. And I had a whole lot of stubborn, all of which had been turned upon my latest project.

Eight dead Irwins. An unknown number of dead bystanders. This wasn't the sort of thing that I could just walk away from. It never had been.

'I'm aware,' said Ben. He didn't sound angry, just confused. Out of everyone on our team, Ben was the one who'd known me longest, and was the most aware that I was always going to be what I was: the sort of person who walked, open-eyed, into danger. Maybe this had been an ambush, but if I had been outside the attack zone, I would have been the first to run toward the sound of screams. 'What's your point?'

'I just sent you a video Jody took of a Blackburn rally she and her team attended.' Blackburn was in fact Kilburn's choice for Vice President: The two of them formed the first all-female team from a major political party to make a run for the presidency. People were already saying they didn't have a chance, and Chuck was having a field day coming up with fire-related campaign slogans based around the word 'burn.' Fire was cleansing, after all. There were worse images for a post-zombie campaign to build on.

'It's on my screen,' he said. 'What am I looking at?'

He sounded so matter-of-fact that I wanted to throw my arms around him and hug him until he couldn't breathe. No matter what else was going on in the world, I could always count on Ben to look at the facts of the situation before he made up his mind. 'Third row back from the camera, see the woman in the bright orange blazer? Bad perm, looks like she's wearing one of Mat's eye shadow designs?'

'Got her.'

'Now look at this.' I dragged and dropped another video, splicing it into the space next to the first. 'Blazer's gone, but she's got the same makeup on, see? It's just smudged. She must have used the stuff that doesn't come off unless you use paint thinner on your face.'

Ben's eyes widened in slow horror. 'This is the same woman.'

'Not just her. I've identified almost all the zombies from the first mob as being part of that rally – sixteen total, which means some of the others probably were as well. It was held three days before the convention. One of their buses never reported back. I think someone hijacked and infected them, then released them out into the woods. Look at the zombies. It took me a while to see it, because I wasn't look-ing right. You see a zombie and that's it, it's a zombie, it's a problem but it's not a person, yeah? You're not trying to figure out their story. You already *know* their story.'

'Ash, I don't understand what you're getting at.'

'None of them are missing any pieces,' I said. 'Look at their arms and throats and faces. Those are the spots most often bitten during initial attacks, but none of these people have been bitten. We have some scratches and bruises, which are consistent with infected individuals being held in an enclosed space. They're also consistent with roaming around in the woods. There's one male with a piece missing from his shoulder, but it looks like a feeding bite – they didn't have enough to eat, so a stronger zombie took a chunk out of him. There's no defensive tearing. He didn't fight back, because he was already dead when that happened. There is no visible reason for these people to have become infected. I'll give you one heart attack victim in a group that size. Sixteen? No. That strains credulity.'

'What about the other zombies?' asked Ben.

'You mean mob number two? Dropping you another video.' I dragged, released, and said, 'Chase took this one. It's a political protest about fracking in Athens-Limestone County. Seems some people want to see what they can get out of the ground, but doing so would destroy the last community pumpkin patch in Alabama. They take their Halloweens very seriously there, hence the declaration of a *gourd farm* as a historical landmark, which allows them to operate it independent of the public health and safety laws that shut all the other pumpkin patches down. They still trick-or-treat in Athens. It's a major tourist destination, because it's the last "all-American Halloween experience" in the country. Again, look at their faces, and then compare them to this video footage of mob number two.'

I dropped the file into the window. I waited. Ben stared, first at his screen and then at me.

'Same situation?'

'You mean the lack of obvious infection points? Yeah. And again, the protest was held a few days before the convention, and a bus full of protestors disappeared on the way back to the lot where they'd stowed their cars.' I shook my head. 'Local police were looking, but not very hard. They had the whole Democratic National Convention rolling into town. They had bigger things to worry about, things that would mean tax dollars and tourism and positive media attention for their city. Some people who didn't know how to read a map barely rated a search party.'

'So you're saying two busloads of people were abducted, infected, held for at least two days, and then released into the woods to spoil your party. Aislinn, I know you're upset about what happened, and I know all this business with Audrey is making you tense, but don't you think you might be stretching a bit?' Ben frowned. 'I absolutely buy that these attacks are a setup, but this one would require way too much work to put together.'

'They buried the dead in Portland, and left them for us to find,' I said doggedly. 'They spiked the pancake makeup at Wagman's fund-raiser, and when I was talking to Jody – one of Blackburn's Irwins – after the attack, she mentioned that they'd had trouble, too. Something's going *on*, Ben. Something bad. This isn't me being paranoid, although if I were going to start, I might point out that several of these attacks have focused on taking out the candidate's media team as well as the candidate. Social media and Internet news are not friends of people who want things to stay hidden. We never have been. If I were trying to kill someone without getting caught, I'd absolutely focus on killing the people standing nearby with cameras. It would be the only way to have half a prayer of keeping things secret.'

'You're connecting several attacks with no obvious common threads,' said Ben.

'Senator Ryman's family farm was the site of an outbreak as he was accepting the nomination to run for his party,' I said. 'Governor Kilburn doesn't have any family to go after. There's nothing to use to make her sympathetic the way that losing a daughter makes him sympathetic. But killing a bunch of Irwins outside? Especially when

I'm there, and I have a track record that involves scrambling fast responses to bad situations? The attack *makes her look good*. Either she loses a member of her team, or that team member scrambles a response that gets people out alive. It's win-win for public approval.'

'She was genuinely upset when she heard what was going on, Ash. Surely you're not implying—'

I put up a hand to cut him off. 'No, I'm not. She doesn't know what's happening any more than the rest of us do. But I think someone is using a lot of different tactics to get the same end result: a candidate who looks sympathetic, like they've been personally touched by Kellis-Amberlee and will understand the woes and fears of the American people. Whoever it is either can't or won't fix the election, so they're tinkering on both sides. That's why all the viable candidates have been attacked at least once, even if no one's connecting the dots. Zombie outbreaks are still too common for people to see this as the hazard that it is.'

'York wasn't attacked,' said Ben.

'I'm a more viable candidate than York, and I can't legally run,' I said. 'The man never left his house. Not once during the whole process. It was always a grandstand for him, and he was never going to get the nomination. No, the focus was on the candidates who mattered.'

'We don't know whether there was an attack on Tate, either,' insisted Ben.

'Wagman had a better shot at the nomination than Tate did,' I said. 'People want to make it out like it was always going to be either Tate or Ryman, but that's not what the polling data says. You know that, and if you *don't*, it's because you bought into the whole "Wagman's a self-obsessed whore" narrative that some of your colleagues were trying to sell. I thought better of you than that. I thought you liked looking at the *facts*.'

'I have been looking at the facts!' protested Ben, cheeks darkening with embarrassment. 'There is some really strong evidence that Wagman plays on her sexuality for power, like say, showing up for work wearing nothing but frilly lace and a smile. If it's not all right for men to do it, then it's not all right for women to do it.'

'It's not right for anyone to be forced to weaponize sexuality, or to take choices away from someone else, but are you seriously going to sit there and tell me that by keeping the promises she made when she was elected, Wagman made herself *less* trustworthy as a politician?' I shook my head. 'This isn't about feminism or the men's rights movement or anything else like that. This is about the fact that she said "if you elect me, I will do this," and when they elected her, she did it. How many politicians can you say that about? Her poll numbers were always good, because even the people who hated what she stood for knew she'd do what she promised. The Republican race was Wagman or Ryman, with Tate in a close third, just like the Democratic race was Kilburn or Blackburn. Honestly, I'd be happier if Ryman had tapped Wagman as his VP. At least then we might not be getting an isolationist zealot that close to the Oval Office.'

I glared at Ben. Ben glared back. Then, to my surprise and relief, he laughed.

'I've missed fighting with you,' he said, turning his attention back to his screen. 'You've been so wrapped up with looking through all this footage that you've barely spoken to me in days. Good job, by the way. You might have a future in Factual News.'

'If I had anything to throw at you right now, I would throw it,' I said gravely. 'Please assume that you're under siege from a barrage of flying objects even as we speak.'

'Ouch, ouch, please stop,' he deadpanned. Then he sobered. 'To recap, you're saying that attacks on all four of the major candidates were staged to make them more relatable to the American people. That implies that someone, somewhere, doesn't care *who* winds up being elected; they just care about how that person will be regarded, and whether that person will be sympathetic toward the infected.'

'It's sort of hard to stay a "soft on zombies" politician after they've tried to chew your face off a time or two,' I said. 'Even people who started out saying that they'd like to improve conditions in the research facilities, and increase the size of the fenced-off hazard areas, well. A change in that attitude makes plenty of sense after the dead have tried to get a chunk or two out of them, yeah?'

'Yeah,' said Ben. 'Have you shared this data with anyone?'

'Not yet,' I said. 'I wanted to run it all through you, and be sure that I wasn't missing something. You're the first.'

'Not quite,' said a voice from behind me. Ben and I turned to see John standing in the bedroom door. He was clothed; either he'd been awake for a while, or he'd taken to sleeping with his pants on. It was difficult to say which I thought was more likely.

He looked almost sad. 'I heard everything you said.'

'That's a nice trick, since I *know* that door was closed when I started.' I kept my voice light, but alarm bells were sounding at the back of my head. There was something about John's eyes that I didn't like one bit, something cold and distant and oddly regretful. If the eyes were the windows to the soul, his were filled with broken glass and cobwebs. 'You got a listening device on us, Johnny-boy?'

'Yes,' said John, startling both me and Ben into silence. 'I got access to plant the bugs weeks ago. This is the first time you've used the keywords to activate them. The trick to proper data scanning isn't to flag every instance of a trigger; that gives you too much data to be useful. It's to flag the *third* within a short period of time. That's when you know you've found something worth listening in on. You just had to go and analyze that data, didn't you, Mrs North?'

'Wait,' said Ben. 'You actually bugged our RV? You're not joking?'

'You should really sweep for listening devices more than once a year,' said John. 'Don't you people have corporate espionage in your little industry?'

'We swept yesterday. How the hell did you plant bugs that Mat couldn't find?'

Ben half-rose. 'This can't be happening.'

'Sit down,' said John.

Ben sat.

'I've got nothing for anyone to listen in on,' I said. John was eight feet away, give or take; I'd never actually measured the interior of the RV. It had never seemed important. I silently promised myself that I was going to measure *everything* once this was over, no matter how unimportant it might seem. I was going to measure the goddamn air ducts, if that was what it took. 'All my work is in the field. Can't scoop getting bitten by a zombie, you know? It's actually the definition of the unstealable moment. So I do okay. And Mat works mostly on video. You need to see what they're doing with their hands if you want to get the full effect of their tutorials.'

There was a closed door between us and the driver's compartment. Long gone were the days when the driver could have casually leaned back and joined a conversation. Safety regulations allowed for things like RVs and buses – they had to, people still had to get from one place to another – but that didn't mean they hadn't made some changes to the interior. Mat was effectively cut off from the rest of us. Maybe that was a good thing. They were a fast thinker and a fast talker, but they didn't do well when challenged by authority. Especially authority that was this much bigger than us.

'Does Governor Kilburn know you bugged our RV?' demanded Ben. He was starting to sound angry. This was all sinking in for him, and he didn't like where it was going.

'Susan? God, no. She would never have tolerated it. She invited you to join us because she wanted to emulate Ryman – he's been this cycle's golden boy from day one, and I'm jealous as hell of the boys who got assigned to *his* detail – but she's always wanted to run a clean campaign. Let the people make up their own minds. That means not spying on her precious journalists. Good thing, too. I would have needed to find a way to spoil her data, and that always looks so suspicious.'

The math of the situation was clear. If Ben hadn't put it together yet, it was only because he'd never been an Irwin: His usual opponents were words and images on a screen, which were less likely to bite when he made them dance for his bidding. I had the field experience to know what this looked like, and I didn't appreciate it. 'Lots of things can look suspicious,' I said, beginning to stand. 'You popping out of the bedroom telling us all about how you bugged the place, for example. Plenty suspicious. I know I'm not feeling too good about it. How about you explain what you're on about, and we'll see if we can't make you feel better?'

His hand moved, and there was a gun in it. Under any other circumstances, I would have been asking how he'd done that. Given that he was aiming the gun at *me*, I didn't really care.

'How about you sit back down, and I don't explain a damn thing?' he asked pleasantly. 'Here's how this is going to go. You're going to call Mat, and tell that weirdo that we need to make an emergency stop, because Ben isn't feeling so well. I'm going to shoot you both. When Mat stops the RV, I'll get out, and tell him Ben amplified and infected you, and I did what I had to do to protect myself. I'll tell him how sorry I am. I'll tell your girlfriend how sorry I am. Lots of sorry is going to get handed around.'

'Not seeing that we'd even consider going along with this,' I said. My voice was low, quiet; I wanted him to stay focused on me. Leave Ben out of this. Ben, with his quick, clever fingers, and his keyboard, and his active Internet connection. The man could type almost two hundred words a minute, when he needed to get something out fast; he could go even faster when he was just swiping his fingers across a screen. This seemed like something worth getting out.

'If you don't, I'll still shoot you both, but then I'll be forced to activate the vehicle's safety alerts, and when Mat pulls over, I'll shoot him too,' said John. 'Save your friends or don't save anyone. The choice is yours. I know what I'd do, but then, I think I have a bit more loyalty than you do. I never married a man I didn't love, or toyed with a woman I could never really be with. You're a piece of work, you know that?'

'It takes one to know one, and Audrey turned you down fair and square,' I said. His continued misgendering of Mat was beginning to wear on my nerves. 'Not my fault you went after a woman who wasn't available. You never worked for the governor at all, did you? Who's pulling your strings, love?'

'Shut up and call him,' said John.

I gave Ben a sidelong look. He nodded minutely. All right. If he was going to call the play, I was going to roll with it as hard as I could.

I tapped my ear cuff, activating the connection, and waited for the cycle to complete before I said, pleasantly, 'Mat? You there, love?'

'Hey, Ash, what's up?' Mat sounded curious but not distressed. They had no idea that anything was wrong. I felt a brief stab of envy. It must have been nice to just be rolling down the road, not looking at a man with a gun and wondering whether you were about to die.

'Oh, not so much,' I said. I kept my voice light and easy, and my eyes on John. 'It's just that Ben's not feeling so well, so I'm going to need you to *hit the gas as hard as you can John is back here and he's got a gun!*'

There was no hesitation. The RV accelerated, hard and fast enough that anything that wasn't nailed down went flying. That included John, who stumbled, falling back into the bedroom doorway before he caught himself. I was already in motion, shoving myself out of my seat and racing toward him. My own gun was in its holster on the rack, and I didn't have time to get it, no matter how much safer and more comforting that would have been. I was the only weapon I had. I was going to use me.

My shoulder hit John in the chest, and his first shot went wild. I heard it hit the ceiling. I didn't turn to look. I was too busy trying to grab for his gun, keeping him off balance and distracted.

'He's not shooting bullets!' shouted Ben. 'Be careful!'

The urge to look and see what Ben was talking about was almost unbearable. I didn't have time. I kept grabbing for the gun. It went off again, and this time I heard the difference in the shot, which was too quiet for the caliber of the weapon: It sounded more like an air pistol than an actual firearm. Mat was driving faster and faster, having apparently found a new gear that the rest of us had been previously unaware of, one which allowed the RV to break the laws of physics. Or maybe it just felt like that because I was on my feet and wrestling a trained security professional over a firearm.

'Get down!' I shouted.

I heard Ben's chair fall over, and heard him start muttering a moment later. He had called someone. Hopefully the authorities. Or John's mother. Under the circumstances, I'd have taken anything that would make him *stop*.

'You're a bastard and an asshole and a bunch of other things I don't feel like thinking of right now,' I shrieked, and kneed him in the balls. John grunted, but didn't collapse. The man must have had the pain tolerance of a charging rhino. Just my luck. 'Give me the goddamn gun!'

'Fuck you, bitch!' he shouted, and fired again.

He had to lower his arm to shoot, which meant it wasn't as well braced in that brief second. I jumped, grabbed his elbow, and twisted until the gun was aimed directly at his throat. His face went pale, eyes widening to an almost comical degree.

'No,' I said. 'Now give me the gun.'

John paused. For a moment, it was like he had just . . . just stopped. There was still resistance in his body; he wasn't giving up. He just wasn't moving, either. He was taking a breath. Then he moved his hand slightly, as far as my grip allowed, and pulled the trigger.

What shot out of the barrel wasn't a bullet: It was a thick silver needle, maybe four inches in length, which embedded itself in his throat. He made a choking noise. I let go of his arm and grabbed the gun from his suddenly unresisting fingers. He stumbled backward. Not far; just a half step, just far enough that I saw my opening. I planted a foot at the center of his chest and shoved as hard as I could. He fell fully into the bedroom. I grabbed the door and slammed it shut.

There were a lot of things that could be delivered via dart. Drugs and poisons — and viruses. It didn't take a genius to guess which of those things John was likely to have been shooting at us. 'Ben?' I turned. 'You okay?'

'He missed me,' said Ben, crawling out from under the table. One of the silver needles was embedded in the floor. Ben started to reach for it.

'No!' I shouted.

Ben stopped, pulling back his hand and giving me a bewildered look. 'What do you mean, no? We need to know what this is.'

'It's a hollow dart,' I said. 'They're used in animal conservation. You can drop a sedative payload into a deer from twenty feet away. You really think he came in here to shoot us with sedatives? Grab a hazmat kit and pick the damn thing up with a Kevlar sleeve if you must, but do *not* touch it with your hands.'

Ben's eyes widened. He looked to the closed bedroom door and then back to me. 'You're not saying . . .'

'I'm not saying *anything*, but I'm implying one hell of a lot, and I think it's time we get out of here. Whatever you had in the bedroom is a loss. Sorry about that, but I don't think it's going to survive decon.' The RV was small but the bedroom was smaller; most of our clothing and equipment was stored in the main living space. Thankfully. I tapped my ear cuff as I moved toward the nearest closet. 'Mat, it's Ash. Stop the vehicle, send out a distress call, and get the hell out. This is an evacuation. Anything you want, you tell me now, because I don't think we're coming back here.'

'Ash, what are you talking—'

'John just tried to kill us both. I'm pretty sure he finished by shooting himself with live Kellis-Amberlee, to make it easier to cover his tracks.' There was a loud thud from the bedroom. I amended: 'I'm *positive* he shot himself with live Kellis-Amberlee. He's amplified, he's locked in the bedroom, and he's hungry. Now stop the damn car.'

We began slowing down. My ear cuff beeped with another

incoming transmission. I jerked my head hard to the side. 'You're go for Ash.'

'Ash, are you okay?' Audrey's recent anger was gone, replaced with borderline panic. 'We just got the weirdest transmission from John—'

'Did someone record it? I want to hear that bastard amplify,' I said, pulling things out of the closet and piling them on the floor, as far from that damned needle as I could. The other one was embedded somewhere. We were going to have to leave it behind. We were still slowing down. We'd be stopped soon, and I couldn't justify staying in the vehicle after that. This was a hot zone now. 'What did he say?'

'He said Ben was sick, and that you were standing in front of him so John couldn't shoot, even though Ben was about to amplify,' said Audrey. 'What's going on over there? Are you all right? Is Ben . . . is Ben . . . ?'

'Do you have our GPS coordinates? How close are you?'

'Um, about a half mile back. Ash—'

'I love you, I'm sorry I nearly got myself eaten, and you're going to find me, Ben, Mat, and as many of our things as we can salvage on the side of the road,' I said. 'I'll explain when you get here.' I killed the connection. I hated to hang up on her – this wasn't going to help the fight we'd been having, at least not in the way I wanted it to – but I needed to focus on the tasks at hand. Like emptying our weapons locker into a rolling suitcase. I paused long enough to strap my gun to my thigh.

'Remind me never to sit around unarmed again,' I said. 'I don't care if we're in the most secure location in the world, we're not getting caught this way twice. Once was once too many.'

Ben had been tearing down our computer equipment, moving with quick efficiency only slightly undermined by the way his hands kept shaking. He looked in my direction and said, 'I didn't have my weapon either. This isn't just on you.'

'But see, Ben, you're about the facts, and I'm supposed to be the wall that stands between you and the things that want to keep those

facts from getting out. I am supposed' – I slammed the locker shut –
'to be' – I opened the last closet and began yanking out the rest of
our clothing – '*the wall.*'

'Ash.' A hand touched my shoulder. I jerked away, pulling my arm
back as I readied a haymaker, before I realized the hand belonged
to Ben: He was the only option. The RV was finally, finally pulling
to a stop, and Ben was standing beside me, a worried expression on
his face. 'This wasn't your fault. None of this has been your fault. If
this is on anyone, it's on me; I was the one who decided we needed
to follow a presidential campaign if we wanted to make it to the big
time, remember? This is on me. You're doing a wonderful job. You're
keeping us all safe.'

'For how long?' I pointed to the needle jutting out of the floor.
'We're up against people we don't know, who will use whatever
weapons they can get their hands on to hurt us. John was supposed
to be our *friend*. When even our friends can do this sort of thing . . .'

'It's worse than that,' said Mat's voice in my ear. I straightened,
blinking. Ben did the same. 'Sorry about overriding the com locks,
but I can't get the side doors to unseal from the dash, which means
we're going to need to do blood test protocols.'

'Makes sense,' said Ben. 'We have a biohazard in here.'

'Right,' said Mat. 'Well, you're not the only one. We've got a double
whammy of a problem, and we're going to need to get to cover like,
five seconds after you get out of the vehicle. I'm serious. Bring the
baggage we can't leave behind, and be ready to run like fuck. We're
talking *Jurassic Park* and the raptors are on your ass levels of running
for your life. If you don't, you may not have a life to run for.'

'What the hell are you talking about?' I asked. 'Did you park us
in the middle of an outbreak?'

'Georgette Meissonier – you know, the Fictional who travels with
the Masons? Well, she's dead. There was an accident while their
convoy was moving, and she got bitten by a member of the campaign
staff, and she died.'

'That's tragic, but I don't see what it has to do with us,' I said. 'Sorry if she was a friend of yours. Not trying to be heartless. Just trying to keep breathing. Which means we need to pick it up, and you need to be working the exterior lock.' A clean blood test from outside would activate the interior testing panels, and allow me and Ben to check ourselves. It was a convoluted system, but it was one of the only things that allowed the nation's RVs to stay on the road. If the driver tested clean, they could at least attempt to get their passengers out. If the driver didn't, the passengers stayed inside, isolated and supposedly safe.

'Supposedly' was such a big word.

'That's why I'm telling you this.' Mat sounded about as frustrated as I felt. They were clipping their words, swallowing the vowels until everything turned staccato and hard. 'Her death was confirmed and uploaded to the Wall *fifteen minutes* after she was reported dead to the CDC.'

'How do you know what was reported to the CDC?' asked Ben.

'A friend of mine watches for anomalies like that,' said Mat, a little less tensely, and a little more evasively. 'She says time-stamp glitches can happen, but fifteen minutes? No. That's too big. That's not an error, that's an intentional report that someone has been infected. So I asked her to keep an eye out for anyone else related to the campaign who might get hit with a glitch like that. She called me five minutes before you asked me to stop the vehicle.'

My stomach sank until it felt like it was going to drop out of my body and keep falling, passing through the floor, to the very center of the planet. 'We got reported as infected and dead, didn't we?'

'We did,' said Mat. 'All three of us.'

'At least now we know he was lying when he said he'd spare you,' I said. I closed my eyes for a moment, trying to steady myself. 'What of Audrey?'

'She's not listed.'

'Ah, thank whoever's listening, and thank the dumb bastard's crush besides.' I opened my eyes. 'All right. Come get us out, and then we run for cover. It might be we'll die today, but if we do, we'll do it running as hard as we can, and we'll shame the devil on the way down.'

'On my way,' said Mat. They didn't kill the connection. We could both hear the RV door slam, and the crunch of footsteps on the ground. I listened as intently as I could, waiting for the moaning to begin, or for the sound of gunshots. This was all too easy.

Or maybe my idea of what was easy and what was hard was flawed. I had wrestled a gun away from a man who wanted to infect before he killed, because he needed our deaths to look natural – or at least as natural as the deaths of those who had attacked me in Huntsville. I had learned too much, and shared what I knew, and triggered some sort of extermination protocol. 'Easy' was no longer a part of the plan. Survival was all that mattered.

There was a beep. I looked around before I realized it had come through the open connection, and not from inside the RV. Mat muttered something under their breath. The beep came again. 'Uh, guys?'

'What is it, Mat?' asked Ben.

'The locks won't disengage. Somehow, the old blood tests Mallory had disabled are back online, and PS, they're broken. I'm checking out clean – it knows I'm not infected – but it still won't open. I can't get you out of there.'

'Why the hell not?' I demanded.

'When John attacked you, where was he before that?'

'He was asleep in the bedroom.' Except he hadn't been sleeping the whole time, had he? He'd come out as soon as I'd said enough that he knew it was time to take us out of the equation. John could have been awake for hours, and we'd have no way of knowing. I amended, 'In the bedroom, anyway. He was definitely in the bedroom. Why?'

'Because it's possible to upload malware to a locked-loop testing system. They're not unhackable. Too many open ports. I'll call you back.' There was a click, and the connection was cut.

John was still banging on the RV's bedroom door. He was fully amplified by this point. He knew there was a source of food nearby, and he wanted it. The slow, viral intelligence that had replaced his humanity would never give up, not until his body broke down, and that could take days. He'd die of thirst before anything else, and that wasn't a fast process.

'He'll break that down in an hour or two,' I said, looking toward the door. 'It's not built to take this sort of abuse for long periods.'

'I want a divorce,' said Ben.

I turned toward him, blinking. 'Excuse me?'

'I said, I want a divorce.' Ben smiled a little. 'You're not going to ask me for one. Mom just died, you're still adjusting to being a citizen, there's a lot of great reasons for you to put it off. I know that. But you need this more than I do. And hell, maybe I need it too. I met some really sweet Newsie girls at the convention, and I couldn't figure out how to get them to see past the ring on my finger.'

'You don't wear a ring,' I said.

'They're Newsies,' he replied. 'They all know it's there, even if it isn't visible, and most of them aren't looking to join a harem. So let's get divorced. You can marry Audrey. I know you want to. And I can finally start looking for someone I want to marry. Someone who's funny, and sweet, and likes me for me, and isn't a lesbian . . . '

'See, it's that last one where you lose me,' I said.

His smile widened. 'It's that last one where I never had you. I'm fine with that. I've always *been* fine with that. But maybe it's time for both of us to start asking for more. So can I have a divorce?'

'I'll see if Amber can recommend a good lawyer,' I said. I knew what he was doing. This was a distraction, a way of keeping me from focusing on what was happening to us. I appreciated it, even as I wanted to shake him and tell him we had more important things to worry about. Instead, I forced myself to smile back, and said, 'It wasn't so bad being married to you. If I had to be married to a man, you're the one I would have picked, no question about it.'

'We're a good team,' he said. 'I didn't necessarily think this was where things were going to wind up going when I decided to fly to Ireland and help you out—'

'If you'd predicted this future, we would have needed to have a nice long talk about how people are not playthings and Sherlock Holmes is not a life coach,' I said.

Ben laughed. It was an incongruous sound when set against the steady thumping from the bedroom. 'Yeah, I know. But we did okay, right? We did some good. We had some fun. We didn't break too many things that shouldn't have been broken.'

'You're very sentimental. I don't like it.' The new voice coming through my ear cuff was female, with an accent that somehow combined the oddest aspects of both French and Russian. I wanted to hear her recite poetry. 'Stop it right now, or I will leave the two of you in that tin can to rot.'

'Excuse me?' I stiffened. 'Who is this, please? This is a private channel.'

'There is no such thing as a private channel, sentimental girl, and if you believe in the existence of such things, then there's no wonder you've been targeted for extinction. You're a technological dinosaur, and the comet is coming.'

Mat sighed. Apparently, we had become a party line. 'Tessa, please don't torment my teammates just because you can. Ash, Ben, this is my friend Tessa. Tessa, these are my teammates.'

'They are dinosaurs. You belong to a team full of dinosaurs.'

'I know,' said Mat. 'Now can you let them out? Please? I called you because I need you to let them out, and because I don't know anyone else who could do this remotely.'

'Wait, what?' Ben frowned. It was a general expression, since there was no one but me around to see it. 'What do you mean, do this remotely?'

'I am very far away from you, dinosaur, and I am happy with that situation.' The sound of typing came through my ear cuff. It was fast: This Tessa woman knew how to move her fingers. 'You will never see my face, you will never taste my cooking, and I will be nowhere near you when the comet hits. But you're friends of my dear Mat, and that means I can be merciful to something that will soon become extinct. See how kind I am?'

There were several beeps – this time from *inside* the RV, as lights I had never seen before came on above the doorframe. There were five in total. Each of them started yellow, cycled to red for two seconds, and turned green, remaining steady.

The last light was red when Tessa said, 'Technically, this is a felony, since I am manipulating the outcome of an official blood testing system. This isn't transmitting to any of the servers meant to keep and collect this data; they'll think you're still inside your vehicle when they come for it. And they're coming. A team was dispatched from your local office five minutes ago. Do me a favor and don't eat anyone, won't you? I'm not in the United States, but I still don't want to become a terrorist because you got hungry.'

'We're not infected,' I said.

'Sweet dinosaur, oblivious to what's coming, don't you know? Everyone's infected.' The red light turned green. The door swung open, and there was Mat, standing next to the RV, an anxious look on their face and a backpack over their shoulder.

'Well?' they said. 'Come on. I don't know how long that's staying open.'

'We're coming,' I said.

We tossed our bags out the door and jumped out after them. Mat was there to help us grab as much as we could, and we took off down the median, running as fast as we could away from the RV. We didn't discuss it: We didn't need to. If the CDC thought that we were infected and contained, they were going to do the most sensible thing, and prevent the infection from spreading. They were going to blow up the RV.

There was an abandoned rest stop less than a quarter mile up the road. I gave Mat a questioning look as we ran, not wasting my breath.

I was the strongest of the three of us, and I was carrying the bulk of our weapons and equipment. It was a fair division of labor, but it didn't leave me with much breath to waste on things like asking questions.

'I thought we might need to run,' said Mat, gasping for air between words. 'We can hide here.'

So could the dead, but the thought was sound, and it wasn't like we had any more options at this point. We charged down the exit leading to the rest stop, getting under cover of the trees bare seconds before the sound of helicopter blades came churning through the air, chopping the wind into bite-sized pieces. If the leaves were too thin, or the helicopter flew directly overhead, we were done for. Mat was wearing lime green pants, and my hair was a burning brand, notifying them of our presence. All we could do was keep running, and hope for the best.

My ear cuff beeped. Audrey. I jerked my head to the side, and said, as softly as I could, 'We're alive, we're not infected, whatever they're telling you is a lie, we're alive, we're not infected, please, believe me, love.'

'Ash, where are you?' Her voice was tight as a plucked bowstring, drawn taut and ready to snap. 'We just got a sympathy note from the CDC.'

'Who's with you?' *Please don't say the governor, please don't say the governor . . .*

'Governor Kilburn, Amber, and Governor Blackburn.'

All the people who might know about what was going on, from the wrong direction. The only one I was even half-sure wasn't working with John's true employers was Governor Kilburn. I had a choice to make, and I didn't have much time to make it. 'I'm going to have Mat send you our coordinates,' I said. 'Back off, wait an hour, and then come for us. Bring whoever you think we can trust. I'll trust you to make the right call. We need to talk. All of us. I love you.'

This time when I cut the connection, she didn't call back. We kept running. Ben was to my left, Mat was to my right, and the crumbling shape of the rest stop was ahead of us, all broken windows and neglected brick. I began to think we were going to make it.

The blast from the explosion when the CDC blew up our van reached all the way to our location. A hot concussion wave hit me from behind, driving me to my knees on the broken ground. My head hit the concrete, and everything went quiet.

People are going to tell you we're dead. They're lying.

People are going to tell you we're terrorists. They're lying.

People are going to tell you we're trying to draw attention to ourselves, that we resent the fact that our ratings aren't at the top of the charts, that we're angry about the way our candidate and her accomplishments have been shunted aside by the drama happening on the Republican side of the house. People are going to tell you a lot of things. People are going to expect you to believe them. Don't.

You don't have to believe me either. After all, I clearly have a lot to gain if you don't listen to them. I have my life, and the lives of my friends, to gain. I have a future to gain. And if you don't believe me, I have everything to lose. But really. Which of us is telling the more believable story here? Me, or the people who tell you that I'm the enemy?

It's time to pick a side. I genuinely hope you'll pick the correct one.

—From *That Isn't Johnny Anymore*, the blog of Ben Ross,
April 25, 2040

Fourteen

I don't think I ever fully lost consciousness: That would have required a harder blow, a softer head, and a weaker constitution. I wasn't put together to be a fainting flower. I pushed myself up from the concrete with trembling hands, mind racing to catalog the scrapes, bruises, and cuts on my palms. There was a first aid kit in one of my bags, complete with pseudoskin sealant. If the ground wasn't contaminated, I might still be all right. The others, however . . .

Ben was a Newsie. He never did anything outdoors if he could avoid it, and he was soft from spending most of his life in the glow of his computer screen. Not that he wasn't brave – he was; I'd known that from the moment he hopped onto a plane and came to bail me out of Ireland – but bravery doesn't count as much as sturdiness when you're actually out in the world. All the bravery there is won't stop a bullet, or block the shock wave of a CDC-triggered explosion. Mat was a little more fit, because Mat needed to be able to lift heavy equipment when there were repairs to be done, but again, that might not be enough.

Both of them were sprawled facedown on the concrete. My hands and knees were bleeding; if I flipped my friends over to see whether they were bleeding, I might infect them. Any zombies in the area would be moving toward the sound of the explosion, drawn by the noise. I couldn't hear moans. I couldn't hear flames crackling, either, just a distant ringing that made me suspect my ears had been damaged by the blast. Not badly enough to rupture an eardrum, since I couldn't feel anything running down my neck, but badly enough that I was temporarily deaf, while also temporarily exposed and contending with two motionless people I couldn't touch without endangering.

'If only this had been planned, I might get a Golden Steve-O out of this,' I muttered, mostly for the comfort of hearing *something*, even if it was just my own voice echoing through bone conduction.

Bone conduction. That was the answer. I tapped my ear cuff three times, triggering it to call Ben. It beeped: He wasn't picking up. Well, I'd been expecting that, hadn't I? I tapped it again, signaling the software to treat this as an emergency and kick off Ben's screamer. It wasn't a privilege I abused, largely because *his* phone was implanted inside his head: bone conduction, rather than ordinary communication. He could never take it off or put it down, and when I forced a connection open, he *had* to deal with it.

'Benjamin Ross, this is your courtesy wake-up call,' I said quietly, counting on bone conduction to do the amplifying for me. 'I recognize you're probably enjoying the pain-free haze of your recent concussion, and do not wish to wake up. Bollocks to that, we may be eaten if we do not get under cover, and I'm bleeding, so I need help if I'm going to get our things to the main building without contaminating them. Again, Benjamin Ross, this is your courtesy wake-up call. Now wake up, before I start kicking you in the kidneys.'

Ben groaned. I couldn't hear it, but I saw his mouth move. My stomach knotted. The classic Kellis-Amberlee moan comes with a very distinctive mouth motion, accompanied by an overall slackness in the face and an emptiness in the eyes. With Ben still facedown against the concrete, I couldn't tell whether there was any tension left in him. If he'd hit the ground wrong, if he'd broken something, the virus would have done its best to wake him up again. That was what Kellis-Amberlee *did*. It would have been a pretty poor zombie virus if it hadn't.

The average time from contact with contaminated fluids to amplification varied according to the height and weight of the person who'd been bitten or spat on, which was why smaller people always seemed to be the first to go. Mat was in more danger than I was, and I was in more danger than Ben. But if a person died, disrupting their body's electrical field in the process, amplification and resurrection were just this side of instant. I took a step backward.

Ben lifted his head, tracking me. One arm of his glasses was bent, the titanium frames hanging off his face at an awkward angle. His mouth moved, forming words I didn't understand.

'Sorry,' I said. 'Sort of temporarily deaf from the blast, and I don't read lips. I know you can hear me because of the bone conduction. Can you understand what I'm saying right now?'

Ben nodded.

'Good. Very good. Look.' I held up my hands, showing him my skinned and shredded palms. 'I need medical care before I touch anything. How are your hands? We've got to wake Mat and get under cover before the CDC circles back.'

Ben gave me an exaggeratedly confused look. I sighed.

'Big explosions draw the infected, because it's a huge, unfamiliar sound that might mean food. Standard protocol after you blow a compromised site is to wait fifteen minutes before circling back and taking out all the zombies you've flushed out of hiding. Sometimes you get nothing, sometimes you get great whopping mobs and make the whole county safer. But I don't know how long we've been out. They could be here any second.'

Ben nodded, looking alarmed, and showed me his unscathed palms before turning and starting to shake Mat by the shoulder. There was an impressive scrape on his shoulder, but since it was more oozing than actively gushing blood, that wasn't as much of an issue as my hands. I moved to start collecting bags, trying to slip my fingers through the straps without actually touching them.

At first, Mat didn't respond. Then, laboriously, their body began to twitch. I blew out a gust of air, relieved. 'Get *up*, Mat,' I called, and grabbed the last of the bags.

Mat's head lifted, revealing the blue-black bruise spreading across much of their forehead. It looked like they'd cracked their skull when they fell. Mat's mouth opened. And while I still couldn't hear, it turned out I didn't need to, because that mouth shape was so perfectly characteristic that sound was not needed. I knew what I would have heard, and I was suddenly, painfully grateful I didn't have to. No matter what happened next, I would go to my grave never having heard my friend and teammate moaning.

Ben danced backward, eyes wide and cheeks ashen. It would have been comic under any other circumstances. Considering where we were standing and what was going on around us, it wasn't funny at all.

'Grab the bags and run!' I shouted, letting the duffel I'd just picked up fall back to the ground before yanking the gun from my thigh holster. *One more thing to sterilize when this is over,* said the small voice of practicality and heartlessness, which was sometimes the loudest thing in the entire world. I wanted to hate myself for having thoughts like that, but I knew they were necessary: They were the still, cold place that I could go to when my job turned bleak. Without them, I would have been lost long before I had come to America. I would never have survived to make it out of Ireland.

But oh, it burned to know that I was the sort of person who could worry about getting blood on my gun when someone I cared about was picking themselves up from the concrete, face slack and pupils gone wide and black as oil. Mat's backpack was dangling by one strap. Their computer was inside, I knew; that would have their contact lists, and any data that hadn't been backed up elsewhere. We might need it.

'Oh, fuck me,' I muttered into the strange silence, and bolted forward, switching my gun to my left hand as I reached out and snatched the backpack with my right. Mat's arm bent under the pressure, offering no resistance: They didn't understand what was happening anymore. That part of Mat was gone, forever.

Newly risen zombies still had intact joints and the potential to be both swift and dangerous. That was bad. At the same time, they were often disoriented, caught up in the process of being rewritten by the virus that had taken over and crystallized inside their brains. Mat had been dead for a very short time, and had been a zombie only shortly longer. Because of that, they weren't moving quickly or reacting well. That was a good thing. That was maybe the only good thing left in the world.

I didn't have my mag. I couldn't record this, and on some level, I was glad. Mat deserved to be remembered laughing, brightly colored and gloriously alive, not moaning and shuffling toward me like an invalid. They weren't reaching for me yet, but they would be. They would be. There was no love between us now. Only my love for Mat, undying and still burning bright as anything. It wasn't fair. It wasn't right. It wasn't something that could be taken back.

'First time I met you, I asked if you were a boy or a girl,' I said. 'You laughed at me. Said I was a bit of a bigot, but I was a good-hearted one; you thought you could beat it out of me. I don't know if you ever did, darling, but I like to think you got pretty far. I'm never going to forget you. I'm so, so sorry.'

Mat took another step toward me. This time it *was* a step, not a shuffle: They were adjusting to the changes in their body. It was time.

'Your name was Mat Newson, and you were brilliant. If there's an afterlife, if there's a God, you make sure you tell the old bastard that. Tell him Aislinn North said you were awesome, and you deserve the best of what's on offer. The very, very best.'

Mat took another step toward me.

I dropped the backpack, switched the gun back to my dominant hand, and pulled the trigger.

The nice thing about close shots is that sometimes, the entry wounds are textbook, small and polite and almost unobtrusive. A hole appeared in the middle of Mat's forehead, no larger than a nickel. I could have stopped it up with my thumb. Not that it would have changed anything. A thick runnel of blood dripped from the hole and ran down the bridge of Mat's nose.

Mat blinked once. Then, gracelessly, they fell. I didn't hear them hit the pavement. There were some small mercies about this day. Very small.

Grabbing Mat's backpack and the rest of the supplies, I ran after Ben.

Once upon a time, the rest stop had been intended for weary truckers and families with overstuffed cars. Rusted, tilting signs entreated me to keep my dogs on their leashes and clean up after them. Ben was nowhere to be seen, but there was only one main structure still standing, a brick-walled, octagonal thing that had probably been the heart of the visitor's center. All too aware that my temporary deafness was becoming more of a hindrance with every step I took toward the convenient hiding spots the walls and crannies represented, I kept going, looking for signs that Ben had been through here.

Someone had nailed plywood over the bathroom doors. It looked like it had been done from the outside. Shutting something in, or making sure nothing could *get* in? It was hard to say. I kept circling, trying to keep my gun in position without letting any of the things we'd worked so hard to save fall. It was odd, but I felt like losing Mat's backpack now would be disrespectful to their memory, adding insult to the injury of their untimely death. The human mind is not always logical under stress, sadly. I was no exception.

Ben was behind the center, using a hammer from our portable repair kit to pry the nails out of another sheet of plywood. I stopped and frowned at him. He shook his head, pointing at the nail he'd just extracted. I continued to frown. He shoved the nail in front of me, pointing more fiercely, and I finally saw.

It was rusty. Deeply, thoroughly rusty, the sort of decay that only comes from being exposed to the elements for year after year, untouched and undisturbed. 'Did you check for other ways in?' I asked, trusting the bone conduction to keep him hearing me, even if his ears were still stopped up.

He nodded vigorously, flashing a thumbs-up around the haft of the hammer. I nodded more slowly.

'I'll keep watch, then,' I said. 'Get us inside.'

Ben went back to work.

The word 'zombie' accurately describes the victims of Kellis-Amberlee. They rise from the dead, hungry for human flesh, if only because the virus that drives them wants so desperately to spread itself. They're just as happy eating cows, or squirrels, or anything else hot and fast and mammalian enough for the virus to recognize. But here's the part the movies got wrong: Our zombies are *alive*. They breathe and sneeze and shit and age. The oldest zombies still alive – 'oldest' in terms of length of post-amplification existence, not in terms of chronological age – were bitten during the Rising and corralled on government research facilities all over the world. The main research center in Ireland collected mostly children, viewing them as easier to contain due to their small size. Some of those kids are still among the technically living. They've undergone puberty and entered adulthood since their hearts stopped for the first time. For all anyone knows, they'll eventually die of old age.

They'd die a whole lot faster if they were denied access to food and water. Even the dead need to stay hydrated, and while they get most of their fluids from the people they devour, even zombies have been known to die of thirst. If there were no other entrances to this little stronghold, and the plywood had been in place for years, there would be no zombies inside to ambush us. There might be bodies, but we lived in a world where corpses were commonplace, barely more important than anything else. As long as those bodies were too dried up to ooze and no longer capable of independent movement, we'd be fine.

My ears were starting to ring, and more, they were starting to *hurt*. There was still no dampness on the sides of my face, so I was choosing to interpret that as my hearing coming back, and not anything worse or more disturbing. I kept my gun up and my eyes moving, scanning the surrounding trees for any sign that we were about to be attacked. It felt like someone had set iron bands around my heart, sealing it off from the rest of me. Mat's death was going to hit me like a freight train once I had time to process it. I knew that, even as I knew this wasn't the time. If I wanted to stay alive – if I wanted to keep Ben alive – I needed to stay as cold as I could. That was the only job I had now. To be cold, and to kill, and to hold my ground.

A hand touched my shoulder. I whipped around, and for one terrible moment, I was doing the thing every firearms instructor screams at their students not to do: I was aiming a loaded gun at an ally, someone I had no intention of shooting. Ben's eyes went wide, but he didn't flinch away. He held his ground, waiting for me to lower my pistol and start breathing again.

The plywood had been removed from the broken door behind him, and it gaped like a toothless mouth, inviting us inside. I motioned for him to stay where he was and stepped past him, into the dark.

The dark didn't last long. The plywood had been nailed over a little alcove – a smoking area, judging by the kicked-over ashtrays near the wall. It was no more than three feet deep, terminating at a pair of sliding glass doors that weren't sliding anymore. Their power source had died long ago. 'Ben, come inside and get these doors open,' I said. I didn't want to pry the doors apart with my bloody fingers: the less contamination I was responsible for, the better. 'First area's clear.'

Ben's head appeared around the rectangle of light that looked out on the rest of the world. Then he crept inside, moving slowly and cautiously even after I'd given the all clear. He brightened when he saw the closed, undamaged glass doors. If there had been a major battle here, they would have been shattered. Maybe we had managed to find a decent bolt-hole after all.

It took him almost three minutes to pry the glass doors open, finally wedging himself between them and pushing as hard as he could. I itched to help, even as I knew that I couldn't. I didn't dare. Finally, he stepped aside, and I entered the visitor's center.

It was a mostly circular room: The octagonal walls of the exterior had been smoothed down and evened out by tricks of insulation and architecture, creating a pleasing, unbroken expanse of wall. It was surprisingly well lit, thanks to the skylights that made up most of the ceiling; one of them had broken, scattering glass across the tile floor and allowing leaves and other debris to drift in from outside, but as there was no blood in the mess, I guessed it had been a storm or other natural disaster, rather than a zombie raccoon out for a stroll. I paused long enough to drop the bags and Mat's laptop against the wall, adjusted my grip on my pistol, and resumed my slow circuit.

There were no signs of a struggle here. Ancient vending machines were tucked discreetly away near the interior entrance to the restrooms, and they too were intact, even though everything inside them was probably long since spoiled. The water might still be safe to drink, but the sodas and juices would be sour and flat, and the candy and chips would be stale. Even so, their presence was a good sign that this place was secure.

The bathroom doors were shut. I nudged the women's-room door open with my foot, revealing the dark space beyond. The ringing in my ears was still there, but sound hadn't quite come back yet, apart from that. I watched the gloom, waiting for movement. None came. Finally, I pulled my foot away and let the door swing shut again. If there were zombies in here with us, we'd deal with them after we were patched up and capable of rational thought again.

Fear and panic can make zombies of us all. We act without consideration for the consequences. We run, and we don't look back. Which is why it's interesting how much investment this world has in keeping us afraid.

I repeated my check with the men's room before I turned and walked back toward the door. 'We're clear,' I said. 'I've mostly managed not to bleed on things, but I need medical care, and we're going to need a lot of bleach.'

Ben stepped into the visitor's center, stopping long enough to force the doors shut again before turning to face me. I put my gun carefully down on the shelf that had once been covered in visitor's brochures and maps of the area before I held up my hands, mutely showing him my bloody, shredded palms. They were mostly numb by this point, too angry with my treatment of them to communicate with the rest of the body. That was a bit of a relief. I didn't need to feel them to know that they were damaged.

"Okay," mouthed Ben, and went for the bag that held our first aid kit. He made a show of checking it for traces of blood, more to reassure me than anything else. I was grateful. The icy bands around my heart were beginning to crack under the pressure, and I could feel the tears threatening to fall. When they started, I wasn't going to be any good to anyone for quite some time. It was important that we get this taken care of before I turned useless.

Ben pulled out the familiar white box of our first aid kit, motioning for me to take a seat in one of the hard plastic chairs studded around the room. There was something obscurely comforting about settling myself on the cold plastic, feeling it press against the strip of skin between the end of my skirt and the end of the chair, and holding my hands out for Ben to repair. He put on a pair of gloves before he touched me, and that was when I finally started crying. Not out of shame or rejection, but out of relief. If he was wearing gloves, it was because he didn't believe himself to be infected yet. He thought he could still walk away from this, alive and capable of fighting the good fight. That was reassuring beyond words. One of us could still walk away.

I wasn't so sure about myself. My heart hurt. I couldn't stop thinking of the look on Mat's face after I had pulled the trigger – that expression of blank nothingness that all zombies shared. Mat had been my friend, and they hadn't even been able to recognize themself when they died. Sometimes I hated the world that we lived in more fiercely than I would have thought possible.

Pain snapped me back into the moment. I bit my lip and hissed, realizing belatedly that I could *hear* the air whistling through my teeth; the ringing was dying down, and the world was coming back into the place it left behind. That was good. I needed to hear if I was going to keep Ben safe.

Speaking of Ben: He was using a pair of sterile tweezers to dig bits of gravel out of my hand, dropping them, one by one, into a waiting biohazard bag. The chunks were irregular and jagged, and most of all, small; it wasn't worth the time or effort it would take to scrub them clean. Instead, they would go to a waste disposal site and be incinerated, burnt at a temperature high enough that everything – bone, rock, metal – was destroyed. I watched the bits of gravel fall, biting my lip and trying not to think about how much of the natural world we were stripping away, year upon year, in our efforts to stay safe.

'We should move to Australia when this is over,' I said. My voice was starting to return to normal as my ears resumed their normal function. It was nice to hear myself properly, and not just through bone conduction. 'We could get a nice place on the beach, watch the zombie whales harass the sharks. Maybe even learn how to surf. They still know how to have fun in Australia. Think they'd let us in?'

'Probably not,' said Ben, and while his voice was distant and thin, I *heard* it. I could have wept with joy, and probably would have, had I not already been weeping with sadness. 'You, maybe. They like expatriates. But the immigration process is hard to get started, much less survive, and they don't like Americans very much. They never want to let us in.'

'Who can blame them? You're all dreadful.'

He had finished digging the rocks out of my skin. Ben looked up and flashed me a quick, strained smile before holding up a sterilizing wipe. He was making sure I knew what was about to happen, and I appreciated that, even as I wanted to slap the wipe out of his hand and say that no, I was fine, I was great and dandy, I was anything that kept that stinging shit away from me. I didn't. I just nodded, and ground my teeth together. What came next . . . I deserved this. Mat had died on my watch. I deserved whatever happened to me, and no matter what it was, I probably deserved ten times worse.

In this case, it was just a caustic antiseptic that removed the blood from my skin and helped to protect me against infection. It could have been formulated to be just this side of painless: We had the technology to do things like that. But most people don't *want* painlessness. Oh, they say they don't enjoy being hurt. They just don't mean it. The prick of a needle during a blood test or the sting of a sterilizing chemical mean the same things to the people who feel them: They mean 'you are alive.' They mean 'you can feel this, and the dead can't, so you're better than they are. You're still in the percentage of the population that gets to feel pain, that gets to bleed and cry and laugh and live.' Pain is important to the people who never left their rooms to see how bad the world was – or how beautiful.

I didn't need calibrated pain to remind me that I was still alive. The aching in my chest and the bruises on my knees did that better than a little antiseptic ever could. I endured Ben's careful cleaning without pulling away, until he sprayed the pseudoskin over my palms and locked them away from the rest of the world. I raised my hands, flexing them carefully as the skin dried and hardened into place. There was no loss of sensitivity with this brand, but there could be a loss of flexibility if you didn't move fast enough to show the sealant how your fingers were supposed to work. It was better for body wounds than it was for hands. It was what we had, and we were going to make the best of it.

'Any cuts?' I asked, as I reached for the first aid kit with my clean hands and dug out another sterilizing wipe. My knees weren't as bad off as my hands, but they needed attention, and I didn't want Ben interacting with my injuries any longer than absolutely necessary. It's hard for a body to infect itself. Not impossible, but . . . hard. It was safer for me to see to myself, now that I could.

'Some scrapes, and I tore up my chest a little, but nothing major,' he said. 'I was wearing pants, remember?'

'So sorry that my fashion choices are sometimes inconvenient when it comes time to run for our lives,' I said. There was blood down my left shin. I scrubbed it away, switching to a new wipe as soon as my skin was clean. 'To be fair, people aren't usually blowing things up behind me and hitting me in the back with concussion waves.'

'We're lucky we made it as far as we did. Any closer, and we might have been hit with shrapnel.'

I managed not to look up from my legs as I said, 'Let's go tell Mat how lucky we are, shall we? I'm sure they'd be thrilled to hear it.'

'Dammit, Ash, you know that isn't what I meant.'

'I know. I know.' I dropped my second wipe into the biohazard bag and reached for the sealant. The idea of looking Ben in the eyes was somehow impossible to consider, and so I didn't do it. I just kept working on my legs. 'I'm glad we both survived, I really am. I'd be gladder if it had been the two of you. I'm supposed to be the one who keeps you all safe. Isn't that what you have me for? Keep an Irwin nearby to draw fire, and everything will be all right. But I didn't draw fire. I didn't connect the dots quickly enough. Mat is *dead*, and we don't know if anyone's coming for us.'

'Mat knew what they were doing when they took this job,' said Ben. 'Aislinn, look at me.'

Raising my head was one of the most difficult things I'd ever forced myself to do. Ben was still sitting on the floor in front of my hard plastic chair, a grim expression on his face.

'You want to start slinging blame around? *I'm* the Newsie. *I'm* the one who should have started digging into where those people came from. I got wrapped up in the nominations process instead, and in documenting the campaign. That seemed more important to me than people who were already dead and gone. You think I'm proud

of myself for leaving you to do what should have been *my* job? You're
smart, Ash, but you're not a researcher. That isn't what you do.'

It was part of what I did, but I didn't argue with him. This wasn't
the time for arguing.

'If I'd realized what you were doing – if I'd listened when you tried
to talk to me – we might have figured all this out days ago. We might
have been able to get help. Mat . . . oh, God, Mat might be alive.' His
voice broke on the last word. I found myself wishing that my hearing
hadn't recovered. Maybe then I wouldn't have had to hear him on the
verge of shattering. 'This isn't just on you. This is on all of us.'

'Then it's on all of us to make this right.' I stood. 'I need to change
my clothes. This dress is contaminated. We'll have to burn it.' We'd
sterilize the things that could be sterilized, and destroy the rest. That
was standard protocol out here in the field. 'I can change here with
you, or I can find out whether the bathrooms are safe. Your call.'

'Change here,' said Ben. 'I can handle a little nudity better than I
can handle you walking off alone.'

'Cheers,' I said, and moved to start rummaging through my bag.

Keeping most of my wardrobe in the RV's main living space meant
I had choices – a word that felt almost self-indulgent, under the circumstances. I didn't deserve choices. None of us did. Mat should have
had all the choices, and Mat was dead.

Beating myself up about it wasn't going to bring them back. I
considered putting on trousers, and decided against it. If I was going
to die out here – and there was a more than good chance that we were
both going to die out here, facing one last disaster with whatever grace
we could muster – I wanted to do it looking as much like myself as
I could manage. Let the last pictures the world saw of me match the
image I had worked so long and so hard to create.

Let them choke on it.

The sundress I pulled out was already bleach-damaged, pattered
in mermaids with come-hither smiles. I draped it over the nearest
chair and pulled my contaminated dress off, avoiding contact with

the fabric as much as I possibly could. Which is why I was virtually naked when the sliding glass doors slammed open and three people in full body armor stormed into the room, their assault rifles aimed at my chest and their faces concealed by mirrored visors.

Ben froze. I cocked my head to the side, making no effort to cover myself. It wouldn't change anything. If this was how I died, well, so be it.

'It was a good run,' I said, philosophically, before I raised my voice and said, 'Well? If you're here to shoot us, shoot us. That's a much more neighborly thing than standing there, all silent and militant, and waiting for us to do something interesting.'

'Is either of you infected?' asked one of the soldiers. Their voice was distorted, probably by an air filter. No one's ever found a way to make those fully operational without also making people sound like Darth Vader. Which may have been part of the point, now that I thought about it.

'Not to the best of my knowledge,' I replied.

'Has either of you been exposed?'

I rolled my eyes. 'We've all been exposed long since. We breathe air, remember? If you're a mammal and you breathe air, you've been exposed. Ask a slightly less useless question.'

'Dammit, Ash, can you be serious for once?' Audrey's voice wasn't distorted. She walked in from behind the soldiers, and she wasn't wearing body armor, but she was wearing a black tactical suit, with a Kevlar vest over the top of it. She was holding the largest gun I'd ever seen in her hands. 'This is not a good situation.'

'No, it's not,' I agreed. 'Do you know what's going on?' I felt strangely peaceful all of a sudden, like this made perfect sense – or, if not that, like this had crossed a line into making so *little* sense that I no longer had to worry about it. I was Alice down the rabbit hole, and madness had become the new sanity. There was something faintly reassuring about that. It meant I didn't have to worry myself about the details anymore. The details could worry about themselves.

'I do,' she said stiffly. 'I'm sorry, but there's something I have to do first.'

I raised an eyebrow. 'And what's that?'

She said possibly the last thing I would ever have expected to hear come out of my girlfriend's mouth: 'By the authority vested in me by the Epidemic Investigative Service, you are under arrest for falsification of test results and crimes against the government of the United States.' Audrey sounded calm, if mechanical, right up until the end, when she said, 'All of you will be coming with me.'

'I don't—' I began, and then the tranquilizer dart hit me in the middle of my chest. This time, I lost consciousness. This time, I was glad.

Ben's already made his big, impassioned plea about not believing the bullshit people are going to pile up in front of you, making 'yummy yum' noises and patting their stomachs as they try to get you to dig in. You should read it. He's better at saying these things than I am, or at least he's better at saying these things without swearing than I am, and sometimes that's important. You can't tell people they're being fuck-headed assholes without them feeling a little judged. I'm not supposed to be judgmental in my op-eds. Apparently, that turns my opinion from 'acceptable' to 'cruel,' and then no one wants to listen.

Fuck them.

If you think this sort of thing is right, or just, or fair; if you think we deserve what's been done to us for the crime of trying to tell you the truth, when that truth was being obfuscated and concealed at every turn; if you think we've turned strident and unacceptable, that this makes it all right to click over to a site where things are nicer, gentler, or at least more suited to whatever your opinions about the world happen to be, then fuck you too. I've run out of the strength it takes to be nice – and niceness is not an innate quality of the human race. It's a façade we construct to make ourselves seem a little less terrible, a little less like wolves. We were never designed to be nice. We were made to be kind, when it suited us, and cruel, when it didn't.

I'm terribly afraid that kindness doesn't suit me anymore, and that you'll be dealing with the realities of that change. I hope you choke on me.

—From *Erin Go Blog*, the blog of Ash North, April 25, 2040

Fifteen

Tranquilizer dreams are like nothing else in this world. There are people who say the best, most vivid dreams come from oxycodone and absinthe, and maybe they're right about the 'best' part, but the most vivid dreams? Those definitely come from high-test tranquilizers, the kind developed by the government to knock a person out before they can twitch. The kind that don't just *put* you under, they *shove* you under with the force of a geologic shift. I ran through the unending dark for hours, pursued by the decaying phantoms of everyone I'd ever loved and lost. Mat was at the head of their cruelly rotted army, a sniper rifle in their hands and a cold expression in their eyes. Every time I slowed down, even a little, they would fire on me and howl, keeping the rest of the dead on my trail.

I whipped around a corner and nearly slammed into Audrey, as dead and rotting as the rest of them. Like Mat, she still seemed to have human intelligence, because there was recognition in her eyes — recognition, and loathing. She looked at me like I was less than nothing.

'You should have been the one who died,' she hissed, and hit me in the center of the chest, and I was falling, falling forever, down into the dark where I belonged.

The thing about dreams is that no matter how vivid they are, they end. I woke up facedown on a soft surface, with my hands cuffed behind me and my legs zip-tied at the ankles. I made a small sound of protest when I realized what had been done to me, and another when my attempts to flip over caused the hem of my hospital gown to ride up, and I realized that someone had undressed and redressed me while I was knocked out.

'Not all right with this,' I said, voice muffled by the fabric beneath me. Stretching my arms as far back as I could, I found the edge of the mattress. It was thin, covered with scratchy, industrial sheets. A cot, then, probably not anchored to its frame. I grabbed the edge, using it to anchor me while I pushed my legs in the opposite direction. They found empty air. I let go of the mattress and rolled, winding up stretched across the center of the cot and staring at the ceiling. From there, it wasn't *simple* to sit up – 'simple' would have implied it was easy, or enjoyable, and not harder than I cared to contemplate. Insult to injury, when I did finally get myself into a seated position, my hair was in my face, blocking the majority of my vision. I got the impression of an empty room, white walls, and industrial lighting.

'I know I'm being watched right now,' I said, trying to sound brave and tough and fierce, and not like a handcuffed woman with her hair covering her face. 'You people don't tranq someone and then dump them in a room without supervision. A little help here, if you'd be so kind? Before you get me *really* ticked off?'

There was a long pause. I heard the sound of footsteps coming toward me. The cadence was familiar, but the echoes were not. Whoever it was, they were wearing unfamiliar shoes, weighted in a way I couldn't reconcile with my vague memories of someone who walked that way. These were heavy boots, field-rated by the dull thud of them, with metal toe and heel protection. It clinked, ever so faintly, every time a foot hit the floor.

'God*dammit*, Aislinn, why did you have to dig without telling anyone what you were doing?' The voice was Audrey's, filled with weary exasperation. 'I could have helped you. Or steered you away from something that you shouldn't have been prodding. This isn't the way I wanted you to find out.'

'Audrey?' Hope warred with betrayal in my tone, filling the syllables of her name with conflict. That was good. That matched what I was feeling, and quite nicely. 'What the fuck is going on here? Why am I cuffed? Why did you have me tranquilized?' *Why did you claim to have authority with the EIS? What have you been hiding from me?*

'You're cuffed because that's standard protocol when dealing with a prisoner in an unsecured location. I had you tranquilized because you were a walking biohazard zone, and I couldn't risk you touching or attempting to touch anyone who hadn't already been exposed. It was the kindest way.'

'The kindest—!' I tried to stand without thinking about it. My zip-tied ankles refused to hold my weight, and I toppled back to the cot, glaring through my hair in the general direction of Audrey's voice. 'There's nothing *kind* about waking up in the middle of a bizarre medical bondage scenario with my girlfriend saying things like "standard protocol." As to why I dug in without telling you, you weren't *speaking* to me, remember? I kept trying – Lord, how I kept trying – and you just kept going back to your bloody sulking place. I'm sorry I nearly got eaten in the woods, and I'm sorry I wouldn't leave my colleagues for dead while I hied it up the nearest tree, all right? Now don't you damn well go blaming *me* if you didn't know what I was doing. The silence started with *you*.'

There was a long pause before Audrey said, 'You're right, and I'm sorry. I shouldn't have frozen you out like that. You'd never scared me that way before. I still wish you'd tried harder to tell me what you were doing.' Her tone shifted slightly, moving away from coldly official, and toward the warm concern I'd always heard there. She sounded like the woman who had kissed my bruises and massaged my shoulders after a bad field run. She sounded like the woman I *loved*, and somehow, that just made me angrier. She didn't get to sound like that anymore. Not after she'd betrayed us.

'Why? So you could have stopped me?'

'I would have tried.'

That brought my thoughts to a screeching halt. I hadn't been expecting honesty: not from her, not under these circumstances. 'Why? Why in the world would you want to stop me from pursuing a story? Pursuing stories is what I *do*. And you — what are you doing claiming to have authority with the EIS? Audrey, what's going *on*?'

'Because I knew this story would get people killed, that's why,' she said. There was a clumping sound, boots against the floor, as she came closer. 'This isn't the sort of story that changes a local government or protects a state park, Ash. This sort of story changes everything, and that makes it dangerous. Too dangerous for people like us.'

'I don't think there's an "us" here, Audrey,' I said. I didn't raise my voice. I didn't shout. The words fell between us like stones, and I knew that the wall was under construction at last. When it was finished, there would be no breaching it.

'Ash . . .' She stopped, not seeming to know how to continue.

That was fine. I could continue for the both of us. 'You need to start answering questions, and you need to start answering them *now*, or there's going to be a reckoning when I get untied. Why are you speaking for the EIS? Where am I? Where is Ben?'

Ben was dead. That was the only reasonable explanation for why Audrey had separated us. I hadn't been careful enough about preventing blood exposure, and he'd managed to catch Kellis-Amberlee from the smears I'd left all over our gear. Ben was dead, Mat was dead, Audrey was apparently working for someone else, and I was the last man standing. I had always suspected that it was going to end like this — well, without the 'my girlfriend sells us all out' part. That, I hadn't seen coming.

I'd just hoped it would take longer for me to wind up alone.

'Ben's in another room, still sleeping,' said Audrey. A ripple of amusement moved through her voice. 'Congratulations. Your system shrugs off tranquilizers faster than his. Don't get too impressed with yourself, though. You're still within the human norm. Once he's awake, we'll be able to debrief you both.'

'I don't want a debriefing, I want an *explanation*,' I said. 'You know those aren't the same thing. They never bloody well have been.'

'No, they're not,' she said. 'As for what you said before ... you can hate me, you can break up with me, you can do whatever you want, but there's always going to be an "us," because we're not as different as you're currently thinking we are.' Audrey's hands brushed my hair away from my face, clearing my field of vision. I glared at her. She didn't look away. 'I'm one person. One person is an easy thing to kill. So yeah, this is the sort of story that gets people like us killed.'

She was still wearing the black tactical suit and Kevlar vest she'd had on when she came into the visitor's center – that, or she was wearing another suit exactly like the first. Her hair was pulled back in a severe ponytail, the bleached streaks from decontamination radiating around the outside of it like the world's worst highlights. Her boots were knee-high, but not in the sexy way; in the 'I might need to wade through rivers of blood, and I want to be ready for every eventuality' way. She didn't look anything like herself. In some ways, she looked more like herself than she ever had before. This was what she'd always been meant to wear, not her paint-stained jeans and comfortable T-shirts. This was the real version of her.

The room was as I'd assumed from the short glimpses I'd been able to catch before: small, white, square, and effectively featureless. The only furniture was the cot beneath me. It looked like the sort of thing that could be put up and torn down in an hour, a mobile interrogation unit. There were two doors, both in the wall opposite where I was sitting. Both of them were closed. Neither was flanked by a blood testing unit. That just reinforced the impression that this – whatever it was – was a temporary thing, somehow assembled around me. Everything was spotless, but the smell of bleach was faint, like no cleansing protocols had ever been carried out here.

'You said you were ex-military,' I said. 'You said you'd been given an honorable discharge because of your PTSD, and that you'd changed your name to keep anyone from connecting you to your past. You lied to me.'

'I edited for you,' she said. 'I *am* ex-military. I *do* have PTSD. I don't take all those antidepressants for show. They're the only things that get me through the day. But I was a military doctor, and I went to work for the CDC after I left the service. That's what broke me. Not the army; the people who were supposed to be protecting us here at home. The CDC . . . they're not the angels everyone makes them out to be. They're not our friends.'

'So blow a whistle next time, instead of betraying your girlfriend,' I snapped.

Audrey just looked at me, expression so profoundly weary that the part of me that was accustomed to comforting her immediately sprang to attention, demanding I make it better. The fact that my hands were cuffed behind me was the only thing that kept me from reaching for her before my rational mind could step in and remind my instincts that I was angry.

'People who blow this whistle die,' she said. 'They aren't martyrs to the cause. They don't change the world. They don't reveal the big truths and make everything different. They die.'

'How's that any different from any other story we've ever told?' I demanded. 'Maybe fiction doesn't get you killed – although we both know *that's* not true, you Fictionals have had your share of obsessive fans who think they deserve you more than anyone else – but chasing down the news has always had the potential to end badly. We signed up for that. We knew what we were doing when we logged in.'

'You're not *listening*,' she said, sounding frustrated. 'The people who chase these stories die, and they don't come back, not even virtually, because they get discredited on their way out the door. Remember that big scandal last year? The Newsie in New Hampshire who hung himself right before the FBI revealed him as the head of a child pornography ring? His wife and kids didn't get the insurance money, because it was a suicide. They've been harried out of their hometown, they're living with her sister in Oklahoma now. They're probably going to have to change their names and disappear, once they realize this is the sort of thing that doesn't go away.'

'He blew the whistle?' I asked, horrified.

'Someone who was good – *really* good, better than Mat, God rest their soul; we'd need a Georgette Meissonier – might be able to find his original reports. The ones where he talked about corruption at the CDC, and conflicting accounts about research into the cure for Kellis-Amberlee. He'd been talking to the wrong people. People who knew too much, and weren't as careful about sharing it as they should have been. Most of them are dead now, too. It's a real shame. There were some brilliant minds on his contact list.'

'You can add Georgette Meissonier to the ranks of the dead,' I said. 'There was an attack on the Ryman convoy. She was killed.'

'I know,' said Audrey. 'The rest of her team is in CDC custody right now. They may not get out alive. It depends on what kind of long game the people in charge are trying to play. And that's my point, Ash, all right? If the Masons had known where to look, if Meissonier had known where to dig, they *might* have been able to get the information out before someone shut them down. They had a chance of getting the real data and going viral. We never had that. We were the second ring of this circus, and no one was ever going to watch us when they had the chance to watch the elephants.'

I looked at her for a long moment before I said, 'You could have warned us.'

'I did my best.'

'You could have warned *me*.'

'I couldn't risk it.' She shook her head. 'You kept my secret, and I am and will always be grateful for that, but the secret I gave you to keep was full of holes. It wasn't *dangerous*. You could have told the world I was ex-military and hiding in a commune in Alameda because

I couldn't stand the smell of cordite, and it wouldn't have changed anything. A few Newsies might have come sniffing around to find out whether I'd been involved with any of the big cleanups that weren't open to the public. You and Mat would have shut them down, Ben would have threatened to start writing about the things *they* didn't want to have shared, and it would have passed. It would have blown over. If you'd been able to say that I was EIS, on leave, not actually retired, people would have come looking for secrets, and *these* secrets are the things that get you killed. How many ways do I have to say that before you'll start listening to me?'

She almost had me convinced. Almost. But almost only counts in horseshoes and hand grenades, as my mother used to say, and I wasn't buying it. 'Come off it, Audrey. They were trying to kill us – all of us – long before I started prying into anyone's secrets. We lost more than half the Irwins at the convention before I'd ever pried into anything. They didn't start this because of my investigating. You really think they'd have stopped if I'd gotten distracted by a shiny thing and wandered off?'

'I can hope,' she said, almost in a whisper.

'You want to fix this? Start giving me actual facts, and not just vague woo-woo "oh they'll kill you, oh I did it to protect you" bullshit,' I said. 'I'm not some fainting flower who needs to be protected. What I need is for you to tell me what's going on. And maybe to unfasten my hands. That'd be a start on me trusting you ever again.'

'Uncuff her, Agent Sung,' said Governor Kilburn. I turned my head and there she was, standing in the leftmost doorway. It was open now, and on the other side I could see a dim room with broken glass on the tiled floor.

'We're still in the visitor's center,' I said.

'Yes,' said Governor Kilburn. She stepped into the room, looking to Audrey. 'I sent Frances on ahead with the rest of the campaign. She thinks we've stopped to look for survivors. I don't know what I'm going to tell her.'

'Neither do I,' said Audrey. She looked back to me. 'That's sort of up to Aislinn.'

I felt my eyes widen to comic proportions as I stared at the two of them. 'Are you seriously standing there and implying you're going to have me killed if you don't like what I say? Because I can guarantee that if that's the case, you're *not* going to like what I have to say.'

'Mouth like a sailor,' said Audrey, with such obvious affection that I wanted to slap her across the face. She didn't get to sound like she loved me. Not now. 'We're not going to kill you. I couldn't if I wanted to. I love you.'

That was the final straw. 'If you love me, take these cuffs off,' I snapped. 'If you're not going to do that, stop pretending to give a damn.'

'All right,' said Audrey. She put a hand on my shoulder, pushing me forward. I didn't resist. 'My name isn't "Sung" anymore, Governor. It's "Wen." You know that.'

'Sometimes I wonder if you didn't choose that name purely for the puns it afforded you,' said Governor Kilburn.

'So what if I did?' There was a click as the handcuffs were removed from my wrists. Audrey straightened, clipping them to her belt before she reached for my ankles. I pulled my hands around in front of me, massaging each of my wrists in turn as I tried to get the circulation back to normal. I hadn't been cuffed tightly enough to hurt, but I'd been putting all my weight against my hands for long enough that they were numb and aching.

Audrey produced a knife from her belt, slicing easily through the zip ties. 'Puns are the highest form of humor, and anyone who tries to tell you differently has never found a way to make a joke resonate through three languages at the same time.'

I kicked her. Or rather, I tried to kick her: My bare foot whisked through empty air, and Audrey wasn't there anymore, having somehow rolled back three feet while the muscles in my calf were still tensing. She gave me a sympathetic look.

'I know you're angry, but I'm still your girlfriend, I still love you, and we're not supposed to solve every problem with our fists,' she said.

'That wasn't my fist, it was my foot,' I said. 'Completely different.'

'My little Irwin.' Audrey looked over her shoulder at the governor, and said, 'This is on you, Susan. You decide what gets said and what doesn't.'

'I'll go get Benjamin,' said the governor, and disappeared, leaving me alone with Audrey. I glared at her. She looked at me, and sighed.

'I tried so hard not to have to lie to you,' she said. 'I thought we were signing up with the lowest-rated Democratic candidate. We weren't supposed to make it this far on the trail. We were never supposed to be having these conversations.'

'Who did you think was going to win?' I asked. 'York?'

'There was a fourth potential candidate. Senator Darren Hart of Pennsylvania was supposed to be running. Based on his numbers and his performance, he would have wiped the floor with Kilburn and Blackburn both. He would have done the same thing Susan did, and chosen Blackburn as his VP candidate, and we could have all gone home.'

I'd heard about Hart. He'd featured heavily in the pre–campaign cycle buzz, and Audrey was right; everyone had expected him to run. And then, sometime between Ryman announcing his candidacy and Blackburn announcing hers, he'd just dropped off the map. There hadn't been a peep from his camp since all this had started. 'What happened?'

'His wife got sick. Staph infection leading to multiple organ failure. Can you believe it? We cure cancer, which used to be the big reason people didn't have the chance to do things; we replace it with zombies, which become the big new reason people don't have the chance to do things; and the world finds new ways to keep the hospitals open.' Audrey paused. 'I'm sorry. That was insensitive of me. Every human life matters. Every human life should be respected.' It sounded like she was reciting a mantra, rather than espousing a long-held belief.

I leaned as far from her as I could without getting off the cot. My hands were still tingling, and my legs felt faintly loose. I wasn't sure they'd hold my weight just yet. Better to wait than to stand and fall. 'What did you do for the CDC, Audrey?'

'Terrible things,' she said. 'And then I left them for the EIS, where I did more terrible things, but at least I did them for the right reasons. The EIS is still working for a better future, even if the CDC isn't. Please don't ask me what those terrible things were. I'm afraid . . . I'm afraid you won't love me anymore, if you ask me, and I need you to love me right now. Even if you're so angry you could spit, I need you to love me. It's the only thing that's allowing me to keep going.'

'Oh, I'm too angry to spit right now,' I said primly. 'I'm saving all my precious bodily fluids for when I might actually need them. I'm not too mad to glare, however, or to tell you that we're going to be having some serious conversations about where we go from here, when all this is over.'

'Since that implies we'll both still be breathing, I'll take it,' said Audrey. Her expression softened, becoming more like the Audrey I knew, the one who cooked me dinner and kissed my bruises and loved me, sometimes fiercely, sometimes with restraint, but always, and continuously, to the end of my days. Seeing that look on her face when she was dressed in military gear and her hair was pulled back in a practical, field-ready style made me feel off balance, like the whole world had shifted, and was never going to shift back.

'What should I call you now?' The words came out before I could fully consider their meaning.

Audrey looked away. 'Margaret Sung died when I walked away from the EIS. That was our agreement, in exchange for the things I knew not being released into the public eye. I couldn't be her and function in a world that had morality and believed in the sanctity of human life. Please, call me Audrey. That's who I am now. That's who I intend to be for the rest of whatever time I have left.'

'All right, Audrey. You want me to keep loving you? Tell me what you did.'

She looked back to me, eyes large and liquid in her too-pale face, and asked, 'Are you sure?'

'Yes.'

And she told me.

Told me about the experiments with serotyping the virus and introducing new strains to volunteers, political prisoners, and the dead; about the way they'd rendered Kellis-Amberlee terrible and new, about the fires they'd set and the facilities they'd cleansed to keep their new strains from getting out. About the way the new strains had gotten out anyway, leading to zombies that didn't moan.

Told me about the infants born to infected mothers kept chained down for their entire pregnancies, born unamplified but legally already dead, perfect guinea pigs for the things the CDC felt were necessary. About the lies, and the deaths, and the manipulation of the media. About the reasons she didn't sleep anymore. And when she was done, she looked at me, and waited.

'I still love you,' I said softly.

She leaned in to kiss me, and stopped as something clattered from the second door. It opened, revealing Ben. He was sitting in a wheelchair, slumped in on himself, and Amber was behind him, pushing. She looked exhausted, and her eyes were red; she had been crying recently. That wasn't a surprise. Whether she was crying for Mat or John or both, we had all lost someone today.

Like Audrey, she was dressed in military black. That made me tense. Amber caught the look and shook her head.

'I don't work for the EIS,' she said. 'They just have protocols before they'll let people into the field, and I needed to come with Audrey when she brought a team to retrieve you. I needed to see that you were safe. I'm so sorry, Ash. I'm so, so sorry.'

'Not your fault,' I said, and shifted my attention to Ben. 'Hi,' I said.

Ben's eyes were red too, but they were alert, and he was sitting up fully, taking in everything. His face had relaxed into true neutrality, betraying nothing of what he might be thinking. It was a trick I had always envied. Must have been nice to be able to hide everything away like that, keeping it on the inside until it was safe to let out.

'Hi,' he said. 'You okay?'

'A little numb, but apart from that, I'm fine,' I said. 'They had me all cuffed and zip-tied like a cartoon supervillain. You?'

'I guess they think of me as slightly less dangerous, probably because sedation makes me pukey,' he said. 'All I had was one hand cuffed to my cot.'

'Not sure whether I should be flattered or pissed off right now,' I said. 'So I'm going to default to "pissed off." It's generally safer.'

'We're sorry about that,' said Governor Kilburn. I turned. She was standing in the other doorway, expression weary and normally perfect hair in disarray. Unlike Amber and Audrey, she wasn't wearing black; she was still in one of her campaign pantsuits, this one slate-blue and accented with blue topaz jewelry. Chuck and Mat had probably worked together to select it for her, basing their color palette on Mat's makeup designs. The thought made my chest ache. Mat was never going to be doing another makeup design, or rebuilding another transmission, or anything. Mat was over. Mat was done.

Distance wasn't going to make this better. Distance was only going to transform new injury into immobile scar tissue. I was never, never going to forgive the people who had taken them from us. There was something pleasant about that realization. It meant that I was a little less shallow than I might have been, and a little more prepared to do whatever needed to be done.

'But really, come on,' said Amber. 'If you hadn't been cuffed all to hell and you'd woken up before one of us could get in here to monitor you, you'd have like, kicked a wall down and gone rampaging around the place, and there are a lot of people with guns outside, keeping things locked down and keeping the CDC out.'

Audrey shot her a quick glare. Amber smiled sunnily instead of glaring back, expression wholly unrepentant. I looked between them before looking to Ben.

'Have they been doing this to you, too?' I asked. 'Implying that the CDC isn't on our side and then clamming up like they've done something messy on the carpet?'

'I think they've been talking a little less freely in front of me,' he said. 'I got freedom of movement, you got freedom of information. It's almost like they knew what our respective strengths were and wanted to be sure that they didn't give away more than they intended to.'

'Funny thing, that,' I said. My hands were no longer tingling. My legs still felt weak, but I forced myself to stand, ignoring the way my short hospital gown barely covered the tops of my thighs, and walked across the room to take the handles of Ben's chair from Amber. 'I also notice that you got a full set of scrubs, while I got this stupid surgical nightie. If anything's been implanted in me, I'm going to be *very* cross.'

'Benjamin didn't have any wounds on his lower body that were actively bleeding,' said Governor Kilburn. 'You, on the other hand, had badly scraped knees. The pseudoskin set better without fabric in the way.'

'I can accept your logic without liking it,' I said, as I wheeled Ben over to my cot. Those same knees were knocking, trying to buckle under the strain of supporting the rest of me. It was a relief when I reached my destination without falling down. I parked Ben, turning his chair so he could face the others, and sat, smoothing my too-brief gown as far down over my legs as it would go.

The divide in the room had never been clearer. Ben and I on one side, Amber and Governor Kilburn on the other, and Audrey in the middle, seeming more than a little lost as she looked between us.

Then Governor Kilburn stepped fully into the room, moving out of the way of a tall, brown-skinned man with long brown hair that grazed his shoulders despite being tucked behind his ears. He was wearing khaki slacks and a black tank top under a startlingly white lab coat.

As was so often the case, my mouth engaged before my brain got a vote on the subject. 'How often do you bleach that thing? Every fifteen minutes? It's like you're wearing a toothpaste commercial.'

He looked down at himself and laughed. It was a genuinely amused sound. It didn't make me relax one bit. 'I guess that *is* pretty white, isn't it?' he asked. 'It's new. That's the secret to keeping things clean: recycle them before they have the chance to get dirty.' He looked back up, studying me and Ben before he said, 'I'm Dr Gregory Lake. I used to be Dr Sung's supervisor. I'm glad to see that you're both awake and alert – the lingering effects from the sedatives should wear off shortly – and I came to answer any questions you might have about what's going on here.'

There was a pause before Ben said, cautiously, 'When you say "answer any questions," you mean—?'

'I mean I'm going to answer your questions, and I'm going to explain what would happen if you released any of the information we're about to give you.'

Information ... I sat bolt-upright, heart suddenly pounding against my ribs. 'Where's my laptop?'

'All of our equipment is safe,' said Audrey. 'We were able to decontaminate and save almost everything. A little clothing was lost, and one of Mat's eye shadow palettes tested positive and had to be destroyed for safety's sake, but all the equipment is fine.'

'How much of it is being accidentally erased?' asked Ben, earning himself a moue of displeasure from Audrey. He shook his head. 'I'm not sorry about asking. You've been lying to us this whole time. I need to know our data will be intact when we get it back.'

'I thought you trusted me more than this,' said Audrey.

'And I thought your name was "Audrey Wen." This is a day where everyone gets disappointed, isn't it?' The nasty edge on Ben's voice would have seemed more natural on mine. I couldn't blame him. More than anything, he hated being lied to. Finding out Audrey had been lying to him right after losing Mat had to be devastating.

'Everything is as we found it,' said Dr Lake. 'We haven't even accessed your files. If there's any damage, it didn't come from us.'

'I'll believe that when I see it,' I said.

To his credit, Dr Lake nodded. 'I can understand that,' he said. 'This has all got to be very confusing, and not very comforting. I'm sorry about your friend. We recovered her body, and—'

'Mat's preferred pronouns were "they" and "them,"' Audrey interrupted. 'Please respect that. Just because they're dead, that doesn't change who they were.'

Dr Lake nodded again, more slowly. 'My apologies. Your friend's body has been destroyed, I'm afraid; it was necessary, for both biological and logistical reasons. There was no way to falsify your remains, so your disappearance has been reported to the CDC – all three of you. While they're trying to locate you in the surrounding countryside, we'll be able to keep you safe, at least for a short time.'

'And this changes the shape of the search,' I said. 'Three people don't move as quickly as two. Or as unobtrusively. Especially not when they're running and loaded down with all manner of equipment. You're trying to keep them off our trail. Why? Why not tell them that we're alive, and fine, and a bit pissed off, thanks awfully?'

'Because the people in charge of the CDC are not your friends,' said Audrey. 'I don't know how many ways I can say that before you'll start believing me. If they caught you, they'd kill you.'

'You said the Masons were in the custody of the CDC,' I said. 'Did you mean it when you said they might not make it out alive? I thought you were saying that they might have been exposed.'

'The CDC has lost track of its primary mission,' said Dr Lake. 'They became . . . confused, some time ago, and have been drifting further and further astray as time has gone on and they have managed to go unchallenged. At this point, nothing short of a miracle is going to loosen their hold on the government.'

'That's tosh,' I said. 'They're a government *agency*. That's not how politics work in America. I just took my citizenship classes, I *know* that's not how politics work in America.'

'They have a lot of money, a lot of lobbyists, and a remarkable amount of public support,' said Dr Lake. 'Tell me, Miss North, when was the last time you heard someone speak out against the CDC? Without being branded a crank and a liar, and finding themselves thoroughly discredited in the aftermath of whatever information they'd managed to release?'

'There have been a few Newsies who have tried to do less than flattering exposés on the CDC,' said Ben. 'Most of them have been laughed at. It's ... interesting that you're putting it the way that you are, because I knew a few of those bloggers before they got interested in the Centers for Disease Control. They did good work. But after the fact, when people started looking at their older pieces, they were full of holes and errors and outright fabrications. It didn't match up with the way I remembered their work. I never pursued it. It didn't seem that important, and on some level, I was ... ' He stopped, looking unsure of how he should continue.

'You were afraid,' said Audrey. 'You didn't want to say anything and turn yourself into a target, and you didn't want to think about what that fear meant, so you kept pushing the fear aside and focusing on things that didn't seem as potentially dangerous. You made yourself feel like it couldn't possibly be important, because if it was important it deserved your attention, and if you gave it your attention, you'd be making yourself a part of it.'

Ben looked at her levelly. 'Yes,' he said. 'Did you feel the same way?'

'I know what my fear means,' she said. 'I used to work for the CDC, and when I couldn't take it anymore, I joined the EIS, and when I couldn't even handle *that* anymore – when I started waking up screaming because of the things I'd seen – I walked away from my life and found someone else to be. I did it because I was afraid.'

'John recognized her,' said Amber. 'He worked for the CDC too, a long time ago. He was security for one of their bigger labs. Not a doctor. I don't think he'd ever actually said two words to her when they were both there. But he knew who she was. He told me he did. Said he was going to see what it was like to nail an epidemiologist. Er. Sorry.'

'It's all right,' said Audrey.

'No it's bloody not,' I said.

'He still worked for the CDC,' said Dr Lake. 'They have people embedded with all the major campaigns – even York had his ringers. The Ryman campaign, ironically, lost theirs during the first engineered outbreak. They've been running largely without supervision. The rest of the candidates have been monitored since the day they started.'

'I knew we had a mole,' said Governor Kilburn. 'I thought it was Amber for a while. No offense, Amber.'

'None taken,' she said. 'I would have assumed it was me, too, given my aunt and everything. Not sure you're who she would have asked me to go work for if she was trying to spy on someone, and not sure I'd have agreed to do it, but I can't blame you for thinking it was me.'

'Hold on,' said Ben. 'How did you know we had a "mole," and why in the world wouldn't you fire that person as soon as you figured out who they were?'

Governor Kilburn looked at him. Her eyes were weary, filled with shadows I couldn't name and didn't want to. 'I knew because sometimes the things I put in the press releases were inaccurate on purpose, and yet several groups always seemed to have the correct information. They were all groups with government ties, which to me, said we had someone reporting back to one of the other candidates, who was then leaking the things I didn't want to say.'

'Instead, it was the CDC leaking things, because they wanted witnesses to every move you made,' said Dr Lake. 'They can't fix the elections without getting caught – the voter suppression and voting machine scandals of the last few elections before the Rising made that sort of thing much harder – but they can guide the results. The attacks on the candidates weren't all intended to kill. They were meant to shape public opinion and sympathies, without showing too much of an early hand.'

Speaking of hands: I put mine up like a schoolchild hoping to be called upon. I didn't wait. 'If they weren't *all* intended to kill, which ones *were*? Since it seems you're telling us things to make us trust you, and all.'

'The Ryman ranch was never intended to harm the candidate. Neither were the attacks in Eakly, or outside the convention center. I'm fairly sure whoever's in charge of this program expects a Republican win, since the Democrats only rated a single group attack by that stage, while Ryman was still getting tailored attention. The attack in Portland . . .' Dr Lake trailed off. 'Miss North? Is something wrong?'

I was so angry it felt like my eyes were crossing. I knew my cheeks and the tips of my ears would be turning red as the blood rushed to my face, gradually blending into my hair. One of the many reasons I've never tried to hold down a job that required any subtlety: Subtlety is not a part of how I was made. 'You said those attacks were *not intended to kill*,' I said, and my voice was harsh with the effort of not screaming every word at him. 'Would you like to tell that to the survivors of the dead? Either those used as weapons, or those the weapons were used against? *I knew those people.* Some I knew because we worked together. Some I knew because I could have been them, so, so easily. They were me, and now they're dead, and you're going to stand there in your fine white coat and tell me that the *intended target* is what matters here, like that somehow makes everything – or anything – better. It does not.'

'My apologies,' said Dr Lake. He sounded sincere. Somehow, that didn't help as much as I wanted it to. 'It's hard to work with the CDC and avoid falling into their ways of thinking. Most of the doctors who work for them are good people who went into medicine because they genuinely wanted to help. You don't make it through medical school and all the hoops that are required to get a CDC job if you don't really, really want to make the world a better place. But they're myopic there, in some very specific, very targeted ways. They see the world in columns. "Avoidable loss" and "acceptable loss" run down every page. Those attacks were either intended to kill the candidates or they were not. In this scenario, in this situation, that was the only loss that mattered. Everyone else was background noise.'

'It doesn't take that much pressure to separate a man's scrotum from his body,' I said pleasantly. 'If I demonstrated on you, would that be an "acceptable loss" or an "avoidable loss," d'you think?'

'Dr Lake is on our side,' said Governor Kilburn wearily.

'Dr Lake has just described the attacks on you, and on my aunt, as both intentional and possibly intended to kill the candidates involved,' said Amber. 'In the absence of anyone else to take responsibility, I say we let Ash rip his balls off.'

'You're all talking in circles,' said Ben quietly. 'Why is the CDC committing acts of terrorism to guide the leadership of this country, and why do they have preferences among the candidates?'

'They've been trying to steer public opinion toward the candidates with families,' said Audrey. She looked at the floor. My heart ached to see her looking so gutted, but I didn't move toward her. I wasn't sure she was mine anymore. I wasn't sure I wanted her to be. 'Ryman has a wife and two surviving children. Even if the children had died during the attack, he would still have had a wife. Tate has a wife, but they haven't been seen in public together for years, and it's generally accepted that they've remained married only for the sake of his career. Not a good lever if you need to move him.'

'Kirsten is unmarried, no kids. Her sister, however, has three children, and Kirsten has always loved them like they were her own,' said Governor Kilburn. 'Frances has a husband and two children. I never married. I never had the time for it. If I had, I suppose I'd be like Tate; holding on to the ring because I wanted the benefits it offered, but not really embracing the institution.'

'Portland was meant to kill you,' I guessed.

Dr Lake nodded. 'It was one of the two scheduled candidate fatalities. Both failed. The trouble with using the infected to do your dirty work is that once they're loose, they can't be controlled, and they'll go where they like, do what they want. Neither candidate died.'

I didn't ask who the second attack was meant to kill. It wasn't relevant to my survival, and so I didn't care. If Ben wanted to know, he could ask for himself. Instead, I narrowed my eyes and said, 'You're still talking circles. I don't like it. What's the CDC's interest in all of this?'

'There is never going to be a cure for Kellis-Amberlee,' said Dr Lake, and the world shifted, and there was nothing I could say. Nothing at all.

The bell above the door rang when Li Jiang slipped inside, betraying her as her cat-soft footsteps never would. She stopped where she was, allowing the door to close behind her, and waited with ill-concealed impatience for the curtain behind the counter to be pushed aside and the mistress of the house to appear.

The House of the Rising Moon was not a place for a respectable woman to be seen, either by day or night, for there were no 'working hours' in a den of ill repute. If the door was open, the house was open for business, and whatever strange pleasures or stranger pains a person sought could be purchased within. Li Jiang had no quarrels with those who walked these halls for either personal or professional reasons, but her position in the city was tenuous enough to make her uncomfortable standing where she stood, with all the eyes of man and Heaven seemingly turned toward her.

The curtain was pushed aside, and a woman carved from polished amber stepped lithely into the shop front that served as one of the house's many staging areas. Her hair was a river of molten metal, and her skin was gilded with paint and pastes, until she glittered in even the dim light, as precious as any concubine of Midas. Her gold-rimmed eyes widened slightly at the sight of Li Jiang. Nothing else betrayed her surprise as she leaned against the counter, displaying her cleavage to its best advantage, and smiled.

'Why, Lethal. I didn't expect to see you here again so very soon. Have you tired of your current entertainments, and come looking for something sweeter to gild your evenings?' Her tongue played across her upper lip, turning innuendo into blatant solicitation.

Li Jiang had known the lady for years, long enough that she took no offense at the attempt. 'I will tire of my Grace shortly after the stars blow out and the night sky turns as black as your heart,' she said. 'I am here because there has been a murder, Demeter, and we need to talk about the funeral arrangements. I am ... I am sorry. I wish I were here for more pleasant reasons.'

The madam called Demeter straightened, flirtation gone. 'Who has died?'

'I'm sorry. Your youngest child, Clio, is gone.'

Alone in the entryway to the grandest whorehouse on the West Coast, the lady of the manor wept, and Li Jiang tried, as best she could, to comfort her.

—From *Those Who Are Gone But Never Lost*, originally published in *Wen the Hurly Burly's Done*, the blog of Audrey Liqiu Wen, April 28, 2040

Sixteen

The silence didn't last. Ben lurched to his feet, taking a wobbly step toward Dr Lake. His lack of balance made him look alarmingly like one of the infected, but his expression was fierce and angry, not raw with hunger. I sat frozen, unsure how I was supposed to react, or what I was supposed to do, or . . . well, or anything. This was a new territory, one I didn't know how to navigate. I just sat, waiting to see what happened next.

'What do you *mean*, there's never going to be a cure?' he demanded. 'That's what the CDC is *for*. All their resources, all their attention, it's all going toward the development of a cure. We've been diverting half the government's budget to them for decades—'

'Because they say they're going to fix this problem any day now,' said Dr Lake. 'But that doesn't account for the diseases we don't know how to fight anymore, does it? Take away Kellis-Amberlee and cancer comes back. How many oncologists are left in the world right now? How many will be left in another five years, or another ten? That doesn't even begin to touch on the number of deaths we used to see annually from respiratory infections. The flu alone killed ten thousand Americans every year before the Rising. Now, we lose half that many to zombie attacks. The math says that a cure is bad for America.'

'So why don't they come out and say that?' It took me a moment to realize that the voice saying those words was mine. I was committed now: I was in the conversation, and I wasn't going to be able to back out a second time. 'Just tell people there's not going to be a cure but that's all right, because they're actually a great deal safer than they used to be – and never mind. I just answered my own question, didn't I?'

Dr Lake nodded grimly. No one said anything. Not even Ben, who had stopped at the middle of the room, wobbling like a reed in a high wind.

Fear wasn't just an American pastime: It was a global addiction, and industries of every size existed to satiate it. Some of them were obvious, like the blood tests shoved in front of our faces at every possible turn, or the heart monitors some parents insisted their children wear before they were allowed to leave the house. Others were more subtle. Even I was in an industry designed to feed into the culture of fear. All Irwins were. We went out into the world and brought home the twin illusions of accomplishment and exposure. Someone who'd seen Ireland through my reports never needed to go there, not really; they could watch the videos any time they liked, marvel at how green the hills were, and go to sleep feeling like they'd traveled the world. Why would they ever leave the house when there was nothing left to see?

Internet journalism hadn't risen to the heights it had despite the mainstream news trying to keep us down. We'd done it *because* of the mainstream news. Because having us to contrast with the 'approved' reports turned us into an outlet and a funnel for the fears of the world. Because we were supposed to be unfiltered and raw and hence *real*, and reality was terrifying to most people. We were a tool. We always had been.

'I'm still mad at you Audrey, but I could really use a hug right about now,' I said, in a small voice. She walked over to the cot, sat down beside me, and put her arms around my shoulders without saying a word. She smelled right, salt skin under decontamination bleach. If I closed my eyes, I could pretend she wasn't dressed like she was getting ready to lay siege to everything I'd ever loved. I closed my eyes.

Closing my eyes didn't make the world go away. In the darkness, Ben said, 'This is impossible. This is . . . it's too big to hide. You can't cover up something like "the CDC isn't looking for a cure." The World Health Organization would find out. They'd tell everyone.'

'The WHO is aware. The world's medical organizations came to the conclusion that the cure would be worse than the disease more than a decade ago. Everything they – we – have done since then has been geared toward one of two ends: management, or control. The EIS wants to manage Kellis-Amberlee. Humanity engineered this disease. We can find a way to live with it, one that doesn't mandate destroying the natural world or living in constant terror. The CDC wants to keep the virus at the forefront of everyone's minds.'

'Why?' asked Amber. She sounded as baffled as I felt. I decided not to hate her quite as much as I hated everyone else.

'Because as long as the world is looking at Kellis-Amberlee as their greatest threat, the CDC and organizations like it will continue to have control, and we'll keep getting along, while the rich keep getting richer on the back of everyone else's fear,' said Ben wearily. 'Am I right, Dr Lake?'

'Sadly, yes,' said Dr Lake. 'The dead rising didn't put an end to war. We fight over things like race and religion and public decency. But we fight online. We fight virtually. The Internet is real, and things said there genuinely cause damage – I'm not trying to minimize the issues of cyber harassment or stalking. They're still a far cry from the days when our government would call in drone strikes under the thinnest of possible pretenses. Now, when the enemy doesn't stay dead, it seems better to negotiate with the living.'

'So the world is healthier and more peaceful and the only cost is that we have to live in terror all the time?' I opened my eyes. I didn't pull away from Audrey. 'You'll forgive me for saying so, but this isn't living. This isn't decency. People shouldn't be lying like this. They should let people make their own choices, and let the world do as it's going to do.'

'The EIS agrees with you, Miss North. The trouble is, we're a small group surrounded by large groups, and many of them have no scruples about making sure viewpoints they disagree with go unheard.' Dr Lake shook his head. 'You may be wondering why I'm telling you all this. Why I'm saying things that are virtually impossible to believe.'

'I'm going to guess it's because you know none of us are recording right now, since you're the ones who stripped us down and decontaminated us while we were unconscious, and you've already made it more than clear that we can't leak this information without the wrath of the United States government falling on our heads,' I said wearily. 'If we don't want to be branded as pedophiles or murderers or something even worse, we can't say a word where anyone could hear, because we're smaller than the things we're up against. Isn't that so?'

'It is,' he agreed.

'Then here's what I want to know, and you'll need to use small words, if you don't mind; I'm an Irwin, we're not deep thinkers, we're mostly interested in what's available for us to hit,' I said. 'You've told us why we can't tell anyone. But you haven't told us why you're *telling* us.'

'He's telling you because I asked him to,' said Audrey, pulling away from me. She stopped when she was far enough to look me in the face as she said, 'He owed me some favors. I called them in, because I needed you to understand why I was going to ask you to run.'

'What?'

'Run.' Audrey shook her head. 'We have to run. We have to run fast, and we have to run far, because you looked in the wrong direction, and you triggered their cost-benefit analysis unit. Now John is dead, and that means the CDC is going to be watching the rest of the Kilburn campaign for signs that we learned more than we were supposed to know. They've always been watching. My presence guaranteed that. Now they're going to be waiting to see who we told, and how many of them need to be shot.'

'What Dr Sung isn't saying is that it was her presence that allowed you to learn as much as you did without interference,' said Dr Lake. 'She's still considered a member of the agency in good standing, and she's never violated her NDAs.'

'Not directly,' said Audrey. 'My stories have a lot of coded data in them. I've been communicating with some doctors in Canada who think they may have figured out the protein coding that Kellis originally designed for his cure. It's not much, but it could be key to understanding the way the viral structures interlocked.'

'That is a topic for another time,' said Governor Kilburn firmly. 'I've been approached by the CDC. They were concerned about my lack of family, and wanted me to know that they would have my back on the campaign trail. It was fairly patently a reminder that they always knew where I was going, what I was doing, and how to get to me. This is not an exaggerated danger. I got you into it. I am going to get you out of it.'

'But I don't want to run,' said Ben, sounding baffled. 'We just buried my mother. My sister, she needs me. I was finally going to fix up the house . . .'

'Your sister needs you to run,' said Dr Lake. 'If you don't, she's going to die. Do you understand what I'm trying to tell you? There will be an outbreak. It will be a tragic loss of life.'

'Don't threaten my family,' said Ben. The bafflement was gone, replaced by cold steel.

Dr Lake sighed. 'I'm not threatening anyone. I'm telling you what the CDC will do, what they'll *have* to do to keep their secrets, if they even suspect you know how deep this goes. You'll be discredited, and then you'll be destroyed, and they won't have the luxury or the compassion to make sure that the people around you aren't caught in the blast. Sometimes the people who stand against them just die.

That's terrible, and it's tragic, but it has a very low immediate area of effect. You've been *digging*. You *know* things, and as reporters, you have a tendency to share them with people – to back them up in places that most people won't know how to find. That means the CDC can't just arrange for an accident. They have to destroy whatever goodwill you might have with the general population, and then they have to destroy *you*.'

For a moment, we were all quiet. Finally, Ben turned and walked back to his wheelchair, sinking down into it with a defeated sound. It wasn't a sigh or a moan: It was somewhere in between, indefinable and heartbreaking. It made me want to go to him, and hold him, and lie to him about what was going to happen next; it made me want to do all the things that wouldn't help, but felt like they should. I didn't move.

'What do we do?' asked Ben. 'You're saying the CDC will go out of their way to destroy us, and I don't want to believe you, which I guess proves that I should. We're in a prefab isolation chamber in the middle of nowhere. Mat's dead. What do we do?'

'As far as the CDC is concerned, right now, you're all dead, or you're all about to be,' said Governor Kilburn. 'We've reported you as missing. That means you were either killed in the explosion and reanimated, or you ran. They'll assume the first – it's the most reasonable – and start by looking for you among the local dead. When they don't find you, they'll start looking farther afield.'

'I'd say we have about forty-eight hours to get you as far from here as possible before that happens,' said Dr Lake briskly. 'I can't provide an EIS vehicle – our profile needs to stay low for the time being, and while I'm happy to help Dr Sung, within limits, there's only so much I can justify endangering our operation. We do, however, have a small off-roader that was purchased from a private owner in anticipation of a situation like this one. It will be left in the woods nearby. Some supplies will "accidentally" be left with the vehicle. If anyone intercepts you, you can produce papers showing it was owned by a man who died in an outbreak two weeks ago, making it legal salvage as long as you're within a hazard zone.'

'You really want us to run,' I said quietly. There were so many things I wanted to say – so many words, and so many of them meaning absolutely nothing, because all the decisions had been made before we'd even woken up. We were small fish that had somehow ended up in the ocean, and I supposed I should feel grateful that a helpful wave was nudging us back toward the shore. Gratitude simply couldn't seem to fight its way through my anger. I've never much liked being told what to do.

'No,' said Governor Kilburn quietly. We turned to look at her. She shook her head. 'I *need* you to run.'

'How long have you known about all this?' asked Ben. 'Did you bring us on board knowing what it could mean – what it *would* mean?' He was asking her whether she had knowingly destroyed our lives, and to her small credit, she didn't look away.

'I started making phone calls after the convention.' Her laugh was small and bitter. 'That's what I do. I'm sure you've figured that out by now. When the going gets tough, the tough start calling everyone they've ever met and asking for help. I knew something had to have gone terribly wrong for that attack to have been possible. I thought maybe I could find out what it was, point you in the right direction. This isn't altruism speaking; I wanted you on point, focused on my campaign, and not on what had happened to your friends. So I needed to know what happened. I guess I called the wrong people.'

She turned her face toward the floor, and for the first time, I appreciated what a good job her makeup artists did with her. I could see fine lines around her eyes, a cobweb of fissures etching her age across her face. She hid them so well. How many of them were new, sprouted since the start of this campaign?

'The CDC showed up at my hotel room last night,' she said. 'They had pictures, of people who are important to me. Not as many as they might have had if they'd been coming for someone with a larger family, but still. They made it clear that they knew everything about what we knew, and what would hurt me, and that my silence was valuable enough to keep my people safe. They don't mind the idea of my becoming President, even though they think it's unlikely – my chances are "witheringly small," according to their analysts. Imagine! Coming to my hotel room and telling me, to my face, that I'm not going to win, but if I do, I'll belong to them. The nerve of it all.'

'I found her in distress,' said Amber. 'She wouldn't tell me what was wrong. I told Audrey and John that the governor seemed to be under some sort of stress. John must have gone and checked in with the CDC, and gotten his instructions about you.'

'And I called the EIS,' said Audrey.

It seemed both messy and pat, like things had been crashing toward a breaking point for quite some time. I wanted to put my head in my hands, to block out the world for a while – just long enough for me to get my bearings back. I did no such thing. Instead, I sat up straighter, and asked, 'Where do you think we're going to go?'

'That's up to you,' said Dr Lake. 'I can't get you any farther than "away." But I have faith in the two of you. I know that you can find a way out of this.'

'The three of us,' said Audrey. 'I'm not coming back to active duty just because things got ugly. I meant it when I went on psych leave. Where Ash goes, I go.'

I gave her a sidelong look. 'I'm still mad at you.'

'I've been mad at you for weeks,' she said. 'I suppose we can balance out each other's anger, hmm? Figure out where we're supposed to go from here.' Then she smiled, small and shy and just a little hesitant, and my anger didn't matter anymore. She was going to come with us. In the end, that was the only proof of loyalty I needed.

'The four of you,' said Governor Kilburn. We all turned to her, varying looks of confusion on our faces.

'Mat's dead,' said Ben. 'We're not abducting a random EIS doctor.

I'm pretty sure that's the sort of thing that gets us arrested. So who—?'

'Me,' said Amber. 'That's what you mean, isn't it?'

'Yes,' said Governor Kilburn. 'The CDC knows you're Kirsten's niece, and that you're close to this team. Maybe she's not a candidate anymore, but things can change, and I don't want them to use you against her – or against me. They don't know how much you know. And I'm not comfortable sending our bloggers into the wilderness without someone I know has common sense to keep them safe.'

'I can't really take offense at that,' I said. 'I want to, but I can't.'

'I know.' Governor Kilburn sighed, running a hand through her hair before she said, 'I am so sorry. If I'd had any idea . . .'

'If you'd had any idea, you would never have run for office,' said Amber. 'I don't think anyone would. Who wants to be a puppet for a bunch of asshole scientists? Uh, no offense, Dr Lake.'

'None taken,' he said. 'I think "asshole scientists" is an excellent descriptor for our group as a whole. I wish you all luck.'

'How are you not worried about letting us leave when we know this much?' I blurted.

Dr Lake paused for long enough that I thought he wasn't going to answer. Finally, he said, 'Because the truth isn't worth the screen that shows it these days. What matters is the fear, and what you have to say is frightening, but it's not as frightening as the world outside. You say "the CDC is lying to you," and people will have to look at the world with new eyes, eyes that don't forgive them for all the things they've done wrong in the name of keeping themselves safe. You're trying to sell a story no one wants to buy. It would take a miracle to make people listen – and right now, you don't have a miracle in you. None of the campaign journalists do. I'm sorry. It's the truth. I can let you leave because you can never speak. You'll be written off as cranks and conspiracy theorists if you try, and then the CDC will find you, and they'll destroy you. Not just you: everything you've ever loved.'

'So you told us all this because . . . ?'

'Because you had to understand why we can never, never come back,' said Audrey wearily. 'We have to run, Ash. We have to run and not look back. This is where the story ends.'

I looked at her, and then at Ben, and I said nothing.

There was nothing left to say.

I'm not supposed to be posting here. It takes time and energy to boot up a connection and compose a sentence, and Ash tells me we can't afford either of those things anymore. She says what matters is finding our way back to civilization. I don't have the heart to tell her I'm not going to make it that far. My leg is broken and turning septic. We can't get a stable enough connection for GPS triangulation; we're lost in the wilderness, and we're going to die out here. Or at least, I am. Mat's already gone. I hope they're on the Wall, grinning for the whole world, putting on eyeliner with a master's hand. I'll never know. The only reason I can get these posts out is because they're pure text, piggybacking on the old SMS networks and bypassing all the high-traffic choke points.

I'm not supposed to be posting here. I don't care. I'm so sorry. I'm going to miss you all.

We did our best. It wasn't enough.

—From *That Isn't Johnny Anymore*, the blog of Ben Ross,
May 3, 2040

Seventeen

The all-terrain vehicle trundled through the woods like an armored bear: fast enough to be better than walking, bulky enough to make driving a continuous adventure, and sturdy enough to give no fucks when I overcompensated for the slopes and sideswiped a tree – something that happened on a regular enough basis that we'd all stopped exclaiming about it. Amber rode shotgun, rifle braced against her shoulder, ready to shoot at the first sign of danger. Ben and Audrey were packed into the backseat, buffered by piles of clothing and equipment, hunched over their respective tablets. Ben was tapping out another of his increasingly fictional 'man versus wild' blog posts, all of which were being dropped online with doctored location tags that would guide the CDC farther and farther down the coast. Audrey was monitoring the various mailing lists that she still had quasi-legal access to, thanks to her CDC background, looking for indications that anyone was looking for us. Anyone at all.

It had been almost four days since we'd left the rest stop and the presidential campaign behind, and if anyone was going to care enough to come looking, they hadn't started yet – that, or they were smart enough to realize Audrey might be watching for them, and they had taken their communications to another channel. That was the trouble with suddenly finding ourselves dropped into the middle of some sort of disturbing spy thriller: There was no way of knowing what was going to happen next, or whether we were even doing the right thing. The world had become a never-ending carousel of bad plans and worse luck, and the ride operator didn't seem inclined to let us get off.

Four days of driving an ATV through the coastal woods of California, heading up the coast toward Oregon, where Amber said she knew some people who might be able to help us get to Canada. Four days of taking turns behind the wheel, because we didn't dare stop for longer than it took to refuel and use the bathroom. The last thing we needed was for all of us to fall asleep and wake to find that our vehicle had been surrounded by the hungry infected while our eyes were closed.

At least the 'supplies' we'd been promised had included almost twenty gallons of petrol and a map of the black market stations farther up the coast. Our fuel consumption was running slightly higher than the estimates, probably due to the irregular terrain and our need to avoid major roads, and on some level, I was relieved; if the estimates had been perfect, that would have said something about how long this plan had been under construction, and I would have needed to pull Audrey aside for a talk about what was really going on. Thus far, the man from the EIS seemed to have been on the up-and-up. Ben wrote posts detailing our slow progress down the coast, the ATV devoured the miles on the way up the coast, and Audrey and Amber took turns keeping watch, their eyes locked on the tree-clotted horizon as they waited for the other shoe to inevitably drop.

'We're going to need to stop in an hour or so,' I said. I didn't need to raise my voice to be heard. The ATV was virtually soundless as it rolled through the forest, thanks to a hybrid engine and a whole lot of carefully designed sound baffling. Anything that was intended to be driven off-road needed to be that kind of quiet, to avoid attracting the dead. The motion was bad enough. It would have been better if we could have hovered above the ground, flying in some sort of magical science-fiction machine, rather than our Prius of the woodlands.

We kept the windows cracked as we drove, trading the risk of being overheard for the advantage of being able to hear if someone was coming. Birdsong had become our near-constant soundtrack. When it went silent, so did we, creeping along and listening for either the moan of the dead or the crunching tires of the living. Both could spell disaster at this point. We'd chosen to believe the EIS – and to believe Audrey – when we'd agreed to run, and that meant the CDC could be sweeping the state trying to find us and prevent another outbreak. Or they could be preparing to cause one, to take care of us once and for all.

It was a little arrogant, assuming the CDC would waste time and resources on us. Sure, we'd found some things they might not want getting out, for whatever reason – and thanks to the EIS, we now knew more than was really safe for *anyone* – but they were still a national organization with better ways to waste their time than trying to find three missing journalists and one former security guard as we raced for the Canadian border. Yes, Canada. There was no better place in North America to disappear, and from there, we could get virtually anywhere in the world if we had the money, the patience, and the willingness to make a deal. Touching our accounts while we were in America would have been suicide, but there were hackers in Canada, people who'd be happy to get the money in exchange for their cut. There were hackers in America, sure. The CDC had jurisdiction in America. None of us were willing to risk it.

Ireland didn't have an extradition treaty with the United States anymore. We might not wind up charged with a crime, but if we did, there were worse places for us to run. I'd sworn once that I would never go back there. I was willing to reconsider that decision if it meant we got out of this alive. I was willing to reconsider a great deal if it meant we got out of this alive. We could always move on again after we had our feet under us.

'Map says there's a fuel depot ten miles ahead, if we get out of the woods and switch over to a frontage road,' said Audrey, looking up from her tablet. 'It's supposedly secure. Part of the black market network that distributes medical supplies to the people who've been living off the grid on the coastal highways.'

'I don't believe there are really people living out here,' said Amber. 'No one would do this to themselves voluntarily.'

'Says the woman who just walked away from her entire life,' I said.

She was quiet for a moment before she said, 'You needed me. I didn't have anything to stay for except for my aunt, and I'd be putting her at risk at this point. She doesn't deserve to be put under pressure because of me. She's already done so much, you know? Mom's not a good lever. Aunt Kiki has always been super open about how she helped Mom with her gambling problems and helped to take care of us kids. There's not much that can be done to make Mom into a tool. And my little brothers, they're little brothers. Kids. Jake's going to be eleven in August. Joe's not even seven yet. The only thing they can be threatened with is no ice cream before bed. If I stick around, I'm a much better target. I needed to remove myself from the field.'

Privately, I thought that there was plenty that little boys could be threatened with, if the person doing the threatening had no scruples and didn't care about looking like a monster. Children are always the most vulnerable part of any conflict. I didn't say anything. Amber thought she was doing the right thing, and even if she wasn't, it was too late now; there was no going back for her. For any of us. We'd run from the CDC. Ben and I were legally dead, thanks to whoever at their office had transmitted those fake test results before John opened fire; Audrey and Amber were missing, which had to look suspicious as all hell. Ben was laying a false trail for me and him farther and farther down the coast, with the intent of ending it with our 'deaths,' since they knew by now that no bodies had been found. By the time the CDC got to wherever we 'died,' our supposed bodies would be gone, but that was nothing new. In the post-zombie world, dead bodies got up and walked away all the time.

'Aislinn?' asked Ben. 'What do you think?'

I thought a lot of things, only a few of which could be repeated out loud. 'Give me the directions and I'll head for the fuel depot,' I said. 'We need to start making contacts if we're going to make it to Canada, and I'm worried about how much fuel we have left in the back. They gave us trade goods for a reason.' Not money — money held little weight in the badlands — but medicine and prophylactics, chocolate and small, canned things with elaborate names. Caviar and tinned asparagus and pears in heavy syrup were what passed for a credit card out here.

It was difficult not to wonder whether my companions had stopped to really *think* about what that meant for our futures, or at least the part of our futures that would take place on this long, semideserted road to the Canadian border. There'd never been much money in our home, but we'd gotten by. Audrey knew how to stretch a single chicken into three meals without anyone going to bed hungry, and my frugal upbringing had left me capable of twisting a grocery budget until it screamed. Ben and Mat had been left to keep the power on and the Internet running, and they'd never needed to worry about how the food got onto the table. Now there was no power to worry about. We recharged our electronics off the ATV's battery, and recharged the ATV by means of the solar panels bolted to the roof. It could run forever, if we kept supplementing it with gasoline. The world was a sea of free Wi-Fi signals and cell phone towers. We had always been swimming in it, and now we were finally taking proper advantage, piggybacking on a hundred signals to make it to the outside.

Things were getting pretty grim out there. As we rolled up the coast, the campaign for the presidency continued. Governor Kilburn was polling well, but not well enough to win; she'd made a few gaffes and missed a few political cues that anyone who didn't know her would take for inexperience, and anyone who did would take for careful, measured refusal to play along. She was bowing out, but privately; publicly, she was continuing to fight, at least in part to give us the time we needed. The Masons had survived their time in CDC custody and come out full of fire and brimstone and the absolute conviction that they were on the road that would lead them to the truth. I envied them their certainty. I envied them their soft hotel beds and easy access to hot tea a hell of a lot more.

'Turn left; there should be a road about twenty yards to the east of our current position,' said Audrey.

'On it,' I said, and hauled hard on the wheel, sending us bumping and jittering through the forest, which ended abruptly at a small embankment. I drove down that, ignoring the way the ATV bounced – what was the point of driving an all-terrain vehicle if you weren't going to drive on *all* the available terrains? – before our tires hit the broken concrete, and we were suddenly rolling down something comparatively smooth.

It was amazing how much easier it was to control the wheel once I was no longer off-roading through an endless parade of tree branches. Amber looked over her shoulder at me.

'Huh,' she said. 'Look at that. You can drive.'

'Did you want to walk?' I asked pleasantly. 'I could stop the car long enough for you to hop out. I'm sure the zombie deer around here would just love the chance to chat about my driving with you.'

'Aislinn, please don't kick Amber out of the car,' said Ben.

'I'd love to see her try,' said Amber.

'Just follow this road until you come to a large fence and a lot of people start threatening to kill you,' said Audrey.

We all stopped bantering. Threats of sudden death had a tendency to kill a mood. Ben recovered first, asking delicately, 'Why will they be threatening to kill us? We're not with the CDC, and we're not here to arrest anyone. We want to buy gas.'

'Because that's the standard means of greeting strangers out here. Think of this entire network as being Aislinn when she has to wake up at seven in the morning. She's not *really* going to remove your kidneys with a fork and fry them up for you before you die, but she'll come up with a lot of interesting ways to threaten to do it.' Audrey shook her head before reaching up and pulling the hair tie from her ponytail. Her hair fell into its usual place, framing and softening her face. She was still wearing her black EIS gear, but that little change made her look almost infinitely more approachable. 'Of course, these people *will* kill us if we force the issue. Don't force the issue. Don't pick fights, don't talk back, and if they ask you a question, answer it. There are no training wheels on these social interactions. They will back up their threats with pain.'

'I'm good with people,' said Ben. 'That's why I'm the Newsie.'

'You're *great* with people,' said Audrey. 'You're great with the kind of people who looked at the shape of society and thought "I should be a part of this thing." These are not those people. These are the people who looked at the shape of society and thought "this is a trap, I'm getting out while I still can." They haven't been playing by the rules you know for years.'

I glanced at her in the rearview mirror. 'I suppose these are the rules *you* know?'

Audrey shook her head. 'No. Not really. I did some surveys in these communities – not this one in specific, I was working on the East Coast at the time – to find out what medical issues they face, what resources they have the most need of, that sort of thing. It was all informal, under the EIS "monitoring and management" purview. We said we needed to know what diseases were circulating in the country, even if we had no way of addressing them. A lot of parents who choose to live off the grid will agree to have their children vaccinated, for example, if they can be sure that they're not going to lose them. You know Doctors Without Borders? Well, this was Doctors Without Borders in Appalachia and the Pine Barrens, looking for people who needed us, but who were never going to come out and say it. I learned enough about their rules that most of the folks I dealt with didn't want to shoot me on sight. That was as far as I got. They don't like outsiders in these places. They have no reason to.'

'Aunt Kiki used to work with the folks who live on the reservation out in Nevada,' said Amber, taking her eyes off the road as she rejoined the conversation. 'Something like seventy percent of the Native American population has refused to leave their land for protected cities, and only forty-two percent of the nation's reservations have modern security structures in place. People keep trying to take their kids away, because they're not properly protected. Aunt Kiki was always trying to make sure that wouldn't happen. She said "if you can thrive in this country when it's full of wolves and bears and white assholes, you can handle a few zombies."'

'So there are lots of different communities of people who shouldn't be alive out here and will happily blow our heads off if we look at them funny,' I said. 'That's splendid. I am delighted to hear it. Tonight, I'll say a special prayer to the Tooth Fairy to thank her for giving me so many opportunities to knock teeth out of heads in her honor.'

'Just try not to insult anyone, all right?' Audrey actually sounded nervous. I wanted to reassure her. I no longer knew how to do it.

I'd known since we got together that she hadn't told me everything about her past: That was one of the first truly serious conversations we'd had, sandwiched right between heavy petting and 'we're finally ready to take our clothes off.' That may make it sound like I hadn't really been listening, but nothing could have been further from the truth. I had been so desperately, head over heels in love with her that I'd been willing to listen to anything she said, even if I wasn't necessarily prepared to believe it all. She'd wanted me to know, she'd said; she'd wanted me to understand what I was getting myself into. So I had listened, and she had spoken, and at the end of it, I had said that I was in for the long haul. No matter what she did, I wasn't going anywhere.

I truly hadn't been trying to lie to her. It was just that she'd been lying to me, at least by omission, and now that I was facing the consequences of that omission – all the little pieces she'd left out, all the things she hadn't trusted me enough to say – I didn't know how to feel. She knew this world, because she had been in it before. That was great for our ability to navigate, but what did it say about my ability to forgive her?

Maybe it was small and selfish of me to be dwelling on my relationship status at a time like this, but I'd always appreciated my ability to distract myself from my own impending demise, and so I didn't try too hard to make myself stop. As long as I was thinking about Audrey, I wasn't thinking about the fact that I was driving, knowingly and with intent, into a dangerous future.

The road curved, leading the ATV inexorably into a deeper patch of woodland. If I squinted, I could see the place where old concrete had been chipped away and new concrete had been laid down, artificially weathered to keep this stretch of abandoned roadway from looking any different on a satellite view. It must have taken years of careful curation to bend the road to where they needed it. I respected the work, even as I became increasingly tense. What we were driving into . . . this wasn't an amateur operation, something we could defeat with logic and a couple of bullets. These were people who put survival and freedom ahead of everything else. We needed to be careful.

Then the road curved sharply, and ended at a large chain-link fence with razor wire strung across the top and a padlock holding the gate closed. I stopped the car. The trees provided cover here, but they had been hacked back harshly from the fence itself, making it impossible for anything that had managed to climb up there to leap over cleanly. The razor wire would stop whatever tried to jump, shredding it where it hung. It was a dandy way of dealing with the issue of zombie raccoons, even if it was the sort of fix that required a lot of bleach.

The fence had been constructed around an old service complex, gas station and attached mini-mart and freestanding farmhouse, all about twenty yards from where we were stopped. It looked like the complex had been independently owned before the Rising, explaining the lack of logos or large signage. An RV was positioned at an angle next to the farmhouse, providing extra space for the people who lived here. People who were nowhere in evidence.

'Are we sure this place is open?' asked Amber. 'Maybe they're on vacation.'

'Where do survivalists go for vacation?' I asked. 'It's not like they have a lot of travel options.'

'No one does,' said Audrey. 'Wait.'

We waited. Seconds ticked by, enough that I became restless and reached for the door handle. My fingers had just closed on it when the dogs appeared, half a dozen of them racing from behind the main building with their ears flat and their teeth gleaming white in the light that filtered down through the trees. They were barking madly, and the sound seemed to travel straight from my ears to my nerves, galvanizing them.

'Holy shit,' whispered Amber.

Ben leaned forward until his head and shoulders were in the front seat, his hands braced to keep him from falling. 'That's a Great Dane, those are German shepherds – that looks like a Bernese mountain dog. Who still has Bernese mountain dogs?'

'They're dogs, the lot of them, and all above amplification weight,' I said, unable to keep the whine of fear out of my voice. 'What are they doing here?' Zombies, gunfire, and hostile terrain, I could handle. The idea of zombie raccoons was charming and novel. But dogs? Dogs were running delivery systems for teeth and tearing and terror. Dogs were the enemy.

'A lot of people went off the grid in the first place because they didn't want to give up their dogs,' said Audrey. 'For them, the relationship between man and canine was more important than the amplification risk – and to be fair, most dogs never bite people. We domesticated them for a good reason. There are people who felt that killing them all because we had made a mistake wasn't just wrong, it was monstrous.'

'No, that *dog* is monstrous,' I said, eyes locked on the fence. 'How can it be so big? I don't believe it's really a dog. I think it's a bear that someone is pretending is a dog, because that someone is seriously damaged.'

A person appeared from the same place the dogs had come from. He was tall enough to also qualify as a bear, the sort of man who, were he to amplify, could take out an entire medical response team before someone managed to drill a bullet through his forehead. His hair was long, blond, and untied, making it all seem distressingly biblical.

'If he says his name is Samson, I'm turning this car around and we're going to go find a *different* illicit petrol station,' I said.

Ben laughed. Audrey snorted. Amber, who hadn't moved in several minutes, did nothing. Her eyes were fixed on the approaching man, and when I glanced her way, I could all but see the math she was running in her head about how many shots she'd need to take him down before he could open the gate and release the dogs. Maybe for the first time, I appreciated how much attention she'd always paid to her job. You don't get hired to protect a potential President because of your connections. It happens because you know how to do whatever it takes to keep people alive.

The man reached the fence and made a cranking gesture with his left hand before pointing to the windows. He wanted us to roll them down.

'This is a terrible idea,' I said.

'Yes,' agreed Audrey. 'Now roll down the window.'

I rolled down my window.

'Afternoon,' said the man, through the fence. 'You folks lost? Because I'm afraid this is private property.' He had a pleasant voice and a mild accent I couldn't quite place. It was definitely American, but apart from broad regional differences, all Americans sounded pretty much the same to me.

'No, sir,' said Audrey, rolling down her own window and leaning very slightly out in order to address him. 'We're looking for gas. We understand you might be willing to barter for some.'

The man's eyebrows raised in an expression of almost comical surprise. 'Is that so? Because I don't remember putting myself in the local yellow pages.'

'What's a yellow page?' I asked, glancing to Ben. He shrugged, a look of blank confusion on his face.

'We got your location from a friend, sir,' said Audrey. 'He assured us he was only giving the location of establishments that would be willing to talk before they opened fire.'

'Four gunmen in the tree line,' said Amber, speaking for the first time since we'd stopped. 'Two snipers in the trees themselves. We're not getting out of here alive if they don't want us to.'

'You say the sweetest things,' I muttered, and stuck my own head out the window, flashing the man my brightest smile. It was the look that had launched a thousand stories, and I just hoped he wasn't immune. 'Hello! I'm Ash. Nice to meet you.'

The man's eyebrows raised further. 'Irish?'

'Born and bred,' I said. 'Look, we're running short of fuel, and we've sort of torqued off some folks in your government, so it's important we keep heading for the Canadian border if we don't want to wind up shot and buried in a ditch somewhere. You seem a reasonable sort. Possibly insane, if the dogs are anything to go by, but lots of crazy people are lovely and reasonable and quite capable of selling us some petrol without shooting us in the head.'

Slowly, the man blinked. 'You've done what to the government?'

'Made them really, really angry with us, which is why we need your petrol,' I said. 'You don't like the government, the government doesn't like us, and that makes us friends. We have trade goods, we don't want to be fed to your dogs, and no one with hair as nice as yours can be a woodlands cannibal, so if you'd just call off your snipers and open the gates, we could continue this conversation in private, hey?'

The man continued to stare at me for several seconds, his expression broadcasting a mixture of confusion and disbelief, like we were absolutely the last thing he had expected to roll up at his gates. Finally, he asked, 'What sort of trade goods?'

Amber cranked down her window and stuck her head out. If someone wanted to start shooting at us, there would now be nothing about the ATV's frame to stop the bullets. I found myself wanting to hand out Kevlar helmets, just in case. I kept smiling. A bright smile on a pretty face can disarm just about anybody. It's not a sex thing, at least most of the time. It's just that humans are inclined to be kind to pretty things, and we read smiles as friendly, deserving of our attention and acceptance. It's harder to shoot somebody who's smiling.

'Good ones,' said Amber. 'We're happy to be fair with you if you're happy to be fair with us, and nobody needs any trouble.'

'You know, this isn't the best place for unescorted women to come rolling up,' said the man.

'We're not unescorted,' I said, sensing the test in his words and refusing to play along. 'We have Ben – he's in the backseat, where you can't see him so well, but he's there – and we have a *lot* of guns. I find a semiautomatic makes an excellent chaperone under virtually any circumstances we're likely to find ourselves in.'

The man laughed. 'All right, I yield to your superior logic. I'm Scott. Welcome.' He produced a key from his pocket and unlocked the gate, swinging it open. The dogs promptly surged out and surrounded the car, barking, sniffing, and jumping.

One of the leggier dogs stood up on its hind legs and stuck its muzzle through the open window of the ATV, investigating my face with a huge wet nose. It had a mouth large enough to hold my entire head, if it decided it wanted to. I went very still, clenching my hands on the wheel as I tried not to betray my raw terror. This was a *carnivore*, a sharp-toothed killer of men, and it was—

'Claremont! Get out of there!'

The massive canine gracefully dropped down from my window and went trotting back over to the man, where it leaned against his hip and gave him an adoring look. The rest of the dogs followed. Pack behavior was apparently a genuine thing — that, or his pockets were full of dried turkey.

'You can come in now,' called the man.

'Snipers are pulling back,' reported Amber. 'Either this is legit, or it's a really complex trap. Either way, we should go in before he changes his mind.'

'We're going to be ground up and fed to dogs,' I said, starting the engine. 'What a terrible demise for a bunch of really lovely people. We deserved so much better. How tragic. The dogs deserved better, too. They're all going to amplify, the poor things.'

Ben snorted but didn't say anything, and I rolled us forward, past the gate, which the man — Scott — swung shut behind us.

There was parking behind the farmhouse. There were also gas pumps behind the farmhouse, positioned such that they would be almost impossible to see from the road, and absolutely impossible to see from the air. The people who lived here must have been working for years to get the trees exactly the way that they wanted them, turning them into natural cover without blocking the solar panels on the roof so completely that the lights went off. It fit with the custodianship implicit in the road: slow, careful, and built to last forever, if that was how long this crisis went on.

'Do we leave the guns in the car?' asked Ben.

'No,' I said firmly. 'You never leave your guns in the car unless you've been *told* to leave your guns in the car, and even then, you do your best to figure out a way to smuggle a gun under your clothes. Never walk unarmed into a situation you don't know anything about.'

'Won't that escalate things?'

Amber came to my rescue. 'If there's something to escalate, you're already screwed. Bring your weapons.'

The four of us walked across the lush grass toward the front of the building where Scott, and all the dogs, were waiting. Not quite *all* the dogs: A new one appeared around the corner of the building, almost hip-high and covered in ropy black fur. It made a suspicious chuffing noise deep in its throat, like it was trying to decide whether barking its head off would do any good.

'Oh, look,' said Amber. 'I always wanted to meet a Muppet in the flesh.'

'He's not a Muppet, he's a Briard,' said a woman, appearing around the corner of the house. She was tall, wiry, and leaning most of her weight on a surgical cane to keep herself upright. The dog promptly went to her side and pressed against her left leg, shoring her up. 'They were herding dogs, originally. He just wanted to check and see whether you needed to be herded.'

'We're not sheep, thankfully,' I said. 'Dumb as hammers, sheep are, and likely to stand on your foot for no good reason when you want to get across the pasture.' Wool was still a major export for Ireland — what else were we supposed to do with all that pasture and protected land? But zombie sheep were a real problem, which made their pastures and paddocks prime Irwin territory.

I'd never expected to miss the sheep. Looking at the enormous black dog, with its fur hanging to hide its eyes and keep me from knowing what it was going to do next, I found myself thinking longingly of herbivores and their blunt, non-ripping dentition.

'I can see that,' said the woman. 'I'm Beth. You've already met Scott, and most of the dogs. There are eleven people in the woods nearby, watching you through their scopes right now. If you twitch in a way I don't like, you're going to be a contamination risk for my dogs. I'd rather avoid that. Why don't you explain exactly what it is you're doing here, and what it is you think we can do for you?'

'Hello, ma'am,' said Ben, stepping up beside me. I willingly faded back. She seemed a bit more focused than Scott, and whether that was a 'good cop, bad cop' routine or simply the difference in their approaches, Ben was the better match to her. 'We're journalists.'

'I'm not,' said Amber.

Ben shot her a hard look and continued, 'We learned some things we shouldn't have known, and attracted the attention of certain factions within the government. Since we don't want to die, we're heading for Canada. Some friends gave us a map of places we could stop for gas along the way without revealing our location to anyone who might have reason to hurt us. We have trade goods, since we understood that money wouldn't be the primary means of exchange out here. Medicine, and some food, that sort of thing.'

'What friends?' asked Beth.

'A doctor from the Epidemic Investigative Service, who wishes to remain nameless.' Audrey stepped up on my other side, putting a hand on my elbow. It was unclear whether she was doing it for my comfort or her own. 'He said we could trust anyone who appeared on his map.'

Beth gave Audrey a dubious look. 'We don't really hold with people who wish to remain nameless out here. This isn't the sort of place that rewards anonymity.'

'Yeah, but it rewards minding your own business and letting others mind theirs, doesn't it?' I asked. 'His name's Gregory Lake, by the by. Besides, none of that matters, because we have peanut butter. I bet you miss peanut butter.'

'I remember Gregory – nice guy – and I *do* miss peanut butter,' said Beth. 'What's to stop us shooting you and taking it, since you seem so happy to flaunt it?'

'It'd be rude, and nobody who has so many nice doggies would be that rude,' I said. 'Nice doggies with lots and lots and *lots* of teeth and how do you sleep at night? I think I'd never sleep again if those were in the house with me.'

Beth laughed. The tension that had been hanging in the air lightened, and Scott came walking around the corner of the building with his attendant swarm of dogs, like he had been waiting for his cue to return. 'So,' he said. 'Who wants lunch?'

Twenty minutes later we were seated around a folding table in the farmhouse garage, surrounded by dogs, with plates of apple slices and fish sandwiches in front of us. The sandwich filling was an interesting mix of local seafood – catfish and bluegills and crawfish – blended with homemade mayonnaise and a small but tasty assortment of spices. As far as 'living off the land' went, these people were doing it right.

Scott and Beth weren't the only people eating with us. Six more had come out of the trees and onto the property to join us. They were an even mix of men and women, and none of them had said a word since they'd come inside. That was apparently the job of the leaders: They were just here to eat and, if I guessed right, to provide backup if things got ugly. That made a certain amount of sense. Living out here had to engender a certain amount of paranoia, and not everyone who looked friendly was going to be.

'You said you were heading for Canada,' said Scott. 'Do you have a goal in mind after that? Most of the communities close enough to drive to and safe enough to approach aren't looking for journalists. You're going to run out of trade goods sooner than you probably think.'

'I'm still an Irish citizen,' I said. 'We can get ourselves onto a plane and go back to the Republic. Let the people who don't like what we have to say come and try to blast us out of my homeland.' Even as I said the words, I began to feel uneasy about them. Dr Lake had implied that every major medical organization in the world knew about the situation with Kellis-Amberlee – and they'd have to, wouldn't they? At least in the start, there had been a race on to find the cure. Every doctor on the planet had been trying to be the one whose name went on that all-important step toward salvation. And somewhere along the way that had all slowed down, until no one really noticed when people stopped talking about it. We'd all had other things to worry about.

The CDC didn't have much power in Ireland, but the World Health Organization did, and they weren't going to let us walk away if we started talking about what we knew. Maybe we could get out of the country and maybe not. Regardless, our lives were never going to be the same.

And there was always Australia, if it came to that.

'I'm a doctor,' said Audrey. 'That's always going to be a trade good.'

'Assuming someone doesn't try to take you for their own, and dump the people you're traveling with in a shallow grave.' Scott made the statement sound almost casual. There was no way he could remove it from its context, however. We were in an enclosed space with dogs and strangers. If he wanted to turn that comment into a threat, he could do so very easily indeed.

'Ash and Amber are both very, very good shots,' said Audrey, sounding unflustered. 'Ben isn't the best gunman I've ever met, but he manages data manipulation and signaling remarkably well. If someone tried to take me, they'd either wind up dead or with their location broadcast to the entire world. A Pyrrhic victory, sure. It's still a victory. If it came to that, we'd take it.'

'I like you,' said Beth. 'You're not fucking around, and I respect that. So I'm going to give you a little advice: Go back to your lives. If there's any way you can make this right with the people you're running from, go back. You're nice kids, but that's exactly what you are right now. You're kids. You think you know what you're getting into, and you don't. Go back to your comfortable, confined lives, and let this be the only glimpse you get of the way the rest of the world lives. We're a nice enough outlier. We're more Norman Rockwell than Norman Bates, at least, and that's more than I can say for some of the folks you'll find out here.'

'There used to be a farming community over the ridge,' said Scott, waving a hand to the east. 'They figured since women don't infect themselves when they menstruate, and kids don't infect themselves when they lose a tooth, that the trick to avoiding amplification was drinking each other's blood. They all donated a pint a week to the cause, and drank big ol' glasses of the stuff. Yum yum vampirism.'

'That worked?' asked Ben, sounding horrified and fascinated at the same time.

'That makes no medical or scientific sense,' said Audrey.

Scott snorted. 'Hell no, that didn't work. Virus is virus, and being resistant to your own blood doesn't make you resistant to anybody else's. They drank their special protein shakes and thought they were building up an immunity, right up until the first person with a cut in their mouth took a swallow. Amplification, zombification, and slaughter followed, in that order. It took the rest of us months to track down all the stragglers. Their fence wasn't as good as they thought it was.'

'Charming,' said Amber.

'Normal,' said Scott. 'Do you follow? We're the weird ones out here. We went into the woods because we weren't going to let them take our dogs away, and we've been breeding and placing pups ever since. We don't hurt anyone. We don't take things that aren't ours or force people to take things that aren't theirs. We're just in it for the dogs, and for the chance to live our lives the way *we* want to, not the way we're told to.'

'There are costs,' added Beth. 'Don't start thinking this is some idyllic paradise for the individualist. It's hard as hell out here. There are always pirates and raiders around, and you have to keep a close eye on what's yours, or chances are that it won't be yours for long. I was a marathon runner once. Not Olympic level, but I did okay. I enjoyed myself, and I wasn't willing to stop running just because the world was locking the doors. Hell, I got through the Rising because I ran faster than the dead did.' There was a faint, wistful note in her voice, and for one shining moment, I felt like I could see it: the woman with the cane and the big, floppy dog, stripped of two decades of time and consequences. She would have been twenty, maybe twenty-five, fleet as the wind and light as the moon, racing down the streets of a dying world with mobs of the infected running in her wake. She must have been amazing. When you're running that kind of race, you only get to come in second once.

'Broken leg?' asked Audrey.

'Broken leg might have been all right; those are easier to set when you're the only doctor you're going to get,' said Beth. 'Broken ankle. I couldn't figure out how to immobilize it safely, so I wrapped it as tight as I could and walked another two miles to the nearest safe house. By the time I got there, the damage was done.'

'That could still be corrected, if you went to a hospital,' said Audrey. 'Titanium implants are safe.'

'Surgery is never safe,' said Beth. 'I haven't been near "real society" in more than fifteen years, not since they started rounding up and outlawing any dog that weighed more than twelve pounds. I'm not going back because I miss going for a jog. Not when there's a chance I could be followed back to the compound.'

Ben tilted his head, looking at Scott, and asked, 'When you let us in, were you planning on letting us leave again?'

'Not necessarily,' said Scott. 'You did make a point of how you had trade goods. We try to be decent people here. We try not to prey too much on the ignorant and the underprepared. But we can't afford to have you go telling anyone where to find us.'

'The EIS knew where to find you,' said Audrey.

'There are some people at the EIS who slip us medication for our population and our animals in exchange for certain medical information,' said Scott. 'Dogs are a unique population. There are plenty of pigs being studied, but dogs? Those have basically gone the way of the dodo.'

'I see.' Audrey reached into her pocket and produced a slim black wallet, which she tossed onto the table in front of Scott. All motion at the table ceased, and I had the distinct, uncomfortable feeling that we had all just moved a lot closer to being shot. 'My badge. I'm EIS – or at least, I used to be, and I still have a lot of friends there.'

'Is that so?' Scott picked up the wallet, flipping it open. He showed its contents to Beth, who whistled. 'This isn't a recent picture.'

'Like I said, I'm retired.' Audrey held out her hand. 'You're going to give us the fuel we need and let us leave, aren't you?'

'I guess I am.' Scott slapped the wallet back down into her palm. 'I'm also going to give you some unasked-for advice. Don't go flashing this around. Most people aren't as friendly toward the government as we are.'

'You know, every time you say that, I become more convinced that you're going to kill us all, grind up our bodies, and feed them to the dogs,' said Amber.

'They can try,' I said stiffly.

Scott laughed. 'We don't want our dogs to get a taste for human flesh. That's Life With Carnivores 101. We feed them fish and poultry, neither of which can carry the Kellis-Amberlee virus. But it's good to be cautious. You need to know that this world is not on your side.'

'It never has been,' said Ben. 'Now. About that gas . . . ?'

The bartering process went fast, once we got started. Over sandwiches and surrounded by dogs, we agreed to swap two bottles of painkillers, some condoms, and a dozen jars of caviar for ten gallons of gas. I felt like we were taking advantage. From the way Beth kept looking at anything but us, so did she, which meant that this was really a relatively fair exchange. If both parties come away feeling like they got the better side of the deal, then things were done correctly.

Scott escorted us back to the fence. He paused before opening the gate, looking toward our over-packed vehicle – which was less tightly packed now, if not measurably so; still, the holes we had opened in our supplies spoke of more holes to come, and a journey that wouldn't end until we were exhausted – and shaking his head. 'You don't have to go,' he said. 'We can support some more settlers here, and there's always a need for more people who can use their hands. You've got enough trade goods in that trunk of yours to get well situated before we have to put you to work. And you wouldn't have to go back out there. That's the best thing I can offer you. The chance to *not* go back out there. The world isn't kind to runaways anymore, if it ever was in the first place.'

'Thanks for the offer,' said Ben, who had taken Amber's place in the front seat, at least for the next stretch of road. 'We have places to go and stories to tell, and it wouldn't be safe for us to stay with you.

There are people after us; we'd get you hurt. Still, we appreciate the fact that you were willing to let us. It means a lot.'

'You're going to learn just how much,' said Scott. He sounded . . . not disappointed, exactly, but grim, like he had been expecting this answer and had made his offer anyway, more out of obligation than anything else. 'Good luck. Try not to die.'

'We will,' said Ben.

Scott opened the gate and we drove on, back out into the green world that had replaced so much of California. I heard the gate close behind us before I hit the button to roll up the windows, and we rolled on, heading into the future.

Book IV

Where You Own
What You Build

I used to want to be an actress. Before that, I wanted to be a fairy godmother. I guess 'paid killer' was a compromise between the two. Kids are weird, aren't they?

—AMBER BURTON

We never got to be the heroes. Now we're just going to be statistics. That's the worst part of all.

—AISLINN 'ASH' NORTH

Everyone's asleep but me. This is my watch, and I suppose fulfilling it by the glow of my tablet is as good as anything. The windows are polarized: The light won't get out, won't attract anything that might make our lives harder than they already are. So it's just me and these words, which I can't share with anyone except the people around me, and none of them care. That's not meant to be a complaint. Why should they care what I write down when they can just ask me what I think? We're living in each other's pockets. We're getting to the point where even the casual conversations to fill the silence of the woods aren't needed. Soon I guess we won't be talking at all. I'm a little worried about what happens after that.

We've had to stop driving straight through, start taking these breaks. Without them, we'd have collapsed from exhaustion by now.

The woods are remarkably alive. I've seen two deer come stepping through, long, graceful things with ears that never stop moving. A third deer came through at a run, and this one was matted and bloody, clearly infected. So the virus is remarkably alive here, too. But this is a good, green world, and it's finding its own balance without us. It will endure, even if humanity never comes to take it back. Maybe it will endure better *because* humanity isn't coming to take it back.

We're mostly cut off here, in the woods, but the sky was clear enough above the compound with the dogs that we were all able to download the latest news. We're all dead, according to the various sites: Ben and I in the accident, Audrey and Amber when they went looking for our bodies. They picked a lovely picture of me for the Wall. I look so happy. I have my arms around Audrey, and she's smiling, and Ben's standing off to one side watching us, and we all look like we're going to live forever. Maybe it's better this way. We get to craft the narrative of our afterlives. How often does anyone get to do that?

Maybe more often than I think. The EIS has probably done this before. We're true exiles now. No country, no past. No future.

Just the truth.

—From *Erin Go Blog*, the blog of Ash North, May 4, 2040
(unpublished)

Eighteen

Our days fell into an easy, if unpleasant, rhythm. We drove through the woods as much as we could, inconveniencing the wildlife rather than risking exposure. Amber and I split the time behind the wheel, with Ben and Audrey spelling us when we needed a break. They weren't sitting idle while we drove – they were watching the forest, scanning for signs of danger, and looking for signs of new growth. Audrey had already spotted two virtually collapsed structures, and searching them had rewarded us with some as-yet-unspoiled cans of food to add to our collection. There were even four cans of old tinned beef, which was a treasure more valuable than gold or jewels in the post-zombie world. Meat prepared before the Kellis-Amberlee virus got into the air was clean; it couldn't infect or trigger conversion. There were people who'd pay dearly for the chance to taste flesh again.

The animals we saw were bold, with no fear of man. Deer grazed as we drove by, their satellite dish ears swiveling constantly, and didn't run away. Opossums watched us from the trees, pale flashes of fur amongst the branches. Audrey exclaimed every time she spotted one. Sometimes 'Look, it's another possum' was the only thing she'd say for hours at a time. They were worth exclaiming over. Before the Rising, they'd been purely nocturnal. But the sun blinded zombie eyes, enough so that most of the dead chose to hunt after dark if they weren't actually starving. Opossums were too small to amplify. They weren't too small to be a snack for something larger and maddened by the disease. So they'd started coming out more and more during the day, shrugging off centuries of evolution in favor of staying alive long enough to evolve a little further. It was a remarkable adaptation. It probably mirrored similarly remarkable adaptations happening all over the world, largely unobserved now that people left the woods alone.

I was honestly sick of hearing about it.

'What's the next safe house on the map?' I asked Amber. She was wedged into the passenger seat, rifle in her lap, eyes scanning the trees constantly as we rolled along. So far, we'd used very few bullets, but the constant knowledge of where we were was grinding us all down.

'No gas stops for another two hundred miles,' said Ben, from the backseat. 'There's a medical stop marked off in a business park about another fifty miles up the coast. No guarantee that they'd have fuel to spare, but they might have showers.'

'*Showers*,' breathed Amber, making the word sound like something holy. It didn't take much effort. None of us had bathed in days, and so we left the car less and less, trying to avoid fresh air. If we breathed in too much of it, we wouldn't be able to stand the thought of getting back into the car with ourselves, much less with everyone else. We were marinating in our own stink, and while that was probably a metaphor for the human condition, I doubt any of us *cared*. We just wanted to be clean. And showers meant civilization, the chance for hot food and soft beds and questions answered about what was going on in the world.

Still . . . ' Do we know anything about it beyond "a medical stop"?' I asked. 'Not to be a party pooper, but I'd rather not have my kidneys harvested because I decided to pull into the wrong parking lot.'

'Your kidneys are probably terrible anyway,' said Amber. 'Not worth stealing. I, on the other hand, have excellent lungs.'

'Oh, yes, this is exactly the conversation I was hoping to get involved with today,' deadpanned Audrey. 'Tell me more about the delightful condition of your delicate lung meats.'

'There's no need to be sarcastic,' said Amber. 'I'm just stating facts.'

'According to what I have here, it's a research station, independent, run by a former associate of the CDC known to be well inclined toward refugees, especially refugees the CDC doesn't like,' said Ben. 'The doctor's name is Shannon Abbey, no gender given, specialty is virology and genetic manipulation. Which sounds like the absolute best thing to run toward. You, too, could be at the center of a new outbreak.'

'But we'd be *clean* at the center of a new outbreak,' protested Amber. 'Remember being clean? Clean was amazing. Clean was like having your birthday every day of your life, and the party was in your pants, where your crotch didn't smell like a dock.'

'That is an image I could have gone the rest of my life without,' said Ben. 'Can we find something else to talk about? Or not talk about? We were all being quiet before, and I enjoyed that quite a bit.'

I laughed and kept on driving. 'Just give me directions, and we can angle toward this Abbey person. Maybe they'll trade us some shower time for topping off their antibiotics, and we can ask what's been going on with the campaigns.' We didn't dare download anything truly in-depth with our makeshift network. There was being a small wireless booster in the middle of nowhere, and then there was being a small wireless booster trying to download specialized information. One of them told the CDC that Ben's increasingly fictional reports were exactly that – fiction – and brought the world crashing down on our heads. No, thank you.

We stuck to the coastal forest for as long as we could, keeping company with the wildlife. When we reached the point at which the woods became impassable, I turned onto a narrow frontage road, branches reaching out on all sides to snag at our windows and slow our progress. According to the maps Ben had, we were less than fifteen miles from the business park where we'd find Dr Abbey, and maybe get our showers. From there, we just had to get through Oregon and Washington to hit the Canadian border and disappear. Freedom was close. I could almost taste it.

The road curved. I turned the wheel to follow it. Things began happening very fast after that, seeming to collapse together, leaving no room for anything but reaction. The trees to either side of us exploded with motion as people launched themselves out of the woods. They were riding what looked like modified Jet Skis, heavily armored, with lances and cowcatchers affixed to the front. I hauled on the wheel as hard as I could, sending us into a spin. Amber was shouting. Ben was shrieking. Audrey was curiously silent, and I had just enough time to worry about that before we slammed into the first of our attackers. There was a sickening crunch from the front of the ATV, the engine giving an audible whine that broke through the sound shielding.

Amber had cranked her window down and was firing into the fray, pulling the bolt back on her rifle and pulling the trigger again and again. There was a particularly loud crack, and something whizzed past my head, tracing a hot line of danger in the air, before shattering my window. Bits of glass flew outward and away. Amber screamed, rage and pain and fury, as the bullet went through her shoulder and into the seat behind it.

Audrey leaned into the front seat, a pistol in either hand, and began firing through the shattered window, giving Amber time to get her equilibrium back. I wanted to shout at her, to order her back into her own seat, but I said nothing. I was fighting with the wheel, Amber was fighting shock, and Ben didn't have the kind of marksmanship that the situation required. We needed to get out of here.

More people poured into the open, shaking the trees. One of the raiders popped up in front of us. I hit the gas, slamming into his Jet Ski as hard as I could. He went flying. Something in the engine made a crunching noise, and we lost forward momentum. I could steer, but we were losing speed fast.

Amber got her senses back and braced her shotgun against her unwounded shoulder, using her dominant hand to steady the barrel as she fired again and again. Two more raiders went down. The car continued slowing.

'Can you speed this fucking thing up?' Amber demanded.

'I wish I could,' I said.

'Then I'm buying you time,' she snapped, and unfastened her seat belt.

Until my dying day, I will swear I didn't know what she was about to do, and until my dying day, I'll be lying, because part of me *did* know, part of me *did* understand, and that part of me – that terrible, remorseless part of me – *approved*. Reducing our weight might be the only thing that kept us moving, and we'd slowed enough that it wouldn't hurt her worse than she'd already been hurt. And she'd been hurt badly. She was trying not to show it, but the seat behind her was soaked through with blood, and she was still bleeding. The bullet had severed something essential.

We were a rolling biohazard now, and Amber didn't have much time. That's what I told myself as she unlocked her door, as Ben realized what she was doing and shouted for her to stop.

She didn't stop. Unbuckling her belt, she kicked the door open and tumbled out into the clearing, shrieking like a madwoman as she brought her gun up and continued firing. The ATV picked up a little bit of speed as her weight was subtracted from its total. For a moment – a single, shining moment – I thought we might stand a chance.

The back of her shirt was black with blood, shining in the sunlight. She fired twice more before the raiders gunned her down and she collapsed, a bullet through her skull guaranteeing that she wasn't going to be getting up again. Amber was gone.

It might still have been worth it, if we hadn't been slowing down again. If her blood hadn't soaked through the seat where she'd been shot, rendering the vehicle unsafe. Even if the engine wasn't dying, we couldn't have stayed where we were long enough to get away. She'd died for nothing. No: not for nothing. She'd died so that she wouldn't amplify in an enclosed space with her friends. She'd died so that we'd stand a chance of surviving. We had to honor that.

We had to find a way out of this.

'Ash . . .' said Audrey, looking over her shoulder at me.

'I'm sorry,' I said. The engine rattled and died. The raiders had us surrounded. Some of them were wearing black and silver pre-Rising football gear with snarling men blazoned across the back. They looked like a gang out of an old movie, and they had us outnumbered ten to one. Even if Amber – oh, God, Amber – had still been alive, we would have lost. There was no way this could have ended any differently.

Ben reached up from the backseat, putting his hand on my shoulder. I took my hands off the wheel and put them up, signaling our surrender. Then I turned, and pulled Audrey as close as I could while avoiding the spreading stain of Amber's blood, and I kissed her like the world was ending. I kissed her like I was never going to have the opportunity to kiss her again, and ah, her lips were sweet, and ah, our tears were bitter.

The door opened behind me. Hands grabbed my shoulders, yanking me out of the car. I saw Amber's body, crumpled on the broken road. Then my head slammed into the pavement, and everything stopped for a little while, like a clock whose hands had been removed.

Tick.

Tock.

Tick.

I opened my eyes on blackness. For a moment – just a moment, but a terrible one – I thought I'd gone blind, or that they'd put my eyes out. That had happened before, to Irwins who stumbled into the wrong part of the underground network of black markets and illegal communities crisscrossing the world. We could be valuable as organ donors, sources of information, and . . . other things. I didn't like to think about those other things. I didn't *want* to.

But these people had killed Amber. Sure, she'd been firing on them at the time, and she'd been an excellent shot; I knew just from the bodies I'd seen fall that she'd managed to hit at least two of her targets. They could still have found a means of taking us without shooting her. Whoever these people were, they weren't interested in harvesting slaves. The fact that I couldn't see probably didn't speak to any permanent damage, so much as it spoke to the space that I was in.

I tried to sit up. I couldn't. Something was strapping me down, crossing my chest and legs and pinning me in place. All right. I clicked my tongue. The noise didn't travel far, but it did sound hollow as it returned to me. From the sounds of it, wherever I was wasn't large, and was at least somewhat disconnected from whatever else might be around us. Stretching out my fingers – which *did* move, albeit reluctantly – allowed me to brush them against a cold metal wall. I winced, closing my eyes again. I was in a cadaver drawer. It was the only thing that accounted for everything I was experiencing, from the darkness all the way to the faint reverberation in every sound. It was a good place to store prisoners. Even if one of us amplified, we wouldn't be able to get to anyone else to infect them, and we could be withdrawn and tested one by one, all without removing the straps. There was no telling how many people had lived and died in this exact position.

There was no way of knowing whether I was about to be one of them.

I steadied my breathing, trying to deduce as much as I could about my situation from what little information I was getting from my own body. My head hurt. I couldn't move it much, but when I did, the ache came from the side of my head and the back of my neck, implying that someone had kicked me after I fell. That would explain the conclusive nature of my blackout. It was hard to deal with two different types of trauma at the same time. Nothing else seemed to hurt, and when my hands brushed against the tops of my hips, I felt fabric. I was still dressed, then.

Wait — still, or again? I breathed in, and smelled nothing but antiseptic and citrus cleaning products. I should have smelled my own funk, which Amber had so gleefully described not long ago. Whoever had taken me had also washed me. It was a terrible thing to realize, accompanied by a profound feeling of violation and rage. In a way, I was almost glad for that. It chased away some of the grief.

Amber was dead. Of that much I was sure: I'd seen her die, and there was no way she was coming back, either as herself or as one of the walking infected. Kellis-Amberlee can fix a remarkable amount of damage in the process of getting the body up and running, but it can't fix a hole in the back of the skull, or the attendant brain damage. Thankfully. If zombies could survive head shots, we would have lost the Rising, and those of us who had managed to survive to the present day would never have been able to stand a chance.

So fine: Amber was dead. I wasn't. If I wasn't dead, it stood to reason that some of the others might not be dead, too. Audrey might not be dead. And if Audrey was alive, I couldn't stop fighting. Not for a minute, not for a *second*. I had to get back to her. Whatever it took, I had to get back to her.

My captors may have taken the time to re-dress and — presumably — decontaminate me before shoving me into a drawer, but they probably hadn't given me back my weapons. That would have been too much to ask. All logic said that I was unarmed, and that they'd be expecting me to be unprepared when I awoke. I couldn't do anything about the first part. My field training meant I was better equipped than most to handle the second.

I began calmly and systematically tightening and relaxing the muscles in my arms, legs, and back. As a meditation technique, it was supposed to help relieve tension and prepare the body for a long, restorative sleep. Sometimes it helped with my nightmares. I wasn't meditating now, and I didn't want help with my nightmares: I wanted my nightmares to help *me*. I was thinking the darkest, least relaxing thoughts I could, trying to keep myself primed to move.

None of the straps were tight enough to cut off blood flow. That was good. I wanted to be ready to leap into action the second I had the opportunity to do so.

Eventually, they were going to have to open that drawer. There was no point in taking us alive if they were going to leave us in here to die – unless, murmured a small, traitorous corner of my mind, they were looking for zombie gladiators. I'd heard about the underground fighting rings, like something out of a horror movie, where the fresh infected were pitted against the unprepared living. Most of the time, the 'fighters' would have the same weapons that the dead did: teeth and fingernails and desperation. But while the zombies were desperate to feed, the living were desperate to escape, and those two goals were never going to be compatible.

No. I was being silly. If they'd taken us for the sole purpose of killing us, they'd *do* it. Allowing us to die of starvation or thirst would just leave them with a bunch of substandard zombies. No sport or show in that. The sort of people who'd swarm our ATV, shoot Amber, and seize the rest of us were absolutely the sort of people who would think zombie pit fights to be the height of sophistication. They'd know how to make it as interesting as possible.

On some level, I knew I was doggedly pursuing this idea – born of purest supposition, with no evidence whatsoever to support it – because the alternative was to let myself consider that maybe the raiders had only taken me. Some of the folks who chose to go off the grid in modern America were racial supremacists of one stripe or another, and all the faces I'd seen during the assault had been white ones. It was less of a stretch to assume I was alone than it was to assume that we'd all been taken. But if that was so, if I was the last one standing, then I wasn't going to be standing for long. The people who'd put me in this drawer were going to learn, in short order, that it was better not to fuck with the Irish.

I don't know how long I lay in the dark, methodically tensing and relaxing my muscles to keep myself warmed up and alert, my eyes open and staring into nothingness. It was long enough that the beat of my heart seemed to be impossibly loud, echoing in my ears like a countdown to some terrible inevitability.

Something clanked, the sound of a great key being turned in an even greater lock, pulling back some unspeakable tumbler. This time when I tensed, I did not relax. Things were about to start moving again. I was going to rejoin a world where things happened, and those things were going to happen to me. That seemed inevitable.

The second clank was smaller, and closer, coming from the end of my drawer. I squinted my eyes shut just in time to block out the majority of the light as someone pulled the drawer open and the sterile hospital glare of the former morgue came flooding inside. No natural light here; this was all man-made and cruel, as unforgiving as anything.

'I think she's awake,' said a voice, female and a little awed, like finding a prisoner already conscious was unheard of. Maybe it was. Maybe they usually supplemented their head trauma with the sort of drugs that required a counteragent before they could be thrown off.

Lucky me, I'd gone with the pure 'concussion' package. 'Sure, and I've been awake for hours,' I said, eyes still virtually closed, hitting my Irish brogue as hard as I could. If these were white supremacists, they might take my foreign origins as a sign of 'purity,' which could buy me the time to find out where they'd taken Ben and Audrey. If they were just bandits, they might panic at the thought of kidnapping a foreign national. Either way, the less American I could sound, the better off I would be, at least for right now. 'What took you lot so long? I was starting to get bored in there.'

'Awake, and a snotty little thing,' said a male voice. It was deep and surprisingly smooth, the sort of voice that should be accompanied by a glass of good Scotch and a blazing fire. A hand touched my cheek. It was a light contact. It was still enough to feel like a violation. My stomach did a slow roll in protest. 'Pretty, though. Look at this skin.

Red and white all over. Are your eyes blue, girl? Are you a living American flag?'

'I'm Irish,' I said, and opened my eyes, which struck me as suddenly traitorous. I didn't want to be blue-eyed for this man, whoever he was. He had the power to let me *out* of the drawer, which meant he'd probably been the one to put me there in the first place.

The light stung. I blinked repeatedly, eyelashes growing damp with unshed tears. Eventually, the room came into focus, bringing the two people I'd heard speaking into focus with it. The female voice belonged to a gawky brunette with short-cropped hair and a tattered lab coat. Faint brown stains down one lapel said 'blood' to me, even though it had clearly been bleached until the protein strands broke down. She'd tried to cleanse herself. She just hadn't been able to replace her coat once she was done. We were in a place that had supply-chain issues, then, where things couldn't be thrown away for the sake of something as petty as mental or emotional distress. Lots of people had panic attacks at the sight of bloodstains. They meant death, danger, and exposure. All good reasons to get a new damn coat.

The man was tall enough that I had to crane my neck to see his face. Tattoos covered almost every inch of his exposed skin, leaving only the palms of his hands and most of his facial features unmasked. 'Most' because the skin above his left eyebrow was tattooed with a dense block of Cyrillic text, and a lightning bolt scar was tattooed under his right eye, standing out green and black and painful against his pale skin. His eyes were cold, and his hair was buzzed so short that I couldn't quite tell what color it would have been if allowed to grow out to a proper length. A white tank top strained to contain his massive chest, and camo pants covered his legs. A real tough-guy type, it seemed, and one who was better left uncrossed.

Too bad I've never been good at leaving better off alone. 'Got a few tats there, haven't you?' I asked. 'Must not have much of a problem with needles. Brave of you. Brave enough that you ought to be able to unstrap an unarmed Irish girl, not worry about whether I'm set to claw your eyes out.' My grammar was slipping, becoming a parody of itself. I was almost grateful. The nice thing about having an accent in America was the way people would forgive my words for getting jumbled: It was like they thought there was no way I could put a proper sentence together, and were hence happy to have their prejudices proven.

Or maybe that was just the nice thing about having a *white* accent in America, one that came from 'the old country' and not one of the places good patriots still assumed were hemorrhaging immigrants onto American soil. As if there would have been a modern America without immigration, people coming from far away and trying to make a home for themselves amongst the stones and the sky. The people who'd owned the continent before Columbus showed up would probably have had a few things to say about immigration. I doubt any of them would have been very pleasant, or very welcoming.

'Undo her straps,' said the man.

'But sir—'

He turned to the woman in the stained lab coat, the skin around his eyes tightening until it was like gazing at a shark: cold, implacable, and deadly. 'I'm so sorry, Jill, I missed the announcement that you'd deposed me. Tell me, was it poison? A sliced artery that's been bleeding for the last hour without my noticing it? Have you science types finally mastered nanotechnology? Am I about to be reduced to a pile of quivering gray goo?'

'N-no,' she said, voice shaking. She didn't step away from him. I had to admire that, even as I thought it was likely to get her killed. Put more stains on that lab coat of hers, these ones too deep to be washed away. 'It's just that she doesn't know the situation here, and unstrapping her could be dangerous.'

'Ah. Worrying about my safety, then, so a tiny British girl doesn't somehow overpower me and take what's mine as hers.' The man glanced back to me, eyes lingering on my midriff. I didn't know whether it was covered or not, but in that moment, it didn't matter. I glared at him, hating the fact that he'd called me a Brit, but I didn't speak. 'I think I can handle myself. Undo the straps now, and I might be able to forget that you ignored my first order.'

'Yes, sir,' said the woman – Jill, her name was Jill – before starting to unstrap me. Her hands were trembling. I couldn't blame her. Somehow, this didn't strike me as the friendliest of working environments.

'Besides, she's not going to make any trouble for me, are you, Ginger?' The man grinned at his own joke, displaying surprisingly white, even teeth. 'She's a smart little thing. She'd have to be, to have made it this far from civilization. Not *too* smart, however. She would have chosen a different route and less breakable traveling companions if she'd been *too* smart.'

My heart sank at the mention of my traveling companions. I forced it back up again. They weren't dead. They *weren't dead*. I wouldn't allow it. I sat up as soon as the straps allowed, making a show of rubbing my wrists, like they'd been chafed.

'I'm not here to make trouble,' I said. My change of position had answered the question of what I was wearing: My sundress was gone, replaced by a white sports bra and a pair of running shorts. Good gear for working out. Not good gear for much of anything else. Still, under the circumstances, I was grateful. I could as easily have been naked. 'Sorry to have blundered into your hunting party, or whatever that was out there. If you'd return my people and my vehicle, we'd be thrilled to get out of your hair. We won't come back, I promise.'

The man blinked, looking like he couldn't believe what he was hearing. Then, to my annoyance – and relief, which annoyed me even more – he burst out laughing. 'Oh, I *like* you, Ginger. You have a sense of humor. You have no idea how rare that is around here.'

'Given that you've had me shoved into a cadaver drawer for the last little while, I'm not even at my best right now,' I said. Finding the right balance between cocky and insulting was never my strongest suit. I wished desperately for Mat. Mat would have been better at walking this tightrope, saying the right things without crossing the line and going too far. 'Look, I don't mean to be a bother, but we have somewhere we need to be. It's quite important we make it to the Canadian border before the elections.' Once the elections were over, we'd know how much trouble we were really in. If Ryman won, the Masons would draw the majority of the attention. If Kilburn won . . .

People might start wondering about our conveniently timed deaths. They might start asking why no one ever found the bodies.

'Then you're in luck, because the elections aren't for months,' said the man, with another flash of those straight white teeth. 'I'm Clive. This is my place. While you're here, what I say is what goes, and what I say is that you're going to stop asking about things that don't concern you anymore. You're going to be staying with me for a while, Ginger.'

He reached out and gripped my chin between his thumb and forefinger, tilting my head back until my eyes were locked on his. I didn't look away. I didn't dare. When a man like this started throwing his weight around, it was better to hold my breath and ride it out.

'You're pretty,' he said. 'I like the way you roll your "r"s. Makes me think you must have a clever tongue. If you can learn to control it, we might be able to make a go of it.' He shoved me when he let go, sending me back down to the bunk where I'd been strapped. I managed not to cry out when I hit the metal, still warm from the weight of my body. It was a near thing.

'Get her cleaned up and explain how things work around here,' he said to Jill. 'I'll be back.' He turned and strode toward the door, leaving us alone.

'What—' I began. Jill's eyes widened and she held up her hand, signaling me to silence. I closed my mouth and waited.

After a count of twenty, Jill's shoulders relaxed. 'He always waits a few seconds,' she said. 'It lets him be sure the people he's walking away from don't immediately start plotting against him. I think he read it in a book of management tips somewhere, that if people are going to talk behind your back, they'll do it quickly, before they lose their nerve. He likes self-help books. You wouldn't think it to look at him, but he does.'

I pushed myself upright again, giving her a bemused look. 'You're talking a blue streak, but you don't seem to actually be *saying* anything,' I said. 'Where am I? What is this place? Where are my friends?' The last question was really the only one that mattered, and the only one I was afraid of having answered. If they were dead . . .

Well, if they were dead, I could burn this whole place down, and not worry overly much about whether or not I made it out. I wasn't the suicidal sort, but some things were worth risking for a good revenge.

'The man you came in with is in general holding. The woman has been removed for further study,' said Jill, her eyes darting to the side. 'When you hit your head—'

'You mean when the people who pulled me out of the car slammed my head into the pavement, after shooting another of my friends dead,' I corrected gently.

'Um. Yes, that. When you got hurt, the woman started saying she was a doctor and trying to get to you. If she was telling the truth, she's valuable, and she won't be hurt. If she was lying to make them spare her, she's . . . she's in trouble.' Jill swallowed as she turned back to me. 'Clive doesn't like liars. He says someone who lies once will lie again, no matter how good their reasons may have seemed in the beginning. So liars don't get to stay here for very long.'

'And I'm guessing, from the look on your face, that they don't get to walk away clean and easy,' I said, with a grimace. 'Well, Audrey's a real doctor, so I suppose she'll be valuable to you lot. I'm still going to want her back before I go. Both of them. I'm attached to them, you see, and I can't really see walking off and leaving them behind.'

Jill laughed, taking a step backward. 'I can't tell whether you're brave or just stupid, but it doesn't matter, because you're not going anywhere. What Clive wants, he takes, and what he takes, he keeps. This is home now. What kind of home it is, well, that's up to you.

It can be a pretty nice one. It can also be hell on earth. It's your call either way.'

'No, see, that doesn't work for me.' The throbbing in my head seemed to be the whole of the pain: Nothing else had been damaged when I was taken. Maybe there was something to be said for concussions. 'We're on our way somewhere, and while this is a fascinating pit stop for our memoirs, it's not the sort of place that winds up holding our bones. We've escaped from bigger men than your boss. It's in everybody's best interests if we're just allowed to go on our merry way, and we won't make any trouble for those of you who choose to stay here.'

Jill gaped at me, openmouthed and disbelieving, before she began slowly shaking her head. 'I can't tell if you're thick or just stubborn, but the end result is going to be the same: your head on a pike.'

'My issue is that you can utter that sentence without seeing how bloody idiotic you sound,' I shot back. 'Where *are* we? How did we get here? Where are my people, and how do I get us out of here?'

'God forbid you listen for two seconds.' She turned and began rummaging through a black bag on the nearest counter. 'What's your vaccination status? Any recent infections or illnesses? Are you on a contraception implant, and if so, which one?'

'To answer your last question first, I'm a lesbian, so contraception has never been high on my list of things to do.' I tried to make my answer sound airy and unconcerned, but she was rattling me. Usually, my steamroller approach to diplomacy is enough to gain me a little ground, even if it doesn't always get me what I actually want. Jill seemed to be shaking off every attempt I made at forward momentum, locked as she was in her own version of whatever all this was.

She turned and looked at me flatly. 'You're an Irwin, aren't you? There was a license tag in your things when they brought you in, you've got a lot of minor scarring on your knees, fingers, and palms, and you have the skin tone of someone born pale and kept pale by high quantities of sunscreen, rather than indoor isolation like the rest of us. The bleach damage to your hair is too extensive to be explained by normal washing, which means you've gone through a lot of decontamination cycles. Either you're an Irwin or you're with a governmental group – and I assume that if your group was here to try infiltrating us, we'd be meant to keep the Chinese woman. That would make you the expendable brute force. You're a *terrible* bruiser. Too short, too skinny, too wearing a floral dress when they pulled you off the road.'

'Her name is Audrey, she's my girlfriend, and we're not here to infiltrate you; we don't even know where "here" is,' I said. 'We're heading for the Canadian border, as I've said. Repeatedly.'

'You *were* heading for the Canadian border,' said Jill. There was a hint of sympathy in her tone, like she wasn't happy to be the one hammering this point through my thick skull. 'This is where you are now, and if you want to live long enough to see your friends again, you're going to start answering my questions. Do you have a contraceptive implant or not?'

'Yes,' I admitted, sullenly. 'Five-year, standard issue from the nice folks at Immigration. It was supposed to keep me from giving birth to an American citizen before they'd finished processing my paperwork and decided they were going to let me stay.' It all smacked a bit of xenophobia and paranoia to me – even Ireland didn't insist on temporarily sterilizing their new citizens while things went through proper channels – but as I'd never intended to have a child with Ben, I hadn't protested as loudly as I could have. Besides, not having to suffer through my period anymore was a joy, especially for someone who spent as much time in the field as I did.

'How much time does it have left to run?'

It would run out in six months. There was something I hadn't considered: What was I going to do when it ran out? Not that I was suddenly going to turn heterosexual and start romping about with all the boys in Dublin, but I didn't know how long we were going to be trapped in Canada before we could find a plane to take us to Ireland,

and menstruation was messy, difficult, and smelled of blood. Most normal humans couldn't detect it if the person doing the bleeding kept their trousers on. The infected, with their increased sensitivity toward both the living and the smell of blood, could. If we were still in Canada in six months, without a permanent residence with walls thick enough to keep the dead out, our lives were going to get a lot harder.

I opened my mouth to answer.

Jill cut me off.

'Wow, the full five years? That's rough. I mean, good thinking having your meds topped off before you went out into the field, but Clive's not going to be thrilled to hear that even if he sweet-talks his way into your panties, he won't be getting any little redheaded babies for a while.' She produced a capsule injector from her bag, and mouthed "Hold out your arm."

My eyes widened as I put two and two together and came up with the potential that she was going to help me – help *us* – after all. I stuck my arm out, only tensing a little as I asked, 'Is he the sort who takes what he wants, then?'

'Yes and no.' The barrel of the injector was cool against my skin. She knew her stuff: Without prodding, she chose an injection site several inches above the spot where the Immigration Authority had inserted my last implant. I was briefly worried about the effects of getting a double dose for the next six months, and then decided I had much, much better things to be worried about. 'He wanted your group and so he took you. He wanted a lot of the things you had – you had some great medications, thank you for those – and so he took them. But if you're asking whether you need to be worried about him pushing the issue, no. That's the one area where he'll take no for an answer.'

There was a brief stinging sensation as she shot the contraceptive implant into my arm. She pulled the injector away, looked critically at the already-bruised circle of skin, and handed me a gauze pad.

'Put this on and tape it down,' she said brusquely. 'If anyone asks what happened, it's one of your injuries from the road. If you point the finger at me, no one's going to believe you.'

'Why are you helping me?'

'In general, or with this?' Her expression hardened. 'Clive won't force you. He won't slip anything into your drink or put his hand up your skirt to see what kind of underpants you're wearing. His ego won't let him resort to that. But he'll pursue, and he'll do it a lot more energetically if he thinks you're fertile. He's an empire builder, is Clive. He wants an army of little Clives to be running around long after he's gone. A woman who might be able to bear his children, it doesn't matter how beautiful she is, she'll be essentially off-limits to everyone – and I do mean *everyone* – until he's sure it's never going to happen. Or, in your case, until her implant wears off. He'll want to know that you're healthy and STI-free when that day finally comes.'

'Won't he just dig the implant out of my arm?' I'd heard of that happening when good Catholic girls visited countries with less restrictive rules about birth control and came home ready to have sex for reasons other than procreation. Some people thought it was a hoax, but I'd seen the scars.

'No,' said Jill. 'We don't believe in unnecessary medical procedures here. Infection is enough of a risk that we try not to cut people open when we don't have to. I really do hope your friend is an actual doctor, and not just telling stories. We need all the help that we can get.'

'She's a doctor,' I said. 'A good one.' Or she had been, to have been recruited by the EIS. The fact that she hadn't practiced in years was beside the point. *Please, let her remember how to do the things they're going to ask her to do.*

'Then she'll probably be all right.' Jill thrust a piece of paper at me. 'Write down all your vaccinations, and when you had them. Try to be as precise as you can. We'll get them updated, and then we'll follow up with a full physical exam. Once that's done, we can talk about what your life here is going to be like.'

I took the paper and began writing. Protests seemed useless. What

I needed now was a plan, a means of getting the hell out of here while we were all still breathing.

When I was done, Jill plucked the paper from my hand, scanned it, and offered me a tight smile. 'Excellent. I'll prepare the injections. In the meantime, welcome to the Maze. It can be a bit of an adjustment, but I think you're going to learn to like it here.'

'And if I don't?' I asked.

She looked at me with tired eyes. 'Then your life just got a hell of a lot harder, because you're not going anywhere.'

I saw a calendar this morning. I think I wasn't supposed to – we're not meant to know or care about what time of year it is, because it's not like we're ever going to see the sun again. We're not worthy of the outside. (And I wonder how many rich assholes would think this was the perfect society, just with the status markers flipped. Let the most prestigious live in their rat holes while the proletariat venture forth to bring them back the things they want and need. Morlocks and Eloi for a new world. H.G. Wells got so much right, even in the process of getting so much wrong.) But my work group was passing through the medical center, and someone had left a door open, and I saw a calendar.

It's been more than a year since we buried my mother.

I barely have the mental acuity to wrap my mind around that thought. I'm writing this longhand on a yellow legal pad that I bartered from one of the janitors, and I know the guards read every word while I'm at work, because they leave thumbprints on the margins and make nasty comments about how I should save my strength, and none of that matters. Let them mock me as much as they want. It won't change the fact that I'm a prisoner, and it won't bring back my mother, or tell my sister I'm alive. As far as Governor Kilburn is concerned, we're in Canada and long gone by now. If she thinks it's strange that we stopped posting before we 'died,' well, she probably has better things to worry about. The campaign is still going. Elections aren't until November, and she has a long road ahead of her.

I'm not worried about Clive – the man who runs this place – figuring out who we are and trying to ransom us back to the governor. We've been very clear about the fact that she sent us away, and that she wouldn't pay to get us back. (I recognize that I write this sentence once every three entries, but I feel it remains important enough to bear repeating. We cannot be sold back to our powerful friends. They have washed their hands of us. We are not a lever. We're barely even tools.)

But I really do wish I'd been able to visit my mother's final resting place, and leave her flowers. I wish I could have been there when my sister scattered her ashes.

I wish a lot of things.

—From *That Isn't Johnny Anymore*, the blog of Ben Ross,
July 23, 2040 (unpublished)

Nineteen

It was surprisingly easy to fall into the habit of captivity. A guard unlocked my bedroom door every morning at six o'clock. As one of Clive's fancy-to girls — as in, the girls he'd taken enough of a fancy to that he wanted us kept safe, secure, and locked away from other blokes — I got my own bed, crammed into a narrow space that probably started as a supply closet. I also got a door that locked, keeping me in and keeping the rest of the population out. I'd felt trapped at first, but as the envy of the less favored girls in my working group became more and more apparent, I'd started to see that door as the blessing it was. When it was closed, I was safe. That was more than could be said during working hours.

Once the door was open, I was expected to wait while the guard finished letting the others out. About half of us had private supply-closet bedrooms. The others slept on pallets on the floor, and they always woke up looking exhausted, like they hadn't gotten a lick of sleep. There were dangers in the Maze at night, dangers I didn't have to know about as long as I was in favor.

I was torn, really, on whether it would have been better to know or not. Knowing would have meant restless nights spent on the floor in a room packed with other bodies; it would have meant exhaustion. It might also have made finding a way out easier, assuming I was awake enough to take it.

We would all gather by the door and proceed to the showers, where we'd each be given a towel, a bottle of all-purpose wash, and a blood testing kit. As soon as I was confirmed biologically clean, I was allowed to make myself physically clean, showering alongside ten to twenty other women ranging in age from their midteens to their late fifties. I wasn't sure whether there were any children here, and if so, where they were kept, but as none of the teenagers seemed to think there was anything strange about the way things were done, I had to assume they'd grown up inside the Maze. Twenty years since the Rising; at least ten years since Clive had set up camp in this abandoned rural hospital, spreading his resources and his recruits out until he owned most of the area. A sixteen-year-old girl could easily have been raised within this community, never knowing anything else, never recognizing how odd it would all seem to an outsider. In that regard, being here was a lot like being in a commune, or a cult.

There were female guards. Not many, but enough that they could watch us shower, keeping the men at a respectful distance. It was nice to have the privacy. It was also distressing, a reminder of why Clive kept so many pretty women around. Maybe he didn't force the issue, and maybe he didn't insist, but anyone who looked at us could tell that we were essentially his harem. We belonged to him, and he was keeping us as pristine as possible.

The one time I'd seen a male guard near the showers, I hadn't seen him again after that. Not in our space; not anywhere in the compound that I was allowed to go. He'd simply vanished, like mist, and the remaining guards had been on edge for days, making me believe that he hadn't just been reassigned. Breaking Clive's orders was not something to be done lightly, or at all.

After the showers, we'd return to our rooms – either solo or communal – to find our clothing for the day waiting on our beds, along with whatever toiletries we required. I got a hairbrush, and sometimes a hair tie or two, depending on Clive's mood. We didn't have uniforms, thankfully; our clothes were drawn from a communal wardrobe, assigned according to a chart that must have existed somewhere. I'd been given a day's use of several of my sundresses, and had seen others on girls I didn't know, catching glimpses of familiar fabric from across crowded rooms or down darkened hallways. Nothing was wasted here. At least a few of us wore patchwork blouses and twice-mended trousers every day, and no one complained. What good could it have done?

That was an attitude that was also surprisingly easy to fall into. What good could anything have done? We were trapped, and while we were together, we were each and every one of us alone.

Breakfast was surprisingly varied, mixing canned and dried goods with fresh fruits, vegetables, and fish, obviously harvested from the surrounding land. There were work crews that went outside, either to hunt or to farm, and while I had yet to be allowed to go with them — and might never be, considering my dual status as newcomer and woman Clive eventually wanted to fuck — it was clear they covered more ground than I would have thought possible. We ate salmon, catfish, and small, heavily stewed scrod that could have been from virtually any freshwater species. Blueberries, blackberries, and tart red huckleberries were a major part of every meal. At least scurvy wasn't going to become a concern any time soon. The amount of vitamin C we were getting, even before our supplement pills, was astonishing.

For the first week or so, I'd watched everything like a hawk, waiting for the opportunity to make a run for it. That opportunity had never come. Clive's people were well trained, methodical, and most of all, loyal. Whether that loyalty was born of contentment or fear didn't matter, because the end result was the same. And at the end of that week, I had been deemed sufficiently settled, and had been put to work.

My work crew was responsible for basic maintenance and light cleaning. We weren't janitorial, to be doing all the big muck-outs and major decontamination, and we weren't tasked with the small but constant repairs to everything in sight. We . . . dusted. We did dishes, and moved items from one place to another. It felt like make-work to justify Clive's airy claim that everyone contributed to the whole, and it was no surprise that every single person I worked with was an attractive female of childbearing age. People looked at us and snickered, or rolled their eyes and looked away. It made my palms itch, my hands aching to ball into fists and start breaking noses.

It didn't help that I still didn't know whether Ben and Audrey were alive or dead. I'd tried, several times, to convince my fellow workers to help me, and my pleas had fallen on deaf ears. It wasn't until the end of my second week that one of them took pity and turned on me while we were washing the mirrors in the communal bathroom, saying, 'Look, we all know you're the new favorite, and we know it's not going to last. Half of us were the favorite once, when Clive liked blondes, or brunettes, or girls with pierced navels. That doesn't mean we're going to help you get things he doesn't want you to have. Maybe you're only going to be in the hot seat for a little while, and maybe that makes you greedy or maybe it makes you scared – it's hard to say, with you new girls – but either way, we're not going to attract attention to ourselves just because you feel like you deserve more than just the boss man's eyes on your ass.'

It was a reasonable, even rational response to my agitating for more information. That didn't mean it didn't sting, or keep me from viewing my interactions with the other girls in a new, more negative light. They'd never been nice to me, and that had always been fine, because I wasn't overly interested in being nice to *them*; civility was the best I had to offer, and the best I was hoping to receive. But if they were looking at me as temporary competition, destined to age out of my current status and join them in whatever the next step down on the ladder of local status was, then they had no reason to be even friendly. I was a rival, not a fellow prisoner.

We were all trapped here, even those of us who would never see the bars on the windows as anything more than protection.

Jill moved through the work crews like a ghost, rarely interacting with anyone unless it was to deliver a cup of pills or a sudden injection of some unidentified substance. There was never any warning before one of those 'medical interventions' occurred: Three times, I saw girls in the middle of a shift stop, roll up a sleeve, and receive a needle to the arm. They never spoke to her more than they absolutely had to, which struck me as odd. Where I'd come from, a little joking around with the company doctor would have made sense, and maybe taken some of the sting out of the injection itself.

Then she came for me.

I was working with the others, sorting crates of pre-Rising liquor according to some mysterious chart that didn't seem to be based on any known properties of alcohol. Scotch and vodka would have made sense – they didn't mix well outside of a Long Island Iced Tea, but they were powerful intoxicants, and anything that put people on the floor clearly had its uses here. But Scotch and grenadine? Tequila and white wine? It was like we were filling a dozen different orders, all made by people who should never have been allowed to mix their own drinks. I wanted to ask if anyone knew what the hell was going on, but I kept my mouth shut. Questions never got me answers here. They only got me rolled eyes and stifled scoffs, and honestly, I was going to put somebody's teeth out if that happened one more time.

'Aislinn?' There was nothing querulous or quiet about Jill's voice. I looked up. She was standing in the doorway, still in her stained lab coat, looking at a clipboard, like that would keep her from needing to look at any of the rest of us. 'You need to come with me. It's time for your exam.'

Giggles and low 'ooo's broke out around me as I put down the bottle I'd been cataloging and pushed myself to my feet. Even a week ago, I would have swaggered, or at the least talked back. Now, I simply walked, head and shoulders down, to join Jill in the doorway. I had finally found the answer to what it took to break me: unrelenting, unforgiving exclusion, and nothing I could fight against. This was my hell, and I was trapped, like a rat in a cage.

'Excellent.' Jill lifted her head then, looking at the rest of the work crew. 'Clive wanted me to inform you that Aislinn will be gone for an extended period, on his order, but the deadline hasn't been shifted. He has faith in you.'

There was some grumbling. To my deep relief, it wasn't directed at me. They were apparently used to Clive pulling one or the other of them off the crew according to his whim, and while they might wish to be in my position – and I would gladly have traded with any, or all, of them; let me sort the bottles alone, while they went off to fraternize with the boss – they weren't going to blame me for being the target of his affections. Thank the good Lord. The last thing I needed was for them to get even more unfriendly than they already were.

That, alone, showed how much my world had narrowed since my arrival. There was a time when I'd had much better things to worry about, and much more legitimately, than the hostility of a few women who wouldn't even speak to me. My life had been all about survival, and now it was all about trying not to alienate the people around me. Maybe it was those rose-colored glasses that people always slapped on their pasts, but I genuinely missed the adventure, and the companionship, even if it had come with the constant knowledge that we were all about to die.

Jill turned and left the sorting room, giving me no choice but to follow her. I was still looking down, and I realized that she walked with a slight stagger. It wasn't pronounced enough to be a limp, not quite, but there was a distinct catch in her stride.

'How long ago did you lose your leg?' I asked.

Jill glanced back at me, apparently startled. Then she smiled and said, 'Years ago. I grew up on a community farm. Your food has to come from somewhere, you know. Only I got my foot caught in a wheat separator, and by the time my uncles were able to shut the machine down and extricate me, there was nothing that could be done to save anything below the knee. Ruined a whole crop of winter wheat, too.' She sighed. 'We had to buy a new separator. Industrial accidents are the primary cause of dismemberment and loss of limbs in both the United States and Canada, now that we've removed cancer and car accidents from the equation.'

It took me a moment to realize we'd removed car accidents from the equation not because they didn't happen anymore – if anything, people get less safe behind the wheel every year, because fear motivates them to speed – but because getting medical intervention to someone who's been hurt in a wreck before they either bled out or amplified is virtually impossible. Even EMTs won't risk their own lives for nothing.

'Sorry,' I said, the word feeling mealy and inappropriate in my mouth.

'Don't be,' she said. 'It was a long time ago, and I don't so much miss my original leg as wish there'd been a way to get me into the hands of decent doctors without cutting it off. I would never have gone into medicine if it hadn't been for that accident. I'd be a good farm wife by now, with four or five children of my own, and all this' – she waved her clipboard – 'would be nothing but a bad dream.'

I didn't say anything. My brief associations with Jill had given me no reason to think she was on my side, apart from her update to my contraceptive implant, and even that could be self-serving as much as anything else. Maybe she wasn't entirely on Clive's side – it would be hard to think of anyone who'd known a world outside this compound as being entirely on his side – but she certainly wasn't on mine. Silence was my best defense.

Jill either agreed with my assessment or had nothing else to say. We walked through the halls of the old hospital, passing other work crews and people running hither and yon on whatever errands they'd been assigned. As always, I scanned the people around me, looking for familiar faces, and as always, I didn't find them. I did find three of my sundresses, two being worn by women reasonably close to my height and build, and one being worn by two little girls in the company of an older woman who was apparently their nanny. It had been cut in half and refashioned into cute pullovers for the children, and seeing it broke my heart a little. Not because the children weren't adorable – they were – but because if our things were already being recycled into the greater community, then it was finished. We were never getting out of here.

The people grew farther spaced as we walked, becoming less and less frequent, until we were the only ones walking along a dimly lit white hallway. 'This used to be part of the oncology ward,' said Jill, sounding distracted. 'It's not very well connected to the social areas, I suppose because people didn't really want to think about cancer when they had a choice. Kellis-Amberlee did us a lot of favors, if you stop and compare the world that was to the world where we're living now.'

'Oh, yes, this is a fairy-tale wonderland filled with candy floss joy,' I deadpanned.

Jill turned to flash me a quick, self-satisfied smile. 'I think you're closer to the truth than you realize,' she said, and stopped, and opened the nearest door.

The room on the other side was small, lit by the stark electric glow that had become the norm, with no windows. The shelves were virtually empty, holding nothing but a few boxes of surgical gloves and tongue depressors. Either this wasn't a place they used very often, or the medical staff was on tight rationing, forced to justify everything they requested from supplies. The truth was probably somewhere between those two disparate solutions, and the truth didn't *matter*, none of this *mattered*, because Audrey, *my* Audrey, was in the middle of the room.

She was wearing a stained lab coat, much like Jill's, over ill-fitting hospital scrubs. Her hair was loose and her eye was blackened and she was crying, and I noticed all those things later, after I'd gone to her – crossing the space between us in three long steps, each faster than the last, until I was virtually running – and put my hands to either side of her face, and pulled her close, and kissed her for all that I was worth. She returned the kiss with equal urgency, her tears increasing in both volume and speed. Her lips were chapped. That seemed like such a small detail to fix on, but something about it bothered me. I kept kissing her. There would be time to talk about such things later. Or there wouldn't be, and either way, I didn't want to be the one who had pulled away first.

There was a click from behind me as Jill closed the door. 'Sorry, but you're going to need to rein your hormones in,' she said, sounding utterly non-apologetic. 'I know it's hard, and I wish I could let you keep going, but we have very little time, and we have a lot we need to talk about.'

I pulled away from Audrey. I still didn't turn to face Jill. Instead, I put my hands on Audrey's shoulders, and said, 'You're alive. I was afraid I was never going to see you. I'm so sorry. I missed you so much. I love you.' That last part seemed like the important one, and so I repeated it: 'I love you. Never scare me like that again. What happened to your eye?'

'Clive,' she said. 'He wanted to test me on what I knew. I got an answer wrong. He said if it had been two, he'd have blackened them both. Three, and I would have lost one.'

'Well, I'll just have to kill him, then,' I said, keeping my voice soft to quiet the roaring fury in my gut. 'Have you seen Ben? Is he all right?'

Audrey laughed, voice thick with tears and snot. 'My violent girl,' she said. 'I saw him once at a distance, while we were on our way to do a count in the drug room. He looked okay. No casts or visible stitches. I don't think they've hurt him.'

'They haven't,' said Jill. I finally turned to look at her. She looked amused, like she'd been expecting to be ignored for a while when she got me to the room. 'Audrey is a special case; Clive thought she was a liar. He doesn't torture his workers, not even the new ones whose loyalty hasn't been proven yet. That would be counterproductive. He keeps them or he kills them, full stop. Your friend is still alive, so that means he's been toeing the line, at least thus far.'

'That's not going to last,' I said. 'Ben's one of the most stubborn people I know.'

'Then we need to move up the timetable.' Jill glanced past me to Audrey, then back to me. 'She was telling the truth about being a doctor.'

'I told you,' I said. 'Bit odd that she's already monitoring your drug usage, what with her being new and all. Nothing in this place makes a lick of sense.'

'It all makes perfect sense, once you consider the name,' said Audrey. She sounded tired. I turned back to her. 'He called it the "Maze." Why would he do that, when there were so many other names he could have chosen? Hell, he could have called it the Free Nation of Clive, and no one would have been able to stop him.'

'When you put it that way, I'm surprised he didn't,' said Jill. 'His ego would really appreciate having a country named after him.'

'Mazes are where you keep rats when you're trying to condition them,' continued Audrey. 'It's where you train them. Teach them to go for the cheese and not the floor with the electric shocks. Clive doesn't expect me to be loyal, not now, and maybe not ever. But he does expect me to follow directions and do as I'm told, and part of how he can make sure that happens is by putting me in the path of temptation. So I get to count the drugs that someone else has already counted, and then he checks my math, or has it checked, and if I'm wrong . . .'

'Is that why he had me filling ludicrous alcohol combinations today?' I asked, looking at Jill. 'To see whether I'd really give someone good Scotch and bad beer?'

'You're Irish,' she said.

I wrinkled my nose. 'That's a foul stereotype. Really, if anything, it would be the fact that I have *taste* that kept me from filling out some of those combinations.'

'It doesn't matter whether you're stealing or deciding that you know better than the person giving the orders: Intentionally breaking the rules will get you punished,' said Jill. She hesitated before asking, 'You didn't, did you?'

'No.' I shook my head. 'I *wanted* to, but I used to date a girl who thought pouring that powdered candy sugar you get at amusement galleries into her vodka was a good idea. There's someone who likes everything, and I wasn't going to be the one to interfere with somebody's favorite drink.'

'That's good,' said Jill. 'Drugs, alcohol, chocolate, sanitary supplies, and meat are the big trade goods here. They can be used like cash, if you can get your hands on them. So the newbies are put in contact with the supplies as quickly as possible, to weed out the ones who can't be trusted.'

It seemed like an underhanded method of testing loyalty, especially since 'newbies,' as she so charmingly termed us, were motivated by fear and the hope of someday escaping from their new prison. Still, I couldn't deny its efficacy. Someone who would steal eventually would probably steal at the first opportunity they got, because some things didn't change with time. 'Then I'm glad I didn't start correcting the horrors before me,' I said. 'Thank you, for bringing us here. I needed to know that she was still alive. That both of them were. Now what do you want?'

'Well, I tried asking Dr Sung for a letter of recommendation to the CDC, but she said they weren't likely to give it much credence, what with her being legally dead and all,' said Jill. 'Then I suggested she team up with me to gather data on this place, and she said she wouldn't do it unless I was willing to approach you as well. All of which brings us here.'

'Here being . . . ?'

'A small, rarely used examining room. Mostly, this is where we take the really bad cases of gangrene, so no one else has to deal with the smell.' Jill said the words with a certain amount of relish. I tried not to turn green. 'It's amazing how long people will let wounds fester if it means they can minimize the potential for bleeding. Too bad they don't realize that pus is an infection risk as much as blood is. Anyway, we're unlikely to be disturbed here, at least for a while, which lets me make my recruitment pitch.'

'Recruitment pitch?' I was starting, slowly, to become annoyed. 'If you have a recruitment pitch, why didn't you give it to me before?'

'Because I didn't know whether I was going to have anything to hold over you,' she said, with a bald honesty that I couldn't help respecting, even as it made me want to introduce my fist to her nose. 'You said she' – she nodded toward Audrey – 'was really a doctor, but of course you'd say that, you were trying to save her skin as well as your own. You'd already managed to catch Clive's eye, which meant I needed you to act as normally as possible for the first few weeks, if only so he didn't catch on to the fact that I don't really work for him. Once I knew Audrey was actually Dr Margaret Sung from the EIS, and fully qualified to help us vaccinate pig farmers against their own fuck-ups, I knew I had something I could use. I just needed to wait before I approached you so that my separating you out from the others wouldn't look so suspicious.'

'Please tell me you're not working for the CDC,' I said wearily. 'I'm getting a trifle tired of them jabbing their noses in all the damn time. It's like being in an American spy movie, only somehow the doctors have taken the jobs that should have belonged to the CIA.'

'No,' she said. 'I went through their base level recruitment program, but they refused to give me a field position because of my leg. I wouldn't have expected the largest medical research organization in the world to be a bunch of ableist assholes, but there you are. Sometimes the world doesn't live up to your expectations.'

'That's the truth,' I said. 'Who *do* you work for, then?'

'Someone I don't feel like identifying by name while we're still in here, and there's a chance you could flip on me,' she said, with perfect calm. 'I have access to your girl. I can get her out when I go. I can't promise the same about your friend.'

'He's my husband, actually,' I said.

Jill raised an eyebrow. 'What happened to your whole "I'm a lesbian" routine? Clive is not going to be happy if he finds out another man has a claim on you. And when Clive is unhappy, nobody around him gets to stay happy for very long.'

'I *am* a lesbian, and Audrey is the one I love, but Ben is the one I married when I needed a way out of Ireland,' I said. 'I can't go anywhere without him. I owe him too much. I wouldn't be here if not for him.' I reached out and took Audrey's hand, like I was trying to reassure her – or maybe reassure myself – that 'here' was where I wanted to be. Oh, I could have done with a little less in the postapocalyptic warlord department, but we never get everything we dream of in this life. That would make things dull.

'You said your real employer would be very excited to meet me,' said Audrey. 'I warned you Ash wasn't going to go for leaving Ben behind. And I told you I'm not going anywhere without her.'

'This isn't a choose-your-own-adventure salvation, all right?' said Jill. 'This is a short-term, onetime offer that I am risking my own neck to make. I can get you out of here at the end of my assignment. I only have another two weeks to go, and then I'm a memory, and this place is just a bad dream.'

'So wait,' I said. 'You're offering to get me out, even though I seem like way too much trouble – especially given Clive's interest in the contents of my pants – because Audrey won't go without me, and you want Audrey. Probably due to her EIS connections, I'm guessing. You're a real doctor. Whoever you work for must be one too, or they wouldn't have been able to risk losing you. You're looking for more data. Audrey represents data. Am I warm?'

'I told you Ash was proof that "Irwin" wasn't a synonym for "stupid,"' said Audrey mildly. She squeezed my hand. 'We go together or we don't go at all.'

'I swear, loyalty is going to get us all killed,' said Jill. She shook her head. 'I don't control where the work groups are assigned. I *can't* set things up so you can talk to your friend. But I'll try to pull him aside for an exam, and see whether he's willing to risk it. Is there anything I can say that he'll believe came from you? Any password or pointless in-joke that will buy me his attention?'

'Tell him the sunrise is beautiful over Newgrange this time of year,' I said. 'It's the truth, so there's that going for it, and he'll know it came from me.' Better still, he'd know it had come from me without my needing to be tortured. There were lots of things I might say while people were hurting me. None of them would be about the ancient monuments of Ireland – not unless it was in the context of where I was going to hide the bodies.

'All right,' said Jill. 'I'll do my best, but you may have to make a call as to whether your friendship is worth your freedom. Clive hasn't lost many people from the Maze. It took us a year to plant me here, and I promise you that when I run, he's going to tighten security to the point where you will never see the sun again.'

'Then we'd better act fast,' I said blithely.

Audrey and Jill exchanged a look before Audrey leaned up onto her toes and kissed my cheek, leaving her lips pressed there for a long moment. Finally, she dropped down onto the flats of her feet, and said, 'I love you. Don't be a hero out there. I want to get out of here together, all three of us. I'm tired of burying the people I care about.'

'You and me both,' I said. I tried not to think about Mat and Amber most of the time. Thinking about them meant remembering they were gone, and that we were never going to get them back, no matter what. I'd seen death before. I didn't know anyone who had lived past the age of eighteen who hadn't. But I had never lost people I cared about so deeply, and it still hurt. I was starting to suspect it always would.

'Audrey, you wait here,' said Jill. 'I'm going to get Ash back to her work group. If anyone comes in while I'm gone, tell them I have you monitoring my vitamin D stores, due to recent pilferage. Try not to sound accusatory. They'll fill that in themselves.'

'Got it,' said Audrey. She leaned up and kissed me one last time, this time full on the mouth, before pulling reluctantly away. She was only doing it so I would be willing to leave. I knew that, and yet my heart ached anyway, even as I had to fight not to reach out and hold her.

Watching the door swing shut and block her face from view was one of the hardest things I had ever done.

Jill and I walked silently back down the halls, this time moving from isolation into greater population density. I would have needed to be blind or oblivious to miss the tension in her shoulders, or the way her eyes darted from side to side, taking in every aspect of the space around us. She was waiting for something to go wrong, that much was clear. I'd seen that posture before, on Irwins who knew things had gotten too quiet while they were distracted. I just wasn't sure what she thought was going to happen.

Then Clive loomed out of an open doorway, filling the hall in front of us, and I no longer needed to question what she might be frightened of. The most terrifying thing in the world was standing *right there*, brows raised in seemingly innocent question, eyes cold enough to make it clear that there was nothing innocent about him.

This was the man who'd hurt Audrey. Who'd ordered Amber killed. I wanted to kill him for what he'd done. I wanted to run like hell and never look back. The conflict was enough to turn my stomach.

'Funny thing, doc,' he said. 'I went by the liquor closet to check on my new pretty thing, see how she was settling in, and she wasn't there. But Catherine was more than happy to tell me about how you'd swept through and carried my pretty thing away. I checked her records. You said she'd already been given all her vaccinations, and she's not due for a physical. So what are you taking my toys for?'

The skin around Jill's eyes tightened, a slight, involuntary betrayal of her panic. Whoever had been willing to send her here and risk her life hadn't considered that some people are just shitty liars. There's no two ways about it. 'I don't suppose you'd allow for doctor-patient privilege?' she asked.

Clive's eyes narrowed. 'Oh, now you're just *asking* for it,' he rumbled.

'Um, actually, I am,' I said. Clive's head swung around as he transferred his gaze to me. I broadened my brogue and spoke faster as I said, 'I'm asking for it, not her. I asked her not to tell anyone. I was embarrassed, and it's been a while since I've had reliable access to a doctor, and I didn't want the other girls to make fun of me. Not that they're nasty or anything, I mean, they sort of are, because I'm new so they're standoffish and everything, you know how girls are . . . '

'Sweetheart, I like you, and I'd like to get to know you a great deal better, but that doesn't mean you somehow get access to a dimension where I am possessed of infinite patience.' Clive stepped closer to me, looming like a mountain in my path. It was just this side of terrifying.

I swallowed hard, and asked, in a squeaky whisper, 'Do you promise not to get mad if I tell you?'

'No. But I promise I *will* get mad if you don't.'

'Um.' I slanted a glance at Jill. I didn't need to fake my concern, just magnify it until it seemed like borderline panic. Returning my attention to Clive, I said, 'We were on the road for sort of a long time, and we tried to keep clean, but hygiene wasn't a top priority, and my, um, bits were, you know, starting to itch, and . . . '

'Are you saying you had a yeast infection?' he asked.

My cheeks flared red. It was nice to know that certain unwanted aspects of my upbringing – like my tendency to blush any time a man mentioned my genitalia – could still come in handy. 'Yes,' I said. 'I didn't want to tell you, because well, you're a man, and men don't always want to think about that sort of thing.'

'Real men aren't that easily disturbed, sweetheart.' Clive reached out and cupped my chin in his hand. It was an almost tender gesture, for all that it was intensely proprietary; he wasn't just offering comfort, he was reminding me that out of all the men in the world, he was the only one allowed to touch me. 'I'm sorry you were all itchy and sad. Did the doc take care of it for you?'

'She gave me a pill, and some ointment that I put on my, um, you know, and I'm supposed to go see her again in a week, to make sure everything is healing up okay.'

Clive glanced to Jill, who nodded. She was doing a better job of hiding her relief than she had of hiding her dismay, maybe because we weren't out of the woods yet.

'It should clear up easily, but I want to keep an eye on it, just to be sure,' she said. 'Those infections can cause extreme discomfort, and that sort of thing is disruptive.'

'Not to mention painful,' said Clive. He looked back to me, giving my chin a squeeze before he let me go. I took a half step backward, fighting the urge to scrub at my skin until all traces of his touch were eliminated. 'I understand why you might have thought you were doing the right thing. Some men are awfully squeamish about perfectly natural things.'

I relaxed a little more. 'Yeah, that's—'

His open hand caught me across my right cheek, hard enough that my head snapped to the side before gravity caught me and pulled me to the floor, where I landed in a heap of limbs and agonizing pain. I raised a hand to feel my jaw, tracing the spot where the skin was already hot and swollen.

Clive loomed over me, and there was nothing of kindness or sympathy in him now. This man was not my friend. He was my jailer, and hoped to one day be my lover – but that wasn't the right word, was it? The stallion doesn't love the mare. He only mounts her. He hoped to one day be my *master*, and anything more than that was just so much romantic nonsense.

'Never lie to me again,' he said, in that same calmly measured tone. 'I don't care if you have diarrhea so bad you can't feel your ass, when I ask you what's wrong, you tell me. I am an understanding man. I am a patient man. I am a man who knows that we are all lucky enough to be in the possession of bodies – beautiful, temperamental bodies that sometimes do things we didn't expect. But I am not a man who can forgive liars, or those who sneak around behind my back. Do we have an accord?'

'Yes.' I didn't have to work to whisper this time: My voice refused to rise above a harsh rasp. I just had to hope Clive was cocky enough to take my fury for regret.

'Good,' he said. He turned to Jill, who flinched. He sighed. 'I'm not going to strike you. You did a doctor's duty, and I should be grateful. I *will* be reducing your rations for the next three days, to remind you of who's in charge here. Nothing more than that. You can relax, doc, and you can treat her again next week. I want to be sure that nothing harms my newest guest.'

'Yes, sir,' she said.

'The CDC's been sniffing around. Not close enough to worry about, but close enough that if you fuck with me, I'll leave you for them to find. In pieces. Maybe that'll send them a warning about getting underfoot.' He turned back to me. 'Feeling better?'

'Yes, sir,' I squeaked, and my voice was so much like Jill's that I was ashamed.

He knew it, too. He laughed as he turned and walked off down the hall, moving with the calm, self-satisfied stride of a man who knew exactly what he wanted out of life, and was confident in his ability to get it. I stayed where I was until he had gone around the corner. Then, slowly, I pushed myself back up to my feet and stood. My knees were shaking as the adrenaline began draining from my veins, leaving me feeling weak and terrified.

'Still want to wait for your friend?' asked Jill in a low voice.

'More than ever,' I said. 'We can't leave him here.'

'Then we're going to have to move,' she said. 'Come on.' She resumed her passage back down the hall. There was nothing I could do but follow her.

Translated from the Cantonese

I am expected to keep notes as part of my medical practice. No one reads them. No one reviews them. They are slipped into patient files and ignored, not consulted even when someone who has been seen before is brought in for a new consultation. The senior doctor here, a man named Cowell, sees all the patients with chronic conditions, I think because there's little chance he's going to lose one of them unexpectedly. The man is a coward. There's nothing wrong with cowardice, under the right conditions. Here, it means that everyone who is not suffering from a slipped disk or sciatic pain is offloaded onto myself or Dr Benson – Jill. She has been here a year now, and is finally afforded a small amount of self-determination in what patients she takes. The expectation seems to be that she, like he, will filter out those who are least likely to devour her, and leave the remainder for me. Junior doctors do not last long in this setting. Perhaps that is why I am expected to keep notes. But no one has said I must keep them in English, and as no one else here reads Cantonese, I feel I can write freely. Maybe someday these papers will be found, long after I am gone, and some peace can be offered to my family.

Aislinn is alive, as is Ben. Both of them have been put with work crews and set to slaving for the man who keeps us here. Dr Cowell speaks highly of him, calling Clive a 'visionary' and claiming that without him, all human life in this part of the state would have been extinguished long ago. I do not get the feeling, speaking to the good doctor, that he has been outside this compound in more than a decade. His is the fear of a man who saw the world burn, and did not dare to stay and help put out the embers. I would feel sorry for him, were he not so comfortably complicit in what happens within these walls. So long as the fire is not for him, it seems he has no concern with who is wounded.

We have to get out of here. We have to avoid the poison promise of the firebreak, and remember: This is not the world for us.

—From *Wen the Hurly Burly's Done*, the blog of Audrey Liqiu Wen, July 6, 2040 (unpublished)

Twenty

The girls on my work crew were still in the liquor room. They shot me suspicious looks when I came back in. A few smirked at the bruise blooming on my cheek, apparently content with the mischief their tattletale ways had wrought. I wanted to hate them for what they'd done. I couldn't work up the energy. Clive had me shaken and cowed after one encounter in the hall and one show of force. How many encounters had these women suffered through? How many times had the hand risen for them? I couldn't hate them for being the victims he'd trained them to be. I couldn't save them either. Maybe there was a time when I would have thought leaving them behind was punishment enough, but if that was so, then I hated the me who would have felt that way. She had no charity.

I had charity. I had buckets of the stuff. I also had a bruise on my face and a spike of cold ice in my stomach, and all I knew about my future was that I was getting out of here. One way or another, I was getting out of here.

The dinner bell rang. We put down our bottles and our lists and moved on to the cafeteria, leaving the guards to lock up the liquor. It was a short walk from the room where we'd been working to the food line; we were the first ones there. Piles of trays flanked the door. I picked one up. Dinner wasn't likely to be inspiring – fish, potatoes, and steamed greens – but it would fill my belly until morning, and that was what mattered.

One of the women from my crew positioned herself next to me in the line. 'He only hit you once, huh?' she asked, a thin veil of friendly concern stretched across a great chasm of greedy nosiness. 'That's pretty good. Usually he really goes to town for the first offense. Sasha lost a tooth. She'll never sneak cookies back to her quarters again.'

None of the girls on the crew had visibly missing teeth. My fear of Clive increased. He knew how to hit so any permanent injuries would be concealable: That spoke to special training, and special training often came with increased pain tolerance. There had always been a question, at the back of my mind, of whether he'd come from a gang or military background. I was finally ready to cast my vote with 'military,' probably United States Marine, where he would've learned how to hit and how to block and most importantly, how to conduct his life with the sort of ruthless discipline that would have been utterly necessary when he was seizing control of the Maze. He looked to be in his late thirties, too young to have been here before the Rising, but this community clearly stretched back that far; a raw recruit in the beginning, then, fresh out of basic training – or whatever the jarheads called it – and following his platoon into the uncertain dangers of the zombie apocalypse.

I was willing to bet that if I pulled the records for military units dispatched to the California-Oregon border during the Rising I'd find him, smaller, skinnier, and less hewed out of the living flesh of some distant mountain, with a little more exposed skin and a few less scars. Desertion had been *easy* during the Rising. Every nation in the world had been finding members of their military scattered around in farmhouses and shopping malls since the dead began to rise, because all the media we'd had to go by had insisted that playing warlord was the only way to win. Build your walls high enough and leave the rest of the world to burn. Fuck 'em all, they sent us out here to die, that had been the philosophy of the deserter.

In his own way, Clive was no different from the laughing, milk-pale girls in the showers, the ones who'd grown up inside the compound, never seeing the sun. This place had become his world during the Rising, and he'd somehow risen to the position of heir apparent. Maybe he'd become leader the old-fashioned way, waiting for his old mentor to die and then stepping up. Or maybe he'd gotten tired of standing in the shadows and arranged for a quick, brutal assassination. Come to think of it, that was the old-fashioned way too. Everything was fair in love and dictatorship.

'He only hit me once, yes,' I said primly, sliding my tray along the counter to the milk and desserts. Blackberry trifle again. There were days when I was astonished we didn't all piss purple, the lot of us. 'Not too hard. He fancies me, and I was just trying to make sure I wasn't going to be too sick to be of use. I don't suppose he's too thrilled with the folks who made him do that.'

'Obedience—'

'Obedience has to be learnt, sure, but do you really think of Clive as the sort of man who *enjoys* beating a defenseless woman because she didn't know he needed to be informed about her itchy vag?' I gave her a withering look as I picked up my tray. 'I'd hoped we could be friends. Now I'm not sure that would be a smart choice on my part. You're clearly the sort who spend all their time looking for an opening, and I have better things to do than spend every waking moment watching my back. So I'll offer you this olive branch: Leave me the fuck alone, and I shan't start watching you for things to tattle about the way that you've clearly been watching me.'

Her mouth hung open as I turned and walked away from her. I didn't stop. This was a calculated gamble, and one I needed to have pay off if I was going to get the freedom to go looking for Ben. Convince them that spying on me was not only bad for them, it was counter to their best interests, and I might be able to start moving around this godforsaken place without the fear they'd go running to Daddy the second I stepped out of the room. Part of that was making sure they thought of me as the biggest threat going, next to Clive himself.

I sat with my back to them and waited. Clive was watching us, I knew that: He didn't generally grace the cafeteria with his presence, but he had his ways, and made appearances when he felt something needed to be defused. I'd seen several small fights break out between the other girls, one of which had ended with a broken nose. That had summoned him, all right – summoned him to kiss the winner and tell her he loved a girl with spirit. They hadn't gone after me thus far, but I'd been playing meek and keeping my head down. Maybe more importantly, Clive hadn't gone at me before. Oh, he'd pushed me during our first meeting, but I didn't get the feeling that counted for these girls. That had been an . . . introduction, almost, the sort of thing that said 'hello, welcome to the neighborhood.' Now that he'd written a bruise across my face like proof that I was no longer the new girl, I was fair game.

They were good, these Maze girls: I barely heard the scrape of chair legs being pushed back on the tile floor, and I heard that much honestly only because I was pretending to chew, lifting an empty fork methodically to my mouth over and over again. I steeled myself for what I was about to do. If Clive didn't take this as well as I was hoping, I might be seeing Jill again sooner than expected, as a patient. But I had to try. If I wanted to be free to look for Ben, I had to try.

The lead girl's hand was barely an inch from my shoulder when I whipped around and buried my fork in her leg. She howled, mouth forming a perfect 'o' of surprise that snapped closed when my fist slammed into her jaw and sent her crashing over backward. It was a textbook takedown, and I should have been proud of myself, but there wasn't time, there's *never* time when a real fight is going on. Seven girls on my work crew, and six of them set against me – unfair odds, even with that first girl on the floor. She was between them and me, and that was good. The dawning rage on their faces was less good.

I kicked my chair back as I stood, grabbing the second chair at the table and flinging it into the center of their cluster. I wasn't aiming to hit anyone, and I didn't; the chair sailed past them to clatter harmlessly against the wall. But it *distracted* them for a precious few seconds – long enough for me to pick up my tray and slam it against the face of the next girl in the line. Sasha, I thought it was, and going by the sickening crunching sound the tray made on impact, she might wind up missing a few more teeth after today.

At least their cluster reassured me that I was doing the right thing, and I hadn't just put a fork in someone who was coming to extend an olive branch. Most people don't bring a gang with them when they want to make peace.

A hand grabbed my hair. One of them had managed to flank me, getting into my blind spot while I was distracted with hammering poor Sasha. That was fine. The thing about going into the field with long hair is that the body learns to channel less attention into that sort of pain. I reached back, grabbed the wrist attached to the hand holding me, and twisted until I heard something snap. A girl howled. Another girl slammed her head into my midsection, sending me stumbling backward until my ass hit the table. That was convenient. I let myself rock back farther, shifting my weight onto my elbows, and slammed a foot into the face of each of the two girls coming after me. One of them yelped and staggered backward, her nose gushing blood.

This was it: the moment when Clive would get involved if he was going to save them from me. I knew he wasn't going to save me from them. Scenes like this one had probably played out a thousand times before, each unfolding in its own unique configuration, but with one constant – the new girl at the center, fighting for her place in the pack. Well, I didn't *want* a place in the pack. I was going to kick, claw, and sucker punch my way to outsider status, and if they didn't want to let me have it, I'd settle for being the biggest, baddest bitch on the block. The one no one questioned, because she might nut them if they did.

Part of me understood that I was just making myself more appealing to Clive, and increasing the chance he'd try to run me down when

I got away. I shunted that part aside and kept on fighting. Playing the weak sister wasn't going to save my neck, and if my greatest fear was being too attractive to a man who wanted to destroy me, well, I could learn how to cope. Coping was a skill I was becoming increasingly practiced at.

The girl who'd tried to chat me up in line screamed and ran for me. I waited until she was almost close enough to do some real damage. Then I straightened my hand and aimed it like a knife at the soft center of her throat, letting her momentum do the rest as she slammed herself into my rigid fingers. The jolt traveled up my arm to the elbow, forcing me to pull my hand back. I folded it into a fist, waiting for the next blow.

There wasn't one. She wobbled, going pale, before she folded up and toppled to the floor, where she joined the other three girls that I'd managed to knock down. The three who were still standing hung back, glancing at me and at each other, like they were trying to figure out what happened next.

What happened next was I flipped my hair nonchalantly back, lowered my fist, and asked, 'Did you lot want to go again? Because I can. Or we can wipe up all this blood before somebody amplifies and we have to explain the situation to Clive.'

Slow applause started from the doorway. I turned, unsurprised to see Clive standing there, one shoulder against the doorframe, clapping with what seemed like genuine enthusiasm. I took a chance and dropped a quick curtsy in his direction. To my surprise and traitorous pleasure, he laughed.

'That was brilliant,' he said, starting across the cafeteria toward me. He cast a hard look toward the girls on the floor, shaking his head. 'Some people never learned the first rule of starting trouble. Don't do it unless you're absolutely sure of the final result.'

'Aw, go easy on them,' I said, trying to make my tone light and flirtatious to cover my genuine concern. 'They were coming at me six to one. They had good reason to think they'd win, don't you think?'

'And yet there's not a scratch on you, and they're bleeding on my floor.' Clive stepped over the unfortunate Sasha, reaching out to smooth my hair back from my face with the knuckles of one hand. I didn't shudder or pull away. For that alone I should have received some sort of an award. 'You have hidden depths.'

'I grew up on a sheep farm,' I said. 'Turns out being surrounded by herbivores big enough to amplify will give you a bloody good motivation to study in your self-defense classes.' There hadn't been a sheep farm within twenty miles of Drogheda, but there was no reason to tell him that. Let his preconceived notions of where I'd come from direct his reactions, and let me keep a slice of the truth in reserve, for when I might genuinely need it.

'I like that in a girl,' he said, and lowered his head, and kissed me.

This was a test. I *knew* it was a test, and even knowing that, it was virtually impossible to stop myself from tensing up and pulling away. He wasn't gentle. He wasn't rapacious, either, but as I hadn't consented to what he probably considered a 'romantic gesture,' the distinction didn't matter. What mattered was making him believe I was enjoying myself. I forced my shoulders to drop and my jaw to relax, pretending as hard as I could that I was kissing Audrey, and that this was all some sort of surreal dream that needed to end as soon as possible.

His tongue touched my teeth. I gasped despite myself. And Clive pulled away, eyeing me thoughtfully. For one terrible moment, I thought it had all been for nothing: that my inability to pretend to enjoy kissing a man I hated was going to blow the whole gig. Then he smiled.

'Poor thing,' he said. 'I know this is moving awfully fast for you. I told you, I'm not going to push, and no one is going to touch you until your contraception implant runs out. But when it does, I promise, we're going to make beautiful babies together.'

Out of the corner of my eye, I saw two of the girls from my work group glaring – at me, not at him. What I had was what they all wanted. Good. They wouldn't betray me when they saw me sneaking out, then, not if it meant I might be dragged back and beaten into going along with Clive's plans for me. Better, far, to let me exit quietly, and let Clive find a new favorite who actually wanted his meaty hands all over her body.

'I'm glad you can wait,' I said, voice a squeaky whisper.

'I'm a patient man. But not' – his voice rose as he turned on the others – 'with people who cause this sort of unnecessary trouble. Aislinn is your sister now. She should be your friend, not your target. I am disappointed in all of you. There will be no desserts for the next week, and the next person I hear has raised a hand against her for any reason will be answering directly to me. Do I make myself clear?'

General murmurs of assent, none large enough to rise above the herd. Clive's eyes narrowed.

'Did I ask you to mumble?'

'No, sir,' said the six girls, in shaky unison.

'Good. Now get yourselves cleaned up.' He tossed me a smile before sauntering calmly toward the door.

'I'll get the doctor,' I said, and trotted after him.

I was testing my limits, but the gamble paid off: He gave me an approving nod, and said, 'That's the way to look after your girls. I'll see you soon.'

Apparently it wasn't sneaking around if I announced where I was going loudly enough to be overheard. That was good to know, and might serve me very well over the next few days. He went one way down the hall. I went the other, gathering speed as I walked toward Jill's office.

The door was ajar. She was inside, along with an older white man I hadn't met before. I knocked on the wall to get her attention, and said mildly, 'There's been a bit of a bar brawl without the bar in the cafeteria. Half the girls on my work crew got their teeth knocked in, the poor wee lambs. Do you think you've got the time to come stop the bleeding and set up whatever decontamination protocols you lot use before there's a zombie apocalypse alongside the mashed potatoes?'

The older doctor recoiled. Jill looked, briefly, amused. Then she clamped her professional expression back into place, grabbed a battered black bag from the counter, and said, 'Lead the way.'

We didn't hurry back down the hall to the cafeteria. We were halfway there when she asked, voice pitched low, 'Did you instigate this?'

'Not as such,' I replied. 'I just didn't do anything to discourage it when I saw it coming. It's easier to move around without anyone tattling on you when they've all decided that you're the boss.'

'I can't wait for you to meet mine,' she said. 'I don't think these techniques of yours will work on her.'

I wanted to ask who she was working for, but I knew it wouldn't do me any good; not while we were still here, passing through who knew what kind of surveillance patterns. It was obvious she knew them well enough to know when it was safe to speak and when the only safety was in silence, but I didn't have that advantage. All I could do was follow her lead and trust that she hadn't been ordered by Clive to lead me astray. The only real proof I had that she was on my side was a needle to the arm and a single meeting with Audrey, neither of which *proved* anything. I had only her word that the injection had been a contraception booster, and if Clive was trying to test my potential for loyalty, putting me in a room with the woman I loved would be an excellent way to do it. I had no potential to be loyal. Not to him, and not while Audrey was still alive.

Jill stopped in the doorway to the cafeteria, looking at the six women inside. The ones I'd hit or stabbed hard enough to cause bleeding were sitting down, having done their best to staunch the flow, but there were red streaks on the floor and red blotches on their clothes. This whole room was a hazard zone now. The women who weren't bleeding or blood-splattered were pressed against the wall as far from the others as they could get, trying to avoid contamination. They looked horrified. I couldn't blame them. Jill looked like she was trying not to laugh. I couldn't blame her, either.

'Ash, please go and find some clean towels and about three gallons of bleach solution,' she said. 'If anyone asks what authorization you're acting on, tell them mine, and Clive's, since he sent you to find me. For the moment, you're going to be my nurse.'

'Does that mean I get to hold a scalpel?' I asked brightly. Several of the women whimpered.

'Maybe later,' said Jill. 'Now go.'

I went.

This was the most freedom of movement I'd been granted since my capture, and I was going to use it to its full effect. I took mental notes as I trotted down the hallway, trying to connect visible doors, air vents, and junctions to my growing internal map of the place. I knew we were in an old hospital, pre-Rising, probably midnineties, if the shape of the walls was anything to go by. Any Irwin who spent a lot of time poking around in pre-Rising outbreak sites learned to enjoy architecture. A few of us have even written books about it, since we're the closest things to experts the world has left in certain schools of design. We lost a lot of hospitals when the dead rose. A lot of business parks and hotels. Not the sort of places that inspired the passion of, say, an art deco art gallery, but there was love in those buildings too. Even the most cookie cutter development had passion behind it, if you knew where to look.

The trouble with passion was the way it could muck up an otherwise straightforward blueprint. No mental map would ever be one hundred percent accurate, because no finished product was ever going to be one hundred percent to spec. That was one more thing for me to work around. It would be fine – it had to be fine – but I would have been a lot happier if I had turned a corner and found myself in the clearly labeled, helpfully staffed hall of records.

Instead, I turned a corner and found myself faced with something even better: a cleaning crew, dressed in tatty, bleach-stained clothes, in the process of swabbing down an apparently clean stretch of hallway. None of them so much as looked up at the sound of my footsteps.

Not even Ben. *Ben*, who was not only alive, but here, intact, a mop in his hands and a scowl on his face. I had never been so happy to see him, not even when he got me out of the institution.

He'd saved me, once. Now it was my turn to save him.

I placed both pinkie fingers in my mouth and whistled, short and shrill. The men stopped moving and turned, in unison, to look at me. Ben blanched, normally dark cheeks going ashen.

'Hello!' I said, dropping one hand and offering a cheery wave with the other. 'I'm Ash. It's nice to meet you, good work you're doing there, with the mops and the sterilization and all, but I'm afraid I need to muck things up a bit. Dr Benson needs a mopper. You.' I pointed to Ben. 'Grab your bucket and a bottle of cleaning solution, and come with me.'

'You can't just sweep in here and steal one of our men, lady,' said a cleaner.

'Can, shall, did,' I said blithely. 'Clive's orders. I'm to get the good doctor whatever she needs to keep this place from turning into a Romero movie, and that means a man with a mop. Top of her shopping list, really. Something she simply cannot live without. It's all very important, and I wouldn't want to be the one telling Clive why she wasn't able to finish her decontamination. Would you? Because I can go get him—'

'Ben, go with the lady,' said the man. 'Make sure the doctor gives you a note showing when she released you, and then come find us. Maybe if you can wallow in the biohazard long enough, you'll miss us cleaning out the john.'

'Oh, what bliss,' said Ben. He picked up his bucket, securing his mop to the side with a clamp, and grabbed one of the large bottles of bleach solution. Then he turned to follow me, quick and silent, back down the hall toward the doctor.

When we were about ten yards away, he began, in a hushed, shaking voice: 'Ash—'

'It's amazing how well this place is constructed, don't you think?' I asked, in my best, bubbliest tone. 'Lots of air vents. It would be *so* easy to wire the whole place up with listening devices, and then the people under you would never know for sure whether someone was listening in.'

Ben shut his mouth. He always had been a smart one.

'Have you met Dr Benson?' I asked. 'Nice girl. Prosthetic leg. Didn't notice at first, what with the whole "was in a car crash, saw a good friend die" bit. I suppose I was allowed to be distracted, you know? Anyway, she reminded me quite a bit of my old friend Tessa. Did you ever meet Tessa?'

Tessa had been Mat's friend, not mine, but my point was clear all the same. Ben's eyes widened as he nodded. 'Once,' he said. 'She was about to go on vacation at the time.'

'That's our Tess, always bustling hither and yon,' I said. 'I think she's probably packing now. Getting ready for the open road.'

Again, his nod was slight but there. 'Good old Tess. What I wouldn't give to go with her, just once.'

'Maybe someday,' I said. We had reached the cafeteria. I waved him inside. I wanted to tell him everything, to grab him in a hug and promise him this was all going to be over soon, but I didn't have a way to do that. All I could really do was hope that we were really almost finished here. I knew where everyone was. Dr Benson was supposedly on our side. We might get out.

We might.

I have all the information I'm going to be able to gather while here, and after a year, three weeks, and six days, I'm finally convinced that there's nothing left for me to learn. That's it, boss; that's the final transmission and the last scrap of secret intel on asshole Clive and his stupid Maze. Final verdict: baby warlord who's never had to *defend* anything, which makes him incredibly dangerous, because he doesn't understand that sometimes, you need to back the fuck off if you want to live to fight another day. If and when he comes for us again, he's going to come hard, and he's not going to back down. And that assumes he never figures out that you were the one who sent me. If he catches on to *that* little piece of delicious gossip, he's not going to settle for killing us. He's going to take us alive, and he's going to burn everything you've ever built to the ground. We knew this was a risk when we started. I don't think we could possibly have known how *big* a risk it was going to be.

Now's the part where I complicate things: Clive caught a former EIS doctor, Margaret Sung (now going by Audrey Wen) and her companions during one of his raids. She may have information you don't about what's been going on during the campaigns, and she certainly has no love for the CDC. But she won't come unless I bring her friends, so we're going to need an extract for four at the predetermined time. Try to keep body and soul together until I can get there, boss, and remember that I'm only in this mess because I didn't read the fine print on my employment contract. Don't fuck this up.

—Letter by Dr Jill Benson to Dr Shannon Abbey, July 10, 2040

Twenty-one

There were no alarms, no flashing lights or distant moans. There was only a hand shaking my shoulder, and a voice whispering, 'Ash, wake up. It's time to go.'

I'd been sleeping without my drugs, alone and on edge, for long enough that I swung for the speaker before I could process the voice. Luckily, I'd been sharing a bed with Audrey for a long time before that, and she was accustomed to the fact that I often woke up skittish and inclined to violence when I didn't have my pills to take the edge off. She danced out of range of my fist and said soothingly, 'I know, honey, I want to punch things too, but this isn't the time for senseless violence. This is the time for sneaking quietly out the back entrance before the man in charge catches on.'

'Audrey?' I blinked rapidly, trying to encourage my eyes to adjust faster to the dark. The figure in front of me was the right height and build. I sat up, pushing the covers aside, and lowered my voice. 'What are you doing here?'

'We're leaving,' she replied, and tossed a bundle onto the bed. 'I snatched some clothes for you. Get dressed.'

That was all the encouragement I needed. I slid out of bed and opened the package. It had clearly been packed by Audrey: I couldn't see well enough to identify the pattern on the sundress, but the straps were Kevlar-reinforced, which meant it was one of my field outfits. There were undergarments, boots . . . and a thigh holster. I snapped it on and held out my hand, relieved when the weight of a gun dropped into my palm. We were really getting out of here. That, or we were planning to die trying.

'Did you get to Ben?' I asked, holstering the gun before easing the underpants on over it. It might have been easier to do this in the other order, but I'd be damned if I was going to disarm myself again.

She nodded. 'Dr Benson has him helping her do an all-night inventory. There are three guards watching us. They've all been drinking coffee for the past six hours.'

There was a note of smug satisfaction in her voice. I ventured a guess, and said, 'You made the coffee, didn't you?'

'Slow-acting sedatives with a gradually increasing dose. They'll be losing consciousness right about now.' Audrey stepped back to give me room to maneuver. 'Once we get back to the lab, we're out of here.'

'Where are we going?'

'Dr Benson is taking us to her employer. After that, it should be a straight shot to Canada.'

'Here's hoping.' After everything we'd been through, it was no longer so easy to see Canada as the great solution to our problems. Amber had died to get us this far, and we had so far left to go. I wasn't sure how many more bodies I could take.

But Ben and Audrey were counting on me, and I was the only bruiser we had left. If there was going to be any chance of them making it, I had to stay with the program. I finished dressing before following Audrey out of the dimly lit closet, through the communal room, packed as it was with bodies, and into the much brighter, more dangerous hall.

We walked fast, keeping our steps light to prevent them from echoing. It wasn't quiet enough: An unmarked door swung open, and there was Sasha, eyes still blackened from our fight in the cafeteria. She looked at me. I looked at her. The world narrowed to that one woman, that one door. I had a gun. I could silence her, but I couldn't silence the shot. Which was I more afraid of? Her screams, or my giveaway gunshot?

Then she smiled, a little sadly, and closed the door. In her own way, she let us go.

I grabbed Audrey's hand tighter than ever and we kept going, quiet and slow.

There were two guards outside of Jill's lab, both slumped over and snoring. We stepped inside to find a third guard curled up against the wall like a big dog. Someone had shoved a wadded-up lab coat under his head to act as a pillow. 'How sweet,' I said.

'No time,' countered Jill, stepping away from Ben and shoving a backpack into my arms. 'Guard this with your life.'

Guard with your life . . . ' Mat's laptop,' I said abruptly. 'Did anyone manage to save Mat's laptop?'

'I got all our computers to Jill and she got them to our escape vehicle,' said Ben. 'We have to move.'

'It took me weeks to find this window, and we can't afford to let it close,' said Jill, picking up her own pack. 'Clive doesn't like your friend, thanks to him coming in with two women who rightfully belong to Clive' – she nodded to Ben – 'and is planning to have him on farming duty inside of the month. Turnover in farmers is incredibly high. They get to see the sun, sure, but everything that lives under the sun gets to see *them*. You said you wouldn't leave without him. That means we go *now*.'

'All right,' I said. 'Lead the way.'

With Ben's help, Jill moved a shelf away from the wall, revealing a swinging door on the other side. We squeezed through the opening, hampered by our various packs. They had been assembled with our limitations in mind. All of us wore backpacks, and Audrey also carried a small case. Jill probably didn't have as much stability as Audrey did; the chances of her falling were higher, and so she needed to be able to catch herself if necessary. It all made sense, and as we ran down the dusty, unused back hall of the hospital, I began to hope we might get out of this with no further complications.

Then Clive stepped into our path, cracking his knuckles for effect. He looked too calm to have just intercepted us: He'd been waiting, preparing himself to make his grand entrance. I appreciated a man with a theatrical turn of mind. I just didn't appreciate the fact that he was standing between me and freedom.

'Oh, Jill, Jill, Jill,' he tutted, shaking his head. 'I really thought you'd get this silly "running away" nonsense out of your head before you decided to pull the trigger on it all. What is there for you out there? Just a short, brutal life, and a hard, brutal death.'

'As opposed to a controlling brute who doesn't allow anyone to have a dissenting opinion,' said Jill. 'I didn't come to work for you because I wanted to. I came because you captured me.'

'It was a setup from the start and you know it,' said Clive, starting to sound annoyed. 'Did you really think you could keep passing notes around *my* place, under the noses of *my* people, and never have me catch on? I've known what you were for almost a year. It was just a matter of seeing whether common sense could trump whatever it is you pretend passes for loyalty.'

If Jill was surprised that Clive had been keeping tabs on her for so long, she didn't show it. She reached behind herself, producing a pistol, which she aimed unflinchingly at his gut. 'If you know that much about me, you know I was just trying to find out where the cases of polio we've been seeing in the local communities were coming from. We can't vaccinate what we can't reach, and people are dying.'

'Could've walked in openly and asked for that information,' said Clive. He looked untroubled by the gun. That was a bad sign. I began scanning the nearby vents and corners, looking for the sniper. There had to be a sniper. There always was, when a big man appeared without weapons and decided to make a show of things.

'No, I couldn't, and you know that,' said Jill. 'You're the reason half the underground communities on the West Coast have stopped sharing information with each other, even when that information could save their lives. Everyone's afraid of you.'

'I worked hard to make them that way,' said Clive. He cracked his knuckles again, looking almost regretful as he said, 'I figure stringing you across the fence line will make sure people understand that I haven't gone soft. I'll send your head to the CDC. Two birds, one stone.'

There: a flash of light from the mesh grid set at the top of the wall. Given the angle, the shooter had to be close; you couldn't use a real sniper rifle in that sort of enclosed space, there just wasn't *room*. But this was close range enough that a pistol would get the job done, so the techniques and tactics still worked just fine. I shifted positions, trying to make it look like I was nervous. Then, without changing my expression, I grabbed the gun out of my thigh holster and whipped around to fire three times at the grating, falling backward to avoid a return shot as I did. I was trusting Ben to catch me, and catch me he did, strong hands hooking under my arms before I could drop more than a few feet. There was a strangled scream from the vent, followed by silence.

Gun still held out in front of me, I whipped around to face Clive, who looked more stunned than anything else: When he'd set up this grandstanding little ambush, he hadn't been figuring on Jill having backup. 'Hi,' I said brightly. 'Who feels like getting shot in the throat today? Is it you? Because I'm sorry to say that right now, you've the best odds of the lot of us.'

Clive growled – actually *growled* – before he said, 'You're making a big mistake, little girl.'

'Am I? Because to me, this looks like the only reasonable course of action.'

'You want reasonable? I can be a reasonable man. Shoot one of them' – Clive indicated my companions with a sweep of his hand – 'and I'll take you back. You can be my girl. Protected, cosseted, no troubles or worries, ever again. I'll forgive you everything, if you'll only pull the trigger.'

I pulled the trigger.

Clive went down hard, clutching his knee with both meaty hands, like he could somehow keep the blood inside his body through sheer force of will. He made a shrill, confused keening sound. This wasn't what he'd been expecting. He'd created a culture of violence and fear, trained and cultivated it; it wasn't supposed to act against him.

Audrey stepped up next to him and slammed her joined hands into the base of his skull, sending him crashing to the floor in a boneless heap. 'He'll wake up with a raging headache in a puddle of his own blood,' she said. 'He shouldn't amplify if he doesn't roll over and inhale the stuff, but he's going to be *pissed* when he comes to.'

'And we're not shooting him because—?' asked Ben.

'Kill a petty tyrant, create a power vacuum, destabilize the region we're fleeing through,' said Audrey. 'We can't afford the distraction.'

'Because him coming after us is *so much better*,' snarled Ben.

'It is, yeah,' I said. 'He'll distract the holy hell out of the CDC, if they're really out there.'

'We move now,' said Jill. There was no reason to argue with her, and several extremely good reasons not to. We grabbed our things and resumed our run, faster now. Taking down Clive meant that we had a better chance of making it to the outside. It also meant that there was a more than good chance someone would have heard the shots and be coming for us.

'How did he know?' I asked, as we ran.

'I told Cowell I was leaving, and why; it was supposed to lay a false trail and keep Clive away from my real employer,' said Jill. 'I knew the old bastard would tell on me, but I was hoping he'd wait before he ratted us out. I should have known better.'

'Yeah, you should have! At the very least, you should have warned us!' The hall ended in a door. Jill looked from it to me, and nodded. I put on a burst of speed and hit it with my shoulder, knocking it open, revealing a worn dirt road with a familiar ATV parked on the shoulder.

'What did you gain by telling Cowell?' demanded Ben.

'A cover story,' said Jill. 'If he'd waited, like he was supposed to, Clive would have been looking for me in San Francisco, where I told Cowell I'd be meeting my CDC superiors and putting in a good word for him. Poor bastard was a country doctor who always dreamt of the big leagues. He had no idea they wouldn't let a woman with a prosthetic leg do fieldwork, much less dangerous insertions.' She reached into her pocket, producing the keys to the ATV, and approached it at a more decorous pace. 'He just blew his load prematurely. Old asshole. I needed that cover story. Still do. Maybe it'll hold and maybe it won't. Too late now, either way.'

'You nearly got us all killed,' said Ben.

Jill smiled without turning, the expression visible only in the sudden tension of her cheeks. 'Yes, but we lived, and now we get to run away. I hope you don't mind that I borrowed your car. It's been thoroughly decontaminated, and the upholstery's been replaced. Clive was going to add it to the raiding fleet; he just hadn't gotten around to it yet. Put your things in the back.'

We did as we were told. Obeying the orders of the woman who had just gotten us out of a would-be warlord's private compound was only common sense, no matter how annoyed we might be at her methods. Opening the back of the vehicle revealed our laptops, and two cardboard boxes full of our personal possessions, wedged into the back of the storage space, alongside two more boxes full of what looked like our trade goods.

Audrey flashed me a quick, pleased smile. 'We've been prepping for this for days. We got as much as we could. I'm sorry we couldn't recover more.'

Mat's makeup box was there. Hot tears rose to my eyes, forcing me to blink them back before I said, in a voice that was a bit too thick to be normal, 'You did perfectly, love. You did more than perfectly. This is . . . this is the world.'

'Get in,' said Jill. She already had the driver's side door open, and one hand on the wheel, making it clear who our driver was going to be. That was fine by me. Stepping outside seemed to have exhausted me on a level I could never have predicted, draining the fight out of my bones. We were free, we were out, and yet we still had so far left to go before we would even approach safety, much less reach it. This all seemed like too much trouble. That was the post-adrenaline fatigue speaking: I'd experienced it before, and I knew the signs well enough to know that I shouldn't listen. It didn't matter. My legs were shaking, and I wanted nothing more than to put my arms around Audrey, lie down on the muddy ground, and sleep until the tremors went away.

Ben could see my exhaustion in my eyes. He got into the front passenger seat without commenting, taking the gun Jill offered him and fixing a weather eye on the window, ready to react to any dangers. Audrey and I climbed into the back, and I closed my eyes, put my head against her shoulder, and slept.

When I woke, the light had changed, going from watery predawn to bright noontime sunlight. That wasn't all that had changed: The trees were different, dense coastal forest replaced by scrubby, over-grown ornamentals. We were driving down the center of what looked like it had once been a residential street. Houses stood to either side of us, although some of them were barely deserving of the name: They were burnt-out husks or collapsed from mold and weather damage. One appeared to have become the host of the largest wasps' nest I had ever seen, so big that it bulged out through the broken windows, buzzing with swift insect activity. I shuddered, wiping the sleep from my eyes, and turned to look at Audrey.

She was awake, her tablet propped on her knees and her fingers dancing across the screen, opening and closing programs and windows with an expert's speed. She smiled at me. 'You've been out for a while,' she said. 'How are you feeling?'

'Stiff,' I said, sitting up. 'Where are we?'

'Almost there,' said Jill. 'I shook a tail about fifty miles back, so we're on a detour right now, to make sure we don't lead any unwanted company back to base. If you're hungry, there's salmon jerky and dried blueberries in the bag by your feet.'

'Does anyone who *isn't* me not find the phrase "I shook a tail" deeply disturbing?' I asked, bending to rummage through the bag she'd indicated. 'It seems to me that being tailed is something to be concerned about.'

'They were from the Forestry Service, based on the logos on their hood, and they weren't doing a very good job of following us,' said Audrey. Her voice was softer than usual, pitched low, like she was trying to keep it from shaking. 'It didn't take much to lose them.'

'Forestry Service is *mean*,' I said. Poaching animals isn't a big business anymore: Few people keep pets, even the kind that can't transmit Kellis-Amberlee, and decorating a home in skulls and pelts is no longer considered exotic or exciting. It's morbid, and unforgivable. Animal-rights activists had been trying to eliminate poaching for decades. All it took was one little zombie apocalypse, and suddenly no one was interested in tasting tiger kidneys anymore. It was a fight to keep people from gunning down anything of amplification weight or above that got too close to a human habitation, but at least people weren't hunting them down and killing them for fun anymore.

No, the real money now is in plant poaching. Rare water lilies and exotic wildflowers are the jewels in the crowns of every private gardener from California to Cancún, and there are people who'll pay virtually anything to have a genuine, wild-harvested exemplar of the species. Concerns about invasive plants and killing the local wildlife by planting things that grew poisonous berries are no longer that important: Many people view killing the local wildlife as just shy of a public service. The Forestry Service has stepped up as much as a limited budget and the ongoing threat of the infected allows, cracking down on black-market garden supply shops and fighting to keep the natural world where it belongs: the wild. Some sheltered suburbanite's back garden just isn't the same thing.

Ben was still quiet. I frowned as I munched on a piece of salmon jerky, trying to figure out what was wrong. Finally, I swallowed, and asked, 'You all right up there?'

'I've been going through my news readers,' he said. 'No transmissions, just downloads. I wanted to know what we'd missed. Whether the news of our deaths had broken, whether anyone was looking for our bodies. I guess it was egotistical of me, but I wanted to know whether anyone had told our families. I hate to think about my sister out there, wondering what happened to us.'

'I know,' I said quietly.

Ben twisted in his seat and glared at me. I managed, barely, not to shy away from the venom in his gaze. 'No, you *don't*. You don't have any idea what's happened, because you were asleep when we found out, and Audrey didn't want to wake you. The whole time we were locked up with that madman, you were getting pampered and treated like a future concubine, while I was working my fingers to the bone, and then when we get out, you're the one who gets to fold up like a house of cards, while I'm the one that has to keep going. You could have kept your damn eyes open for another fifteen minutes. Maybe then we wouldn't have had to cry so quietly.'

'You're not being fair,' said Jill. 'Aislinn was dealing with an adrenaline rush, and those can cause physical symptoms that can't be shrugged off and ignored.' She sounded sympathetic toward both of us, and less upset than Ben – or Audrey, who was still refusing to meet my eyes. Jill had already known whatever it was that the two of them had just learned.

I looked from Audrey to Ben, steeling myself. 'Well, I'm awake now. What is it? What have I missed?'

'Georgia Mason is dead.' There was something small, childlike, and wounded in Ben's voice. He sounded like he'd heard that Christmas was canceled, not just this year, but forevermore. 'There was an outbreak at a political event in Sacramento, and she was shot with a dart like the one John tried to use on us. She managed to get a blog post out before she amplified, and her brother put a bullet through her head to prevent her from hurting anyone else.'

Georgia Mason, dead? The idea was preposterous. Sure, she was a spoiled, overly rigid princess of the news, but that didn't mean she was going to wind up *dead*. She and Shaun had the best of everything. The best equipment, the best positioning, the best leads. She was never going to die. She was going to grow old on the circuit, and wind up with her own television show on a mainstream network, presiding over her own media empire. Shaun might die – he was an Irwin, we don't have the best life expectancy going – but Georgia? That couldn't happen.

And it didn't explain why Ben was so upset over someone who had been an acquaintance at best, and a rival at worst.

I didn't have to wait long for my explanation.

'Listen,' said Ben. He cleared his throat, and read, '"My name is Georgia Mason. For the past several years, I've been providing one of the world's many windows onto the news . . ."'

We all sat in silence, and listened, unmoving, as Ben read us one last postcard from the Wall, entreating us not to be afraid, begging us to rise up while we could.

Dear Rosie;

It's not safe for me to send this now, so I'm going to leave it with the woman we're staying with when we head off to our next destination. Maybe someday you'll get it, and you'll feel a little better. You'll probably also want to track me down and slap me until my ears bleed for making you think that I was dead. I can't blame you for that. I'd want to do the same, in your position.

We got involved in some bad stuff, Rosie. Not bad as in 'criminal' – we didn't do anything wrong, I swear – but bad as in we learned things we were never supposed to know, and there are people who would do anything to keep them from getting out. If you don't believe me, look at what happened to Georgia Mason. They killed her, Rosie. They killed her because she got too close and learned too much, and when I read her last blog post, I realized she didn't even know everything we do. There are these pits everywhere, filled with things people will kill to keep secret, and you can't even know that you're walking toward one until you're already falling.

I love you so much, Rosie. More than anything. You were the best sister I could have wished for, and I am going to miss you every day of my life. But I think that what has happened proves I can't come home. It wouldn't be safe, and it wouldn't be fair.

Take care of the house for me. I always wanted to restore it properly. Take care of yourself. I love you.

I remain, and will always be, your brother.

—Letter from Benjamin Ross to Rosalind Ross,
July 12, 2040 (unsent)

Twenty-two

Jill pulled into an old pre-Rising business park just before sunset, driving around the edges a few times to make absolutely sure we hadn't been followed before turning into an old parking garage. The first five yards were dark, filled with debris and ominous shadows. It was the perfect place to be ambushed by the dead. I stiffened, putting a hand on my gun, and waited for the other shoe to drop as we pulled up to a closed gate.

Then the lights came on, activated by the movement of our vehicle. Jill rolled down her window, leaned out, and slapped her palm against a blood testing unit. The seconds ticked by, and then there was a beep, and the gate began rolling upward, revealing the bright, clean garage on the other side. There was a woman there, short, curvy, and scowling. Her hair was brown, cropped short and streaked with gray, and her skin was surprisingly freckled, implying that she'd spent a more than average time outdoors. All of this paled when set against her electric orange 'QUEEN OF TRAFFIC CONELANDIA' T-shirt, which was only blunted, not obscured, by her white lab coat.

Really, the shotgun in her hands was almost reassuringly normal.

Jill stopped the ATV and hopped out, grimacing as her prosthetic foot hit the ground. Driving all day must not have been good for her.

'Dr Abbey!' she said, beaming. 'Oh my God you have no idea how much I missed your angry little face.'

The woman raised an eyebrow. 'That is no way to speak to your employer, Dr Benson. And I do not have an "angry little face."' She had a Canadian accent, thick enough to be noticeable, but mild enough not to distort her words too much for American ears. I was grateful for that. Americans sounded funny enough; dealing with them dealing with a Newfoundlander might have been more than my nerves could handle.

'You're smaller than I am, it's an angry little face,' said Jill. She beckoned the rest of us forward before switching her attention back to the woman I assumed was her boss. 'These are the visitors I told you about. Benjamin Ross, Internet journalist, Aislinn North, Internet thrill-seeker, and Audrey Wen, formerly Dr Margaret Sung of the EIS.'

'Please, call me Audrey,' said Audrey.

'I take offense at being termed a "thrill-seeker,"' I said. 'I'm a journalist too. Just a slightly messier one.'

'Look, Irish, be glad you didn't wind up termed a statistic,' said Dr Abbey. 'I didn't want to let Jill bring home strays. She insisted. I try to be an understanding employer, so I finally gave in, but you were the one I had the most concerns about.'

All three of us looked at her blankly. It was a relief to be unified once again, even if I had no faith that the moment would last – or that there'd be many moments like this in the future. Losing Mat had broken the thread that had bound us as a functional whole. I didn't think there was going to be any coming back from that, not now, maybe not ever.

'Foreign national, no strong ties to anyone in this country who isn't also in this room, green card marriage to a reporter, long-term romance with someone who might be able to feed you information about the EIS ... this looks like espionage to anyone suspicious enough, and believe me, I have suspicious for days,' said Dr Abbey.

'But Tessa vouched for you when I had her run your backgrounds. She says you used to work with a close friend of hers. Mat Newson. Sorry to hear that they've died, by the by. I never met Mat personally, but from all reports, they were a nice person.'

She used Mat's pronouns with deliberate care, something that used to frustrate me endlessly, but only ever made Mat laugh. 'Education is awkward sometimes, and people are learning,' they would say, like that made everything better. Maybe for them, it had.

'Thanks,' I said dryly. 'I'm not an Irish spy. In case you were still concerned.'

'I'm not,' said Dr Abbey. 'Tessa provided me with a full background. If you're a spy, they did such an excellent job of hiding your training between arrests, lectures from your priest, and minor injuries that I suppose you deserve the chance to dig through my servers.' She reached behind herself, picking up a sealed silver bag, and lobbed it underhand onto the ground between us. 'I'm going to need to see clean blood tests from all of you before we go any further.'

'Now this is starting to feel like home,' said Jill. She picked up the bag, wrestled it open, and turned to offer it to the rest of us. We each reached inside and pulled out an individual blood testing unit. Once we were outfitted, Jill did the same, setting the bag back on the ground to be used as a biohazard disposal unit.

'They won't transmit,' said Dr Abbey. 'All the tests here at my lab have been modified.'

I gave her a blank look. 'What?'

'Normal blood testing units transmit their data straight to the CDC,' said Ben. 'It's supposed to be randomized and filed without your name on it, but people have suspected for years that the CDC could identify who'd given any specific sample.'

'They have computer banks dedicated to just that,' said Dr Abbey. 'There was talk at one point of jamming RFID chips in every American citizen, to make it possible to track people after amplification. It got shut down due to privacy concerns – maybe the last time the American people chose privacy over government oversight – but the people who really killed it were at the CDC. They can already trace every living human through the way they ping on their blood tests. That's power. Nobody gives up power when they have a choice in the matter. Now prove that you're clean. My feet are getting cold.'

One by one, we popped open our blood tests and slipped our fingers into the testing panels. This was a three-point test, sampling thumb, index finger, and pinkie. It stretched my hand into a starfish of flesh, making the bones ache. It was a good sensation. My body was waking up from the forced lethargy of the adrenaline crash, remembering that it had a purpose and a place. I was in the world again. I was moving. This test – this need to confirm that I was clean, because I could have been exposed to things that would make me unclean – proved that I still had work to do.

One by one, we checked out clean and held up our tests for Dr Abbey to see. She nodded, looking satisfied.

'Put them in the bag and follow me,' she said, and started for the door. Leaving an unattended biohazard in her garage didn't appear to be a concern for her. She probably had staff who'd take care of it. Whatever her reasons, we hurried back to the ATV long enough to grab the things that were most important to us, and then followed her. Jill brought up the rear, sedate, smiling, and carrying the two crates of trade goods.

I barely had time to wonder what those were for before the door was opening and we were stepping into something out of a pre-Rising science-fiction movie. The building had originally been intended for corporate use: that was clear from the gutted remains of the cubicle maze that had been incorporated into what looked like a medical lab crossed with an amoeba. Half the equipment was outdated enough that it might have *been* pre-Rising. The rest was clamped together with office supplies, held in place with twist ties, and generally assembled on a wish, a prayer, and a whole bunch of gaff tape.

'Welcome to my lab, don't touch anything,' said Dr Abbey. She led us through the maze, past people both in and out of lab coats — although even the ones who weren't wearing lab coats somehow managed to project the *idea* of lab coats, like it was just unthinkable that anyone could be working here without a certain amount of mad science in their bloodstreams. When we reached a small blue-tiled kitchenette she stopped, turned, and said, 'All right, why am I letting you live?'

'Was that supposed to be "why am I letting you leave"?' asked Ben.

Dr Abbey leveled a flat look on him. 'No.'

'You're letting them live because they brought you nice things,' said Jill, dropping our boxes of trade goods on the table. 'And because they helped me get out of the Maze, and because it's the right thing to do.'

'And because it'll really piss off the CDC,' added Audrey. 'I'm pretty sure they want us dead more than they want Oregon to be not on fire, which is why it's important that we get to Canada as quickly as possible.'

Dr Abbey raised an eyebrow. 'How much do you know?'

'Not enough. I was never inner echelon. I had too much of a sense of morality to go beyond fieldwork, and I never learned anything about the structure of the virus or why we couldn't cure the damn thing. But I know plenty about the funding structure, and where we've been channeling all our money for the past decade or so. I know about the secret testing facilities in Kentucky and Ohio. I know where they're keeping the dead, and I know about the serotype studies they conducted up until I went on leave from the EIS. I'm not a big leak. They'd never have let me leave. But I think I know enough to be valuable, don't you?'

'Especially since they're killing journalists,' said Ben. 'Georgia Mason.'

'She found a way to make people listen, that's for sure,' said Dr Abbey. 'I never thought of martyrdom as a way to keep something from getting buried. But hey, whatever works for you. People know there's a problem now. That's a big improvement over where we were a few weeks ago.'

That could just as easily have been us. We'd discussed what it would take to keep ourselves from being discredited, our names ruined and our families devastated; we'd never considered that letting ourselves be killed might be the answer. It wasn't worth it. Maybe the Masons would think it was, but the Masons were zealots. They'd been born to the news, and if they died making it, they wouldn't think their lives had been wasted. I didn't want that. I wanted to live. I wanted to grow old with Audrey by my side, watching Ben teach his grandchildren to operate a ham radio. I wanted to see a thousand things I'd never seen, do a thousand things I'd never done, and not become a footnote for the sake of a story that had never really been mine and had never been meant to be.

There were too many bodies littering the road behind us for us to turn back now. John. Amber. Mat. Poor, sweet Mat, who'd only wanted to make the world more beautiful and more fantastic than it had ever been before. Let Georgia Mason be a martyr. Let her brother be the standard-bearer for her cause. We had other stories to tell, other leads to chase. Maybe one day, we'd be the ones remembered for breaking this one, if we could just get far enough away to do it without dying. I wanted to live. More than anything, I wanted to live.

'We need to get to Canada,' I said, reaching out and taking Audrey's hand firmly in mine. 'We'll tell you whatever you want to know, all of us will, but then you're going to help us find a way out of this damn country.'

Dr Abbey raised both eyebrows this time. 'Why would I do that?'

'Because she' – I nodded toward Jill – 'figured you'd want to learn things about the CDC. Secret things. That means you probably like them about as much as we do at this point, and *that* means you're probably in the market for things you can do to piss them off. Getting us out of the country is guaranteed to piss them off. I promise.'

Claws clacked on the linoleum behind us. I turned. A black dog the size of a full-grown ram was standing in the doorway, massive head lowered, ears pricked forward.

'That's Joe,' said Dr Abbey. 'Or, as I like to call him, my "I don't have to do anything I don't want to" card. Joe would like me to ask, again, why I would help you get to Canada.'

'Because Audrey's going to tell you whatever she knows, and Ash is going to help with any home repairs you need, and I'm going to compile everything we have on this political cycle,' said Ben. 'We're going to let you suck us dry, and then you can give the CDC one last fuck-you by showing us to the border. Doesn't that sound like a good deal? You get everything, and you get to know we'll probably survive in case you need us again.'

Slowly, Dr Abbey began to smile. 'All right,' she said. 'Tell me everything.'

Coda

Don't You Want to
See the World?

Sometimes the right thing to do is to walk away.

—AISLINN NORTH

I never said I wasn't a coward.

—BENJAMIN ROSS

Next time someone tells you the American political process is fair, point them to the short career and brutal death of Susan Kilburn. I'm sure they'll find it very educational.

—FROM *IT WASN'T THE WIND*, THE BLOG OF
FRANKLIN GELLER, NOVEMBER 7, 2040

We know who you are. We'll catch you one day. Watch your ass.

—ANONYMOUS COMMENT ON *IT WASN'T THE WIND*,
NOVEMBER 8, 2040

Twenty-three

Everyone saw the footage.

It didn't make as much of a splash as Georgia Mason's last blog post – it's sort of hard to top a reporter reporting their own death by government conspiracy – but everyone saw the footage, because it was the sort of thing you couldn't *not* see. We were living in an abandoned vacation home in the woods of North Vancouver when it happened, running the lights and heat off an old generator that broke down as often as not, stealing wireless from the sky, and we still saw it. It was one of those moments that made the world stop, if only for a few seconds.

The election results had come in, and Peter Ryman was the new President-elect of the United States, with Richard Cousins – that sweet man who had stopped to talk while we were all in Wagman's employee lounge – standing as his Vice President. He'd been giving speeches and shaking hands when someone realized that the defeated Democratic candidate was nowhere to be seen. Susan Kilburn had simply slipped away in all the chaos, ducking her handlers and her disappointed campaign staff.

She reappeared on the roof of her hotel some fifteen minutes later, wearing a bathrobe, with her hair tied neatly back from her face. 'Hello,' she said, and the microphone she had clipped to her collar picked up her voice and bounced it back to the world. People began to turn. Parties began to stop. In our ever-monitored world, she was captured on film as soon as she began to speak.

'Hello,' she said again, and followed it with, 'My name is Susan Kilburn. I am of sound mind and body. I have congratulated my opponent, Peter Ryman, on defeating me. I hope he is a stronger person than I am. What I do now, I do for my family, and for the people I represent. The people who wished to control me will not be able to use them as leverage. Thank you, America, for the opportunity, however brief, to serve. To my poor bloggers . . . I'm so sorry. I hope you can forgive me.'

And then, without turning off the microphone, she stepped off the edge.

Her body burst when she hit the courtyard, some fifteen stories below. That part of the building had been designed to hold private events, weddings and engagement parties; it was architecturally isolated from the rest of the hotel. She died on impact, her organs rupturing and her skeleton shattering. The virus that had slumbered so patiently in her bloodstream could find nothing to resurrect. Like everyone who dies violently, she had created a biohazard, but she neither reanimated nor endangered anyone else. Susan Kilburn was a patriot to the end.

We were not.

People all over the Internet were asking why. Why did she do it, why would she kill herself when she had a cabinet position waiting for her, when she had the world at her feet, and could run again in four years. Me, I looked at the shadows in Governor Kilburn's eyes, the absolute emptiness that lurked there, hiding in the body of a broken woman, and I said nothing. I already knew everything I needed to know. Oh, there were questions. What did they have over Governor Kilburn at this stage, what had they threatened, what could they *do*? But those answers were for someone else to chase down. Someone who was safe; someone who was staying. We were neither.

That night, I rousted Ben and Audrey, got them into the ATV, and started driving farther east. We had a long way to go before we'd reach the Irish embassy in Toronto, and most of the journey would be along the Trans-Canada Highway, long swaths of which were no longer maintained. But we'd make it. We'd get to the embassy, get tickets on the next transatlantic flight, and make for Dublin. I knew people who would take us in, help us get our feet back under ourselves. And Ireland, as I'd reminded myself so many times before, was a non-extradition country. Maybe the WHO would come after us. Maybe the EIS would try to follow. It didn't matter. Whatever happened, we'd find a way to deal with it, and when we had our balance back, we'd disappear again. Australia was supposed to be lovely. Ben and Audrey were Americans, but there were ways around that. There were always ways around that.

Audrey was asleep with her head resting on the window; Ben was in back, lit by the soft glow of his computer screen. My family. Both of them, forever. And I was going to protect them, if it killed me. That's my job. I'm an Irwin, after all.

Our part in this tale was done, and we were getting the hell out. Leave the lies to the living and the truth to the dead. Nothing ever stays buried for long.

About the author

Mira Grant lives in California, sleeps with a machete under her bed and strongly suggests you do the same. Mira Grant is the pseudonym of Seanan McGuire – winner of the 2010 John W. Campbell Award for best new writer. Find out more about the author at www.miragrant. com or follow her on Twitter as @seananmcguire.

Find out more about Mira Grant and other Orbit authors by registering for the free monthly newsletter at www.orbitbooks.net.